No Ri

LAURA WRIGHT

Published in Great Britain 2014
by Mills & Boon, an imprint of Harlequin (UK) Limited,
Eton House, 18-24 Paradise Road, Richmond, Surrey, TW9 1SR

NO RING REQUIRED © 2014 Harlequin Books S.A.

Millionaire's Calculated Baby Bid, *Playboy's Ruthless Payback* and *Rich Man's Vengeful Seduction* were first published in Great Britain by Harlequin (UK) Limited.

Millionaire's Calculated Baby Bid © 2007 Laura Wright
Playboy's Ruthless Payback © 2007 Laura Wright
Rich Man's Vengeful Seduction © 2007 Laura Wright

ISBN: 978-0-263-91214-2
eBook ISBN: 978-1-472-04509-6

05-1214

Harlequin (UK) Limited's policy is to use papers that are natural, renewable and recyclable products and made from wood grown in sustainable forests. The logging and manufacturing processes conform to the legal environmental regulations of the country of origin.

Printed and bound in Spain
by CPI, Barcelona

Laura Wright has spent most of her life immersed in the world of acting, singing and competitive ballroom dancing. But when she started writing romance, she knew she'd found her true calling! Although born and raised in Minneapolis, Laura has also lived in New York, Ohio and Wisconsin. Currently, she has set down her bags in Los Angeles, California, and although the town can be a little crazy at times, Laura is grateful to have her theatrical production manager husband, two young children and three dogs to keep her sane.

During her downtime from writing, Laura loves to paint, play peek-a-boo with her little boy, go to movies with her husband and read with her daughter. She loves hearing from her readers and can be reached at PO Box 57523, Sherman Oaks, CA 91413, USA.

MILLIONAIRE'S CALCULATED BABY BID

BY
LAURA WRIGHT

For Lucca Elliott,
my sweet baby boy…

Prologue

One hour ago Mary had expected to lie back on the king-size bed in the most exclusive bed-and-breakfast in Long Lake, Minnesota, and let Ethan Curtis make love to her, with no emotion, zero response from her body. At that very same time, she'd wondered if he'd be rough, cold, like the unfeeling bastard she'd met in her family's former offices a week ago—the offices he now controlled and ran like a well-oiled, profit-gouging, soul-sucking machine.

His mouth moved over hers, slowly, seductively coaxing her back to the present. Every time his skin brushed against hers, every time his teeth raked lightly over her neck or back or shoulder, she mewled so loudly with desire she was sure the entire inn heard her and knew exactly what she was doing.

Ethan Curtis might've been a bastard, but he was anything but cold.

Moonlight spilled into the room, making it impossible not to see Ethan's face as he pushed into her again, his cut cheekbones, hard mouth, and tanned neck taut with exertion and damp with sweat. His cobalt gaze slipped from her eyes to her mouth, and he lowered his head. Mary's heart hammered in her chest as she tried to force back the rush of desire in her blood when his full mouth found hers and nuzzled her lips open.

The reality of why they were here in bed together, so that her father was now free from any threat of prison, scratched at the door of her mind. She wished she could crawl out from underneath Ethan and leave the room, but her body continued to betray her. Maybe it was because she hadn't been with a man in two years. Maybe she just craved the weight and the closeness and the surge of adrenaline, but she wanted this man so badly she ached with it.

Ethan drifted lazily from her mouth to her cheek, then to her ear. She felt the tip of his tongue against her lobe and shivered, her back arching, her hips arching, her body taking him deeper. Her ears were surprisingly sensitive, and she hated that he knew it, that he was having this power over her—yet loved it at the same time. His tongue flicked back and forth as though he were tending to more than just the lobe of her ear, and she trembled again with sudden spasms she couldn't control. Outside their door, she heard voices, heavy footfall in the hallway, then a door closing. Had they heard her as she moaned with desire, her body begging him for more?

The urge to touch Ethan, grab his lower back and buttocks, sink her fingers and nails into his muscular flesh was almost overwhelming and she fisted the sheets at her sides. It was the one thing she'd prom- ised herself—not to touch him. But the pledge was hurting her far more than it was hurting him, she imagined. His tanned, thickly muscled chest and shoulders had erotic voices of their own and were calling to her as he rose for a moment, then settled back against her breasts.

How could you sleep with a man like this? she heard herself say, though the only sound her throat produced was a deep moan of satisfaction as he lowered his head to her breast and suckled deeply on one hard, pink nipple. *How could you desire a man like this?*

He's a demon.

Shuddering with the electric heat, she wrapped her legs around him and arched her back, pumping her hips furiously. She was close, so close. It had been two incredibly quiet years since she'd been with a man she'd dated for only a few months, two long years since she'd faked release before breaking it off and wandering back into hermit territory and remaining there as the eternal businesswoman. She'd felt the real charge of climax only in her dreams—those dreams of faceless strangers pleasuring her body until she woke up sweaty and frustrated. But there was no faking anything tonight.

Again her thoughts were seized and cast aside by Ethan's touch. He slipped his hand between them, his fingers inching downward until he combed through the pale curls between her spread thighs. As he stroked her, flicked the tender, aching bud, Mary gulped for air. She didn't want to give in to him. He didn't deserve her desire, her complete and utter surrender. But her head fell back anyway as the heat of his hand and the skill of his fingers took her over the edge. She knew how loudly she cried out as he played her, as he sank deeper, but she didn't care. Wounded, desperate and totally unaware of time, she clawed at the white sheets, pretending they were his skin.

Ethan watched her, his gaze feral yet brushed with uncharacteristic concern. Then with a growl of hunger, he pushed deeply inside her, his rhythm steady, his breathing anything but. The force of his release made him shake, made his body hard as iron, and when he dropped gently on top of her, he buried his head in the damp curve of her neck.

It was only moments before Mary's skin started to cool and her rational mind returned, along with her anger. No matter how much her body craved this man, in the light of day this had been little more than a transaction.

A wave of nausea moved through her as she recalled the day Ethan Curtis had made her an offer she hadn't been able to refuse.

"You're one arrogant son of a bitch, you know that, Curtis?" she had said to him.

Ethan had sat back in his leather chair and regarded her with cold eyes. "I think we've established that. Are you going to take the deal or not?"

With his short black hair, sharp blue eyes and hooked nose, Ethan resembled a hawk more than a man. Mary had never seen a man with more arrogance or more presence.

She had stood in his massive office of glass and metal, with its hard, uncompromising edges, and tried to be as much of a hard-ass as him. "I told you I would agree to artificial insemination."

"If I felt that you would actually honor—"

"Honor?" she said, appalled. "We've leaped way beyond that now."

"True." His sapphire gaze had missed nothing, especially the intense desire she had to thwart him in any way possible. "But to make certain your end of the bargain is upheld, we'll do this the old-fashioned way."

"Not a chance in hell."

He'd looked amused. "You may even like it."

She'd given him a derisive glance. "Maybe. But we'll never know. I'm not going to bed with you, Mr. Curtis."

The look of amusement had disappeared and he'd replied gravely, "You want your father cleared of all charges. I want a child. It's very simple."

Simple. The word now crashed around in Mary's brain as the man who'd uttered it one week ago rolled off her in one gentle movement. Nothing was simple about this situation. She ventured a quick glance at him as he sat up, his back to her, ropes of thick muscle flexing as he moved. Was it possible to despise someone yet be intrigued by them at the same time?

His voice cut through her silent query. "Do you want me to go?"

Despite her efforts to remain indifferent, she felt anger bubble up within her. At herself and at him. "Yes."

His jaw tight, he let out a slow breath. "I *will* see you again tomorrow."

Without answering, she got up from the bed and headed straight for the bathroom. She wasn't about to turn over and lie there, sheet pulled up to her chin like a naive girl who'd just been taken advantage of. She'd known exactly what she was doing and why, and had admittedly enjoyed herself.

She turned on the shower to drown out any sound of him getting dressed and walking out, then threw back the shower curtain and stared at the water as it dropped like rain onto the virginal white surface of the porcelain tub. She placed one foot over the tub, but quickly stepped back on the mat. Why the hell wasn't she getting in there, getting clean, getting rid of any sign of him? What kind of woman didn't want to wash off the scent of a man she had sworn to hate—a man who wanted her only to procure a blue-blooded child? Not any kind of woman she would respect.

Mary let go of the curtain and went to stand in front of the full-length mirror on the bathroom door. With nervous fingers, she ran a hand down her torso, over her belly. Had they made a child tonight? A shiver of excitement went through her, accompanied by an intense feeling of dread. A baby. She sighed. There was nothing in the world she wanted more than to build a family of her own, but not this way.

Feeling ashamed, she looked away. Her priorities were what they had always been, ever since she was a child: to fix the lives of others before her own. And right now having all charges dropped against her father was the most important thing. She wasn't getting a family out of this deal, she was keeping her father out of prison.

Her hands splayed on her belly once more and she shook her head. Impossible. The whole damn deal. She was a fool for thinking it would work, just as Ethan Curtis was a fool for thinking that if she did get pregnant, the baby would ever be raised by anyone but its mother.

One

Four Weeks Later.

"Whose idea was it to install a kitchen in the office?" Tess York inquired, the words slightly muffled by a massive bite of eggs Benedict.

Olivia Winston flipped a yellow dish towel over her shoulder and walked her petite, though incredibly curvaceous, frame over to the table with the grace of a movie star. "Ah, that would be me."

"Well, you're a genius, kid."

Beneath a rim of shaggy brown bangs, Olivia's gold eyes sparkled. "This I know."

Tess laughed at her partner's mock display of arrogance, her long mass of red curls hopping about her back like marionettes. "All I want to know is where my mimosa is."

"No drinking before ten o'clock." Mary Kelley sat across from Tess, her wavy blond hair falling about her face as she absentmindedly drew slash marks through the hollandaise with her fork. "Unless disaster strikes."

"I'd say a two-week dry spell qualifies," Tess said slyly, making Olivia laugh.

"It's August." Mary looked from one of her partners to the other. "We're always a little slow at the end of the summer."

"Slow, sure," Olivia retorted, holding a piece of perfectly cooked bacon up like a white flag. "But we're bordering on drought."

Barring these two weeks in August, No Ring Required was normally buzzing with activity. The premier wife-for-hire company in the Midwest had zero competition and one hell of a brilliant staff. With Mary's creativity and business sense, Olivia's culinary skill and Tess's wise budgeting and decorating style, NRR was a highly successful company. The problem, Mary had to admit, was that all three of them were such intense workaholics who cared nothing for a private life that they had no idea what to do with themselves on their downtime. And each time the end of summer came aknocking, the women panicked in their own ways.

"Well," Mary continued, putting down her fork and dropping her napkin over an untouched plate of food. "Clearly this is no time to be picky about clients."

"Yeah, Olivia," Tess murmured with a grin.

Olivia raised her brows questioningly. "And what is that supposed to mean?"

"I think she's referring to your problem with trust-fund clients," Mary offered, laughing when Tess cleared her throat loudly.

Olivia scowled, then reached down and grabbed Mary's plate. "I don't like them, and nothing's going to change that. Trust-funders are boorish, brainless, self-obsessed jerks, who think they not only own the world, but everyone else along with it."

Tess flashed Mary a grin. "Tell us how you really feel."

"Yes," Mary agreed. "I'm not entirely clear on your opinion regarding the rich."

As her partners chuckled, Olivia sighed. "It's not the rich, it's— Oh, forget it." Clearly looking for a way to end the current conversation, Olivia glared at Mary's untouched plate. "Mary, you're not on a diet, are you?"

"What?" Mary said, sobering.

Olivia tossed her an assessing glance before she turned and sashayed back to her beloved Viking range. "You know that I feel as though diets are a total affront to all those in the culinary world."

"I do know that."

"Besides, there's not a grapefruit or bowl of cabbage soup in my fridge, I'm afraid."

As a shot of nerves zipped through her, Mary shook her head. "No diet, Olivia. I guess I'm just not very hungry."

Tess paused long enough to swallow. "As much as I hate to side with Olivia, that's been going on for a while now."

"Yep," Olivia agreed.

"And, well," Tess began awkwardly, "we're here if…well, you know."

Mary nodded and forced a smile. "I know."

Among the three of them, talking about business was an easy, playful and spirited adventure, but when the conversation turned to anything emotional or personal, the women of NRR seemed to transform into the Stooges—a bumbling, uneasy mess. From the inception of No Ring Required there had been a sort of unspoken rule between the partners to keep personal matters to themselves. Odd, and perhaps against every female cliché, for three women to abstain from discussion about history and feelings, but there it was.

"So, what's on the agenda today, ladies?" Tess asked, pushing away from the table and a very clean plate.

"I have a meeting with a potential client," Mary informed them, her gaze drifting over to the clock on the wall. Okay, five minutes were up. The test was done. The zip of nerves from a moment ago turned into a pulse-pounding elephant-sitting-on-her-chest type of situation.

"Maybe not such a dry spell after all," Olivia remarked gaily, her good mood returning. "I also have a client coming in at two whose fiancée ditched him a week before the wedding and he wants help with what he referred to as a "screw her" dinner party."

Tess laughed. "Should be fun."

Mary hardly heard them as the muscles in her legs tensed painfully, as though she was on the verge of a charley horse. The pregnancy test was hidden behind fifty or so rolls of the insanely soft Charmin Ultra that

Olivia insisted on buying. Would there be one line or two? One line or two?

"Big name or big business for you?" Tess asked, staring at Mary expectantly.

"Ah…both actually."

"Sounds great." Olivia set her own full plate down beside Tess, then promptly rearranged her silverware, napkin and water glass to their proper places, now ready to partake in her own breakfast.

Her heart slamming against her ribs, Mary stood and grabbed her purse. "I just have to hit the little girl's room and then I'll be on my way."

"Good luck," Olivia called.

Tess nodded. "Yeah, good luck, kid."

If they only knew the double meaning in her good wishes, Mary thought, each step toward the bathroom feeling as though she was walking in quicksand. She had no idea what she wanted to see when she tossed aside all that toilet paper and pulled out the test. If it was positive, she'd have to make plans to get away from Minneapolis eventually, away from Ethan—that man would never let her walk away with his child. If it was negative, her father's life was over. She felt a sickly sour feeling in her stomach. She had lives to protect, and she wasn't altogether sure how capable she was.

She locked the door behind her, sat on the floor and opened the cabinets under the sink. The mountain of white rolls pushed aside easily as she reached inside and felt for the thin stick. Her pulse pounded in her ears. God, what did she want here?

Her fingers closed around the test and she yanked it back. With one heavy exhale she stared at the results.

It was three twenty-seven and Ethan Curtis was growing more impatient by the second.

He wasn't used to being kept waiting. People arrived early for meetings with him, fifteen to thirty minutes on average. They would sit in his massive lobby until he was ready to see them. For six years it had been this way. He knew his employees thought he was an arrogant ass. He liked it that way.

He punched the intercom button. "Marylyn, when Miss Kelley arrives, have her join me on the roof."

There was a slight pause on the other end of the line. Marylyn had never heard such a request, but she recovered quickly. "Yes, sir. Of course."

Ethan glanced at the clock. Three thirty-one. Where the hell was she? He stalked over to the elevator and stabbed the button. Mary Kelley was a strong-willed, business-first, no-nonsense type of person—not unlike himself. But if she worked for him, she'd be fired by now.

He was not generally a nervous man. He didn't pace, worry or stress before a deal was done. If a client didn't perform or comply the way he wanted them to, he finessed the situation, made it work to his advantage. However, as he rode his private elevator the short distance to the roof, his gut continued to contract painfully, just like it had the day his father had informed him that his mother had taken up with a new man and wasn't coming back.

Ethan walked out of the elevator and onto the rooftop, for which he had hired a world-renowned landscape architect and two botanists to transform into his escape three years ago. The courtyard opened to a Moroccan-tiled fountain and several ancient sculptures, while to the left was a sun terrace, complete with bar and circular planters filled with flax, pyracantha and perennials to keep the urban scene colorful year-round. Red bougain-villea covered several of the arched trellises, and cherry trees flanked the central walkway. It was a strange mixture of ease and exotic, and it suited Ethan perfectly.

He sensed her, smelled her, before he saw her. Fresh, soapy—yes, he remembered. The lower half of him contracted as his mind played the ever-present film of those nights in July over again. Ethan saw himself lying on top of her, buried deep inside of her, his mouth on hers as he breathed in her scent and she moaned and writhed like a wildcat.

He glanced over his shoulder to see her walking toward him. She was average height, average build, but Mary Kelley possessed two things that would make any man stop dead in his tracks and stare. Long, toned, sexy-as-hell legs that he could practically feel wrapped around his waist at this moment, and pale blue eyes that turned up at the corners, like a cat's. "You're late."

She didn't respond. "What's all this, Mr. Curtis?" she said, looking around the garden seemingly unimpressed. "Your bat cave?"

As well as the legs and the eyes, she also had a sharp tongue.

"A sanctuary."

Her brows drew together as she sat in the chair opposite him, the skirt of her pale blue Chanel suit sliding upward to just a few inches above her knees. The late-afternoon sun hit her full force, her blond hair appearing almost white. "And what do you need sanctuary from? All the people you've screwed over this week?"

Yes, a very sharp tongue, though he remembered that it could also be soft and wet. "You think I thrive on making life difficult for others?"

"I think it may be your life's blood."

There was no disputing the fact that she disliked him. No, he could see that clearly. What he couldn't make out from her attitude was if she was carrying his child or not, and that was the one thing he desperately wanted to know.

He walked over to the bar. "Drink?"

She nodded. "Thank you."

"Anything in particular? Martini, soda?" That would give him his answer.

"Something cold would be nice. It's pretty warm."

"You're going to make me work for this, aren't you?"

"Would you really appreciate it any other way?" she said brusquely.

"Martini?"

"Lemonade would be great if you have it. I'm driving."

"Mary—"

"Do you think you deserve an easy answer, Mr. Curtis?" she interrupted coldly. "Think back to how we got here."

He had done nothing but, for the past four weeks, though not in the same way as she, clearly. "We made an agreement."

She laughed bitterly. "Is that what you'd call it? You blackmailed me and I gave in. Maybe gave up is a better way to put it."

Ethan abandoned the drinks and went to stand before her. Her cat eyes were blazing hatred, and her claws were out, but he didn't give a damn if she was angry. He wanted one thing and one thing only, and he would go to any lengths necessary to get it.

"Are you pregnant?" he asked bluntly.

It took her a moment to answer. Several emotions crossed her face, and her breathing seemed shallow and slightly labored before she finally nodded. "Yes."

Ethan turned away, his heart pounding like a jack-hammer. He'd wanted this but had never believed it possible. He had no idea how to react.

"You'll drop all charges against my father," Mary said, her tone nonemotional.

He stood there, his back to her. "Of course."

"And you won't interfere in my life until the baby is born."

He opened his mouth to agree, then paused. He turned to face her again. "I don't know if can do that."

"That was our agreement," Mary countered, coming to her feet, her gaze fierce. "Do you not even have one ounce of honor in your blood, Mr. Curtis? Where the hell did you grow up, under a rock?"

She didn't know where he came from, couldn't know,

but her words struck him hard and he frowned. "I will keep my word."

Seemingly satisfied, Mary grabbed her purse and started for the elevator. "Good."

"But there's one condition," Ethan called after her.

She whirled around, held his gaze without blinking. "There were no conditions."

"This has nothing to do with my child, Mary. This is business."

"I was under the impression that the child was business," she said dryly.

Despite the dig, Ethan pressed on. "I want to hire you."

She looked confused for a moment, then broke out laughing bitterly. "Never."

"You'd turn away business so you don't have to be around me? I thought you were way tougher than that."

"I have enough business. I don't need yours."

The foolishness of that statement made him smile. "Being the heads of two successful companies, we both know that's not true."

"Look," she began impatiently, "my deal with you is done. Unless you plan to go back on your word and not drop the charges—"

"No," he cut in firmly. "But perhaps you also want that sculpture your father risked so much to retrieve?"

"I couldn't give a damn."

"No, but your father does." He gestured to the court-yard and the small sculpture of a woman and child that Hugh Kelley had almost gone to jail for. It had been a gift from the Harringtons, part of their courtship when Ethan took over the company. They'd hated him for buying controlling shares in Harrington Corp., but the company was floundering under their care, and because they still wanted to be involved, they'd forced themselves to act nicely. If Ethan had known the rare sculpture belonged to a family member, he probably would've rejected the piece. For as much as he wanted to be accepted and welcomed into the old money of Minneapolis, he hated family drama. He hadn't been too keen on having Hugh Kelley arrested for wanting the sculpture back, either, but he also wouldn't allow breaking and entering at his company for any reason.

"Why are you doing this?" Mary asked, her cat eyes inspecting him as though he were a pesky rodent. "Why would you care if my father has that sculpture back? You have what you want."

A pink blush stained her cheeks. She was so beautiful, and her temper and passion only made her more so. She was kidding herself and him if she thought they were done with each other. Two things had come out of their nights together: a baby and the desire to have her in his bed again. Both would take time, but he'd get what he wanted.

"I want to be there," he said simply. "I want to be around you and see what's happening to you. I want to see this child grow. That's all." When she said nothing, he moved on. "I have several parties to give and to attend over the next month. And one trip—"

"Trip?" she interrupted.

"To Mackinac Island."

"Not a chance."

"A no."

"Well your refusal doesn't take away from the fact that I need help. I could ask one of your partners—"

She fairly choked on her tea. "No."

Ethan hesitated. It was the first time he'd seen her ruffled during their conversation. Sex didn't shake her up emotionally, and neither did money, business or the subject of her father, but just mentioning her partners at NRR had her sweating.

"You have two partners, isn't that right?" he asked casually.

"They know nothing about you…or this," she said in a caustic tone. "And I want it to stay that way."

"I see."

She put down her glass and stood at the side of the bar. "You want your eyes on me all the time…"

"For starters."

She nodded slowly, as though she were thinking. "All right, Mr. Curtis. You get what you want once again. I'll take the job." She turned away then, and walked to the elevator. "But understand something," she added as the door slid open. "What happened at the lake will never happen again."

"Whatever you say, Mary," Ethan said with a slow grin as the elevator door closed.

It was seven o'clock on the nose when Mary walked into the little Craftsman house at 4445 Gabby Street. She'd grown up there, happy as any girl could be with two parents who adored her and told her

"You don't travel with clients?"

"You're not a client."

"Listen, if it were simply a business meeting, I'd alone, but I have to stay a few days and I'm planni on throwing a party as well."

"And you could find someone to help you with tha anywhere," she said. "Some woman you know? And I'm sure you know several."

His mouth twitched with amusement. "I do."

"A girlfriend."

"No."

"How about a call girl then?" she suggested, flashing him a sarcastic grin.

"I want the best. A professional—and NRR has a sterling reputation. And, quite honestly, it wouldn't hurt having a Harrington by my side to—"

"Right," she said quickly, then shook her head. "I don't think so."

She was so damn stubborn. "Do you know the circles I run in?"

"I could guess."

"The kind that are really good for your business."

She shrugged, shook her head again.

He stepped closer, studied her, then grinned. "You're afraid of what might happen if you're around me."

"Try concerned." She walked away, over to the bar where she poured herself a glass of iced tea. "Listen, Mr. Curtis, I won't deny my attraction to you, just like I won't deny my abhorrence of you, either."

"I appreciate your honesty. But that's still—"

every day. With two such gentle souls guiding her, she should have been a softer, sweeter personality, but clearly there was too much Harrington in her. Instead of hugs, she loved to argue and battle and win. Today at Ethan Curtis's office she'd done all three fairly well. She'd won her dad's freedom, though she'd paid a high price for it.

Mary walked through the house, then out the screen door. She knew where her father was. During sunset, Hugh Kelley always sat in the backyard, his butt in dirt and under a shifting sky, he patted the newly sprung string bean plants as though they were his children. He was sixty-five, but lately he looked closer to seventy-five, far from the strapping man he used to be. Today was no different. He looked old and weathered, his gray hair too long in the back. For the millionth time Mary wondered if he would ever recover from her mother's long illness and death and the arrest that followed. She hoped her news would at the very least remove a few layers of despair.

He glanced up from his beans and grinned. "Never been late in your life, have you, lass?"

Her father's Irish brogue wrapped around her like a soft sweater. "If there was one thing you taught me, Pop, it was punctuality."

"What a load of crap."

Mary laughed and plunked down beside him in the dirt.

"Watch yourself there." Hugh gestured to the ground. "That suit will be black as coal dust by the time you leave."

"I'm all right, Pop."

He snapped a bean from its vine and handed it to her.

"And you know I haven't been on time a day in my life. Neither had your mother. Not you, though. Born right on your due date, you were. Neither your mother nor I ever understood where your timeliness came from. Well, no place we'd admit to, certainly."

Hugh wasn't being cryptic, just matter-of-fact. The rift between Mary's father and her grandparents was old news—though old news he loved to drum up again and again. Not that she blamed him. The Harringtons had never approved of him, and had made him feel like an Irish peasant from day one. Mary just wished things could've been different all around. Bitterness and resentment were such a waste of time.

She took a bite of her bean as the late-summer breeze played with her hair. "So, I have some news."

"What's that, lass?"

"Ethan Curtis has dropped the charges."

Hugh didn't look surprised. "So my lawyer informs me."

"You already knew?"

"Yep. Teddy called me half an hour ago."

Mary studied his expression. Unchanged, tired, defeated. She shook her head. "Why aren't you happy, relieved, something?"

"I am something." His pale blue eyes, so like her own, brightened with passion. "I'm pissed off."

"What? Why?"

"I know you, lass. I know you better than anyone. What did you do to make this happen?"

Her heart jumped into her throat, but she remained

cool as steel on the outside. "I don't know what you're talking about."

"Mare."

"Pop, I talked to the man."

Hugh snorted. "Ethan Curtis is no man. He's a devil, a demon with no soul."

Mary was all set to agree when a memory of the cozy room on Lake Richard flashed into her mind. Ethan was a demon, yes, but there was another side to him—a deeply buried side that held a surprising amount of warmth and tenderness. She'd seen it when he'd talked about his child.

She closed her eyes. *His child.*

"Well he's decided to let it go," Mary forced out. "He agreed that the sculpture wasn't really worth his time and is even willing to give it back to you. After all, it was just a gift from Grandmother, with zero sentimental value to him and—"

"A gift that old woman had no right to give," Hugh pointed out gruffly.

Mary gave a patient sigh. "I know, Pop."

The basket beside him strained with vegetables. No doubt he'd been out here picking for a few hours. Lord only knew what he was going to do with it all. "Promise me you're not in any trouble."

Mary's chin lifted. She'd lied, yes, but she'd done what she had to do. She was no more pregnant than a box of rocks, but her father was free, and protecting him was all she cared about right now.

"I have nothing to fear from Ethan Curtis," she said

tightly. As long as he didn't find out the truth, she amended silently, as she picked up the basket of vegetables and walked inside the house.

Two

Mary wondered for a moment if she'd fallen asleep and was, God forbid, snoring. Every once in awhile NRR got a client who was so dull one or all of the partners would actually find themselves nodding off while discussing contracts.

Today it was Mary's turn to down a third cup of coffee and pry her eyes open with toothpicks. She shifted in her chair and focused on Ivan Garrison, a new client who had hired her to design a menu for a party he was throwing aboard his yacht, *Clara Belle*. For the past thirty minutes the forty-year-old wannabe boat captain had been sorrowfully telling Mary that he'd named the boat in honor of his dead wife, who he'd married for her "outstanding boating skill and formidable rack."

It had taken Mary a good thirty seconds to realize that Ivan was referring to his wife's chest and another ten seconds to contemplate passing him on to Olivia, since the job mainly consisted of culinary planning. But he was one of those trust-fund jerks who made Olivia's skin crawl, and the risk of having her abide by NRR's seventh vow, Do No Harm might be asking too much.

Who knew? If he took Olivia for a ride in his yellow Lamborghini and insisted she call him Captain like he did everyone else, Olivia just might bop him on the head the night before the party and serve him to his guests with an apple in his mouth the next day.

"The date for the regatta gala as you know is the twenty-fifth," he said, touching the brim of the snow-white captain's hat he had worn to both meetings. "I'll have my secretary send over the guest list. Please make sure to refer to me as Captain on the invitation. That's how my friends and business associates know me."

Aye aye, sir! Mary nodded. "Of course."

"I'd like to really pack this party. We always get enough entrants for the race, but the galas aren't as well attended."

"We could make it as a charity event," Mary suggested.

"I'll think about that." He leaned back in his chair and sighed. "Now, have I told you how I came to be called Captain?"

"No." If Ivan was going to come around every week, she'd have to invest in some NoDoz.

"As you know, it's not my given name," he said. "When I was six—wait, no, closer to eight, my nanny, her name was Alisia and she was the one who bathed me—"

"Excuse me. I'm sorry to interrupt."

Mary glanced up and smiled thankfully at her partner. "No problem, Olivia. We were just finishing up here."

Olivia acknowledged Ivan with a quick nod. "Hello, Captain." Then she turned back to Mary. "Your next client is here."

"I don't have—" Mary stopped herself. What the heck was she doing? Her savior, Olivia had clearly noticed her drooping eyelids and coffee-stained teeth, maybe even heard the beginning of the creepy nanny-and-the-eight-year-old's-bath story and was giving her a way out.

"We can discuss the rest on the phone, Captain," Mary said, standing and shaking his hand. "Or if you'd prefer, we could e-mail."

The captain sighed wistfully. "My Clara Belle loved the e-mail. Did I tell you she had twelve computers, one for every bathroom? She wanted to stay connected. I haven't had the heart to remove them."

After one more minute of commiserating about the impracticality of expensive technology in damp places, Mary told Ivan where to find the little captain's room and walked toward the lobby with Olivia.

Mary released a weary sigh. "Thank you so much."

"For what?" Olivia asked.

"The 'your next client is here' save. I'm thankful for the business, but sadly Ivan is only eccentric and strange in an uninteresting way. There's nothing worse."

Olivia looked confused. "Mary, I'm always happy to help with tedious clients, but in this case, you really do have someone waiting." She nodded toward the man sitting in one of the lobby's artfully distressed brown leather chairs.

Mary's breath caught at the sight of him, and she wanted to kick herself for the girlish reaction, but she walked toward him instead. Ethan Curtis wasn't the kind of handsome you'd see on the pages of a *Businessman Weekly*. No three-piece suits or slicked-back hair, no calm, refined demeanor. He looked edgy and ready to pounce, his severe blue eyes alert and ready for a battle. Dressed in tailored pants and an expensive, perfectly cut black shirt, his large frame ate up the leather chair as around them the air crackled with a potent mixture of desire and conflict.

"We didn't have an appointment today, Mr. Curtis," Mary said in a gently caustic tone.

Amusement flashed in his eyes. "Yes, I know. But this is urgent."

Obviously she wasn't getting rid of him anytime soon. "Let's go into my office."

"No. I need to take you somewhere."

"Impossible," she told him sharply.

"Nothing's impossible."

"I can't." Didn't he see that Olivia was still lurking around? If she overheard them, she'd get the wrong idea…well, the right idea, and Mary didn't want that. "I have insane amounts of work—"

"This is work."

Mary pressed her lips together in frustration. She felt caught in a trap. If she refused, made even the smallest of scenes, Olivia would be out here, wondering what was up. That could bring Tess, too. She eyed Ethan skeptically, lowered her voice. "You say this is work?"

"Of course." He spoke the right words, but he stared at her mouth while he said them.

"Better be." She tossed him a severe gaze before heading into her office for her purse.

Mary stepped into the world of trendy layettes and custom chintz toddler chairs and felt her heart sink into her shoes. It was the last place in the world she wanted to be. The fact that not only was she lying about being pregnant but that it would be a long, long time before she came into this type of store for any real purpose weighed on her like an anchor. She eyed the blue and pink bookcases and dressers with cute custom airplane and unicorn knobs.

"This is a baby shop, Mr. Curtis," she said quietly, sidestepping a beautiful whitewashed Morigeau-Lepine changing table.

Ethan dropped into a pale-green gliding chair. "Can we drop the 'mister'?"

"I don't think so."

He raised one brow in a mocking slant and whispered, "Hey, I've seen that tiny raspberry birthmark right below your navel."

A wash of heat slipped over her skin and she could only mutter, "Right…"

"Come sit down." He motioned for her to take the yellow duckie glider beside him. "You never seem to get off your feet."

"I'm fine. I'll stand."

"Ethan."

"Fine. Ethan," she ground out. "Now, are you going to tell me why we're in a baby shop?"

He picked up a lovely piece of original artwork from a nearby table and studied the drawing of two frogs sailing a boat. "I'm thinking we could add one more item to your workload."

"Like?"

"A nursery in my house."

Mary's pulse escalated to a frenetic pace. "You want me to design a nursery for the…our…"

"Baby, yes. I may have unlimited resources, but you weren't far off when you suggested I grew up under a rock. It was a trailer park actually. Dark, dirty and decorated with the curbside castoffs of the rich people on the other side of town. So, I have zero taste. And as you can see, I'm a guy."

She stared at him, not sure how to feel about what he'd just revealed to her. She hadn't meant to insult him with the "rock" comment. Well, maybe she had a little, but now she felt pretty damn snobby. Although, his need to be accepted by the Minneapolis bluebloods, have a child with one, made way more sense now. Not that his actions were in any way forgiven. "Look, I'm sorry about what I said…the rock thing—"

He waved away her apology with his hand, his jaw a little too tight. "It's not important. What is important however is that my child has a place to sleep. So? Is this agreeable to you?"

This wasn't a bizarre request for an NRR client. She'd designed over twenty nurseries and children's rooms over the past five years. Single fathers, gay fathers who had to admit they had no taste, even busy moms on occasion.

"I thought you might enjoy this," Ethan said, coming to his feet.

"Did you?" He wanted her to decorate her own child's room. A child that didn't exist.

She turned away from Ethan and closed her eyes, took a deep breath. What was she thinking? What was she thinking lying to someone about something so important, something as sacred as having a baby? This was getting out of hand. Yes, she'd had to protect her father, and now that he was out of danger, wasn't it time to tell Ethan Curtis that he was not going to be a daddy, suffer his censure, his threats, and get on with her life?

Fear darted into her gut. But what if he refiled charges? That was entirely possible—maybe even probable given how angry and spiteful he'd be if he learned the truth. Her father couldn't survive another arrest. No, there was no way she was allowing that to happen.

Mary fingered a swatch of green gingham fabric. It would work wonderfully for a boy or a girl. Tears sat behind her throat. She wasn't the most maternal person in the world, but she wanted a child. Someday. With a man who loved her…

"Mary?"

She turned and looked at Ethan. "Okay."

"Hello, there." A very perky blond sales clerk appeared before them, her round brown eyes wide with excitement. "So, when's our baby due?"

Before Mary could even open her mouth to say that they were just looking around, Ethan chimed in with "Early to mid April."

Mary's head whipped around so fast she wondered if she'd given herself whiplash.

Ethan shrugged. "I did the calculations."

"A spring baby," the salesgirl said, beaming at Ethan as though he were a candidate for father of the year already. "How about we start with a crib?"

Ethan gestured to Mary. "The lady's in charge."

The girl looked expectantly at Mary. "Traditional? Round? Any thoughts?"

"No thoughts," Mary said, feeling weak all of a sudden. "Not today."

The girl looked sympathetic and lowered her voice. "Mom's tired."

You have no idea, lady.

"I tried to get her to sit down," Ethan said with a frustrated shake of the head.

The girl nodded as if to say, I've seen many a pregnant woman and understood their moods. "We can do this another day."

Mary nodded. "Another day is good." Another year might be good to.

Ethan checked his watch. "It's after one." He eyed Mary with a concerned frown. "Have you eaten lunch?"

Mary shook her head. "Not yet, but I'll get something back at the office—"

"You need to eat now. You wait here. I'll go get the car."

"I have my car," she said, but he was already halfway out the door.

To make matters worse, the salesgirl sidled up to Mary, clasped her hands together and sighed. "You're so lucky."

"Why?"

She looked at Mary as though she was crazy or just plain mean. "That man is going to make a great daddy."

"If he can stop ordering people around long enough," Mary muttered to herself.

"Excuse me?"

Mary smiled at the girl, shook her head, then followed Ethan out the door.

"You know, there was an iffy-looking Thai place next to that baby store," Mary said, sipping lemonade and munching on perfectly tender chicken picata and fresh spinach salad.

Across from her, Ethan waved his fork. "This is better."

Mary shrugged, a trace of a smile in her voice. "Well, sure, if you like quiet, great food and a killer view."

Under the guise of work, Ethan had taken her to his home for some lunch. Worn-out from the experience at the baby shop, and more than a little bit curious about what kind of home a man like this one would choose, she hadn't put up much of a fuss. And her curiosity was well rewarded.

She had expected Ethan's home to mirror his office— glass and chrome and modern—but maybe she should've taken a clue from his rooftop garden instead.

There was absolutely nothing modern about the estate. It was enchanting and secluded, complete with a charming wooded drive that led straight up to the massive French-country style home.

Inside was nothing less than spectacular, but not in a showy, uptight way. Though it was sparsely furnished, the rooms were warm and rustic with lots of brick and hardwood.

Mary sipped her lemonade, taking in the soft summer afternoon on the sprawling deck that nestled right up to the edge of a private lake.

"I thought you should see the space you'll be working with," Ethan said, finishing off his last bite of chicken.

Mary nodded. "You're nothing if not helpful, Mr. Curtis."

A breeze kicked up around them, sending pre-autumn leaves swirling over the edge of the deck into the water.

"Hey, I thought we talked about this back at the baby shop. You were going to call me Ethan—"

"I only agreed to that to get you to stop talking."

"What?" he said, chuckling.

"You were bringing up the past and I wasn't interested in going there."

"The very recent past."

She attempted to look confused. "Was it? Feels like ages ago, like it didn't happen at all."

He glared at her belly. "Oh, it happened, Mary."

Heat flooded her skin, but she forced her expression to remain impassive.

His gaze found hers again and he studied her. "You've got quite an attitude on you."

"With you, yes."

"I'm sure I'm not the only one," he said, one brow raised sardonically.

"Don't you have a room to show me?"

He sighed. "Come on, Mary, can we make peace here? Maybe even start again? Friends?"

Inside the confines of his office, where she could remember who and what he was, Mary felt safe. She had her walls up, double thick. Even on his rooftop or at the baby shop, he still seemed arrogant and ever the dictator. But here, in his home, with nature and softness surrounding him, it was different. His skin seemed bronze and highly touchable, his eyes glistened like two inviting lakes beckoning her to jump in, and his clothes seemed highly unnecessary. Mary felt her defenses slipping. Forget being friends; she wanted him to kiss her again— just once so she could prove to herself that it wasn't as good as she remembered. Sure, he had more depth than he let on, but she could make no mistake about it— Ethan Curtis was a selfish, misguided man, who was solely out for himself.

She put down her napkin and tried not to stare at the lush curve of his lower lip. "I won't pretend that we're friends, or even friendly."

"Fine, but can you really despise me? For wanting a child?"

She laughed, shocked at how obtuse he was being. "Is that a serious question? Of course it's understandable and wonderful to want a child—blackmailing a woman you know nothing about to get one is not."

He leaned forward and with a trace of a growl said, "True."

"You have no excuse for your behavior?"

"None whatsoever."

They stared at each other in stubborn silence, sparks of heat, of desire, flickering between them.

Finally Ethan spoke, "Let's go see the room."

They walked side by side through the house and up the curving staircase to the second floor. Ethan had run these stairs a hundred times, alone of course. He hadn't invited many people to his home, and the ones that had made it past the foyer had never been allowed upstairs. He normally took women back to their place after a date. Less complicated that way.

These upcoming parties were going to be the first time he'd invited a large group to his home, and the thought alarmed him somewhat, though he knew it was the right business decision. If a person was going to switch insurance companies for their billion-dollar business, they would want to see the man who'd be taking it over in his natural habitat—simple as that.

"I chose the room next to mine," Ethan explained as they walked down the long hallway. "If he or she needs me in the middle of the night…" He paused at the door to the nursery and looked at her. "That's how it goes, right? They wake up at night and you go to them?"

"I wouldn't know." Her skin had taken on a grayish

pallor as she stared into the empty room with its beamed
ceilings and white walls.

"Your womanly instincts must tell you something—"
Ethan began, but was quickly cut off by Mary's soft
laughter. "All right, I'm a little nervous about this whole
thing. I want a child more than anything, but I know absolutely nothing."

"You'll get help."

"I don't do therapists."

She released a heavy sigh and turned to face him.
"No, Ethan. Not that kind of help."

"What? Like a nanny or something?"

"Or something."

He shook his head. "All this child will need is me."

"Two seconds ago you were saying you didn't
know a thing."

"I'll learn."

"Maybe you won't be able to give a child everything. I mean…"

"What? What do you mean?"

She gritted her teeth. "Well, you were just talking
about womanly instincts. I mean, don't you think that
a child needs a mother?"

Ethan felt his whole body go numb at her query and
tried to shake it off, but the more he tried to control the
feeling, the anger building inside him, the harder it
attacked him. He heard himself mutter a scornful sound,
then say, "Not from what I've noticed."

Mary's face was impassive, except for the frown lines
between her brows. "What have you noticed?"

His head was swimming, his thoughts as jumpy as his skin. But why, dammit? Why was he reacting this way? The truth was he'd done just fine after his mom ran off. Sure he got into trouble with the law, but he'd gotten a hold of himself, and look at where he was today—no thanks to a mother. No, he and his kid would do just fine.

Mary felt the conflict start deep in her gut. She didn't want to give a damn about Ethan or his past or his feelings on his family, but the stark pain etched on his face was very telling and intriguing. She would never have imagined seeing the hint of a suffering boy behind the overconfident glare of the man. "Ethan," she began softly. "I'm not going to push you on this, but—"

Turning away from her, he lifted his chin and stared into the nursery. He was not about to discuss his past with her. "What do you think of the room?"

"It's great," she said in a soft voice. "Perfect. Any kid's dream."

"I'd like to get started on it right away."

"Sure."

He looked down at her once again, his eyes so dark blue and impassioned she felt her breath catch. "Mary?"

"Yes?"

"Would you mind…" He broke off, shook his head.

"What?"

"Can I touch you?"

Her self-control, always to be counted on, melted like the last bits of snow on a warm spring day. "We agreed—"

"No." He moved closer, until they were nearly touching. "Your stomach."

"Oh."

He cursed darkly. "I know it's ridiculous. Way too early. All of that. But, I…"

Her gaze dropped to her belly. "It is early."

"I know, but I just…" His mouth was close to her ear, that sensual, cynical mouth.

"All right," she heard herself utter foolishly.

Mary closed her eyes, afraid of what she might say or do when his hand gently cupped her stomach. Heat surged through the light cotton fabric of her shirt, and she was flooded with emotions. There was no child here, yet there was an ache so intense she thought she'd collapse if he didn't move his hand up toward her breasts or down between her thighs. Frustrated weakness overtook her and she wobbled against him.

"Are you all right?" he asked, holding her steady.

She had never run from anything in her life, but at that moment she had to get out of his house, away from that room, far from him. "I have to get back to the office."

"I'll drive you back."

She ignored the concern in his voice and pushed away from him. "I followed you over here, remember?"

"Maybe you should sit down for a minute. You seem—"

"The first party is Friday, correct?" she said, running her fingers through her hair, as if that would help quiet her shaking body. "If you can send me the guest list."

"Of course." He attempted to touch her again, but she moved away.

"Thank you for lunch, Ethan." Brushing past him, she walked quickly down the hallway, down the stairs and out the front door, only remembering to breathe once she was safely inside her car.

Three

"What's Olivia making?" Mary asked when she returned to the office later that day. Even in her sorry mental state, the scent she'd encountered when entering the lobby of their office building five minutes ago had made her taste buds come alive. Mouthwatering aromas wafting through their building weren't an unusual occurrence during the week, they just made her want to run up the four flights of stairs to get to the source instead of taking the very slow elevator.

Poised at the front desk, with a full plate of beautifully arranged golden spheres, Tess tried to smile. Unfortunately, her mouth was full and she could only manage a chipmunk-like grin. "Scones," she said on a sigh, pointing at the plate. "Cranberry. Have one."

"I've actually just come back from lunch, so I'm pretty stuffed."

"Seriously? Too full for one of these?"

Tess rolled her eyes, then grabbed one. "Devil."

"Don't blame the addict, kid," Tess replied, reaching for another. "Blame her supplier."

"Where is Olivia?"

"Trying out another scone recipe. Chocolate this time."

"Great."

"She has a high tea to plan. That angry groom wants something beautiful and classic to celebrate the loss of his fiancée."

"How strange, yet lovely."

"He has over sixty guests."

"Lovely for us, too, then."

Tess laughed. "So, where were you?"

Obviously Olivia hadn't told her about Ethan.

"That new client Olivia was telling me about?"

Or not. Mary glanced through the mail on the desk. "Yes. Ethan Curtis. CEO of Harrington Corp. and old-money wannabe."

"Harrington Corp.? Isn't that your family's insurance company."

Mary nodded. "Was. Before Ethan Curtis took it over."

"Interesting that he'd hire you," Tess said nonchalantly, taking another scone, but only fiddling with it on her plate.

"I've got the blue-blood background he's looking for," Mary explained. "In many respects.

"Olivia said he was pretty good-looking."

"I suppose he is."

"A clean-shaven Colin Farrell with the body of a construction worker, is what she said, I think."

"That's incredibly specific. She saw him for like five seconds."

"Just be careful," Tess said, her tone serious.

Such a strong warning from a woman who rarely got involved in the personal matters of her partners made Mary's defenses perk up. "He's just a client, Tess."

"Of course. Sure. But you know, it's always better to be safe, kid. Expect an agenda and you won't get hurt." She picked up her scone and pointed it at Mary. "You never know the true character of a person or what they're really after."

Whenever Tess spoke in this cryptic way, Mary had the burning desire to ask her what she meant by it, and maybe where the cynicism was coming from. But the women of NRR kept their pasts in the past. As for Tess's concern over Ethan Curtis's character, Mary wasn't flying blind—she knew exactly who he was and what he wanted. But her partner's advice was sound. After what had happened today, how she'd felt standing so close to him, as though she were frozen solid and he was a very inviting campfire, she had to be careful—adopt the all-business facade she normally wore with such ease and comfort.

"I'll watch my back." She tossed her partner a reassuring grin. "But in the meantime, Mr. Curtis has given me five days to plan a very swanky event. I'd better get on it." She paused over the plate of scones. "Damn that Olivia," she grumbled, grabbing one and heading toward her office.

* * *

In the past Ethan had used a local catering company for his parties. A boutique-type place, very upscale and guaranteed to impress. Their food had always been good, though at times unrecognizable. But, in his opinion, the menu and service had always felt cold and impersonal, not really his speed. For years he'd gone along with the very fancy, tasteless hors d'oeuvres, prickly flower arrangements and silent waitstaff because, well, he'd been to several events with just that type of vibe and everyone had seemed to enjoy themselves.

Then he'd asked Mary Kelley to plan his event.

When she'd come to him with the menu and details of what she had planned, he'd worried. Would his stuffy clientele appreciate her vision?

Ethan glanced around his home. Clearly, he'd worried for no reason. In five short days she'd transformed the entire first floor of his home into a relaxed, candlelit lounge, and outside on his deck and lawn, she'd created a beautiful Asian garden. It was anything but showy. In fact, the feel of the whole party was classic and elegant and totally comfortable. Smiling, helpful waitstaff milled about with delicious alcoholic concoctions like wet-cucumber and ginger-passionfruit margaritas, and Asian-French treats like miso-braised short ribs, coriander-crusted ahi tuna and Vietnamese sweet-potato fries with a chili cream dipping sauce.

Surrounded by several clients and potential clients, Ethan felt in his element and ready to do business, but he couldn't stop himself from wondering where Mary was. Earlier in the night she'd slipped away to change and reappeared right before the first doorbell chime.

Ethan had been having a difficult time keeping his eyes off her since. His gaze scanned the crowd and found her chatting with two couples, looking at ease and incredibly sexy. Her makeup was smoky and sophisticated, and she'd slicked her blond hair back into a very chic ponytail. But it was the clothes she was wearing that really made his entire body jolt. She looked as though she'd just stepped off a runway in New York. The black crisscross halter top and white pencil skirt showed off her long, slim figure to perfection. Soon she wouldn't be able to wear clothes like this, he mused thoughtfully. Her body would grow with their child, blossom with curves.

He continued to watch her as she gestured to one of the waitstaff carrying those very popular pale-green wet-cucumber margaritas. After serving the couple, Mary made her way over to Ethan and his insurance friends, her light-blue cat eyes bright with success and confidence. "Good evening. Is everyone enjoying themselves?"

The people around Ethan nodded and offered their host and hostess several enthusiastic compliments, then chuckled with amusement when Ethan declared he had to have what appeared to be the last piece of ahi and he was going to seek it out. Feeling oddly possessive in the large crowd of married and single men, Ethan led Mary out on the deck, where guests were waiting for a boat ride around the small lake.

"You haven't said anything about—" she gestured around the room "—all of this."

"Looks good," he said distractedly. The light out on the deck was even more intimate than the candles inside the house. Her neck looked soft and white and he played with the thought of leaning in and kissing her, right where her pulse thrummed gently.

"Looks good?" she repeated. "Is that all I'm going to get from you?"

"Nice choice of words," Ethan muttered, closing the gap between them so they were nearly touching, his chest to the tips of her breasts. Heat surged through Ethan's blood, and Mary must've seen the desire in his eyes because she quickly restated her question.

"What I meant was, is everything satisfactory?"

Ten feet away, around the side of the house, there was an alcove, just dark enough for them not to be spotted. He wanted to take her there, watch her pale-blue eyes turn smoky as he removed her skirt. "The food is amazing, the house looks perfect…yes, all satisfactory."

"Good."

"Great party, Curtis. Really top-notch." Downing a plate of short ribs as though they were going out of style, Ed Grasner, one of Ethan's biggest clients, walked by, no doubt headed for the boats and his wife.

Like a brick to the head, Ethan remembered why his guests were here. It was not to facilitate a seduction—he could do that on his own time. He turned back to Mary, his game face on. "The success of this evening isn't based on how much everyone eats and drinks or how great the house looks, it's based on acquiring several new clients."

Mary looked confused, as though she was watching a chameleon change colors. "Of course."

Ethan nodded toward a couple in their late thirties, sitting at one of the candlelit tables by the water. "Isaac and Emily Underwood. The St.Paul Underwoods. Very old money."

"Yes, I've heard of them."

"They own twenty-five exclusive inns around the Midwest. Get to them, get to the rest of their family. Can your efforts tonight reel in prize fish like that?"

"Is this a business party or the hunting and gaming channel?"

"I want what I want. And ninety-nine percent of the time I get it."

She shook her head at him.

He raised a brow. "I sound arrogant?"

"Arrogant, presumptuous, lacking in finesse."

Her derogatory adjectives caused him to stiffen. "Do you ever not say what's on your mind?"

"Once or twice. But it's a rarity."

Ethan had never been spoken to like this. At least not in the past fifteen years. He wasn't used to it, but for some reason with her, it didn't bother him all that much. In fact, her honesty and candor appealed to him.

"Mr. Curtis?" The pair that Ethan had just been talking about were walking toward him. The Underwoods were a handsome couple, very blond and tanned. Understated wealth oozed from them. They also appeared very much in love, their hands tightly clasped, only releasing each other when Ethan and Mary reached out a hand to greet them.

Emily gave Mary a warm, beautifully white smile. "I hear that you are the one responsible for this party?"

"I am," Mary said pleasantly. "Are you enjoying yourself this evening, Mrs. Underwood?"

The woman looked confused. "Have we been introduced?"

"Not yet. But I've heard much about you and your husband, and of course your lovely inns, from my grandparents."

"Your grandparents?"

"The Harringtons."

The casual warmth from a moment ago morphed into a look of understanding and respect. "Of course. I should have noticed it before. You have your grandmother's eyes. The shape."

Mary smiled, but her stomach churned lightly as it did whenever someone found a similarity between her and her grandmother. She didn't despise the woman like her father did, but growing up she had always been compared with her and had desperately wanted to be compared to her mother instead. But they'd looked so different it was almost impossible to see.

Ethan's hand came to rest on her back and she instinctively leaned into him. "Have you had a boat ride?" he asked, gesturing toward the lake. When they nodded, he asked them if they'd tried the food.

Chuckling, Isaac spoke then, "The food is amazing,

Curtis. Really. Both Emily and I have taken full advantage of your hospitality." He turned to Mary. "We must have the name of your chef. There are a few things we'd love to add to our menus."

"Of course," Mary replied. "The chef is my business partner, Olivia. I'll make sure to give you her name and number before you leave. But first, I see that the wait-staff are bringing out the desserts. You must try the pistachio crème brûlée with orange ice cream."

"Sounds delicious," Emily said with childlike enthusiasm.

Lowering her voice, Mary said conspiratorially, "Heavenly actually." She gestured toward the house. "Let's make sure you both have at least one."

Emily giggled. "At least. Come along, Isaac."

Before Mary could disappear, Ethan grabbed her arm. "Why are you sending them away? I wanted to speak with them about—"

"Relax, Curtis," she said softly, her eyes bright with mischief. "They'll be back. And because they want to, not because they've been hooked, yanked onto a boat and gutted."

Equally shocked and impressed, Ethan studied her. "Very nice."

She inclined her head. "Thank you."

Ethan's gaze followed her hungrily as she walked off to feed crème brûlée to his guests.

Some men resembled excessively tall penguins in their tuxedoes. Some looked awkward and uncomfortable. But Ethan Curtis wore his like a second skin. As he stalked his estate, he looked like a predator in search of his next prey—and he seemed to take his targets down with amazing speed and assuredness. By the end of the night, several potential clients had verbally signed on to Harrington Corp.'s already thick roster, and as Mary had predicted, the Underwoods had come back to him in a sugar haze, asking for a meeting at his office the following Monday.

When Mary found Ethan he was in the kitchen, looking very pleased with himself, his bow tie undone and falling against his open white shirt. Beer in hand, he chatted with the on-site chef, Jean Paul, as the man prepared to leave.

Mary shut her eyes against the sudden and unbidden image of Ethan out of that tux, his heavily muscled, tanned skin pressing down into the cushion of a woman's body—her body. She despised her reaction to him and to the memory of those nights together. Why couldn't she get it through her thick skull that those moments were over? Yes, sometimes he looked at her with a flicker of desire in his eyes, but the moment was over in seconds and he was back to business. He hadn't even commented on how she looked tonight, and she was really working it.

She grabbed her purse from the counter by the fridge. What did it matter? She was the one insisting that nothing romantic ever happen again. She faced him and spoke in her most professional voice. "Well, we're done here. If there's nothing else…"

Jean Paul discreetly returned to his knives, and Ethan regarded her with open respect. "I owe you a very big thank-you."

"You're welcome. It was a success, I think."

"Completely." He came to stand before her, his dark-blue eyes glittering with the satisfaction of a tiger who'd just bagged several hunters for dinner. His sensuous mouth turned up at the corners as he grinned at her, stealing her breath. "In fact, many of my guests are wondering what you'll come up with next."

"They'll just have to wait and see."

"I'm wondering, too." One of his dark brows lifted. "Do I have to wait?"

If he came any closer, she was going to lose it. Feeling irritatingly light-headed, she reached out for the granite countertop to steady herself. "We could discuss the menus and themes at any time."

"How about now? I didn't get one of the boat rides."

"I don't know if the guys are still out there."

His grinned widened. "I think I can manage to take you for a ride myself."

"Ethan Curtis, where have you been?" The slow, whiskey-smooth female voice came from behind Mary, and she turned with a jerk to see a five-foot-nine Playboy playmate, dressed in an orange tank dress.

"Allison, where did you come from?" Ethan asked, sounding more annoyed than surprised.

"Didn't you say eleven? I don't wear a watch, but I could swear I'm right on time." Her voice and body language just screamed sex.

Mary heard Ethan curse, but she didn't dare turn back to face him, not with her neck turning red as she knew it was. He had a date. An after-party date. Of course he did. Why not?

"Wait for me by the pool, Allison," Ethan said, his voice soft but commanding. "I'm not quite finished here."

Finding her nerve at long last, Mary forgot about her red neck and gave the hot blonde a hotter glare. "Allison, is it?"

She smiled. "Two Ls and two Ns."

Brilliant and beautiful, Mary mused dryly. What a combination. "You don't need to go anywhere. Mr. Curtis and I are finished." She turned to Ethan and gave him a fake smile. "I'll call you in a few days, sir—to discuss the next function."

Anger burned in her stomach and, as she walked swiftly through his house and out the front door, she called herself fourteen kinds of fool for even considering him in a romantic way. He was an egotistical, spoiled player who had no idea what he really wanted.

"Mary, slow down." Ethan caught up with her on his driveway and grabbed her hand as she tried to open her car door.

She brushed him off. "I have work waiting for me at home and you have a Barbie twin waiting for you by the pool."

"I made that date weeks ago. Before...well..." He pushed a hand through his hair. "This is awkward."

"Damn right," she retorted in a sharp voice. "So, I'm going to go now before it gets any more awkward."

"No."

"I'm not into threesomes, Curtis."

"I didn't even know you were interested in a twosome."

Gritting her teeth, Mary stared at him. "Ditto."

He took a moment to process her meaning. "If you think I don't want to go to bed with you again, you're wrong."

"Who the hell could tell?"

"What does that mean?"

"You hardly looked at me tonight," she said with a scowl. "Then the cover of *Sluts-R-Us* magazine walks in and your eyes pop out of—"

"I see you, Mary," he interrupted hotly. "I remember every damn detail."

"But?"

"Weren't you the one who said that what happened those nights at the lake would never happen again?"

She hated when the truth was tossed in her face. "Yes." She wrenched open her car door.

"And it's complicated, isn't it?" he continued. "What we did? What we made? Who I am."

"Who you are? I can't figure it out."

"The bastard who blackmailed you…basically."

His words shocked her. The easy admission of something so base and vile. She got in her car and slammed the door. "So, what? You feel guilty?"

"No."

"Of course not. You see nothing wrong with what you did."

"I don't feel guilty, that's true. But I do feel…" He

cursed. "Conflicted. Protective." He shrugged, as if the truth surprised the hell out of him. "Isn't that the damnedest thing?"

"Protective? Of whom?"

"You."

"You're protecting me from you?"

"Maybe. I don't know."

"Well, stop it," she said caustically, gunning her engine. "Sex doesn't have to be any more emotionally significant than a really charged football game."

The words exploded into the air like fireworks, but she didn't believe them, and she knew that he knew she didn't believe it. What was she trying to do? Why couldn't she abandon this idea of him and her, one more time, or two or three? What was she? A masochist?

"Mary—"

"Go prove my point to Allison in there," she said bitingly before shoving the car into Reverse and taking off down the quiet, wooded drive.

Four

Mary sat in Little Bo and Peep's baby shop, up to her eyeballs in terry cloth, stretch cotton, bouncy seats and black and white mobiles. For the past twenty minutes, she hadn't been able to pick out a single thing for the nursery. She knew exactly what clothes she loved, what crib and bassinet she wanted, she even knew the drawer pulls she would pick out if this were all real. But designing a nursery for a child that didn't exist was next to impossible. She felt like a total fraud and she wanted to give up.

The doorbell over the shop entrance jangled merrily, and Mary watched a young couple come through the door with excited grins. They oohed and aahed as they moved from one quaint set of nursery furniture set to the next, hands clasped tightly, the woman's round stomach looking like a sweet watermelon. She wanted that. A real relationship, a real baby...something impossible to have with Ethan Curtis. Mary's mind rolled back to the party and how it had ended. For the past two days she'd thought of nothing but him and that blonde, and her own irrational need to be with him again. She'd wondered what had happened after she'd left. Had Ethan met her by the pool? Did they go for a swim together? Allisonn—two Ls, two Ns—hadn't seemed like the kind of woman who thought swimsuits were all that important.

Beside her, the young mother pointed at a tiny Minnesota Twins baseball cap and squealed with delight, catching Mary's eye in the process. Mary forced a smile, then moved on to look at bathtubs and safety accessories. Why the hell did she care what Ethan did? Or *who* he did, for that matter? She had to get over this.

The saleswoman walked by her again with that look all salespeople give a person when they think you're lingering without purpose.

Are you stealing or just indecisive?

"Right, I get it," Mary grumbled under her breath as she abandoned the bath supplies and headed to the front of the store. Nothing was going to happen today. She wasn't about to do any work on the nursery in her state of mind. If Ethan asked her how she was progressing, she'd just have to stall and—

"Mary?"

Coming into the shop just as Mary was exiting was a very elegant woman in her midseventies, dressed in a thin crepe navy blue suit, her white hair swept off her mildly wrinkled face in a tightly pinned chignon.

"Grandmother? What are you doing here?"

Grace Harrington surveyed her granddaughter, her perfectly arched brows lifting at the sight of Mary's plain black pantsuit and slightly scuffed heels. To Grace Harrington, clothes were like Ziplock baggies, only good for one use.

"Pearl Edicott's granddaughter is expecting twins," her grandmother said in a pinched tone. "Pearl has the most horrific taste. It's a very good thing she knows it."

"Very good thing," Mary repeated, smiling in spite of herself. Grace Harrington was an over-the-top snob, and if Mary had any sense, she'd probably detest her. After all, Grace wasn't all that warm either, more days than not she found something wrong with Mary's clothing or hairstyle, and she treated her help like they didn't breathe the same air as she did. And then there was the fact that she had cut Mary's mother out of her life when she'd married Hugh.

Yet, with all of that, Mary felt a connection with her, a strange admiration that went far beyond her wealth. Grace was smart, well-read and a stickler for speaking her mind. Mary could really respect that. She and her grandparents were rarely *simpatico*, but they were her blood, and had always wanted to be a part of her life, and strangely Mary's mother had never discouraged her from seeing them.

Grace picked up two twin chenille baby robes that cost a hundred dollars each and eyed them closely. "And what are you doing here, my dear?"

"Designing a nursery for a client."

"Ah, yes, your business. How is that going?"

"Great."

Grace forgot about the robes for a moment and focused on Mary, her lips pursed. "This isn't for one of those two-father homes, is it?"

"Not this time."

"A couple, then?" She didn't give Mary a chance to answer as she clucked her tongue disapprovingly. "A mother who doesn't want to create her own child's room. How modern."

Mary was about to ask her grandmother if she herself had actually designed her own daughter's nursery or if she'd hired three or four interior designers to make it happen, but she knew she'd probably get an answer that resembled something like, "It was my vision. As usual, the help was only there to execute it."

"The nursery is for a single father actually," Mary told her.

"Anyone I know?"

Mary's brow lifted. "Now how many single fathers do you socialize with, Grandmother?"

Grace gave her a blank look. "None…that I know of." Spotting a beautiful pink-and-blue blanket draped over one of the handcrafted armchairs, Grace turned her back on Mary. "Well, this chenille is lovely. It reminds me of the very one your mother carried around for years. If the maid even spoke of washing it, she would…" Grace stopped abruptly and cleared her throat.

Mary was grateful not to have to see the woman's

face in that moment. Turning toward a row of onesies, she quickly changed the subject. "Babies are really no bigger than dolls, are they?"

"For a short time, yes," Grace replied softly. "But before you even realize it they are grown and deciding what they will wear and who they will marry without any input from you."

"There you are." A booming male voice broke through all the femininity. "I called your office and Olivia said you'd be—"

"Ethan?" In the heaviness of her conversation with Grace, Mary hadn't heard the bell over the door. If she had heard—and seen—who was about to enter the shop, she would've been out the door in a matter of seconds. This was not good.

Ethan spotted Grace and changed instantly from casual guy to cynical business mogul. "Mrs. Harrington. What a pleasant surprise."

"I doubt that," the older woman said dryly.

Before her grandmother could connect the single father with Ethan, Mary said quickly, "I'm organizing several functions for Mr. Curtis."

"Is that so?" Grace said, pursing her lips as if she'd just gotten a whiff of rotting fish, or as if the thought of her blue-blooded granddaughter working for the upstart who had basically stolen her family's company made her want to throw up. "When did he hire you?"

In other words, how long has this been going on and why was I not informed?

"Just a few weeks ago," Mary replied.

"And he has a meeting with you in a baby boutique?"

"No."

No doubt sensing that Mary was floundering, Ethan jumped in to save her. "We were supposed to meet at the restaurant next door, but I saw your granddaughter in here and wanted to start early. As you know, Mrs. Harrington, I have little patience and zero time. I was in the neighborhood seeing a client and there was something I needed to discuss with Miss Kelley that couldn't wait. Luckily she agreed to meet with me."

"Luckily for you she agreed to take you on as a client, Mr. Curtis," Grace said frigidly.

He nodded. "Your granddaughter is very talented."

"A fact of which I am well aware."

"Knowing that your granddaughter is planning the event, maybe you'll reconsider the brunch on Saturday."

"Perhaps," she said tightly, then turned to Mary. "I have to run, my dear."

"But the gift for the twins…"

"This shop is a little too new money for my taste, and you know how I despise that." She didn't have to look at Ethan to get her point across. "Your father is out of harm's way now, I hear."

"Yes," Mary said, surprised her grandmother would bring something like that up, much less care.

"Nasty business, that. But we were in no position to help, unfortunately." After two air kisses to Mary's cheeks and nothing whatever for Ethan, she left them.

"That woman couldn't hate me more if I spit on her shoe," Ethan muttered.

"Oh, yes she could, but I wouldn't advise trying it."

"You'd think I stole the company right out from under their noses."

"Didn't you?"

He gave her a haughty look. "Harrington Corp. was in trouble. Your grandfather was really slipping. Clients weren't getting serviced the way they had in the past and many were threatening to walk. I didn't steal anything. If anything I saved that damn company."

"Pretty much the same as stealing it, to my grandparents." Mary took her cell phone out of her pocket and showed it to him. "Now, you have my phone number, right?"

"Yes."

"Couldn't you have called me instead of tracking me down?"

"Why? Did I embarrass you?" he asked coldly.

"Don't be so thick, Curtis. I'm in a baby shop. I had to dance fast with my grandmother about why I was here, then why you were here—"

"*I* danced fast on that one," he interrupted.

She ignored him. "You know I want to keep this quiet. I thought we both did."

"I never said I wanted to keep anything quiet—"

"Hello, there." The saleswoman who had been watching Mary for the past thirty minutes in annoyance joined them, completely smiley-faced and enthusiastic at the sight of Ethan. "Daddy's here."

Ethan looked pleased with the comment and nodded. "He is."

"Would you and your wife like some lemonade before you get started?"

Mary snorted derisively and said, "I'm not his—"

"Yes, we would," Ethan said, cutting her off before following the saleswoman to a small refreshment area.

For the next twenty minutes Mary sat beside Ethan and watched as the saleswoman laid blankets and rugs, hats and booties, washtubs and soothing lullaby CDs at Ethan's feet as though he were the sultan of Bruni.

Feeling close to exploding if she stayed in the shop one more minute, Mary leaned in and whispered to Ethan, "I have to get back to the office," then grabbed her purse and headed for the door.

He caught up with her, placing his hand on her arm. "We need to talk."

"About?" she asked, trying to ignore the heat of his fingers searing into her skin.

"The brunch."

"Call my office and we'll set something up for tomorrow—"

"No, I'm the client. You can come to my office." His jaw hardened, letting her know there was no denying his command. "Today, four-thirty."

As she struggled to maintain her calm exterior, Mary fought the desire that simmered beneath. "Fine. Four-thirty."

"You look exhausted."

Not exactly the first thing a woman wants to hear

when the man she finds overwhelmingly attractive opens his office door.

"Thanks," Mary uttered sarcastically.

Ethan grinned, gestured toward the chocolate brown leather couch. "Sit down."

"I'm fine."

"We're not going to discuss the brunch while you stand. This could take a while."

"How long are you estimating?"

"Why? Do you have a date or something?"

Standing on either side of the coffee table, like two gunslingers, they stared at each other.

"Not the best joke I've made this week."

"No."

"Come on, have a seat," Ethan said, dropping onto the plush leather and grinning.

On a weary sigh, she plunked down on the couch. "Okay, I'm sitting, now let's start with the menu. I think we should go for a southern theme. Olivia has this New Mexican menu— Wait, what are you doing?"

Before Mary could stop him, Ethan had taken off her shoes and placed her feet in his lap. "I'm helping you to relax."

"Why?"

"Why not?"

"I'll tell you why not. I'm here for business not for pl—" She came to screeching halt, which made Ethan's eyes glitter even more wickedly.

"If this helps," he began. "Rubbing your aching feet is business. Technically."

"I can't wait to hear this."

"It's my job, my duty—my business, if you will. Or so I've read."

She looked surprised. "You've been reading books on…"

"Pregnancy? Yep."

"Seriously?"

He nodded. "Pregnancy, baby care, labor, postpartum, breastfeeding—"

"Okay, that's enough," she said, relaxing back into the couch as Ethan's strong hands worked the tired knots in her arches. "Five minutes max."

He laughed. "I've learned many useful things."

"Like?" she asked, trying to keep her eyes open and the soft, cozy sound out of her voice.

"Like nausea and strange cravings are very normal in the first trimester."

"Uh-huh."

"So are leg cramps and exhaustion."

"Yep."

"And an unusually high sex drive."

Her eyes flew open and she sat up, swung her legs to the floor. It took her a moment to tamp down the tremors of need running through her. She felt the urge so strongly, all she wanted him to do was continue touching her. She wanted his mouth on hers, nudging her lips apart with his tongue… "All right," she said breathlessly. "Southern food, maybe Southwest or Cajun. What about having an autumn-barn-dance theme for your brunch?"

"A heavy sex drive is nothing to be ashamed of, Mary." She tilted her chin up. "I've never been ashamed of it."

What she was saying dawned on him almost immediately, and his eyes lit with mischief, his lips parted sensuously.

"Now, can we get back to this?" she asked coolly.

He wouldn't allow her to look away. "Nothing happened with Allisonn."

Her heart skipped and she swallowed nervously. She wanted to tell him that she couldn't care less about blondie, but he wouldn't believe her. "This doesn't sound like brunch discussion."

"Mary…" he began, his voice the husky baritone she remembered from those nights at the lake.

"Listen, Curtis, what you do in your house, bedroom, pool, etcetera is your business. Let's just get on with this."

"Why are you so hard?"

"Bad genes," she responded succinctly which made him laugh. "Not from my parents. They were angels. But they say attitude skips a generation."

Shaking his head, he stared at her for a moment, then he stood up and reached for her. "Dance with me?"

"You've got to be kidding."

"We'll make it business related. Show me what you're talking about with this barn concept. There's got to be some dancing involved on my deck, right?"

"Yes, but there's no music."

"I could turn some on, but I don't think we need it," He touched his temple with his index finger. "It's all in here."

Laughing, she took his hand and let him pull her to her feet and into his arms. "You have country music playing up there?"

He pretended to be insulted by her query. "Blues, baby. Only the blues for me."

Her toes sank into the plush carpet and she sank into Ethan's embrace. His hand gripped her waist, then slid to her back to pull her closer. She felt feminine and unsure, but she didn't want him to release her.

"I don't know how to dance," she admitted.

"I'm not that great at it, either," he said. "But I can manage a few turns and the side-to-side swaying."

His eyes were so expressive, so full of life. They could leap from anger to lust to boredom to amusement in mere moments, but it was these times that made her toes curl, the times when he stared at her with unabashed longing.

As he rocked back and forth, as his hips brushed hers and his palm pressed possessively against her hand, Mary experienced a feeling so powerful, so new it made her heart thump painfully in her chest. She was enjoying herself, with Ethan Curtis, the man who had forced her into— A man she should never enjoy herself with.

Her thoughts dropped away suddenly as Ethan quickened his pace, twirling her first to the right, then the left. With a sinful grin, he grasped both of her hands and gave her a gentle push back, then he turned her and pulled her into his body, so her back was pressed against his chest.

She glanced over her shoulder at him and smiled at the amusement in his eyes. "Tell anyone about this and I'm never dancing with you again."

Laughing with delight, Mary let him sway them both to the right and left, then squealed when he dipped her. When he rolled her out toward the couch, she released him and dropped back on the brown leather cushions. Chuckling along with her, Ethan did, too. For a moment neither of them spoke, then they both turned to look at each other.

"We'd better be careful," Ethan said.

"Why?" Mary asked breathlessly. "What do you mean?"

He reached over and brushed a strand of honey-colored hair from her cheek. "If we don't watch our step we might have fun together—or worse, actually start liking each other."

To Mary's delight, the brunch fell on a glorious late-August day. The trees were starting to contemplate change, their green leaves making room for rich golds, ruby reds and pumpkin oranges. Mary had nixed the Cajun idea, but the pre-autumn Southern barn theme was there and looking fabulous. As she meandered through the guests, who had almost doubled in size since the last party, she took in her handiwork with a proud grin. The deck and surrounding land was deco-rated with an odd but interesting, contemporary rustic charm; hay bales in glass troughs like funky center-pieces, scarecrows dressed like runway models, Tom Sawyer-style rafts in the water, and on and on. Then there was the food. Pumpkin and sage soup in minia-ture pumpkins, fried catfish with a spicy green tomato relish, mustard greens with pancetta, watermelon and pecan pie tartlets.

Everyone seemed relaxed, the stuffy atmosphere of this crowd's customary Saturday cocktail party forgotten. Diamonds still sparkled from ears, wrists and fingers, but the backdrop was denim and Ralph Lauren plaid.

Mary spotted five-star-inns' Isaac and Emily Underwood coming toward her and smiled welcomingly. She knew that, as of last Monday, the couple were now Ethan's clients. "Well, hello, there. Are you two enjoying yourselves?"

"Your creativity is astounding, Mary," Isaac said, gesturing to the backyard.

"Thank you."

"Yes, amazing," Emily added.

Isaac dropped his voice to a conspiratorial whisper, "Even though we don't have to work, the feeling of success can bring great rewards, don't you think?"

Mary's brows drew together. Contrary to what the Underwoods believed was reality, Mary had to work for every penny. The Harringtons didn't help her one bit, never had, nor had she ever asked them to.

"This is a great success," Emily said, two-carat diamond studs sparkling in her ears. "Especially for Ethan. Invitations to his parties will be sought-after now."

"Now?"

Heat spread across Emily's face and she stumbled to explain. "Well, what I mean to say is…"

Isaac quickly covered for her. "Curtis is brilliant,

and he has the client list to prove it, but as far as social-
izing…well, he's not really one of us, you understand."

She certainly did, and she had to resist the urge to
grab the pumpkin out of Isaac's hand and dump the
contents over his head. Lucky for her and for them, the
Underwoods spotted another group of snotty elitists
over by the bar and excused themselves. Why did Ethan
want to be a part of this world? she wondered, heading
inside the house. She scanned the room looking for him,
expecting to find him in the center of a group of wealthy
people who were looking for free advice, but he wasn't
there. She sidled up to one of the waitstaff. "Have you
seen Mr. Curtis?"

"I think he's in the kitchen."

"Alone?"

"No, there's a full kitchen staff in there, Ms. Kelley."

"I mean, was he with anyone? A guest?" she asked
tightly. Like maybe a Tiffany—one F, two Ys?

The man shook his head. "Not that I saw."

As she walked toward the kitchen, the sound of
clanging pots and hustling staff was interspersed with
a shrill, critical voice that Mary instantly recognized as
her grandmother's.

The door opened and as a mortified-looking waitress
rushed out with a plate of food, Mary heard the older
woman's voice again. "You can take my family's company, hire my granddaughter to act as your wife at
parties and invite the top shelf as your guests, but that
will never make you one of us."

Interrupting the conversation didn't sound like a

good plan. She didn't want to embarrass Ethan any
further. So Mary watched through a crack in the door.
The room was busy with waitstaff, chefs and to Mary's
horror, not only her grandmother, but two of her grandmother's closest friends. Grace Harrington stood a few
feet from Ethan, who had his back to the sleek Wolf
range, her friends behind her like a scene from one of
those movies about exclusive high school cliques.

"Breeding cannot be bought," Grace continued, her
tone spiteful and cruel. "Where and who you come from
is in every movement you make. Make no mistake about
it, Mr. Curtis, you wear your trailer-park upbringing
like a second skin."

The room stilled. The chefs stopped chopping, the
waitstaff looked horrified as they tried to stare at anything but Ethan.

White-hot fury burned in Ethan's eyes. "I know
exactly where I come from, Mrs. Harrington, and I'm
proud of it."

"Is that so? Then why try so hard to impress us all?"

"My work makes enough of an impression to sat-
isfy me. These events are a way to gain more clients.
After all," he said with a slow smile, "before I came
along, Harrington Corp. was not only hemorrhaging
money but about to lose seventy percent of their client
base as well."

Grace's jaw dropped, and she looked as though she
couldn't breathe. Ditto with the geriatric sentinels behind her. Mary had never seen her grandmother bested
before, and she felt oddly sorry for her, but knew the

older woman had it coming to her. Grace Harrington could dish it out, and maybe now she would learn to take it.

Mary watched Ethan grab a beer from the counter and tip it toward the threesome. "Good afternoon, ladies. I have every confidence that you can find the front door from here."

And then he was coming her way, in ten seconds he'd bump right into her. Mary dropped back into a small alcove off the hallway and waited for him to leave the kitchen and pass by her. His jaw tight, his stride purposeful, he walked past her and in the opposite direction of the party. After waiting a moment for her grandmother and her friends to leave, Mary followed Ethan. She had a good idea where he'd be.

She climbed the stairs and walked down the hall, unsure of what she was going to say to him when she found him. The door to the nursery was closed, but that didn't dissuade her.

Without knocking, she entered the room. Ethan was lying on his back on the floor, staring out the enormous bay window. Sunlight splashed over his handsome face, illuminating his pensive expression.

Mary sat beside him. Maybe he'd been right that day in his office, after their musicless dance, maybe they were becoming friends. God only knew why, after their history. But the fact was she understood him a little better now, understood what drove him. Her mother had felt some of the same feelings of not being good enough, not knowing where she belonged or who really cared about her for herself and not how much money she had.

"She's right."

Ethan's words jarred her, brought her back to the present. "Who's right?"

"Your grandmother. I'm not worth much more than the trailer I was born in."

"That's not exactly what she said." Mary knew that she sounded as though she were defending Grace, when that's not what she was trying to do at all. She knew her grandmother had been cold and cruel, but Ethan could be that way as well.

"That's what she said, Mary. I've heard versions of that diatribe many times. From my ex-wife, from my own mother. Doesn't seem to matter how hard I work." He shrugged. "I'll never escape it."

"This self-pitying thing has to stop, Ethan."

He sat up, stared at her with cold eyes. "What?"

"Why do you care?" she demanded.

"What?"

"Why do you care what any of them think?"

The anger dropped away, and he shook his head. Just kept shaking his head. "I have no idea."

"Why can't you be satisfied with the life you've created?"

The double meaning wasn't lost on either of them, and in that moment, Mary knew it was just a matter of time before she confessed the truth about her pregnancy. She didn't want to care about him. He'd forced her to make some abominable decisions…and yet…

She put a hand on his shoulder, and in less than an instant he covered it with his own. "Under that layer of pride and arrogance," she said softly, "is a pretty decent guy. I can't help but believe that."

He leaned in until his forehead touched hers. "Even with everything that's happened?"

"Yes."

He tipped her chin up and with a soft groan his mouth found hers in a slow, drugging kiss. Mary opened to him, even suckled his bottom lip until he uttered her name and pulled her closer, his tongue mating with hers.

She protested when he pulled away from her, whispering a barely audible no.

With his face still so close to her own, he regarded her intently. "Are you pitying me, Mary?"

She wanted his mouth, his tongue, his skin against hers and no more questions. "Does it matter?" she uttered huskily.

A long moment of silence passed, and then Ethan groaned, a frustrated, animal-like sound. "No," he muttered, closing his eyes, nuzzling her cheek until he found her mouth again.

Five

Despite the open window, the air in the room had become stiflingly warm. Mary's limbs felt heavy, and she clung to Ethan for support. His mouth was hard on hers, his breath sweet and intoxicating. For a moment she wondered if she was drunk, but then realized she had been sipping seltzer water all morning. Mouth slanting, Ethan unleashed the full strength of his need, his tongue against hers, caressing the tip until Mary was breathless and limp. Whatever he wanted to do, she was a willing participant.

Without a word, Mary started unbuttoning her white blouse, her fingers shaking. Her skin needed to breathe, needed to be touched. As Ethan chuckled softly against her lips, she tugged away at her shirt, wishing she could just rip it off.

"Let me," he uttered hoarsely.

"And this," she practically begged, struggling with the hooks on her pale-pink bra.

"Tell me what you want, Mary."

"You."

"My weight on top of you? My chest brushing against your nipples?"

"Your mouth."

His head was in the crook of her neck, his forehead nuzzling her, his teeth nipping at her skin. "On your mouth? On your breasts? Do you want me to suckle them like I did your tongue?"

"Yes," came her ragged whisper.

Gently he pulled the straps over her shoulders, eased her bra to her waist. She felt as though she were falling, sliding down, down, until she landed against plush, fuzzy white carpet. Her back to the floor, Ethan poised on top of her, his dark blue eyes hungry, almost desperate, Mary struggled to catch her breath.

"Ethan," she rasped.

Ethan paused, his body pulsing with heat. He'd never heard her say his name like that—desperately.

His body tight to the point of pain, Ethan slid his hand up her torso to her rib cage and gently cupped one breast. Instantly hungry for more, he brushed his thumb over her nipple until it stiffened into a rosy peak. His mouth watered. He'd tasted her before, but the memory had been little comfort over the past weeks.

"You are so beautiful," he whispered, leaning forward into the warmth of her body, her skin, his mouth grazing the tender bud.

Gasping, she arched her back, her chest rising and falling rapidly, one hand fisting the carpet. Her skin was so hot, electric, and he couldn't help himself, he covered her with his mouth and suckled deeply.

"Oh…" she uttered breathlessly, cupping her other breast. "Oh, Ethan, please."

Ethan rooted between her ribs to her other breast, over her fingers until he found the sweet, taut peak in the center. Her body danced beneath his, her hips pumped as though he was inside her, and how he longed to be.

So caught up in the moment, Ethan gently sank his teeth into the pink flesh surrounding her nipple as he continued to flick the tight bud. Her breath quickened, and he could hear her heart pounding in her chest. He wanted to make her climax, just with his mouth on her breast, and she was close, so close. But then outside the window came the sounds of people laughing and talking, some loud enough to hear.

"Where do you think Curtis ran off to?" one said.

"Back to the office?" someone suggested, chuckling.

The conversation wasn't lost on Mary or Ethan, and they stilled, looked at each other, their breathing labored. Then after a moment, Mary let out a frustrated sigh and rolled away from him.

Feeling like an ass, Ethan didn't say anything as he watched her dress, but when she finally looked at him, pink-cheeked, slightly disheveled and, judging by her eyes, still on the verge of orgasm, he couldn't stop himself.

"No farther?" he asked gently.

She shook her head, deep regret in her eyes, but from what, he wasn't sure. "We have to get back to the party."

"God, why?"

"They're leaving."

"I don't care—"

"Yes, you do," she said, coming to her feet, smoothing her blouse. "We need to make an appearance, say goodbye to those who remain. You don't want people thinking that you completely disappeared."

"I don't give a damn what they think." Desire still raged through him. He wanted to play caveman and drag her off to his bed and lock the door behind him. "I want to finish this."

"Another time."

He was about to tell her that he didn't want to wait, but he knew that determined look on her face, knew better than to try to sway or push her. "I'm holding you to that," he grumbled.

By the time they returned, separately of course, to the party, most of the guests had gone. There were a few stragglers milling about, and while Mary thanked and paid the staff, Ethan showed his face to the last of the guests.

He was in his office when Mary found him a half hour later.

"Well, the general consensus is that everyone had a good time," she said.

"Everyone?" he asked pointedly, his gaze intense.

She bit her lip, which made his groin tighten painfully. "I should get going."

"Stay until the end," he said.

"This is the end. Everyone's gone, even the wait and kitchen staffs have taken off."

He sat back in his chair. "I meant stay until the end of the night…when it gets light outside and my housekeeper serves breakfast."

"Ethan…"

"You could stay upstairs in my bed. Because you want to…this time."

She sighed, let her eyes fall closed for a moment. When she opened them again, he saw the same look in her eyes as he had upstairs. She wasn't finished with him or what they'd started, but she also wasn't about to agree to stay with him, either. She shook her head. "I'm sorry." Then turned and left the room.

Her ancient Betty Boop bedside lamp clicked on and Mary uttered a tired, "Man…"

Her father's face, bed-worn and confused, stared down at her. "What are you doing here, lass?"

"Sleeping."

"Why?"

She glanced at her matching Betty Boop clock, both it and the lamp presents from her parents for her twelfth birthday. "Because it's four in the morning."

Hugh sat on the bed and dragged a hand through his rumpled hair. "Why are you here and not in your apartment?"

Right. Mary glanced around her old bedroom. Not a thing out of place since she'd found her own apartment at nineteen. Same red-checked curtains and white dresser. She smiled halfheartedly when she spotted her *Xanadu* album in the corner by the old turntable.

Her father cleared his throat, and Mary looked at him sheepishly. "All right, I ran away."

"Did you indeed?" he said, his shaggy brows lifting.

"From a boy." Actually from a man, a gorgeous, fever-inducing man, who wanted her in his bed almost as much as he wanted the nonexistent child in her belly. Mary shook her head. What a mess. She burrowed deeper under her old, white down comforter.

"You won't be telling me why you're running from this boy, will you lass?"

Her lips pressed tightly together, she shook her head like a stubborn toddler. How could she possibly? Her dad wouldn't understand what she'd done—the lengths to which she'd gone to protect him. Or worse yet, he'd understand perfectly, feel incredibly guilty and fall deeper into the chasm of despair he was already stuck in.

"You just need a bit of the old family house, do you?" he asked finally, shooing a tiny insect away from the lamp.

She gave him a grateful smile. "If you don't mind, Pop."

"You know you're always welcome here, lass." He paused for a moment, his eyes concerned. "I just don't want you to be running away from your problems too often. You'll never have time to sit down and take a breath if you do."

"I know."

"I love you, lass."

"I love you too, Pop."

When her father left the room, Mary lay back against her pillow and stared out at the same moon she'd watched change from sliver to crescent to full so many times when she was a kid. What had started out as the only foreseeable way to keep her father out of jail, or from a trial at the very least, had become a nightmare that she wanted to wake up from. She and Ethan had a meeting next week, and no matter how difficult it would be, she was not going to run away from the truth. She was going to tell him everything.

The wind off the lake whipped her hair from side to side, as though trying to make up its mind which direction to go. It was Sunday morning, a day Mary usually reserved for the newspaper, coffee and as many Danishes as she could eat without exploding, but when Ivan Garrison had called and asked her to see his boat, she'd readily accepted. The fact was, she was dying for some impersonal work to take her mind off Ethan.

After seeing his eighty-four-foot yacht, and having a quick discussion about where he'd like everything set up for the gala, the captain had asked her to take a sail on the very boat that he would be racing that day. Mary had been on very few sailboats in her time, and had been a little afraid of seasickness, but after popping a couple of Dramamine, she'd hopped aboard and found life on the water rather magnificent.

After they'd rounded the lake twice, Ivan headed back to the marina. Over the wind and the lapping of the water, Mary called, "This is great! I think your guests will be very impressed, Captain."

Ivan grinned at her. "Not just by the gala, I'm hoping."

Confused, she said, "I'm sorry?"

"I've decided to take your advice and make this a charity event."

Mary nodded. So, the captain did have a soul after all. Shocking, he wasn't just a Lamborghini-driving playboy. She'd have to tell Olivia.

"So all the entry fees will go to charity?" she called as Ivan maneuvered around in the marina, approaching the dock at a very slow speed.

"My financial advisors have told me that this will be a great tax write-off."

So he wasn't exactly Mother Teresa, but at least he had agreed to do something worthwhile. Maybe she wouldn't mention this to Olivia.

"Have you decided which charity appeals to you?" she asked him.

"Cancer's pretty popular."

"True."

Ivan slowly entered the slip, then placed the transmission in neutral and let the wind blow the boat back. "But which one to choose?" he called, securing the boat's front dock line first. "Children? Lung? Breast?"

Mary removed her life vest and placed it beside her on the bench. "Well, how about the Cancer Research Institute? They pretty much cover it all."

"Perfect." Staring onto the dock, Ivan squinted, then frowned. "Is he waiting for you or me?"

Mary glanced up, saw what Ivan was seeing and felt her pulse jump inside her veins. Standing there, arms crossed and looking murderous, was Ethan. "That would be for me."

Six

Ethan's body tightened at the sight of Mary walking down the dock toward him. A white T-shirt, pink shorts and bare feet had never looked so dangerous on any woman. Visions swam in his mind, images of soft skin against his mouth and long legs wrapped around his waist, cute round buttocks cupped in his hands. This intense physical reaction was becoming way too familiar, and he wondered if the only way he was going to get rid of it was to take her to bed again.

Ethan had known many women in his time, but his need for them had faded quickly. Why wasn't it the same with Mary Kelley? Why had the desire to taste her, fill his nostrils with her scent, open her thighs and bury himself deep inside her only intensified over time? Was it the baby or something else, something more?

Her pale-blue eyes mocked him as she came to stand before him, a grin tugging at her mouth. "You are officially stalking me now, Curtis."

"Well, one of us has to protect the baby," he muttered grimly.

"What in the world are you talking about?"

He gestured to the water. "Out there on the open water, no life jacket, no nothing."

"Open water?" she repeated, laughing. "Come on. This is a lake, calm as a sleeping kitten. There's no danger here."

Ethan eyed the man coming up behind her. "Isn't there?"

"Oh, for God's sake," Mary said as her sailboat buddy walked by with a smile and a wave. She waved back and called, "I'll call you on Thursday," then returned her attention to a very annoyed Ethan. "I was wearing a life jacket, and the captain—he's just a client."

"*The captain*," Ethan drawled with derision. "Please don't tell me that he makes you call him that?"

Mary regarded him incredulously. "Let's not get into crazy demands from clients, shall we?"

"Fine," he muttered darkly, following her down the dock and toward the parking lot.

As she dug the car keys from her purse, she asked, "Now, what's brought you all the way out here?"

"Do you have a doctor?"

She stopped, turned to look at him. "Why? Do you have a medical emergency?"

Her joke was lost on him and he scowled. "Be serious for a second."

"I have a doctor, Ethan."

"For the pregnancy?"

Her gaze flickered to the ground then back up, and he wondered if that was too intimate a thing to ask her.

"Yes, I have a doctor," she said finally. "A family-practice type thing. Why?"

He shook his head. "That's not good enough. You need an Ob/Gyn."

Exhaling heavily, she walked away from him toward the lot, but he was on her heels. "I'm serious, Mary."

"I'm going to come to your house and take every one of those books away from you. Foot massage is one thing, buddy, but—" she fumbled in her purse again for her keys "—you're getting way too knowledgeable on *Girlfriends' Guides* and *Mothering and You*, and frankly, it's making me feel a little weird."

Ethan paused. He didn't have those two books, but he made a mental note to get them. "Listen, I have a client whose wife is Deena Norrison."

"Never heard of her."

"She's only one of the best Ob/Gyn's in the country."

When Mary reached her car and still couldn't find her keys, she looked ready to explode. Undeterred, Ethan continued, "She's agreed to see you."

"I have a good doctor, Ethan," Mary assured him, her

hand stuffed inside her purse again, perspiration beading on her brow.

"Good is not great, and Deena's the best. Doesn't our child deserve the best?"

"Aha!" Mary held up her keys triumphantly, but her glee was short-lived when she noticed the stern look on Ethan's face. She sighed. "When is this appointment? This week is swamped for me, and next week we leave for Mackinac Island."

"How's today?"

"Today," she repeated, the blood draining from her face.

"Right now." He took her cool hand in his. "There's no reason to be nervous. I'm sure everything is fine."

"Now?"

"I know. Isn't that great? She's a pretty cool lady. She'll fit you in at four. Ultrasound and everything."

Mary shook her head. "But—"

Ethan didn't give her time to refuse. Once she saw the kid's heartbeat and heard from the best doctor in the country that everything was just as it should be, she'd relax. "Come on," he said, gently guiding her toward his car. "I'll drive."

Dr. Deena Norrison's reception area looked like a photograph straight out of the pages of *Victoria* magazine. Surrounded by cabbage-rose wallpaper, clients sank down into soft and cushy deep-pink sofas with rolled arms. The love seats and chairs, Mary was certain, had down pillows.

Mary sat on one of the love seats, her purse perched on the Queen Anne table before her. The scent of flowers was dizzying and made her feel as though she was trapped inside an English garden at the height of summer.

"Are you okay?" Ethan asked beside her.

"No. I don't know." The deodorant she'd put on this morning had disappeared, and she felt wet and uncomfortable.

"I can get you some water or something?" Ethan suggested.

The woman at the front desk stood, smiled at them and said in a polite whisper, "Mrs. Curtis?"

"Oh, jeez," Mary muttered.

"We can correct that later," Ethan assured her, then turned to the receptionist and said, "She's right here."

"We'll be taking you back soon," the woman informed them.

Mary saw it all in her mind: an examination table covered in a crisp old English linen sheet with exquisite crocheted trim and white slip-covered booties on the stirrups. She giggled a little hysterically.

"You need to relax," Ethan suggested gently.

"Easy for you to say," Mary uttered as the receptionist held out a clipboard with a flower pen attached.

"If you can just fill out this paperwork."

Sensing that Mary was not about to move, Ethan retrieved the papers for her and placed them in her lap. "I could do this if—"

"No, it's fine."

As Mary filled out the forms, the words blurred

together, and she had to stop and take a deep breath. The front door to the office opened and a woman came in. She was really far along in her pregnancy and looked exhausted. She dropped down in the chair beside Mary's love seat and exhaled heavily. When she spotted Mary, she smiled. "Long way to go yet, huh? When are you due?"

"What? Oh…ah…" It was all she could get out. Her heart pounded furiously in her chest, and waves of nausea were hitting her every few minutes. She needed air, needed to breathe something other than that damn flower smell. Suddenly panicked, she stood, dropped the paperwork on the table and ran out of the office. She spotted a stairwell to her left and ran to the door. Down the stairs she flew, her shirt spotted with sweat, her breathing labored. She heard Ethan behind her, calling her name, but she didn't stop. Once she made it to the lobby, she swung the front door open wide and ran to a grassy spot where a few nurses were eating their lunch.

Breathing heavily, she wanted to collapse on the grass, but instead she started pacing.

"Mary?"

She didn't look at him, didn't stop moving. "I can't do this."

"It's okay." His voice was soothing, and she hated him for his concern. He was the one who'd gotten them into this mess in the first place, damn him. "You don't have to see her," he continued. "Use your own doctor. I just thought it would be—"

"It's not the doctor, Ethan."

"Then what?" When she wouldn't stop pacing, he grabbed her shoulders and held her against him, his tone worried now. "What the hell is wrong?"

His chest felt so strong and she wanted to sink into it, disappear inside of it, but he wouldn't allow her to hide. Easing one hand from her shoulder, he tipped her chin up so she had to look at him.

"Tell me what's going on, Mary."

Miserably, she shook her head. "There is no baby."

"What?"

"No baby, Ethan."

He went white. "Did something happen…that boat ride…"

"No." She stared at him, into those beautiful dark-blue eyes she'd believed for so long were soulless. What a damn mess. This whole thing. "I just wanted my father to be okay."

He still looked confused, but after a moment, re-alization dawned and confusion was swapped for a fiercely accusing gaze. "You were never pregnant?"

Shame coiled in her belly and she shook her head. "No."

"You were never pregnant," he repeated.

"I'm sorry."

Ethan stared at her, his eyes wide in fury. "Yes, you will be," he uttered, his jaw knotted with the force of emotion.

"Ethan."

"I should've known."

"Ethan, please, I—" But her words fell on deaf ears. He had already turned his back on her and was stalking toward his car. Feeling as though she'd just assaulted someone, Mary dropped onto a hard picnic bench and watched his BMW leave the parking lot, tires squealing.

Seven

Twenty minutes later, Ethan entered the crumbling stone gates of Days of Grace Trailer Park. As he drove past the shabby office, muscle memory took hold and his BMW practically steered itself to the curb beside number fifty-three. The one-bedroom mobile home his father had sold just before his death looked as though it had been remodeled, as though someone were really trying to make the place a home, with fresh paint, a nice carport and fenced garden.

"About damn time," Ethan muttered, opening his window a crack before killing the engine.

It was ironic. At sixteen, he couldn't have gotten out of this park fast enough. He'd had big dreams, big plans, and he'd sworn to himself he'd never be back. But here he was, drawn to it like scum to bathroom tile. How was it that he felt infinitely more comfortable parked outside his father's trailer than at his home or office? Why was it that he could breathe here? The air was stale and slightly mildewed; nothing had changed.

He shoved a hand through his hair. He should have expected Mary to lie to him. People were never honest, never to be trusted—including himself. Why the hell hadn't he learned that in all this time? Maybe because he'd thought himself worthy of a family, good enough to make a child with a Harrington.

A large man in his early thirties wearing a baseball hat and ripped jeans came out of the house. When he spotted Ethan, he lifted a hand in a wary hello. Wasn't the first time the guy had seen Ethan parked there, but he'd never called security. No doubt the guy knew he could've handled the situation himself if things got out of control. After all, he was pretty big.

Not looking for any more trouble today, Ethan gunned the engine of his sports car and took off back to his self-made world.

Mondays were usually Mary's best day. She was well rested, coffeed-up and excited to get back to work. Today, however, she felt as though a semi had been driving back and forth over her body all night long. She felt jittery and exhausted at the same time—a wicked combination.

As she walked into the office, her hand shook a little around the double espresso she carried. The first person she saw was Olivia. The startlingly pretty brunette was sitting at the receptionist's desk—something she liked to do before Meg, the receptionist, got there at nine. "Hey there, Miss Kelley," she said in a chipper voice. "You're here early."

"And I'm not the only one."

"I have some phone calls to return. I wanted to get to them early." Olivia's eyes narrowed as she stared hard at Mary. "Did you get any sleep last night?"

Mary sighed, placed her plastic coffee cup on the reception desk. "I think somewhere between four and six I dozed off."

"Work…or—" Olivia hesitated, bit her full bottom lip "—something else?"

For a moment Mary contemplated blowing Olivia's mind with the entire story of Ethan Curtis and her. She just wanted to unburden herself with a girlfriend for a few minutes, emotionally puke and have Olivia figuratively hold her hair back. But for good or bad, the partners of NRR just didn't go there with each other— though Mary wondered if any of them wanted to but were afraid to ruffle the feathers of their business.

"I was working late," Mary said at last. "The captain is very demanding."

Olivia laughed at that, her dark eyes filled with mirth. "He seems like a semidecent guy, despite the millions and the bawdy reputation."

"He is, actually. Did I tell you he's donating all the proceeds from the regatta gala to charity?"

"Would it be uncharitable of me to say that he should?"

It was Mary's turn to laugh, though the sound felt a little forced. "Ivan's all right. Not much going on upstairs, though."

"What a shocker," Olivia said sarcastically. "Inherited wealth?"

"Yes."

Olivia rolled her eyes as she stood up and headed into the kitchen. "Do you want something to eat? I made blueberry muffins, and, not to toot my own horn or anything, but both attorneys offices downstairs came up to ask where that amazing scent was coming from."

Mary's stomach rolled rudely at the thought of food and she headed toward her office. "Maybe later."

"Okay. Oh, hey, Mary?"

"Yeah."

"Mr. Curtis called."

Mary felt a tremor of nervous energy move through her, and suddenly she felt unable to breathe. She hadn't spoken to him since Saturday, since her breakdown in the parking lot.

She poked her head out of her office and gave Olivia a weak smile. "Let me guess. He no longer requires my services."

Wielding a saucepan in one hand and an egg in the other, Olivia looked perplexed. "No. Actually, he asked if you could come by his house today at four-thirty."

"What?" There was no way she had heard Olivia correctly.

"Four-thirty," Olivia repeated. "His house."

"Oh. Okay." Well, sure. Why should he make the

trip to her office to can her when he could do it in person? Her heart pounded so hard in her chest the movement actually hurt.

"Is he an inheritance jerk, too, Mary?"

Mary shook her head. "No, self-made all the way."

Olivia nodded. "I thought so. He always sounds down-to-earth when he calls. That's pretty refreshing."

Mary went back into her office on unsteady legs and dropped into the chair behind her desk. She had to be ready to hear whatever he had to say. There was no doubt he was going to fire her, but what if he wanted to tell her that he was bringing her father back up on charges?

The queasy, dizzy, anxiety-ridden feeling she'd been having since yesterday came back full force, and she put her head down on her desk. Her eyes remained open, and even in the semidarkness of her self-made tent, Mary saw what she'd collapsed upon. The plans for Ethan's nursery—a nursery she hadn't even begun. With a groan she pushed the plans off her desk and into the trash can.

Ethan's housekeeper, Sybil, who Mary had only seen twice before—right before the staff and caterers arrived for a party—answered the door with a vexed expression. "Hello, Ms. Kelley."

"How are you, Sybil?"

The woman released a weighty breath. "Mr. Curtis is in the game room. Let me show you the way."

"Game room?" Mary repeated, following behind the housekeeper. She'd been in Ethan's house several times and she'd never seen a game room.

Glancing over her shoulder, Sybil rolled her eyes. "It's where he goes when he's brooding."

Brooding? Mary tried not to register the shock she felt. First of all, she couldn't imagine Ethan showing anyone his emotions—it just wasn't his style. And second of all, did he know that the woman he paid to run his household talked about him this way? She'd bet not.

They passed the dining room and library, then rounded a curve into a hallway that Mary had never ventured down, or even remembered seeing. When they came to a door, Sybil knocked once, then said to Mary, "Here we are."

"Should I just go in?" Mary asked when she heard no answer.

Sybil nodded. "He's expecting you."

After the woman walked away, Mary gripped the knob and pushed the door open. For a good thirty seconds after entering the large room, Mary thought she'd just stepped into kid's fantasyland, Chucky Cheese. But since she didn't smell pizza or see a large, furry gray animal with whiskers, she knew she must be in Ethan's game room.

The room was a perfect square, with one wall devoted to windows that faced the backyard and lake. It was as if the room was meant to have a screen or drape down the center as a divider, as the right side was completely devoted to every arcade game imaginable. Being a fan of arcades from way back, Mary recognized skeet ball right away and smiled wistfully. There was also basket-ball, air hockey, pound the squirrel, racecar games and many more she saw but wasn't familiar with. Then there was the left side of the room, which couldn't have been more different. It was an office, with a very modern desk and furnishings in charcoal gray and chrome, and in the middle of it sat Ethan, reading the newspaper.

She had an urge to turn around and leave before he saw her, but instead she walked into the room and parked herself beside the foosball table. "Quite a setup you got here."

Still hidden behind the *New York Times*, Ethan muttered a terse, "These are all the things I couldn't afford when I was a kid. I wanted to have them now."

Mary Kelley was no genius, but she sure understood his meaning: he'd had nothing growing up and was hoping to give this to his child. The child he'd thought was coming. The child he'd blackmailed a woman into creating with him.

She got it, and she felt Sybil's pain, and she, too, rolled her eyes. Why couldn't he have been in his library beside the bar drinking like any normal pissed-off male?

She fiddled with the handles on the foosball table. "Do you play?"

"I rarely play games," he said, still masked by the *Times*.

Neither did she, and she was having quite enough of this one. "Listen, you wanted to see me."

"Yeah." The paper came down with a snap, and Mary saw his face for the first time since they'd stood outside the doctor's office and she'd told him the truth. As he stood and walked over to her, he looked like a determined, really angry devil, his black hair slightly spiky and his blue eyes fierce with a need to hurt. He stood close, stared into her eyes and said in a punishing voice, "I have never felt such disgust with anyone in my life."

It was a strange thing—in that moment, spurred on by those words, Mary's nerves suddenly lifted and she was no longer afraid of what he was going to do about her and her father. The only thing she felt in the moment was the need to strike back. "I know that feeling. I had it about a month ago. But we were standing in your office, not your playroom."

His eyes blazed. "What you did was beyond low."

"You're right."

"And you have nothing to say."

"Just this. Need I remind you that you basically forced me into—"

"I never forced you to do anything," he interrupted darkly. "It was your choice—"

"Choice?" she repeated. Was he kidding? "What choice did I have? Tell me that?"

"You could have walked away."

"And left my dad to…what? Go to jail. Never." She glared at him. "But you don't understand that kind of devotion, do you? You've never loved anyone that much— so damn much that you'd make a great sacrifice for them."

His gaze slipped to her belly.

She shook her head, not about to pity him. "No, Mr. Curtis. That wasn't a sacrifice. That was a *need* to be met, a blue-blooded medal to hang around your neck to make you finally feel worthy." His nostrils flared, and he looked dangerously close to exploding, but Mary

wouldn't back down. "At least the child would've belonged to the old-money club, right? And maybe you,
too, by association? No, it doesn't work that way." She
was yelling now, frustrated at him, at herself. "They
don't care about association, they only care about blood.
Can you get that through your thick skull?"

When she stopped ranting, they both stood there,
face-to-face, breathing heavily. His eyes had lost some
of their heat and she wondered if she'd finally gotten
through to him. But he didn't answer her, not that she
expected him to. He had too much pride. Instead, he did
as all highly successful business persons do—he went
for the jugular.

"You're wondering if I'm going to file charges against
your father now, aren't you?" he said evenly, his tone cool.

Mary wasn't about to deny it. "Of course."

"I'm not."

Shock slammed into her and she actually stuttered.
"Wh-why?"

With a casual shrug, he left her and wandered over
to the air hockey table where he picked up a paddle and
examined it. "I've decided to close that chapter."

Mary couldn't contain her relief. Her father didn't
have to worry about court or jail ever again. She wasn't
about to thank Ethan, but she could feel the tension drain
from her body and she sagged against the foosball table.

"But I do want something from you."

Ethan's words sent a shock of alarm through her tired
limbs. "What?"

"Mackinac Island."

Oh, no. The trip to the beautiful Michigan island. She was supposed to have planned a party there, served as hostess, but how could that ever happen now? "You want me to recommend someone to take my place, right?" she asked hopefully.

"No."

"You can't be seriously considering—"

He slammed the paddle down and glared at her. "Believe me when I say I would rather bring a python with me on this trip. But your reputation has preceeded you, and I need that party to go off without a problem."

No way. She couldn't. There was too much between them. She shook her head. "No."

"You owe me."

"I owe you nothing," she assured him, straightening up, forcing her legs to hold her weight and not buckle.

His voice dropped and his lips thinned dangerously. "Don't think I wouldn't reconsider opening that paternal book again if I have to."

She shook her head, knowing she was cornered. "You're really good at blackmail."

He lifted one sardonic eyebrow. "I'll protect my business any way I have to."

"Clearly."

"Just as you would, Mary. Mine is administrative business and yours would be personal business."

The idea that they were in any way alike made Mary's blood jump in her veins, but she knew when her choices were few. "This will be our final business endeavor together."

He nodded. "After the last guest has left my party, Ms. Kelley, you and I can pretend that we've never met each other. How's that?"

"Perfect."

Eight

The airport was packed, but Mary maneuvered her way through the crowds with the fierce determination of a woman going to war. According to the itinerary Ethan's secretary had sent over yesterday morning, the plan was to fly to Chicago, then to Pellston Airport in Michigan, then take a cab to the Mackinac Island ferry. After their declarations of mutual disgust for each other, Mary was more than a little shocked that she and Ethan would be traveling together. She could've easily caught her own flight and met him at the hotel, but he'd insisted they make the trip together.

After checking in and making it through security without a body search, Mary headed over to the gate to wait for Ethan. She winced as she slid her carry-on bag off her shoulder and onto one of the hard plastic chairs.

The captain's regatta gala had been successful yesterday, raising a huge amount of money for the Cancer Research Institute, but Mary had forgotten to apply a liberal coat of sunscreen and had managed to give herself quite a sunburn in the process. And the painful moments just kept coming as she spotted Ethan walking toward her, looking anything but the stuffy business traveler in a long-sleeved white shirt and jeans, his large frame and hawklike gaze sending people out of his way without a word from him.

"Ms. Kelley."

Her body instantly betrayed her, her insides jumping with awareness at the sound of his voice. "Mr. Curtis."

"You look well," he said, barely glancing at her striped polo shirt and white cropped jeans.

"Ah…thanks," she muttered with a touch of sarcasm.

Ignoring her tone, Ethan handed her a large envelope. "I've taken the liberty of providing a dossier on the potential clients we're going to see. Their likes, dislikes, food preferences and hobbies."

"Great." Mary couldn't help but notice all the wistful stares Ethan was getting from women walking past. No wonder he could be so arrogant.

"As far as staff to hire for the party goes," he continued brusquely, "I have the name of the best—"

"I've already been in touch with several staff-for-hire agencies on the island," Mary informed him proudly. "I know who I'm going to hire and have already spoken to most of the staff."

The only sign that Ethan might be impressed by her actions was the slight lift of his brows. "You're nothing if not on top of matters, are you?"

Mary couldn't tell if his words were meant as a back-handed compliment or sexual innuendo, but she flashed him a defiant glance regardless. "I'm good at what I do, how about that?"

"Make-believe," he muttered.

"Excuse me?"

"A wife-for-hire agency, Mary?" he stated, as if that said it all. "What is that but pretending to be someone else?"

Mary was silent for a moment, her ire moderated by observation. "You know, I think there's hope for you yet, Curtis."

"I guess it's my turn to say, excuse me?"

"If you can recognize the phony in me, you'll be able to see it in yourself soon enough."

Before Ethan could even react to her words, a woman approached them with a plastered-on smile. "Mr. Curtis, you may board now if you wish. The first-class cabin is ready."

"Thank you."

Ready to follow him, Mary shouldered her bag. "Should I go with you or are we boarding separately?"

A slow grin touched Ethan's mouth, and he nodded at her boarding pass. "Better check your seat assignment first."

Confused, Mary looked down at the ticket in her hand. When she looked back up, Ethan was already on his way toward the gate. How lovely, she mused. While he got pampered with warm towels and chocolate chip cookies in first class, she was going to share a bathroom with forty other passengers in coach.

"What's wrong with your neck?" Ethan asked her once they were aboard the ferry and headed for Mackinac Island.

"It's nothing," she grumbled.

"Nothing my ass," he countered as they walked the length of the deck and back again. "You're moving like a robot."

Ethan was just full of compliments, and she felt like socking him. "It's just a pulled muscle. No big deal."

"You can't meet clients like that."

"It'll pass, okay? Relax."

"How did it happen?"

The wind off the water whipped Mary's hair around her neck as she tried to pick up her pace and shake off the stiffness in her limbs. "Do you really care? Why don't you go inside and have a cup of coffee or a bourbon or something and let me work out these kinks myself."

"I care, okay?" he said dryly. "What the hell happened on the flight?"

She sighed, stopped in her tracks and faced him. "A very large man decided to take a nap on my shoulder, and no amount of pushing and prodding and poking

would wake him up. I was stuck in this insanely awkward position for two hours. I wonder if they have a chi-
ropractor on the island."

Ethan stared at her.

"What?" she asked.

"You poked someone?"

She sighed with heavy patience. "It was just with the
eraser end of a pencil." But, oh, how she had wanted to
do so much more. "Little good it did. It only made him
snore harder. And don't even get me started with the
lady on my right."

"Did you poke her, too?"

"No, but I thought about it." Mary pressed a hand to
her lower back and stretched out her spine a little.

"Wanted to tell you her life story?"

"No. But that would've been okay, life story I
could've handled. I can work up a good conversation
with a stranger." Her memory of the woman was pretty
fresh and a wave of nausea hit her full-on. "No, this was
a lack-of-deodorant thing."

Amusement played behind his eyes. "I'm not going
to feel sorry for you."

"Who asked you to?" she returned playfully, using
every ounce of will to make herself start walking again.

"You belonged in coach."

She gave him a mock bow. "I know that, Mr. Curtis.
I'm an employee, and I'm cool with that. In work and
in life I know who I am and where I belong, and I fully
accept it." She couldn't help herself, the words just fell
out. "Unlike other people."

"What's that supposed to mean?" he asked as they reached the railing.

Only wanting to make a quick dig, not have a full-on fight, Mary glanced over the edge to the choppy sea below and tried to deflect. "Look at that water."

Ethan wasn't having any of it. Not that she expected him to. "Don't go all female on me, Mary."

Mary considered. "I don't think that was as much female as it was passive-aggressive."

"Whatever it was, just say what you've got to say," he said impatiently.

She exhaled and turned to face him. "This is just a thought, but maybe if you'd stop trying to be something you're not, you could actually enjoy your success. Maybe you wouldn't have to resort to blackmailing people into doing what you want. They might come willingly."

He grinned then, his gaze moving lazily over her. "If I remember correctly you came very willingly."

"Don't be crude."

He shrugged, looking like a bad little boy. "I was talking about coming to work for me. But I like where your dirty mind goes, Ms. Kelley."

"If you remember correctly, working for you was something I fought tooth and nail."

"I remember you giving in pretty quickly, actually, as though you wanted to be as close to me as I wanted to be to you."

Were they always going to end up here? Mary wondered. Bantering back and forth, both wanting to outsmart and outplay the other. And to what end…? It was only a few more days. "All I'm saying is that if you'd accept who you are and where you came from maybe you could be happy."

"Who says I want to be happy?"

"Everyone's looking for happiness, in some form or another."

"Not me."

She ignored him. "The problem is you're going about it the wrong way."

He gave his back to the water and lounged against the railing. "And you know the way to true happiness, Mary?"

No, but... "I'm trying. I'm sure as hell trying." She cocked her head to the left to look at the island as it came into view and felt a searing pain in her neck. She groaned.

Ethan cursed softly. "You can hardly turn your head."

"I'm fine. Nothing that a hot shower and a massage won't cure."

He touched her shoulder. "You know, I'd offer to help you with both of those forms of physical therapy, but—"

"But you pretty much hate me right now," she answered, trying to ignore the heat from his hand.

"Nope, that logic doesn't matter so much for a guy."

She tried to look shocked, but laughter quickly bubbled in her throat. "Okay, so what is it, then? You can't help me take a shower because *I* can't stand *you*?"

He considered this for about two seconds. "Ah...no. A guy can get past that sad fact, too."

She laughed again.

His voice lowered to a sexy timbre. "And you don't hate me, Mary."

His arrogance and unflinching confidence could be a real pain in the ass sometimes, especially when his assumptions were right on target. "Well, so what is it, then? Don't tell me you won't assist my shower time out of some misplaced sense of duty."

"No." He faced the coming island and looked pensive. "I'm just afraid it might make me happy, and as I said, I'm not looking for that."

The Birches was an authentic 1890s Queen Anne Victorian, and when Mary first stepped inside the entryway, she thought she'd fallen asleep and woken up in a dream—or at the very least a movie. The nine-bedroom, six-bath original Victorian had beautifully restored hardwood floors, luscious paneled ceilings, three fireplaces, extensive property, and from the wraparound porch, a panoramic view of the Straits of Mackinac, Round Island, Mackinac Bridge and the Grand Hotel.

She couldn't even imagine how much it cost to rent such a place. Harold, the real estate agent Ethan had used for their trip, gestured gleefully around himself. "Here we are, Mr. Curtis. Beautiful home, isn't it."

"Nice," Ethan said unenthusiastically as he checked his Blackberry.

Poor Harold looked so dejected that Mary felt compelled to offer up her best smile. "Well, I think it's lovely."

He gave her a grateful look. "It was rumored that Rudolph Valentino and Nita Naldi stayed here at one time."

"Really?"

"Right after *Blood and Sand*."

"Wasn't Valentino married?"

Harold nodded and said conspiratorially, "To two women, actually. He hadn't yet divorced the other."

"I hate silent films," Ethan muttered, checking his e-mail.

Mary rolled her eyes at Harold. "So, where am I staying?"

Before Harold could even open his mouth, Ethan jumped in with, "I arranged for you to have the house next door."

"What?" Mary looked from Ethan to Harold and back again. "A whole house? Come on, Curtis. I thought I'd just get a hotel room close by."

Harold cleared his throat, his neck growing as red as a ripe tomato as he tried to make eye contact with Ethan. "Actually, sir, we had an emergency, and the family staying there had to remain on. But," he said, brightening, "we have a lovely suite for Ms. Kelley across town at the Mackinac Inn."

"That will be fine," Mary said pleasantly, but she could feel Ethan already shaking his head.

"No, it won't," he informed her. "We have work to do, and you need to be here. Across town…" he said in a tone that sounded as though she were going to stay somewhere in Paris. "You can't even get anywhere around here without a horse or a bicycle. It'll take forever."

"Sir," Harold attempted deferentially. "I assure you that on an island so small, transportation is quick and very easy to—"

Ethan ignored him, his gaze hard and fixated on Mary. "You'll stay with me."

She was getting awfully tired of Ethan Curtis's demands. "No way."

"This house is large enough for ten people," he said.

"Again. No way."

He scowled. "You're acting like a child."

"I'm acting like a professional. Forget for a moment how it looks and feels to me, but how would it look to your clients if the woman you hired is also staying in the home you rented?"

He shrugged. "Practical."

"No." She lowered her voice as Harold pretended to inspect a wall sconce. "Like she's also being hired for another purpose."

They stared at each other, a haze of lust blanketing Ethan's expression. Mary felt helpless, weak for a moment as a quick shiver shot through her. She tried to control the sudden pounding of her heart, until finally the look on Ethan's face dissolved.

"You're being paranoid," he said roughly. "This is business. I'll have offices here and so will you. You can take the entire second floor and I'll remain down here. Barring business, we never have to see each other."

Mary sighed. She didn't want to argue the point anymore, and poor, miserable Harold had all but tried to crawl up inside the wall sconce and disappear. She would figure out her situation on her own. "All right, Harold. Can you show me upstairs?"

The man released a weary breath and started up the

stairs. "There are some beautiful rooms to choose from and incredible views of the water."

Before she followed him, Ethan put his hand on her shoulder. "Make sure you get that shower. You're still walking like a robot." Then he leaned in, whispered in her ear, "And if you need any help…"

Yes, she'd have to find another arrangement as soon as possible. Just the warmth of Ethan's hand made her want to curl into him, nuzzle his neck and remove his shirt, but she detached herself anyway, and followed the agent up the stairs. "Hey, Harold, how old is this house did you say?"

"It was built in 1891, but everything's been updated for your convenience."

"Like the plumbing?"

"Of course."

"And locks on the doors?"

"Every one of them, miss."

She heard Ethan chuckle below, and the sound shot to every nerve, every muscle, every spot that ached for his touch.

Nine

Good thing he'd checked the house's extensive property, or he might not have found her.

The historic barn was only about sixty feet from the main house and featured three horse stalls, food storage areas, tack room, carriage storage room, hay room and small living quarters upstairs. That last bit of information had tipped Ethan off when Mary hadn't come downstairs after a shower and change.

Ethan scowled at her. "You're the most stubborn person I have ever met."

Wearing a white terry cloth robe that showed absolutely nothing except for her feet and about an inch of neck, Mary stood at the barn door, blocking his entrance. "Thank you."

"That agent told you about this place, didn't he?"

"His name is Harold."

"Yeah, well, Harold clearly isn't looking for a good word from me to his boss."

"Don't take it out on Harold," Mary said, trying to force her hair into some type of halo style on top of her head with a couple of pins. She looked like a damn angel and Ethan had an intense urge to be saved.

"Are you going to show me around?" Ethan asked wryly.

Defiance glimmered in her pale-blue eyes, but she took a step back and allowed him to pass. "Do you promise to be good?"

"Are you kidding? Don't you know me at all?"

She laughed, a soft, throaty sound that made him think of the nights they'd shared, the sound that would erupt from her throat every time she climaxed. Blood thrummed in his temples as he followed her past the neat tack room and unused stalls, up the short set of stairs to the loft. There he took one look around and sniffed derisively. "This place is microscopic and—"

"And perfect for one person," Mary finished for him.

The walk upstairs had caused the ties on her robe to loosen, and the lapels were gaping slightly—just enough for him to see a curve of one pale breast. His mouth watered, and he tore his gaze away and glared at the bed. Warm light infused the room, kissing the pale-blue coverlet. It was a soft space, and he felt way too hard to belong there.

"I think it's the best of both worlds," Mary said, mistaking his tense jaw and piercing gaze for annoyance instead of desire. "Seeing how we feel about each other."

How they felt about each other. The idea made Ethan want to laugh. One minute he wanted to shake her, and the next he wanted to kiss her. What he did know was that he didn't want to hate her—not anymore—didn't want to feel pissed off at her. "I don't like this."

She sighed. "We're close enough to work and far enough not to…"

"Not to what?" he asked, wondering how long it would take him to remove that robe. Two seconds? Five? Or maybe he'd want to do it slowly, just a shoulder first. Or maybe he's start at her feet, work his way up to her calves, thighs… "Fall into bed again?"

Pink suddenly stained her cheeks, and she moistened her bottom lip with her tongue. "Something like that."

"It seems like a whole lot of trouble for nothing."

Her chin lifted. "I seem to remember you comparing me to a python. Aren't you glad that the python isn't living upstairs?"

He didn't answer. He walked over to the window and stared out. "There's no view of the water from here."

She sniffed. "I think I'll live."

"You'll be up here day and night…alone."

"Why do you care, Curtis?"

"I don't," he said through gritted teeth. He didn't want to.

"Business won't suffer," she assured him. "I can be up at the house in under five minutes."

If he didn't get the hell out of here right now, he was

going to find out the answer to that robe question of his, and then Mary Kelley would have the upper hand on him and he couldn't have that. He turned away from the window and stalked across the tiny space. "Thirty will be fine."

She studied him, her brows slightly knitted. "What's the plan for the rest of the day?"

"We have a few hours of good light left. Maybe... scouting a location for the party?"

She looked surprised. "I would've thought you'd want it at the house."

"I'm not sure what I want," he said tightly. "I'd like some options."

Her expression now impenetrable, she nodded. "All right. Well, I'm finally going to take that shower I've been looking forward to since this morning, and I'll meet you out front in thirty minutes."

The thought of Mary naked under a waterfall of hot water had Ethan sucking in oxygen, but not enough: his lungs constricted with pain. *She* was going to take off that robe, not him. *She* was going to touch her skin, not him. Women could be masters at torture, but this woman had it down to a science. His gaze shot to the small bathroom to his right. So white and clean and sweet.

His entire body charged with electricity, Ethan turned away and headed back down the stairs.

"We could always walk into town," Mary suggested as she sat in the back of a small black buggy, outside the gates of their rental house.

Glaring at the docile horse, Ethan slowly shook his head. "Nope."

The carriage driver looked straight ahead, smart enough not to get involved, but Mary wasn't afraid to incur the wrath of Ethan Curtis. The late-afternoon sun was starting to mellow into a stunning orangish pink and if they didn't get a move on they'd be scouting locations for the party in the dark.

"Are you going to climb up here or not?" Mary asked as she watched Ethan sidle up to the chestnut mare.

"Just give me a minute," he uttered crossly, reaching out to stroke the animal's mane as he whispered something to her Mary couldn't hear.

When he finally climbed into the buggy and dropped down beside Mary, she was curious as hell. "So, what's up with you and Shirley?"

"It was personal."

The driver clicked his tongue a few times and they were off down the dirt road. "Did you ask for her hand in marriage?" Mary asked, grinning. "Oops, sorry, I mean her hoof?"

"We were just having a little discussion, that's all."

"About?"

"Manners."

Mary laughed. "Did you have a drink before we left the house?"

Ethan crossed his arms over his chest and reclined back in his seat. "I don't want her throwing us, that's all."

"The driver said she's as docile as they come."

"That's what they'd like you to believe," he muttered dryly.

"They?"

"The driver and…Shirley."

Again she laughed. "What in the world are you talking about?"

"I'm not all that into horses, okay?"

"Oh, c'mon. Everyone loves horses. How could you not like horses? It's un-American."

"Okay, they don't like me," he grumbled.

"You need therapy," she said as they passed another horse and buggy on their way to town. The air had chilled considerably since their arrival, and Mary scooted just a little closer to Ethan. "All right, I'm listening. Tell me the whole sad story."

"What story?"

"Give me a break." She inched even closer to him so their legs were touching. "You've got to be freaked out for a reason—what's the story?"

On a curse, Ethan lifted his arm, dropped it around her shoulders. "I was ten. It was Sammy Bishop's birthday party and this sweet and supposedly ancient horse named Izabo was there giving rides to all the kids. With everyone else, she walked slower than a turtle, it was almost funny, the parents were actually referring to her IzaSlow. But as soon as *I* got on her back it was Kentucky Derby time." He lifted up his left forearm. "I fell and broke my arm in three places."

Mary let her head relax against his arm, knowing full well how totally inappropriate they were both being.

"That was a fluke thing and it happened one time. You can't hold that against—"

"Then when I was fourteen," he said as the buggy took a deep hole and they bumped against each other. "My girlfriend dragged me to the circus. Everything was fine until the horse and rider came out. Jezebel the Great freaked out halfway through her routine and stormed the stands."

"No way."

"Oh, yeah. And who do you think she headed straight for?"

"Okay, I'm beginning to see a pattern," Mary said, laughing, the scent of lake water heavy in the air.

"I broke two ribs."

Without thinking, Mary reached over and ran her fingers down the length of his rib cage only stopping when she heard his sharp intake of breath. "Feel fine to me."

His heavy-lidded gaze held hers. "Well sure, they've healed now."

It was a good thing that the driver stopped then, or Mary believed Ethan might've leaned in and kissed her, and she also believed she would have kissed him back. They got out in front of a fudge shop and started walking up Main Street, which had a similar architectural feel to New Orleans, though the scents in the air were totally different. As they passed shops, restaurants and art galleries, Mary missed Ethan's arm around her, the strength of him, and she silently wished he'd take her hand, lace her fingers with his.

"You know what?" she said as they walked to the

west end of downtown where the pedestrians were fewer. "I don't think it's really about the horses not liking you."

"Oh, this should be interesting."

"I think it's a sex thing."

A dark brow lifted over one eye. "Come again?"

"Izabo, Jezebel and Shirley," she pointed out. "It's a female thing. Females have this reaction to you."

Ethan processed this for a brief moment, then burst out laughing. "How the hell did I get mixed up with you?"

She tossed him a taunting smirk. "Do you really want me to answer that?"

They continued down the street, passing a lovely old church, a library and a quaint soda shop—which Mary considered for the party, then quickly deemed too informal. Several blocks down, closer to the water, Ethan pointed to a lovely, small, intimate hotel called the Miran Inn. "What do you think of this place?"

Cocking her head to one side, Mary looked the inn up and down. "It's beautiful, but hotels have been done to death. Not to mention the fact that three of the ten potential clients we're throwing this party for own inns on the island."

"Right."

"Don't you want something interesting and surprising? Something the spouses actually want to come to?"

"Yes."

Mary had been contemplating something since they'd arrived here, and she wanted to pull it out now. "Let's go." Grabbing his hand, she tugged, urging him to follow her.

"Where?"

"Just follow me."

Mary led him off the main street and down a short hill to a bluff, onto the sandy beach. Overhead the gulls were calling on each other to share their fish, and several tourists were taking pictures of a beautiful lighthouse in the distance. Releasing his hand, Mary walked down to the water's edge and lifted her hands to the fading sun. "Perfect," she called, turning back to face him. "A barbecue on the beach. Intimate, casual, great food—and no horses involved."

Ethan glanced around, then slowly nodded. "I like it."

"Great," she said excitedly. It would be her first beachside barbeque and she was going to make it a day to remember.

Ethan came to stand beside her, a look of admiration in his eyes. "I have to admit, you're great at what you do, you know that?"

Her hair whipped around her face. "Thank you."

He tucked one thick blond strand behind her ear, then let his thumb retreat across her cheek. "Very smart, very intuitive. There's just one problem."

Her expression froze. "What's that?"

"You're too beautiful for your own good. A man couldn't get you out of his mind no matter how pissed off he was."

"Don't you mean 'is'?" He was too close. She could feel the heat off his body, and there was no denying the desire in his eyes.

His fingers left her cheek and slid down her neck,

pausing at her collarbone. He didn't move for a moment, and his face looked rigid, as if he was contemplating what he'd just done. Then he dropped his hand and shook his head helplessly. "I'm sorry. I…I have to get back."

Electricity was shooting through Mary's body like fireworks, but she fought for control and nodded once. "Of course."

"I have a dinner meeting."

"And I have a guest list to study."

They walked side by side, up the bluff and back to Main Street to catch a cab.

"You'll be all right on your own tonight?" Ethan asked as one pulled up in front of them.

Mary climbed into the cab and this time sat close to the door. "Have been for the past twenty-some years," she uttered softly.

"What was that?" Ethan asked, not having heard her muffled answer.

She released a heavy sigh. "I said, I'll be just fine."

At night on Mackinac Island something wonderful happens. As the sun sets slowly and exquisitely against the water, the sounds of nature hum rhythmically through an invisible speaker. Forget expensive sound machines to soothe you to sleep, opening a window and stretching out on the bed was all Mary needed for a relaxing evening.

Well, that and some food…and a glass of wine.

With several pillows behind her head, Mary grabbed the delivery menus she'd garnered from the buggy driver and flipped through them. Beside her on the table was the guest list she now knew backward and forward, and she was ready to chill out. She paused on the page of an Italian menu that sounded pretty good and grabbed her cell phone off the bedside table. But before she had completed dialing the number, there was a sharp rap on the door downstairs.

She glanced at the clock. Would Ethan really be done with his dinner meeting by eight-thirty? Maybe it was Harold, come to discuss the history of each barn stall and let her know that Man O' War once sired a foal here. Laughing at her idiocy, Mary loped down the stairs and hauled back the barn door.

Ethan Curtis leaned against the door frame looking incredibly handsome in jeans and a black long-sleeved T-shirt, his sharp jaw dusted with stubble.

"Everything okay?" Mary asked, amusement in her voice.

"Yeah," he began, then took it back. "Well, no. There's a problem up at the main house."

"Seriously? What is it? Did a pipe burst or something? These older houses are notorious for plumbing problems no matter how new the pipes…"

"No. It's not the pipes."

"Fireplace smoking?"

"No."

She just loved it when he was forthcoming. "Well, what is it? Can't figure out which bed to sleep in?"

His eyes darkened. "Something like that."

Instinctively she took a step back, but only managed

to knock her heel against a bucket and feel like a clumsy oaf. "How did your meeting go?"

"Good, fine, boring," he said, his gaze moving over her. "They're looking forward to the barbecue."

Mary nodded, her mouth suddenly numb. If he would only just grab her, make this easy on both of them.

"Oh…" Ethan pulled a plastic bag from behind his back and handed it to her. "I thought if you hadn't eaten…"

"Thanks. I was just about to order something."

"Now you don't have to."

Many different ways of asking, "Would you like to share this with me?" popped into Mary's head, but she rejected all of them. After all, he'd just come from dinner with clients. "Well, I'm going to go and enjoy this."

"Okay." He didn't move.

She raised a brow at him and tried to apply a professional tone. "Do we need to discuss anything or can it wait until morning?"

He walked past her into the barn, his hand brushing over hers as he took the takeout bag from her. "You know what? I don't think it can wait."

Ten

Ethan hadn't been kidding about the dinner he'd just had with two potential clients. The food had been ordinary, the conversation bland, and somewhere around the caprese salad, he'd hoped for a fire in the kitchen so an immediate evacuation would send him back to The Birches.

Mary followed him up the stairs to the loft, her tone warily playful. "Something tells me that inviting you in may turn out to be dangerous."

"Perceptive," he said over his shoulder.

"So if you come in, can we talk about the menu?"

"I'm already in, but sure." At the moment, Ethan could care less about the menu for the barbecue. He was in Mary's room, surrounded by moonlight and the subtle soapy scent of her. Hell, at this moment, he couldn't care less about work, clients or good manners.

Her back to the wall, Mary gestured around the room. "Not many places to sit."

Ethan glanced at the bed, then back at her. "No."

Looking suddenly self-conscious in her pink tank top and matching boy shorts, Mary eyed the bathroom door. "I should throw on a robe or something."

"Don't go to any trouble for me."

"I think I'm already in trouble," she muttered, walking over to the bedside table and grabbing a yellow legal pad. "So, the caterer thinks—and I agree with her—that an all-American barbecue would be best. Ribs, burgers, barbecued chicken, sweet-potato fries, salads, pecan and apple pies. And maybe some local flavors like fresh cherried whitefish."

Didn't she get it? Ethan wondered, dropping the takeout bag on the window seat. She could move across the room, across the yard or all the way across the island and it wouldn't make a damn bit of difference. He'd still come for her, he'd still seek her out—his need for her was that strong.

"Some of the local menu items are interesting," she continued, her breathing slightly labored as she spoke, as though she'd just ran the loft stairs. "We could have a tasting if you'd like."

"I'd like that."

His tone and meaning were clear as the night sky outside the window, and Mary shook her head, her pale-blue eyes uneasy. "We can't."

"We won't."

Mary's skin suddenly felt very tight, as if she'd spent weeks in the sun without protection, and she tossed him a look that said, "Yeah, right." They were leading up to something here, something inevitable, proven even further by the fact that Ethan was walking toward her right now.

"I swear I won't even go near the bed," he said. Ethan brought his hands up and cupped her face, the warmth of his skin melting all of her resolve in an instant. She leaned toward him as he dipped his head and covered her mouth in a series of soul-crashing kisses.

He was so warm as his mouth and his chest brushed teasingly against her breasts that Mary's knees nearly buckled, and she wrapped her arms around Ethan's neck for support. His body responding at once, Ethan groaned at the nearness and gently pressed her back against the wall, cradling her neck in his hand as he explored her mouth with teasing, drifting kisses until she opened for him, gave him a sweep of her tongue.

Mary tried to keep her head, tried to recall what they had said to each other just the other day, the rotten things they'd said, but each thought faded away like fog in the sun. She felt his hand delve under her shirt, felt his palm on her stomach and sucked air through her teeth, her back arching as she silently begged him to explore higher.

Pressing closer to her, Ethan reached around her with his free hand and unhooked her bra, setting her free while holding her captive with his mouth. Mary could hardly remain still. Her skin itched to be touched, and when his hand raked up her torso and covered one full breast, when he slowly rolled the hard peak between his thumb and forefinger, she cried out into his mouth.

The sound had Ethan backing off for a moment, his hungry gaze fixated on her. Thinking he was about to scoop her up and deposit her on the bed, Mary shook her head wearily. "You swore you wouldn't—"

"Go near the bed," he finished for her. "And I'm not."

"Then…what are you—"

She never finished the sentence as Ethan lifted her shirt over her head and artfully cast aside her lacy bra. She stared at him, at his face, marveled at the need there as the lower half of her contracted and hummed.

"I wasn't hungry until now," he mumbled, dipping his head and nuzzling up one pale slope until he found the sustenance he required. His tongue circled her taut nipple slowly, desperately slowly, and Mary could only arch her back again and again, thrusting herself in and out of his mouth until finally he took her between his lips and tongue and suckled deep and hard.

"Oh, Ethan," she whispered breathlessly, her knees weak and the small curve at the top of her inner thigh wet with desire.

Ethan drank from her, his tongue flicking the swollen bud back and forth until her hips began to move, to thrust forward and back looking for his hand, his mouth, something to ease the building tension within her—or maybe to build it even further. His mouth moved down, gently sinking his teeth into her belly and hip bones as his hands brought her shorts and underwear to her ankles, then off completely.

Mary felt a moment of embarrassment, being fully naked in front of him, standing there in slashes of moonlight, her breasts free, one nipple still wet from his mouth, and the lower half of her open and ready for whatever he was willing to give.

On his knees, Ethan spared her one wicked, hungry glance before taking what he wanted. "Open your legs," he said, his warm breath so close to her sensitive flesh that Mary found it almost impossible to hold on to the climax she felt building just inches from his mouth.

She widened her stance and let her eyelids drift closed, tried to calm her body, ease the electric charges running through at a sprint, but when he spread the soft folds back with his thumbs, she couldn't control anything anymore. When he lapped at her with his tongue, Mary groaned and pressed herself against him. When he suckled and nuzzled the tender bud beneath, she cried out his name, "Ethan, please, I can't…"

She had no idea what she couldn't do, if it was hold on to her climax or give in to him or both, her mind was adrift on a sea of all-consuming pleasure. Then his hands came around to her buttocks, squeezing the flesh as he found his rhythm, his tongue flicking the tiny nub over and over as Mary rocked her hips.

"I can't hold on…" she uttered, her limbs weak, her body charged with electricity as the waves crashed and she stiffened—every part of her but her hips. She cried out and rocked wildly against his mouth, shuddering, giving in to release.

Mary sagged against the wall, her hips still bucking,

but slowly now as she sucked air through her teeth and tried to force back rational thought to her mind. When Ethan left her to stand, she felt slightly cold, but he took her in his arms and held her against him, his heart thundering so powerfully she could feel it against her chest. More than anything, she wanted him to take her to the bed, rise up over her and sink down between her legs. For a moment she thought about pushing him back onto the bed and straddling him, taking what she wanted as he had just taken from her.

But she never got the chance. She was still shaking from head to toe when Ethan moved away from her. He walked into the bathroom and came back with her robe, which he gently placed around her. Then he found her gaze and uttered a gentle, "I'll go."

"You don't have to," she said boldly, not really giving a damn that she sounded needful and not the littlest bit desperate.

He ran a hand through his hair and looked uncomfortable, shaken…or was that angry? She couldn't tell. "I really do."

She quickly slipped her arms through the holes in the robe, then nodded at Ethan. What the hell else could she do? "So, tomorrow…"

"Ten. On the porch." It was all he said before heading down the stairs and out of the barn.

Mary went to the window, watched him walk across the yard, her knees still trembling with aftershocks of her climax, the relaxing sounds of nature now replaced by the hum in her body—the need for more. If she'd had her way—and Ethan could've handled it, if he had the same unrelenting desire that she felt for him—he'd be poised above her right now, spreading her legs again, but this time for an entirely different purpose.

The image caused such intense shots of electricity to run through her body that she had to sit down on the edge of the bed.

Mary left City Hall with permits for the party and walked through town, hoping to arrive back at Ethan's place just before their scheduled meeting time. She'd been up since five that morning, planning the party and keeping her mind focused on Ethan's business goals as well as her own—basically anything except what had happened last night. As she passed Ticklers Fudge Shoppe, her cell phone rang, making several passersby frown at the disturbance.

She flipped open the phone and pressed it to her ear. "Hello?"

"Hey, it's Tess," came the voice of her partner. "And Olivia," chirped the other. "We're conferencing you."

Mary had been on several trips, business and otherwise over the past five years and had rarely missed hearing from her partners. This morning, however, she felt incredibly comforted by the sound of their voices. "Hey, there. How are things back home?"

"Same old, same old," Olivia informed her. "And how is Mackinac Island? Insanely beautiful and romantic?"

"She's not there for romance, Olivia," Tess said, a bite of irritation in her tone.

"Of course she's not. I just meant—"

"It's lovely," Mary said with a laugh, passing the small church that was about three-quarters of a mile from The Birches, making her heart jump nervously at the thought of seeing Ethan in a few minutes. "Lovely and incredibly picturesque."

"Well, in that case," Tess began, her business tone smartly in place. "Make sure you take plenty of pictures for our book."

"I will," Mary promised. "So, besides checking on the beauty of the island, anything you two want to discuss—anything going on I should know about?"

"Well," Olivia said excitedly. "We wanted to tell you that we've gotten three calls from men who were at Mr. Curtis's party last week. Two older gentlemen whose wives have passed and who have no idea how to run a social or home life. By the way, they were very impressed with what you did and are desperate to hold similar events for their companies. One of them is selling his home and moving to a waterfront estate— he's terrified because his wife handled all of that type of detail."

"Sounds right up our alley," Mary said, very pleased that her efforts had brought NRR several more clients. "And what about the third?"

Olivia snorted. "One very arrogant thirty-something trust-fund baby."

"Oh, your favorite," Mary said, grinning.

"And Tess palmed him off on me," Olivia added sourly. Mary heard Tess groan in frustration, as though she'd had this conversation ten times already. "He needs your culinary skills."

The wind picked up around Mary, bringing the scent of overcast morning and lake water to her nostrils. "What's his name?"

"Mac Valentine," Olivia told her.

Mary racked her brain for a mental picture of him, then recalled the handsome man Ethan had introduced to her at the first party. Oh, yes. Everything Olivia despised. Family money, total playboy, gorgeous and knew it.

Olivia sighed. "It'll be fine. Just like the rest of you, I refuse to get sucked in by clients. Do my job and do it well, and that's it."

As she walked down the country lane, Mary spotted her "just a client" on the porch of the old Victorian home, mug in hand, and felt a shiver of awareness move through her. If the girls only knew what a mess she'd gotten herself into over this particular client, they'd probably kick her out of the business. "Got to go, ladies."

"Oh, one more thing," Tess said quickly. "Your grandmother has called here three times since you've been gone."

"Why didn't she try my cell?"

"She said she misplaced the number, so I gave it to her again. She sounded pretty agitated."

That's what came from not checking her messages at home or at the office. "She always sounds that way. Agitated is normal. Now if you said she sounded blissful or pleased, I'd be worried."

Both women laughed.

"Thanks for the call. I'll talk to you both later." Mary dropped her phone into her purse and walked through the yard toward Ethan. A scant bit of sunlight had broken through the clouds and was taking up residence on the porch, playing with the coffee-brown highlights in Ethan's dark hair. He looked serious and sexy, dressed in all black, the features in his face all angles and sharpness with a tigerlike stare. Her heart in her throat, Mary climbed the porch steps and sat beside him on the bench.

"Taking a walk?" he asked, his tone rigid.

"Just back from City Hall and a meeting with the caterer and waitstaff. They're really thrilled with the barbecue." She tried to ignore the way his gaze moved over her in a possessive, animal-like way. "The tasting you requested is today at one-thirty. If that works with your schedule."

He shook his head. "I don't need a tasting. I trust your instincts."

"Last night you said—"

"I wasn't talking about food last night, Mary."

His words stunned her, and his reckless, impenetrable gaze had heat coiling through her. Since he had wanted so much to avoid talking about their situation last night, she'd thought to grant him the same courtesy today, but he looked anything but calm, cool and forgetful, so she lifted her chin and said, "Do we need to discuss what happened last night?"

"Only if you want to continue where we left off," he said with a bluntness that matched hers.

Mary's nerves dropped away completely, and the no-

nonsense businesswoman with an attitude took over. She had been open to him in more ways than one last night, and he was the one who'd walked away. She didn't want to play games anymore, back and forth and want and don't want—it was b.s. "All I want right now is to do my job. The best damn job anyone's ever seen."

His eyes glittered with ire. "I have no doubt you'll succeed in that."

"And after I've finished this job, I want to leave here. I want to go back home and…" She paused, unable to finish her sentence. Why couldn't she finish that sentence?

"And?" he asked.

She would go back home and work as she always had, with no more interruptions or complications. No doubt, just like Ethan.

The frustration in her tone was obvious. "Would you like the tasting or should I cancel it?"

"I'll be there. One-thirty, right?"

She nodded and stood. "It's going to be at Fanfare restaurant in town, right on Main Street. Easy to find." She headed off toward the barn. Another shower sounded good, thirty minutes under hot water to clear her head and retune her attitude.

"I'll come by the barn to pick you up at one," Ethan called after her, making Mary stop in her tracks and whirl around to face him. "We can walk this time. No more horses."

"We?" she uttered hoarsely. "No, I don't need to be there. The staff will write down everything you like and don't like and report back to—"

"I want you there," he said, reclining on the bench, looking like the CEO of the world. "And at least until the end of the barbecue tomorrow, you work for me."

Without realizing it, the catering staff at Fanfare had romanticized an event that should have been nothing more than a business meeting. On the walk over, Mary had imagined that she and Ethan would stand at one of the prep stations in the restaurant's kitchen and sample a variety of dishes, writing down their thoughts on a piece of scratch paper in between bites, then they would thank the staff for their service and get out of there. Later, Mary would call the head chef and discuss what worked for the client and what didn't.

This was normally how it was done on the mainland, but clearly things were taken to an entirely different level on Mackinac Island when a hotshot millionaire was throwing a party for the island's upper crust.

On the restaurant's cozy deck overlooking the lake, a table had been dressed with exquisite white linens, funky blue plates, silver, wineglasses and frosted beer glasses.

"I feel like I should've worn a tie," Ethan said with a sardonic grin as he was seated at the table.

"Me, too," replied Mary.

"No. You look too good in that dress."

She smiled.

Taking in the elaborate scene before him, Ethan raised one dark brow at her. "Are you sure they're going to be able to pull off a beach barbecue?"

She tossed him a mock frown as the waitstaff poured

samples of wine and beer. "Are you questioning my abilities, Mr. Curtis?"

Lifting a mug, he gave her a silent toast. "I'd be a fool."

"Damn right." In spite of herself, she grinned at him as several dishes were set before them. "How about we taste and see?"

Amusement glittered in his eyes at the unintended double meaning in her words. "You make me crazy, you know that?"

"Right back at ya, Curtis."

Each item the staff laid before them was whimsical and over-the-moon delicious. Grilled whitefish and chips wrapped in paper, sweet-potato fries with a killer dipping sauce, salads, pork, chicken, desserts. And they sampled it all, along with fresh-squeezed lemonade, interesting wines and rich beer.

At long last, Ethan sat back in his chair and sighed. "I approve."

Mary laughed as she tried to get up from the table. "I thought you might."

After thanking the staff, they walked back to The Birches, thankful for the exercise as they were both stuffed to the gills. Several times, Ethan reached out to take Mary's hand, then stopped himself. They weren't a couple. Sure, there was an intense sexual attraction between them, unfinished business that he wanted to see to, taste again—damn, he couldn't get last night out of his head—but he was kidding himself if he thought they'd just been on a date, that they were starting a romantic relationship.

Once they were in the driveway, Ethan followed her to the barn and paused at the door. Mary's cheeks were flushed and she looked relaxed and satisfied with their day. She took off her sandals and stood there in her virginal white sundress, the same need he'd seen last night in her eyes—the same need that was no doubt echoed in his.

"I think I'm a little tipsy," she said, opening the door.

"There's nothing wrong with that."

She laughed. "It's three o'clock in the afternoon."

"Are you going to be operating any heavy farm machinery this afternoon?"

"No."

"Then you're fine."

"Thanks for walking me to my door, so to speak, but I'm good from here."

Cursing, he leaned against the door frame, feeling frustrated and dense. "Why the hell are we fighting this?"

She shrugged. "I don't think I am."

"Fine. Why am I fighting this?"

"Because you hate me?"

"No, I don't think that's true anymore." He reached out and took her hand. "In fact I don't think that was ever true. I think it's quite the opposite and that's why I'm fighting it." He took her other hand and pressed them behind her back, leaned in and kissed her gently, sensually on the mouth. "Come on," he uttered, leading her inside.

"No more games, Ethan," she said, her tone fragile for the first time since they'd met.

"No." He shook his head, led her up the stairs, but halfway there his need to kiss her, taste her, had him pulling her into his arms.

"The bed…" she uttered hoarsely.

Ethan nuzzled her neck, the curve of her ear, making her moan. "We'll get there."

Eleven

Somehow they stumbled up the stairs, clothes marking their way like Hansel and Gretel's breadcrumbs. Mary clung to Ethan like a rag doll, covering his mouth and neck with hungry kisses as he led them into the bedroom and onto the down comforter. She only knew her shirt and bra were off when her warm back met the cool, soft down and when Ethan lowered himself on top of her, the hair on his chest tickling her, and the delicious, hot weight of him making her heart jump with excitement.

Her skin felt as if it was on fire, itchy, needy, and she couldn't get him to touch her everywhere at once, so she had to force herself to relax as he lazily kissed her throat and breasts, nuzzling one nipple with his nose and cheek until Mary could hardly stand the torture and he finally gave in and suckled her deep into his mouth, tugging at the flesh with his teeth. She was in a dream—she had to be—but she didn't want to be. No matter how she and Ethan had begun, there was real, honest-to-goodness affection here. She was really falling hard for him, and she desperately wanted him to make love to her.

He found her mouth again, and as his hands took over, kneading the undersides of her breasts, cupping them, feeling their weight, slowly circling the firm peaks with his thumbs, Mary moaned, plunging her fingers into his thick hair.

His jeans and the small scrap of cotton at her hips were all that separated them, and Mary couldn't stand it. With deft fingers, she flicked the button and slid down his zipper, her hand delving inside to feel him, hold him, make him as insane with desire as she was.

Ethan sucked in a breath as her fingers wrapped the hard, solid length of him, and Mary smiled as he continued to kiss her. He was like silk, pulsating, hot, steel-hard silk, and she ached to have him inside her. As she stroked him, Ethan hooked his thumbs under the waistband of her underwear and slipped them down far enough that Mary could easily wriggle out of them. This was no sweet love scene; they wanted each other in a primitive way. They wanted to be connected, and Mary reveled in the fact that she felt like a horny teenager at the ripe old age of twenty-nine.

Ethan broke away for one second to pitch his pants to the floor, and when he returned, Mary pushed him back on the bed. She felt sexy and strong and wanted to climb on top of him and take what she wanted, be in control, and Ethan lay back and allowed her that, his hands instantly finding her hips.

She kneaded his chest with her hands, rolled his nipples between her fingers until his erection looked like a marble pillar, then she lifted up off him, pressed her hips forward and sank down until the curls between her legs met the coarse hair at his center.

Ethan uttered a curse, a deep throaty sound that went with the thrust he met her with. "Mary, I don't—"

"Want this?"

A deep, almost wounded chuckle escaped him. "Are you kidding? No, I don't have any protection."

"I do," she said breathlessly.

"You do?"

She pushed off him, her smooth legs brushing against his hair-roughened ones as she grabbed a foil packet from the bedside table drawer. "I'm not going to pretend I didn't want this to happen," she said, grinning down at him. "I came prepared."

Ethan reached for the packet, but Mary wanted to do it herself, wanted to feel the latex as it slid over him, wanted to place him inside her again. After feeling so out of control for so long, she needed this, and for once Ethan let her take what she needed, let her slide back down over him, let her place his hands on her breasts as she rode him, her hips swiveling and thrusting as she tried to feel him from every angle.

"Tell me," Ethan whispered, one hand trailing down her belly to the spot where they were joined, where wet heat made their movements quick and intensely pleasurable. "What do you want?"

Through gritted teeth, Mary cried out, "Yes, right there. Touch me there."

Ethan's fingers moved and played until Mary's head dropped back and her breasts rose and fell. She let him take over, one hand gripping her hips, rocking her back and forth, deeper and deeper, the other hand nestled between them, his middle finger flicking the tender button hidden inside until waves of pleasure so intense Mary could hardly breathe washed over her. Her hands slipped to his chest as he pumped furiously beneath her, guttural sounds erupting from his throat as he followed her over the edge.

Exhaustion flooded her and she collapsed on top of him, tears filling her eyes. She lay there, her heart thudding against his chest, and wondered what she'd been doing for the past two years besides working and remaining separate from the world. She'd never realized just how lonely she'd been, spending her time, energy and focus on the business. She'd completely cut herself off from living.

Ethan slid out from under her, and she gave him her back so they were spooning. It felt so good, so right to be held like this by him. How that was possible, after all they'd been through, she didn't know, but it was obvious to her that they might have a chance together.

Ethan trailed kisses down her back, down, down, raking his teeth against the sensitive spot right above her buttocks. Electric currents shot through Mary's weak limbs, and she uttered a playful, "What do you think you're doing?"

"I'm not done."

"Not done with what...oh."

He flipped her over and sat poised above her, staring down at her with eyes that glittered blue fire, his erection brushing against her leg, hard once again.

Laughing weakly, she grabbed the covers and hauled them up and over her head. "Can't. Tired."

"Mary," he began wickedly. "Do you actually think a few inches of cotton is going to stop me?"

With a little pleasurable scream, Mary saw Ethan appear at the bottom end of the covers, his gaze ravenous as he started at her ankles and crawled toward her, his mouth planting soft, wet kisses up her calves, knees and finally her inner thighs.

"You don't have to do a thing," he whispered, his mouth poised between her now widespread thighs.

Her fingers delving immediately into his hair, Mary lifted her hips tentatively. How could she resist? His head was down, the muscles in his shoulders flexing as he gripped her buttocks. His mouth was like heaven, his tongue...

"Ethan..."

He started slowly at first, just gentle laps at her sensitive sex, long, slow licks from hood to the opening of her body. But Mary's body responded quickly, writhing beneath him, twisting, her fingers leaving his hair to find herself. Ethan said something sexy and dirty as she opened the slick, hot folds at her core, then nuzzled and suckled at the taut bud that ached so badly. Following her rhythm, his pace quickened, moving with the thrust of her hips, until she arched her back and called out raw, insatiable moans over and over again, shuddering against his mouth.

Completely exhausted now, Mary curled over on her side and released a heavy, satisfied sigh, even smiling lazily when Ethan lay facing her on his side.

"I want to stay," he said.

"The bed's too small," she joked.

He draped one muscular thigh over her hips, pulling himself closer. "Is it?"

And they fell asleep that way.

The weather had been sketchy all morning, but miraculously by eleven o'clock the sun had pushed its way through the clouds and had started to warm the sand. Right alongside the staff, Mary helped set up tables, chairs, chaises and umbrellas, all in festive shades of blue-and-white stripes. The beach had been combed beautifully, leaving only the whitest, softest sand for their party, and when noon hit and the guests began to arrive, Mary breathed a sigh of relief. Despite the morning gloom and a night of amazing sex that had left her bone weary, she'd pulled it off.

Dressed in a simple though elegant navy-blue sundress and white hat, Mary walked from one station to another, making sure the drinks were flowing and the food was getting out in a timely manner. Barring one strange and obviously experimental plate of baked-bean custard that she immediately had the waiter send back to base camp, everything looked perfect.

Just as she was inspecting the barbecue grills and the delicious scents wafting from each, Ethan came up behind her and took her hand. She smiled instantly at his touch, and a warm sensation came over her heart as she recalled this morning, waking up together in a haze of touchy, feely, romantic sweetness, complete with breakfast and a killer make-out session at the door as they each complained about how late they were going to be but not really giving a damn.

"Twenty minutes into the party and I have two potential clients flying to Minneapolis next week for meetings," he said, brushing a kiss to her ear. "You're amazing."

He looked calm, relaxed and deadly handsome in white pants and black polo shirt, and Mary felt a strange sense of pride, as if they were actually together. "It's not me, it's the mojitos," she joked.

"No, it's you," he insisted, his blue eyes flashing with admiration. "Or maybe it's me around you."

"That's a nice thing to say," Mary said a little shyly, trying to ease her hand from his in case anyone was watching them. She didn't want to give anyone the wrong idea, especially Ethan. She had never been the kind of woman to have expectations, and no matter how much she wanted to curl into this man and whisper her feelings against his chest, she wasn't about to lay that kind of pressure on him. She may have come to a realization last night about what she had been missing, what she wanted now and how they'd both been stuck in a past that had ruled their actions. But Ethan might not have come to any realizations except that the two of them had just had great sex.

Whatever his beliefs, Ethan held firm to Mary's hand as they walked over to the bar, greeting guests along the way. It was odd. In all the years Mary had been one of NRR's partners, she'd never felt like an actual wife to a client, or wanted to be, until today. For brief moments she even caught herself imagining that she and Ethan were a couple as they circled the crowd.

"I should go and speak with the chef," she told Ethan after about twenty minutes of crowd watching. "We're running low on a few things."

Ethan nodded but didn't release her hand immediately. "Before you go, I have to ask you something."

"Okay."

"I feel like an ass—a romantic ass."

"A whole new thing for you?"

"You bet." Chuckling, he drove a hand through his hair. "Will you stay with me tonight?"

Pleasure circled her belly, and she grinned at him. "I seem to remember us agreeing to something…after the party ended."

He gave her a mock scowl. "No idea what you're talking about."

"Sure you do. Should I refresh your memory?"

"If you say one word about that conversation, I'll have to take drastic action."

Biting her lip to keep from laughing, she said, "After the party ended we were both supposed to—"

Before she could say another word, Ethan hauled her into his arms and kissed her hard and quick. "Don't make me take this to an obscene level in front of all these people," he warned against her mouth. "I'll ruin my reputation."

Mary laughed, a warm, rich sound that totally conveyed how happy he was making her in that moment. "Wasn't I supposed to take off just as soon as the last guest departed?"

"Oh, you asked for it," he said wickedly, taking her hand and slipping behind the bar where it was shady and devoid of party guests.

In seconds Mary had her arms around his neck as he kissed her with all the passion of the night before. When they finally came up for air, Ethan's eyes were glazed and hot and his voice was ragged with emotion. "Whatever we have going here, I want more of it."

All she could do was kiss him, passionately and without holding back.

He held her face in his hands. "Tell me you want that, too."

"I want that, but I'm a little scared."

"Of what?"

"All that's happened."

"That's over, Mary. Can't we decide to forget about it and leave it in the past?"

"I think we've both left too much in the past. Don't you think it's time to deal with it?"

His brow furrowed with frustration just as a loud trill erupted from Mary's pants pocket. With a quick look of apology, she grabbed her cell phone and flipped it open. "Hello."

"Mary, it's your grandmother."

"Grandmother, how are you?"

"Your grandfather has died."

Her heart sunk into her stomach. "What?"

"The funeral is Tuesday. You'll be here?"

"Yes, of course," she said quickly, uncomfortable with her grandmother's unemotional way of giving news. "How did it—"

"I will see you Tuesday," Grace continued brusquely. "St. Agnes, downtown. 10:00 a.m."

She hung up almost immediately after Mary said that she would see her at the church. Still in shock, Mary gripped the phone in her fist and stared at the sand.

"What's wrong?" Ethan asked gently.

"My grandfather died." Why was she feeling so blown away? She and Lars Harrington had never been close, but for some reason the news of his death reminded Mary of her mother's death, and of how short life really was.

"I'm sorry," Ethan said soberly. "How did it happen?"

"I have no idea."

He didn't push her for more. "When are you leaving?"

"Right away. Tonight."

He nodded. "I'm going with you."

"No," she said quickly, not sure why she didn't jump at the offer, but sensing in her gut that Ethan Curtis around her family right now might not be the greatest idea. "You have business to finish up here, people to see and deals to make. It's the reason why we came to Mackinac Island in the first place."

"All of that can wait a few days."

She eased away from him, from his embrace and the intimacy they'd shared only moments ago. "And lose momentum? No way. It was our plan, anyway, that I was going to leave today and you were going to stay. Let's stick with the plan, for now anyway."

Ethan wasn't a mysterious man; he said what he thought and didn't apologize for it. With an understanding but not altogether amused grin, he said, "You're almost as good at this as me."

"Good at what?"

"Pretending you don't give a damn."

They said nothing further as they walked back into the eye of the party.

The cemetery looked like an English garden, with buckets of daisies and vases of tulips and roses everywhere you looked. The woman next to Mary at the grave site had been nervous about what to say to Lars Harrington's granddaughter. She had bypassed the usual offers of sympathy and instead had gone on to explain that Sunday was the heaviest day for visitors to the cemetery, and that all the guilty relatives brought flowers. After a quick, tight-lipped smile to the woman, Mary had moved to the opposite side of the grave, to stand alongside her grandmother, aunt and cousins.

As the priest spoke, Mary gripped the stems of her lilacs—a flower her grandmother had always called "peasant flora" as they grew in just about anyone's backyard—recalling the day that she and her father had buried her mother. The weather had been far better than today, full sunshine and a heavy breeze, but the mood felt similar and, Mary noticed, some of the same crowd was there. But no one except Mary and Hugh had shed a tear that day, no one had left that cemetery broken the way they had.

Staring at the casket as it was lowered into the ground, Mary wondered if she'd actually healed from that whole ordeal: the illness and the loss. She'd always been so worried about fixing her father and helping him to get over his grief that she hadn't even looked at her own. No wonder she'd allowed herself to take that deal of Ethan's—she'd been a little out of her mind.

Ethan. Warmth spread through her and she wrapped her arms around herself. She missed him, missed sparring with him, lying in his arms, feeling alive. It had been a few days since she'd spoken to him, since he'd kissed her goodbye at the ferry and returned to the island.

Mary glanced up and spotted Tess and Olivia standing next to the woman who'd voiced the inappropriate cemetery comment. The two women looked quiet and sad, and even though she hadn't asked them to attend, Mary was thankful for their presence and support. And they weren't the only ones offering their support, Mary noticed as she shifted her gaze to the back of the crowd behind her partners.

Conservatively dressed in a black suit and bright-blue tie, Ethan Curtis stood apart from all the others, staring at her, his gaze solemn as Bible verses were read. At first, Mary felt a jump of excitement at the sight of him, then beside her, her grandmother opened her purse and noisily slipped out a tissue, which she used to dab her eyes. This probably wasn't good. Grace wouldn't want him here and might create a scene.

As soon as the service ended, Mary hustled over to him. He took her hand and kissed it. "I thought you might need...something. I wasn't sure exactly what, so I came instead."

"Thank you," she said, wanting to curl into his arms and let him comfort her. But she knew this wasn't the time or the place, and she needed to get him out of there before he was verbally attacked by her grandmother.

But unfortunately she wasn't quick enough.

"What is he doing here?"

It was as if a cold wind had blown in, encircling them like a tornado. Mary's grandmother walked up to them. She stared hard at Ethan, a sneer on her weary face.

"He came as a friend, Grandmother," Mary quickly tried to explain. "And—"

"He's no friend to this family," Grace snarled. "Your grandfather would be appalled."

"Grandmother, please—"

"You don't need to defend me, Mary," Ethan said calmly, then turned to Grace. "I was offering a little support to a friend, that's all."

Her eyes narrowed into nasty slits. "The blue-collar trash that took his company from him." She turned on Mary. "How could you allow this?"

"I didn't. I'm not. I—"

"Don't bother, Mary," Ethan said with a mild sigh before turning around and walking away.

"I'm surprised at you," Grace uttered to Mary when he was gone.

"And I wish I could say I'm surprised at you," Mary said tightly.

"You will not speak to me in that tone, young—"

"I understand that today is a difficult day, Grandmother," Mary said, feeling strong and in control with this woman for the first time in her life. "But I won't allow you to speak to my friends that way anymore. If you want a relationship with me, you'll need to restrain yourself in the future."

Leaving her grandmother standing there, mouth open, Mary went after Ethan. She caught up to him on top of the hill overlooking her grandfather's grave site. "I'm sorry. It's her grief talking."

"Then she's been grieving for a long time," he muttered.

"This is why I didn't want you to come here," she explained. "I knew she'd—"

"Stop trying to protect me, Mary. I don't need it."

"I'm not…" Even as she said the words, she knew they weren't true.

"Aren't you tired of it?"

"What do you mean?"

"Protecting everyone. Your father, your partners, your grandmother, me, yourself."

She stared at him unable to speak, her brain running a hundred miles an hour. Had he read her thoughts last night? How could he know that all of her life she'd been doing exactly this, hoping her interference would bring peace where there was chaos—and having no life of her own in the process. She could plan her work, her business years in advance, but could never see her personal future because she didn't think she deserved one.

"I have to go," Ethan said, mistaking her silence for indifference.

"No," she said sternly just as Olivia and Tess came toward them, waving.

"I'm so sorry, Mary," Olivia said sympathetically, placing an arm around her friend's shoulder. Then she noticed Ethan and gave him a curious smile. "Mr. Curtis. Hello. What are you doing here?"

"He took over my grandfather's company," Mary said quickly and without thinking. "But he was just leaving."

When Ethan's cold gaze found hers, she realized what she had said and how it had sounded. It was one thing to protect him, but to act ashamed of him... She wanted to explain, but with Tess and Olivia standing right there she knew it would have to wait.

Ethan nodded to both Tess and Olivia. "Ladies." Then turned and left.

Mary's heart sank.

"What happened here?" Tess asked.

Olivia grimaced. "Hope it wasn't something I said."

"No," Mary assured them, knowing it was about time to come clean with her partners. "I'm afraid it was something I said."

Twelve

"Yes, Mr. Valentine, I'll be there." Olivia rolled her eyes as she hung up the phone. "This is his third call in two days. The excessively rich can not only be bossy but paranoid, as well." She swiveled toward Mary and gave her a sheepish expression. "Sorry, Mary. I don't mean you."

It was quarter to five and they were all sitting in Olivia's office going over the appointments and events that were scheduled for the next two weeks. It was September and business was starting to really pick up.

As she sat beside Tess on the other side of Olivia's desk, Mary crossed and uncrossed her legs. "Hey, I'm not rich."

Tess looked up from her notes. "I thought your grandfather left you a small fortune."

"It still doesn't make me rich," Mary said on a laugh that sounded incredibly forced. "Comfortable, maybe— but I've found that rich is an attitude."

"I'll say," Olivia went on. "Just because this guy has a dozen or so women who'd do anything from shine his shoes to act as though they don't know where Darfur is just so he can feel like the smart one, doesn't mean he should expect the same from me." She snorted. "As if I would forget a meeting. The nerve."

"You'll make sure he gets a clue, Olivia, I have no doubt." Tess winked at Mary, who smiled in turn.

The three women had changed during the past several weeks—since the funeral and the three-hour dessert and coffee gab session they'd shared afterward. Exactly ten minutes after Ethan had walked away from her, Mary had broken down and confessed their relationship to Tess and Olivia.

The two hadn't been surprised, but they had asked, no pressure, if she'd wanted to talk about it. She did, and she had. Not that it had changed the situation any, but it had been moderately cathartic and had made Mary realize what she'd been missing in a friendship.

Both Tess and Olivia hadn't mentioned Ethan since, and she was beyond thankful for that because Ethan hadn't contacted her for two weeks except to send a check to NRR for services rendered. There hadn't been a note in the envelope, nothing that would make her think he missed her or had even thought about her at all. For her part, she'd called him to try and explain, but he'd refused to listen. Even so, she hadn't stopped thinking about him.

Tess closed her book with a sigh. "I think that's it. We're all going to be incredibly busy this month, so take every opportunity to relax."

"Agreed," said Olivia pulling out her Rolodex. "And I know just how to start the relaxation process."

Tess groaned. "I can't take another one of those seminars on How to Cool Your Cooperate Stress."

"Seriously," Mary agreed wholeheartedly. "I fell asleep at the last one and the group leader actually tousled my hair to get me to wake up. It was very freakish."

Shaking her head impatiently at both of them, Olivia explained, "I'm not talking about a seminar, I'm talking about Senõr Fred's—tonight." She wiggled her brows. "Spiciest salsa in town and dollar margaritas."

"Oh, I'm so in," Tess said without hesitation, standing up and heading out of the office. "Let me get my coat, finish up some paperwork and I'll meet you at reception in fifteen minutes."

"What about you, Mary?" Olivia asked. "I mean, can anyone really turn down a margarita?"

At that question, Mary wanted to laugh, but she didn't feel merry enough to make it happen. She could turn down a margarita, and pretty much anything alcoholic for the next nine months. She was back to where she'd started, with a pregnancy test hidden behind the rolls of toilet paper under the sink. And this time, she'd actually missed her period.

She scrubbed a hand over her face. How was she going to tell Ethan, or not tell him?

"I'd love to come," Mary said finally, feeling slightly

sick to her stomach at the thought of salsa and chips and happy hour chaos. "But I think I'll stick to soda."

Olivia smiled and shrugged. "Okay."

"But if you two end up completely hammered," Mary said, gathering up her notes and grinning. "Consider me your designated driver."

Dr. Eleanor Wisel was a kind, grandmother type of Ob/Gyn with cool hands and warm instruments and a penchant for delivering news with her eyes closed. Dramatic effect? Who knew, but it was exactly how she'd told Mary that yes, she was indeed pregnant.

With a prescription for prenatal vitamins stuffed in her purse and a small plastic bag of coupons, information and dates for future appointments hanging from her wrist, Mary walked out of the office building and across the parking lot toward her car. Her insides had stopped shaking long enough for her brain to start processing what all this could mean. She didn't have to worry about money or a future for this child—she had her business and the trust. She didn't have to worry about loving this baby, she already felt totally in love with him or her. But what she did have to worry about was the father. She had to tell him, of course, but things were so crazy right now, would it be better if she waited?

She opened her car door and was about to climb in when she heard her name being called across the parking lot. Her skin prickled and her heart raced, and she quickly tossed her free bag of goodies into her car and slammed the door. When she looked up again, he was there, looking incredibly handsome in jeans, a white button-down shirt and a gray brushed-wool blazer. She found herself fascinated with his features, wondering would her baby have his eyes or hers? His hair color or hers? His roguish smile or her quirky one?

"What are you doing here?" he asked in a tone he usually reserved for employees.

"Seeing a doctor."

Concern etched his features and he took a step closer to her. "Why? What's wrong?"

"Nothing." Why did he have to smell so good? All she wanted to do was fall forward, rest her forehead on his chest, tell him how much she missed him and that everything that happened the day of her grandfather's funeral was a stupid misunderstanding. "I'm perfectly healthy."

He looked relieved.

"And what are you doing here?" she asked, suddenly aware of the pregnancy packet laying on the back seat in full view.

"I had a meeting in the building next door, and I saw your car."

"Right," she said, patting the Mustang she'd have to get rid of now in favor of an SUV or something more child friendly.

"Well, it's been interesting." He looked ready to take off, but Mary was not about to let him leave without at least starting the groundwork for a decent future relationship.

"Ethan, I want to apologize for what happened at the funeral—"

He put up a hand to stop her. "No need."

"No, there is a need. What happened was a misunderstanding."

Beside them, a woman was getting into her car, tossing her purse and effects into the back of the car, just as Mary had done a few minutes earlier. But she was not just any woman, Mary realized, her stomach roiling sickly as she turned her head and tried to go unnoticed by the woman she had chatted with in the waiting room of Dr. Wisel's office.

"Oh, hey, there."

Too late.

Mary gave the woman a quick wave and a very tight-lipped smile as she silently begged her not to say anything more.

The woman waved, utter glee in her eyes at having heard good news today, as well. "See you later, and good luck with your baby."

Her heart in her shoes, Mary nodded as they woman got into her car and shut the door. "You, too."

She didn't want to look at him, afraid of what she'd see in his dark-blue gaze: horror, disgust, disappointment. It would be something she'd always remember, but she wasn't a coward, and she faced her child's father with a proud lift of her chin.

"Baby?" he repeated, his face registering utter shock.

"It looks that way. It's very early."

"But…how is that possible? I wore a—"

"I know."

"And the first time we had nothing at all and…well, nothing happened."

"I know."

He looked away, scrubbed a hand over his chin. "God, a baby. Your baby."

"Our baby," Mary couldn't stop herself from saying. She wasn't about to beg, but she loved the guy and she wanted him to want this child and her, too.

"Oh, Mary," he said with a softness she'd only heard when she was in his arms, when he kissed her. "Were you going to tell me?"

"Of course I was going to tell you," she assured him. "But you weren't taking my calls—"

"I would've taken this one."

"I had some things to think about first, some decisions to make—"

He went white as paper. "You're going to…to have it, right?"

Her heart leaped into her throat. How could he even think… "Yes."

He released a heavy sigh. "But you were going to wait to tell me?"

Around them people slammed doors and cars pulled in and out of their spaces. "Ethan, again, we haven't spoken in two weeks. I didn't know if we'd ever speak again the way you were ignoring my phone calls."

"I was pissed."

"I know."

"I had every right to be."

He did. "Okay."

"But that doesn't mean my feelings for you changed."

Mary felt her breath catch in her throat. What did that

mean? What feelings? Besides attraction and a strange friendship?

He continued, "That doesn't mean I didn't think about you every damn minute and want to be with you, around you, inside you."

"Ethan," she uttered, shaking her head.

"I have to know something, Mary."

"Okay."

"Are you ashamed of me, too?"

"What are you talking about?"

"What you did at the funeral—or what you didn't do. Your grandmother treated me like dirt and you stood there."

"You're right. I was an idiot. At first. But after you left, I told her off."

He didn't look as though he wanted that answer, he was still so angry—at her, and maybe at his life and past. "You couldn't get rid of me fast enough around Olivia and Tess."

Sighing, she leaned against the car. "That had nothing to do with shame, Ethan."

"What was it then?"

"I didn't want my partners to know about you."

He looked triumphant. "Exactly."

"No, not exactly. I didn't want them to know that I had allowed myself to be blackmailed by you, that I went to work for you afterward and then that I—" she swallowed "—fell in love with you in Michigan. If I'm ashamed of anyone, it's myself."

"For loving me?" he asked.

She studied him hard. "I'm coming clean here,

Ethan. I'm admitting my failings, how I've screwed up. I should have found a different way to help my father, or allowed him to find a way out himself. I know that all I've ever done is try to keep the peace, take care of everyone else but myself. Then I used it as an excuse to stay away from relationships with people." She looked heavenward. "But no more. I'm done with that. I have a child on the way, and I'm going to teach her by example to run headfirst into life and embrace it, and that the world's problems are not hers to solve." She looked at Ethan. "What are you going to teach her?"

Mary had hoped that her words, her own admission of past failures would jar him, make him see what a fool he'd been and how releasing the past was his only way to have a real future. But he wasn't ready for that, and she had to accept the fact that maybe he never would be.

"I have plenty to teach," he said proudly.

"The art of the deal?"

"There's nothing wrong with being ruthless in business matters—"

"Business matters?" She shook her head, disappointed. "You still don't understand what happened with us—or take any responsibility for it, do you?"

"If we're talking about the bargain—"

"Of course we are."

His chin set, his eyes blazing blue fire, he said, "I did what I had to do."

Mary laughed bitterly as she opened her car door and climbed in. "You know, with how brilliant you are, I'd have thought that by now you'd have come up with a far more creative answer. That one's getting a little tired, and frankly so am I," she said before closing the door in his face.

Ethan Curtis wasn't a big drinker, never packed up his troubles and headed to the nearest bar. Instead he preferred to solve his problems in a clear and rational way. Even in personal matters, this method worked well for him. Today, however, clear and rational just didn't exist.

He drove through the stone gates of the Days of Grace Trailer Park and past the office to the mobile home he couldn't seem to stay away from. The one-bedroom home seemed to stare back at him, wondering why he kept returning to a place that held such bad memories.

Ethan reclined his seat and shut his eyes, remembering the sound of his father cracking open another beer from his second six-pack, hearing the squeak of springs as the old man dropped down on the ratty couch before hurling beer caps at Ethan, along with a few choice words about how Ethan was the real reason his mother had left them.

Why the hell did he keep coming back here? Did he like torture? Did he feel he deserved it?

A loud knock on the window had Ethan awake and alert in seconds and he stared out the side window at the man who now owned the trailer. Still a little foggy with memory, Ethan pressed the button to his left, and the window dropped slowly.

The man had no baseball cap on this time and looked like a badass with his bald head, Iron Maiden T-shirt and sinister expression, but when he spoke there was no anger in his tone, only interest. "Is there a reason you like to park in front of my place or are you just a freak?"

"I used to live here."

The man's brows shot up. "Did you now?"

"With my mother and father—well, actually just my father."

"Yeah, I know about that." The man scratched his neck, said thoughtfully, "I got a boy myself. Teenager. Crazy at that age, but he's real smart. All As, every subject. Maybe he'll go to a good college and get a fancy car like yours."

"Maybe."

"That's why I moved here," the guy confessed. "For him, so he could go to the best public school in the city."

Ethan stared at the guy. He didn't have much, and he seemed to know the curse of a woman walking out on him or maybe never being around in the first place, and yet his biggest concern was his kid's future. Ethan hadn't had that kind of love and commitment from his own father, but he sure as hell wanted to be that kind of dad.

What the hell was he doing? Coming here, feeling sorry for himself when he had made a life that he should feel damn proud of. Mary had been right. He'd been lying to himself all along. The shame he felt for where he came from wasn't about the trailer—that was an easy excuse, and an easy place to throw the blame when he just didn't want to deal with the past. His shame came from a father who'd had no pride in himself and had blamed everyone else for his lot in life.

Kind of like Ethan.

He didn't need blue blood to feel worthy, and he didn't

need to be accepted by those people to feel real success. His real success was growing inside of Mary right now.

Ethan eyed the guy outside his window as he gave a quick wave to what was probably his teenage son on the porch. He'd never known the kind of love this man had for his kid, had no idea what it felt like, so to get it he'd forced a woman to create a child with him by threatening the one thing she loved.

"What a damn fool," he muttered.

"What was that?" the man asked, turning back.

"Just talking about myself, brother." Ethan took out his wallet. "Here." He handed the man a business card. "When your boy starts college, have him contact me."

The man read the card, then looked up impressed. "CEO?"

"Wouldn't have minded a leg up in the beginning," Ethan said. "We always have internships available."

"Appreciate it." The man pocketed the card, then gestured to the trailer. "You want to come in? We're just about to throw some steaks on the barbecue."

"Thanks." Ethan smiled. "But I think it's time I got out of here."

"Back where you belong?"

"That's right." He was only thinking about Mary and the baby when he said it.

Ethan drove away from the trailer park, knowing it was the last time he'd ever be back, realizing that if he wanted any future with the woman he loved and the child growing inside her, he had to leave the past where it was and look ahead to the future.

Thirteen

"I can't believe I'm going to be a grandpa."

Mary sat on the picnic blanket her father had laid out in the backyard beside the vegetable garden, a garden that was now going crazy with bushes of fragrant basil, vines of squash and pumpkin and rows of ripe cherry tomatoes.

"Well, it's true," she told him, taking a bite of her corned-beef sandwich.

He plunked down beside her, looking stronger than she'd seen him look in a year. His color was good, too, and when he spoke, his tone contained that rich, happy sound she remembered from her childhood. "Your mother would be so proud. I wish she could see…"

"I know. But she will, in her own way."

"I like that." He winked at her, then handed her a cookie. "I made these myself, chocolate chip."

She took a bite and sighed. "They're great. In fact, all of this food is wonderful. I may have to hire you to cater for the company."

He chuckled. "Sounds good. But let's wait until after I open my restaurant."

"You're opening a restaurant?"

"More like a roadside place. Sell my vegetables and offer some small meals, homemade ice cream, the cookies…" He grinned. "Who knows, it's still in the planning stages."

"Good for you."

He nodded, then shifting topics. "So, what are your plans? Are you going to stay in your apartment after the baby is born? It's pretty small."

"It is." She didn't know exactly what her plans were, only that she'd be okay and that this child would be loved beyond belief. "Oh, Grandmother called."

Hugh looked surprised. "Really? Even after the scene you told me about at the funeral?"

"She said she respects my choices—"

"She actually said that?"

Mary laughed. "I know. I was shocked, too. She even apologized and said my friends are my own business. Even after I told her who the father was. She wants me to move in with her, have the baby there."

"What did you tell her?"

"Thanks, but no thanks."

"Bet she wasn't too happy to hear that."

"No, but she said she understood and asked me to visit as much as I could."

Hugh munched on a carrot. "Boy, she's certainly changed her tune since her daughter married me."

"I guess so. She wants to be a part of my life and the baby's, and she said she was willing to let go of this feud with Ethan." Mary shrugged. "I'll believe it when I see it, but people have been known to change every once in a while, right? Even in small ways?"

"It's been known to happen," Hugh said, tossing aside his carrot and regarding her with serious eyes. "Did I say I'm not all that happy about the daddy myself?"

"You did." The sun was high in the sky, must be around one o'clock, she thought, reclining back on the blanket. "He made some mistakes, Pop. Some big ones, but then again so have I. So have you."

"Well, if sending that back to me was any indication of change, than perhaps you're right, lass."

Mary looked in the direction that her father was pointing. At the far end of the garden, where her mother had planted a circle of yellow roses, was the sculpture of mother and child that Hugh had risked so much in trying to get back.

"He gave that to you," she asked, stunned.

Hugh nodded. "Brought it by himself. We didn't say much to each other, but it was pretty decent of him."

Mary smiled to herself, knowing that for Ethan, coming to her father's house with that sculpture couldn't have been easy. He'd made a grand gesture.

When she looked up, her father was watching her. "You love him."

"Yes. I just hope that's enough. He's got some demons to exorcise, some new ideas to come to terms with and a life waiting for him. But I'm anxious to see what his next step will be."

Hugh lifted one grayish-blond brow. "And if he doesn't take a next step?"

"Then I'll be very sorry—" she lifted her chin, trying to ignore the ache in her heart "—but I'll survive."

It was Saturday morning around ten-thirty, and all three of the women of No Ring Required were working, sans receptionist. Business was crazy right now, and Mary, Olivia and Tess were all working overtime to accommodate their clients.

Tess stuck her head in Mary's office. She looked slightly anxious, unsure of how she wanted to say what she had come in there to say. "Mary, it's Mr. Curtis."

Her heart leaped into her throat. "Here?"

"No, he was on the phone."

"What line?" she asked, breathless.

"He's already hung up," Tess explained awkwardly. "But there's a message." She handed a slip of paper to Mary. "He asked if you'd meet him there."

"Asked?" Mary repeated.

Grinning, Tess nodded. "Good luck."

After Tess went back to her office, Mary stared at the address on the paper, her pulse pounding in her blood. After all they'd been through, she didn't want to go back to that place, especially now, but more than any-thing, she wanted to hear what Ethan had to say, so she stood up, grabbed her purse and headed out.

Ethan was actually nervous. Like a damn teenager asking out a girl he knew he was not even close to being good enough for. Thank God the baby shop wasn't packed with customers or he'd probably have to pay the owner to shut the place down for a while so he could really talk with Mary in private.

The bell over the door jingled, and he turned to see Mary walk in, looking so beautiful Ethan almost couldn't speak. Her blond hair fell in waves around her shoulders and she wore a cream linen pantsuit with sexy sandals and pale-pink toes.

He picked up a baby blanket from the railing of a nearby crib. "I think we should stay away from anything blue. Even if it is a boy."

With wary eyes she regarded him. "What am I doing here?"

"Sit." Grinning at the command that came so easily to him, he amended quickly, "Please."

She sat in the rocker next to him and waited.

"How are you?" he asked.

"Fine. Curious."

He nodded, knowing he needed to get to the point if he wanted to keep her attention. "Look, Mary, I get it now."

Her brows lifted. "Get what?"

"My hang-ups. All seven hundred of them. I get it. I forced you into a situation that was impossible, all for the sake of feeling like I was worth something. You have every right to be angry with me. But you have no right to be ashamed of yourself."

"I'm not."

"I'm glad."

She gave him a tight-lipped smile. "But thank you for saying that."

"Oh, honey," he said, dropping to his knees in front of her. "That's just the tip of the iceberg as far as confessions go."

Mary felt her pulse pick up speed as hope surged through her for the first time in weeks. Ethan's heart was open to her, completely. She could see it in his eyes, hear it in his voice.

He took her hand in his and kissed the palm. "I know after all I've done that asking you to love me again is asking a helluva a lot, but I'm asking anyway."

Her stomach flipped. She couldn't believe what he was saying. "You don't have to do this. If it's about the baby, you can be a part—"

"Mary, I love you. Finding out about the baby didn't change that fact, but it did force me to face what I've done, what I thought I needed and a past I just couldn't let go of."

Completely overwhelmed, Mary shook her head at him.

"What is it, sweetheart?" he asked, kissing her hand again so tenderly, so reverently it brought tears to her eyes.

"I just never thought we'd get here."

"But we did."

"I know and I'm so thankful."

"You wanted to know what gift I can give this child?" he said, reaching out to touch her belly.

Mary nodded, too emotional to speak.

"I can give the same gift our child's mother gave to me—love."

In that moment all Mary wanted to do was wrap her arms around Ethan and never let go. "I do love you, Ethan. So much."

He kissed her neck, her cheek, her eyelids. "I love you, too. Marry me?"

She laughed, insanely happy and so sure of her future. "Yes. Yes. Yes."

Ethan kissed her, a hungry, possessive kiss that she never wanted to end.

"Hi, there," came a feminine voice from behind them.

Still clinging to each other, Ethan and Mary glanced up and smiled sheepishly at the saleswoman.

"Are we shopping for ourselves or for someone else?" she asked.

Ethan reached in his pocket and took out the most beautiful yellow-diamond ring. He grinned at Mary as he slipped it on her finger. "What do you think, my soon-to-be Mrs. Curtis? Shall we do a little shopping?"

Mary kissed him squarely on the mouth and said happily, "I think it's about time."

* * * * *

PLAYBOY'S
RUTHLESS PAYBACK

BY
LAURA WRIGHT

To Daniel, thank you for seeing me through
this book. You're the best!

One

"Congresswoman Fisher is on line two, Derek Mead is still holding on line three and Owen Winston is on line four."

Mac Valentine relaxed in his chair. His executive assistant, Claire, stood in the doorway of his modern, chrome-and-leather penthouse office, an expectant look on her grandmotherly face. She had been with him for eight years and she was somewhat of a voyeur when it came to watching him work. She especially enjoyed moments like this when he was about to crush someone. She thought of him as a ruthless, unflinching businessman, and on more than one occasion he'd heard her refer to him as a black-haired, black-eyed demon who held each one of his thirty-five employees to incredibly high standards.

Mac grinned. The woman was right. The only thing she'd left out was that if any one of those employees fell short of his expectations, if they didn't strive for the goal of making MCV Wealth Enhancement Corp. the first choice of not only the Minneapolis area, but also the entire Midwest, they were sent packing.

Behind her black frames, Claire's eyes glistened like a child waiting for dessert to be served. "Mr. Winston says he is returning your call, sir."

Mac palmed his BlackBerry. "Tell both the congress-woman and Mead that I'll return their calls. This won't take long."

"Yes, sir." Claire hovered in the doorway.

"And close the door when you go," Mac said evenly. "Today is not a school day."

"Of course, sir." Looking thoroughly disappointed, Claire left the room.

Mac pressed the call button and leaned back in his chair. "Owen."

"That's right," came the irritated voice on the other end of the line. "I've been holding for longer than I care to. What can I do for you?"

Satisfaction rolled through Mac at the slight tremor in the older man's voice. He turned his chair toward the wall of windows behind him and stared out at the view of the Minneapolis skyline. "I won't waste my time or yours asking why you did what you did."

"Excuse me?"

"Or force you to admit it," said Mac. "Attempting to ruin the reputation of a competing firm happens quite a bit in our game. Mostly with the older set. You guys get tired, lose your edge and the clients start looking elsewhere."

Mac could practically see Owen's face darkening with rage. "You don't know what you're talking about, Valentine—"

"You can't help it," Mac continued coldly. "You see these hotshots coming up the ranks with cooler heads and sharper minds and you start to worry that you're not going to be taken seriously anymore. And when you realize it's only a matter of time before you're forced out of business, you panic." Mac leaned forward and said without emotion, "You panicked, Owen."

"This is ridiculous," Owen sputtered. "You don't know what you're talking about."

Mac continued as if he hadn't heard. "A respectable man would recognize his limitations and retire, maybe play a round of golf in the morning followed by a nice nap in the afternoon."

"A respectable businessman, Valentine." Owen laughed bitterly. "A respectable businessman wouldn't give preferential treatment, key information or tips to certain privileged clients. A respectable man wouldn't give that information based on their client's long legs and large breasts."

It was the accusation of a desperate man, total BS, but the rumor had spread like the flu. "You are this close to a lawsuit, Winston."

"That sharp mind of yours would never allow these observations of mine to go on the record in a court of law. Such a long, drawn-out process. Even worse for your reputation, I would think."

It took a few seconds for Mac to respond, then a deadly calm crept over him like the blackening sky before a thunderstorm. "True enough," he said slowly. "Perhaps legal recourse isn't the right way to deal with you."

"Smart man. Now it's late and I have—"

Mac stood and walked across the room. "No, I suppose I'll have to come up with a different way to make you pay for what you've done."

"It's after seven, Valentine," said Owen tightly. "I have dinner plans."

"Yes, of course—get home to your family." Mac opened his office door and gestured for Claire. "Especially that lovely daughter of yours. What's her name again? Allison? Olive?"

Owen didn't answer.

"Ah, right…" Mac raised a brow at Claire. "Olivia. Beautiful name," Mac said as he watched his assistant go to her computer and begin a search. "Beautiful name for a beautiful woman, I'm told. You know, your daughter has a reputation for being a very good girl. Sweet, loves her father and steers clear of anything scandalous. Might be interesting to see how easy or how enjoyably difficult it would be to change that."

Claire glanced up, her expression a mixed bag of respect, curiosity and horror.

"You stay away from my daughter." The once cocky old man now sounded like an anxious pup.

"I'm not a religious man, Owen, but I believe the

phrase 'an eye for an eye' is appropriate here." Mac stalked back into his office. "I may be an arrogant, selfish prick, but I'm no fraud. I give every one of my clients two hundred percent, male and female alike. You went too far."

Mac stabbed at the off button on his BlackBerry and walked to the windows. The bleak, gray light of a hostile rainstorm hovered over the parking lot and street below, making Mac feel as though his threats to Owen Winston might be so powerful they could not only affect the sexual status of an innocent young woman, but the weather, as well.

"She owns No Ring Required."

Mac didn't turn around to address Claire's statement. "How do I know that name?"

"*Minneapolis Magazine* did a cover story on the business last month. Three women—a chef, an interior designer and a party planner—all top-notch business-women who have banded together to create—"

"A service for men who need the help and expertise of a wife," he continued. "But either don't have one or don't want one."

"That's right."

He turned around and nodded to his assistant. "Perfect. Set up an appointment with Olivia Winston for this week. It would seem that I'm in need of her services."

"Did you read the article, sir?"

"I don't remember…I probably skimmed it."

"These are hardcore, upstanding women who are well-respected in the business community. They are adamantly against any and all fraternization."

Mac grinned to himself. "Get that appointment for tomorrow morning. First thing."

Lip pulled under her teeth, Claire nodded and left the room.

Mac returned to his desk and thumbed through the files of the clients that had gone AWOL since Owen Winston's lies had surfaced two days ago. Who knew if they were ever going to return to his company or if their relationship with his firm was dead in the water.

Mac wanted to throttle that bastard—but violence was too quickly given and gotten over. No, it would have to be a rep for a rep. Owen had taken Mac's and Mac would take his daughter's.

Well-respected or not, Owen's little girl was going to have to pay—for the loss of revenue to MCV and its employees, and for her father's stupidity.

Two

Olivia closed her eyes and inhaled. "I'm such a genius...."

"How long are you going to make us wait, Liv?" Tess asked, her stomach rumbling loudly. "I skipped breakfast."

Seated at the table, Mary Kelley stared at the tall redhead's trim belly, her brows drawn together. "Sounds like a train's derailing in there. Very ladylike."

Tess gave Mary a teasing glare. "Give me a break, I'm starving." She pointed to the massive yellow diamond engagement ring on her pretty blond partner's finger. "Not all of us have beautiful men bringing us poached eggs and bacon in the morning."

Smiling, Mary touched her growing belly, her blue

eyes soft and happy. "Ethan's very concerned about feeding his child. If I don't have something to eat every few hours he freaks."

Tess snorted. "That's just a little too sweet for me."

Mary laughed. "Oh, c'mon. You'll change your mind about that someday. Guaranteed."

"Doubtful. I'm too much of a loner—and I like it."

"Well, then we have to get you to go out and socialize more." Mary's eyes lit up. "Maybe you'll meet someone at Ethan's and my holiday engagement party at the end of the month. He has some cute friends."

"No thanks."

"You might meet up with the right guy."

Tess shook her head and laughed. "I don't believe in the right guy, Mare. Now, a truckful of not-so-right guys—that's something I believe in."

Mary poured herself another glass of milk. "You're not old enough to be so cynical. How many men have you dated at twenty-five?"

"Enough to know better," Tess said seriously, then turned to Olivia. "You and I are lucky to have escaped the noose for so long, right, Liv?"

"Oh, so lucky," Olivia drawled as she cut squares of brownie. Olivia tried to ignore the wave of envy that moved over her heart as she recalled the tenderness in Ethan Curtis's eyes that morning when he gave Mary a goodbye kiss at the reception desk before leaving for his office. He had looked so in love, so happy, so over-the-moon excited about their baby.

Olivia didn't begrudge her friend the beautiful man

and solid relationship, but she did wonder if it was possible for someone like her to have half of that kind of happiness. In her heart of hearts, she wanted a man—someone to cook for and love and make babies with, but odds of that kind of life coming her way weren't great. Even though she had grown up in years, she was still very much stuck to the past. In many ways, she was still that depressed sixteen-year-old who had just lost her mother to cancer, couldn't get her father to notice her and had escaped from her pain in the most foolish ways possible—parties and boys and sex.

The shame of what she'd done and how many boys she'd allowed herself to be used by hadn't diminished in the ten years since, but in that time she had grown extraordinarily tough. She had also become cautious and resolutely celibate. Today, her reputation was lily-white—she was a hard-nosed businesswoman who kept the secrets of her past to herself.

"All right," Olivia said brightly, setting two extra large squares of chocolate brownie before Tess and Mary. "These will keep your mouths occupied."

"I believe she just told us to shut up," Tess said with a grin.

Mary picked up her brownie and sighed. "But it was in the very nicest way possible."

"True," Tess said, her pale gray eyes raking the gooey chocolate square. "And for another one of these I will not only give up on the guy and marriage talk, but if asked, I will gladly roll over and pant."

"Before you do," said a husky male voice behind them, "just be aware that you have an audience."

Mary and Tess whirled around in their chairs, and Olivia glanced up. Filling up the doorway with a cynical, though highly amused, expression was a man with eyes the color of espresso. He was tall and broad and was dressed impeccably in a gray pinstripe suit and black wool coat. Olivia found herself clenching her fists as she felt an irresistible urge to flip up the collar of his coat and use it to pull herself against him. The feeling was so out of character that it frightened the hell out of her and made her stomach churn with nervous energy. In the past seven years, since her self-imposed exile from sex, her body had rarely betrayed her. Sure, there had been a few late nights with a good romance novel in her bed, but other than that, nada.

As she looked at this man, every inch of her screamed *Caution!*

"Mac Valentine?" she said, relieved that her voice sounded steady and cool.

He nodded. "I think I'm early."

"Only by a few minutes," she assured him. "Please come in."

As he walked toward them, his stride runway-model confident, both Mary and Tess stood and offered him their hands. "It's nice to meet you, Mr. Valentine," Mary said evenly. "We were just enjoying a midmorning pick-me-up."

"I understand."

"Chocolate is life's blood around here," Mary continued warmly.

"I wondered what that amazing scent was the minute I got off the elevator."

Tess patted Olivia on the back. "Well, that's our resident chef's doing. Olivia makes magic and we all get to enjoy it."

His gaze rested on Olivia. "Is that so?"

Olivia shrugged good-naturedly. "I've never been good at false modesty, so I'll just say, yes, I'm a damn fine cook."

Amusement glittered in Mac Valentine's dark eyes, and Olivia felt a shiver travel up her spine.

"And on that note," said Mary, packing up the rest of her brownie and half-full glass of milk, "Tess and I will leave you in Olivia's capable hands. Welcome to No Ring Required, Mr. Valentine."

"Thank you."

Tess shook his hand again, then when his back was turned grabbed another brownie, before following Mary out of the room.

Trying not to laugh, Olivia watched Mac take off his coat and lay it over an empty chair, then she gestured to the table. "Please, have a seat." She snatched the orange platter of brownies off the counter and held it out in his direction. "Would you like one?"

He glanced up at her. "Do I have to roll over and pant?"

"Only if you want seconds."

Mac Valentine's eyes flashed with surprise at her quick comeback. "I'll let you know." Then he took a brownie from the plate.

She sat beside him and folded her hands primly. She

didn't know exactly why this man was here, but she had a feeling he brought trouble with him—several varieties of trouble. "Now, your assistant didn't reveal much about why you're here today when she made the appointment. Perhaps you could."

"Of course." He sat back in his chair. "I need you to turn my home into something far more 'homey' than what it is."

"And what is it?"

"A lot of unused space."

"Okay."

"I have clients coming in from out of town, and I want them to feel as though they've visited a family man, instead of a…" He paused.

She lifted her brows. "Yes?"

His lips twitched. "Someone who has no idea what those two words really mean."

"I see." And she did. It wasn't the first time she'd worked with a clueless millionaire playboy.

"I think it would be best if you saw my house for yourself."

She nodded, her gaze darting to the untouched brownie before him. "All right. But you understand my main area of expertise is in the kitchen."

"I was led to believe you were a multitasker."

Why wasn't he eating her brownie? "I am, but if it's true homemaking you're looking for then Tess might be a better—"

"No," he said, cutting her off.

She paused and gave him an expectant look.

"I want you," he finished, his face hard.

"Yes, I can see that," she said cautiously. "There's just one problem."

"And what would that be?"

"Your relationship with my father."

His brows lifted, just slightly. "I have no relationship with your father."

"He called me this morning and said you might be stopping by."

"Did he?"

"Yep."

Mac studied her for a moment. "You have the reputation of being a soft-spoken sweetheart, did you know that?"

"Are you trying to tell me that I'm not living up to my reputation?"

That query produced a wry smile from him. "I think I'm going to have a bite of this brownie now."

It's about damn time, she thought as she watched him slip the thick dark cake between his teeth. He had large, strong-looking hands and thick wrists, and she felt a humming in her belly as she wondered what he did with his hands that garnered him such a roguish reputation.

Her father had left her with a big warning about Mac Valentine. But instead of being worried she felt as curious as a one-year-old with an uncovered wall outlet in her sights.

"Good?" she asked, pointing to the half-eaten brownie on the plate.

"Very good."

"I'm glad," she said evenly. "Now, Mr. Valentine, why don't you tell me why you're really here?"

Three

If there was one thing Mac Valentine could spot a mile away, it was a worthy adversary. She may have been only a few inches over five feet with eyes as large and as soft as a baby deer, but Olivia Winston's cleverness and sharp tongue clearly declared her as a force to be reckoned with.

He hadn't seen that coming.

But then again, there was nothing he loved better than a challenge.

He watched those brown fawn's eyes narrow, and knew she would wait all day for the answer to her question.

"Due to circumstances beyond my control," he began, "my financial firm has lost its top three clients. I expect this to change over the course of the next few months when they realize that no one else in this town can make them the kind of money that I can, and did. But in the meantime, I need some help from you in landing a few heavy hitters."

Olivia's gaze flickered to the tabletop. "Do you need my help rebuilding your business or your reputation?"

"I see your father has done more than warn you about me." She didn't confirm or deny this, so he continued, "My business is not in any danger, but yes, my reputation has come into question and I cannot—and will not—allow that to continue."

"I see." Her smile turned edgy. "So, you want these potential clients to stay at your house instead of a hotel?"

"They're the type who appreciate home and family and soft edges—" he waved his hand "—all of that."

"But you don't."

"No."

She stood and took the plate that was in front of him, the plate with half a remaining brownie on it. "I have a question for you," she said, walking to the sink and depositing the dish there. She was small, but all curves, and when she walked it was seduction with every step. She turned to face him, leaned back against the countertop and crossed her arms over her full chest. Mac felt his gut tighten at the picture-perfect sight of her. "You believe that my dad caused your clients to leave your firm, right?" she said, arching her brow.

"Actually it was the lies your father spread that caused my clients to leave," he corrected.

"If you think that, then why would you want to work with his daughter? Unless…"

"Unless what?"

She walked to him and stopped just shy of his chair. If he reached out, grabbed her around her tiny, perfect waist and pulled her onto his lap, what would she do?

Whoever said payback was a bitch hadn't seen this woman.

"Unless you want to use me to get back at him," she said in a voice so casual she might have been reading a grocery list.

He matched her tone. "Is that what he told you?"

"Yes, but he didn't really have to."

"And how exactly would I use you?"

She shook her head. "Not quite sure." When she sat this time it was across from him.

"But your father has some ideas?"

"He's worried about your…" She smiled, thin as a blade. "Obvious charms—I mean, you're a great-looking guy. But I assured him he didn't have anything to worry about."

Well, this was a first. "Really?"

She nodded, said matter-of-factly, "I let him know that I would never be interested."

Mac felt his brow lift.

She laughed. "I don't mean to insult you, but the truth is, I would never go for a guy like you."

"Why do you think I'm insulted?"

The question caught her off guard and she stumbled with her words. "I, well—"

"And what kind of guy do you think I am?"

She lifted her chin. "One who assumes he can have anything he wants and any woman he wants."

Mac was not a man of assumptions, he was a man of words and deeds, and this woman was starting to piss him off. "I go after what I want, Miss Winston, but the people and things that come to me come at their own free will, I can assure you."

"You're just that irresistible."

He sat back in his chair. "Do all clients of No Ring Required go through an interrogation process or is it just me?"

"You're not a client yet, Mister—"

"Ah, Olivia." Tess stuck her head in the office, a confused expression on her face. "Can I see you for a moment?"

"Sure." Olivia turned to Mac. "I'll be right back, Mr. Valentine."

He saw, with vicious pleasure, that she was caught off guard and he couldn't help but grin as he said, "I wish I could say I was looking forward to it."

"If you can't wait…" she began.

"Oh, I can wait." He reached for his coat, and snagged his BlackBerry from the pocket. "I'll make a few calls."

Olivia felt like taking the man's phone and crushing it under her heel, but she smiled and nodded. Once out in the hall, the door tightly closed behind her, she faced her anxious-looking partners.

"What are you doing in there?" Tess said in a harsh whisper.

"Talking to a potential client."

"Insulting a potential client, is more like it," said Tess dryly, her arms crossed over her chest.

"Tess, you don't know the situation—"

Ever the mediator, Mary took over, her tone calm and parental. "Whatever the situation is, Liv, we could hear you all the way from our offices, and it sounded like an attack. Can you tell us what's going on?"

Olivia blew out a breath. "He's not a normal client. Hell, I don't even know if he's going to be a client at all."

"Not after what I just heard," Tess grumbled.

"At ease, Tess." Knowing her partners deserved an explanation, Olivia offered them the simplest one. "He and my father are in the same business, and a few of Mac Valentine's clients have decided to leave him and hire my dad instead. Mac thinks my father went the un-ethical route and told the financial community that he was doling out preferential treatment and tips to his better-looking clients."

"Wow," Tess began. "And did your father do that?"

"I can't imagine. My father's always been at the top of his profession. But the point is, Mac Valentine believes it. He thinks my father is responsible for the loss of three of his best clients, and now he's hiring me to get even."

Tess frowned. "What?"

"How?" Mary said, perplexed.

"I don't know yet, but I intend to find out."

"I don't like the sound of this," Tess said, shooting Mary a warning glance.

"Does he have a legitimate request for us?" Mary asked.

"He's out to bag a few new clients to replace the ones he's lost, and he wants me to make his house homey and inviting on several levels to impress them."

Mary put a hand on Olivia's shoulder. "If you don't feel you can handle him, Liv, Tess or I will—"

"No. First of all, he only wants me, and secondly, I'm not about to run from this man. I'm a professional, and I'll get the job done without getting involved."

Mary put a hand to her belly. "Sounds familiar."

"If I don't take the job, I'm willing to bet this guy would find a way of letting it be known around town that one of NRR's partners isn't a true professional. We don't need that."

Both Mary and Tess begrudgingly agreed.

"Just be careful, okay?" said Mary, squeezing Olivia's arm.

"Always." She gave them a bright smile and a wave and returned to the kitchen.

Mac was just finishing a call when Olivia eased back into her seat at the table, an NRR contract for him to sign in her hand. She took a deep breath. "Sorry about that."

"For leaving the room or for the insults?"

"Look, I'm going to take this 'job' because I am a professional and have partners who are counting on me. I'm also more than a little curious as to what you're going to try and pull. But know this, Mr. Valentine, lay one hand on me and we're done, understand?"

Mac looked amused. "For someone who believes herself so unaffected by a guy like me, you're acting worried."

"Boundaries and rules—good things to have."

After a beat, Mac agreed. "I understand. Now, can we get down to business?"

Olivia slid the one-page contract and a pen across the table. "When would you like me to start?"

"I'm having the DeBolds to my home this weekend."

"The diamond family?" She was surprised. The DeBolds would be a huge score and, according to her father, incredibly hard to land as clients. Mac Valentine had guts and drive, she'd give him that.

"They don't have children yet, but they are very into family, and the lifestyle that accompanies it. I need to make them feel at home with me."

She nodded. "I understand."

"I want home-cooked meals, family activities," he continued. "I want them to see me as secure, a man who understands their needs and desires for the future."

"Okay."

"And I'd like you to stay at the house with us."

She paused and stared at him, hoping her gaze was a cold as her tone. "No."

"In a room upstairs, down the hall from the DeBolds."

"And where will you be?"

"I sleep on the first floor."

Out of patience, she stood from the table and shot him a hot look. "It's not going to happen."

He ignored her as if she'd never said a word, "I want you to be there with us from breakfast to evening."

"Yes, I know. And I will."

In his ever-present calm way, he studied her. "All right, we'll discuss that particular detail at a later date. Now, on to something more important—this contract I'm about to sign, it guarantees confidentiality, is that right? You will not reveal anything about my business, and whom I do business with?"

"Of course." She had loyalties to her father, but her loyalties to the business and her partners came first. "Do you have menus in mind or would you like me to plan something?"

"I'd like you to plan everything."

After signing the contract and issuing a rather substantial check to NRR, Mac stood, towering over her like a statue. The soft scent of fading aftershave drifted into her nostrils and it annoyed her that just a small detail like his scent made her feel off balance. She found herself staring at his lips as he said, "I would like you to come by my house tomorrow, see what you have to work with and what you feel needs to be changed."

She stepped away from him, trying to regain her cool composure. "How's 10:00 a.m.?"

"You have my address?"

"Yes." She looked up at him and grinned slightly. "And your number, as well."

"Clever." He held out his hand, and for just a moment Olivia felt this odd sensation to turn and run from him.

But she knew how ridiculous and childish that thought was, and she confidently placed her hand in his.

There were no sparks or fireworks that erupted inside Olivia at that first touch. Instead something far more worrisome happened; she had an overwhelming urge to cry, as though she'd been on an island alone for ten years and had woken up to see a boat a few miles off shore—a boat she knew in her gut she wasn't going to be able to flag down.

She broke the connection first.

"Until tomorrow then," he said evenly.

She watched him walk out of the kitchen and down the hall, the edges of his wool coat snapping with each stride. Yes, it had been a long time since she'd met a man who affected both her mind and her body, and it was pretty damn unlucky that he happened to be an enemy of her father's.

Thankfully, she had become quite good at denying herself.

Four

Mac had hoped Olivia Winston would be moderately attractive. After all, it would make his goal a little easier and more pleasant to achieve if the woman he was going to seduce was decent-looking. Unfortunately this woman was miles past decent—circling somewhere around blistering hot. She was also intelligent and passionate and pushed sugar. And if he had any hope of seeing his plan through to the end, whenever he looked at her he was going to have to force himself to remember the he and her father were at war. And that her unhappiness and disappointment and permanent scarlet letter would be his justice.

He slowed his car to a comfortable seventy miles per hour as he exited the freeway. But seeing her as an enemy to be taken down wouldn't be easy. Damn, the way she'd looked at him with those fiery coffee-colored doe eyes, as though she couldn't decide if she was intrigued by him or wanted to follow her father's advice and toss him right out on his ass. Mac turned onto Third Street, Minneapolis's restaurant row. Eyeing the line of cars in front of Martini Two Olives, he backed into an open parking space with one effortless movement. Light snowflakes touched down on his windshield as he spotted a tall, cool blonde through the window of the packed restaurant.

She smiled warmly at him as he walked through the doorway. Mac gave her a kiss on the cheek, and above the din of celebratory restaurant patrons, he said, "Hello, Avery."

"Well, Mac Valentine, it's been way too long," she practically purred.

They took a table at the bar and ordered drinks. When a scotch neat was set before him, Mac asked, "How's Tim? You two still in love?"

Avery blushed and smiled simultaneously. "Blissfully. And planning on starting a family next year."

Mack leaned back in his chair and took a healthy swallow of scotch. "I'm a damn fine matchmaker. My best buddy and my firm's geeky ex-lawyer."

"Hey, watch it with the geek stuff. That was years ago. I'm a knockout now."

He grinned. "Yeah. You're all right."

She laughed. When her laughter eased, she grew

serious, her pale blue eyes heavy with sincerity. "You are a great friend, and you did a good thing. We owe you."

"Yeah, well, I never thought I'd have to collect on that debt, but times are a little…unsure."

"Tim mentioned something…"

"He always sucked at discretion."

"What do you need? Anything at all."

"Do you still represent the DeBolds?"

She nodded. "My favorite clients."

"I've heard they're shopping for a new financial firm, and I'd like to show them what I have to offer."

Her fingernails clicked on her glass. "They might've heard the rumors, Mac…. And you know how they are about family, or lack of. They don't want to deal with—"

"I know, I know. That's why I'm planning to be everything they're looking for and more."

She looked unconvinced. "Five-star restaurants and over-the-top gestures won't impress them. If you really want them to take the firm seriously, you'd need to do something—"

He put a hand up to stop her. "Let me tell you what I have in mind, then you can decide to set it up or not."

"All right," she said and lifted the glass of red wine to her lips.

Given the kind of man he was, Olivia had expected Mac Valentine to live in a sleek, modern type of home made of glass or stainless steel or something impervious to warmth. So it came as somewhat of a shock to find that the address he'd given her belonged to a stately, though charming, mansion on historic Lake of the Isles Parkway.

After parking in the snow-dusted driveway, Olivia darted up the stone steps and rang the bell, noting with a smile the lovely way winter's ravaged vines and ivy grew up one side of the house in a charming zigzag pattern. The wintry November breeze off the lake shocked her with a sudden gust, and she was thankful when the door opened. A tall, thin man in his late sixties ushered Olivia inside. He explained that he was the handyman, then told her Mac would be down in a minute. Then the man disappeared down a long hallway.

Olivia stood in the spacious entryway of Mac's home, staring at a beautiful, rustic banister and staircase, and wondering why it felt only slightly warmer inside the house than out.

"Good morning."

Coming down the stairs like Rhett Butler in reverse was Mac Valentine. He was dressed simply in jeans and a white shirt, the sleeves rolled up to reveal strong forearms. Awareness stirred in her belly. She liked forearms, liked the way the cords of muscle bunched when a man gripped something, or someone.

"Find the place all right?" he asked when he reached her.

"Perfectly," she said, noticing that not only did he look good, but he smelled good, too. As if he'd showered in a snowy, pine forest or something. Realizing her thoughts had taken an idiotic turn, she flipped on her professional switch and said, "Shall we get started?"

His eyes lit with amusement, but he nodded. "Come with me."

As Olivia followed him through the house, she noticed that each room she passed was more warm and inviting than the next, with wood paneling, hewn beams and rustic paint colors on the walls. But there was a glaring problem that Mac didn't mention as they walked—every room, from bathroom to living room to the fabulous gourmet kitchen, was bare as bones. There were no furnishings, no artwork, no tchotchkes—no nothing. It was the oddest thing she'd ever seen. It was as though he'd just moved in.

"I'm sensing a theme here," Olivia said with a laugh as they stopped in the kitchen. "You, Mr. Valentine, are a minimalist of the first order."

"Not totally." He gestured to a massive stainless steel contraption on the counter. "I have an espresso machine."

Two perfect cups of steaming cappuccino sat on the counter beside it. Olivia took one and handed the other to him. "And that's a good thing, but it barely strikes the surface of a family home." Her hands curled around the hot cup, feeling warm for the first time since she left the car. "I have my work cut out for me. What's up with all this?"

He shrugged. "I never got around to buying furniture."

It was more than that, she thought, studying him. It had to be. He hadn't put his stamp on anything. Maybe he hated permanence or didn't trust it. Whatever it was, it would be her first order of business. "How long has it sat empty like this?"

"I bought the place three years ago."

She nearly choked on her cappuccino. "That's just wrong. Where do you sleep? Or more importantly what do you sleep on?"

"I have a bed," he said, leaning against the countertop. "Would you like to see it?"

"Absolutely. It's my job to make sure it has that stamp of family charm on it."

"What do you think is stamped on it now?"

"Debauchery?" she said quickly.

He grinned. "There's one more room down here, and in this one, I did put down a few roots. Two, to be exact."

Curious, Olivia followed him down a short hallway and through a heavy wood door. She stopped when she saw it and just stared. The room was, in a word, fantastic. Olivia walked in and stood in the middle, thinking she could hear music playing. One wall was made entirely of glass and she felt instantly at one with the white wonderland outside. Snow fell in big globs off the many tree branches and landed in pretty little tufts below. Birds hopped in the snow, making three-pronged tracks, and squirrels passed nuts back and forth. Inside, to her right were a pair of comfortable-looking navy-blue leather arm chairs that sat before a massive stone fireplace. Mac sat in one of the chairs and motioned for her to do the same.

"So once in a while you force yourself to relax?" she asked, as the heat from the blazing fire seeped into her bones and called upon her to relax.

"A man needs a refuge."

"Well, this is great."

He glanced over at her. "Do you think you can do something with this house?"

"I believe so."

"Good." He dug into the pocket of his jeans, pulled out a card and handed it to her. "Get everything. From sheets to picture frames. I don't care what you spend just make it warm and family friendly."

She stared at the platinum card. "You want me to furnish the whole house?"

He nodded.

"Every square inch?"

"Yes."

"Don't you want your stamp on it at all? Choices in artwork? Television?"

"No."

"I don't understand. Don't you want to feel comfortable here?"

"I don't like feeling comfortable—too much can happen to a person when they get comfortable."

"I'll try and remember that," she muttered.

His voice grew tight and cold. "All I want is the DeBolds, signed and happy."

Olivia was tempted to ask him just where he'd gotten such a desperate need to win, but it wasn't her place to care. He looked so serious, so raw, so sexy as he stared into the fire. Just his presence made the muscles in her belly knot with tension, and she knew that no matter what she told her father, after today, the truth was she was attracted to Mac Valentine. Not that she was going to do anything about it, or allow him to use her in any way, but the attraction was undeniably there.

"I'll do my best to set the stage, sir," she said with just a hint of humor.

He looked over at her then, his eyes nearly black in their intensity. "I hope so."

Her gaze dropped to his mouth. It was a lush, cynical mouth and for a moment she wondered what it would feel like against hers. She turned away. "You need to understand something," she said as much to herself as to him.

"What's that?"

"I know you didn't hire me because I'm a dynamite cook."

He snorted. "That's a little self-deprecating."

"No, it's the truth."

He didn't reply.

"You're looking for revenge. I'm not entirely sure how you're going to go about making me pay for something you believe my father did, but be forewarned…"

"Okay."

She forced herself to look at him. "I'm not going to fall under your spell."

"No?"

She shook her head. "Instead, I'm going to watch you."

"Watching me…I like that."

"And if you get out of line, I'm going to shove you right back in."

"Olivia?" He raised an eyebrow.

"What?"

"What if *you* get out of line?"

The question stopped her…from thinking and from a quick reaction. Mac saw her hesitate, too, and his dark eyes burned with pleasure.

"I think social hour has come to an end," she said tightly, standing. "I have a lot to accomplish in a short amount of time, so let's get to work. Show me the bedrooms."

"All of the bedrooms?" he said with a devious smile.

"Yes."

He stood, shot her a wicked grin and said, "Follow me."

Five

"So?"

"How was your meeting with Valentine?"

Olivia hadn't been back in the office more than five minutes and Tess and Mary were already standing in the doorway to the kitchen, their eyes wide with curiosity.

"Fine," Olivia said from atop a stepladder. She was searching through an upper cabinet, going through brands of cookware. She wanted to buy just the right one for Mac's kitchen. "I'm checking out a few things, then I'll be gone for the rest of the day."

They walked over and stood beside the counter. Tess asked, "What are you up to?"

"I have to furnish his house. The place is practically empty."

"The whole house?" Mary said, fingering the stainless fry pan that Olivia had set on the counter.

"Why do you sound so surprised? We've done similar jobs before."

"True."

Olivia could practically hear Mary's brain working. She glanced down. "What?"

"Are you furnishing his bedroom, too?"

"Oh, for goodness' sake. You have too many hormones running around in there."

Laughing, Tess grabbed a mug from the dish drainer and poured herself a cup of coffee. "We're just worried about you, that's all. If everything you said about this guy is true, he's up to more than just having you refurnish his house to bag a big client."

"Of course he is. I told you both that."

Mary put the pan down, grabbed Tess's cup and took a sip of her coffee. "What if he's having you design the bedroom he's going to try and seduce you in?"

"What? You're both acting nuts. He may be trying to use me, but he's incredibly clever and creative and interesting in his thinking. Whatever he's planning has got to be far more elaborate than—" She stopped at the worried looks on her partners' faces. "What?"

"You like him," said Mary.

"Oh, come on."

Tess nodded slowly. "You think he's 'clever' and 'creative,' and you probably think he's hot, too."

Olivia laughed and stepped down from the ladder. "Of course he's hot. Anyone with eyes could see the guy is hot."

"Oh, dear," Mary began, one hand to her belly as if she were protecting the baby from hearing anything too scandalous.

"Not good," Tess agreed. "I think I should take over the job."

"Will you two chill out?" Olivia grabbed a pen from her drawer and began writing down the names of several pieces of cookware. "Mac Valentine may be great-looking and charming and all the other things I said, but I'm not an idiot. He is also an arrogant womanizer with no furniture and no moral compass."

Tess nodded. "Yeah, that's pretty much what that article I read last week said. But somehow they made it sound like it was a good thing."

"What? What article?"

"Tess, go get it," Mary commanded, then turned back to Olivia.

"Oh, you read it, too," Olivia said.

Mary shrugged. "I was going through all the old magazines for recycle and you know how once I see something I can't stop reading, blah, blah, blah…" Tess returned and handed the copy of *Minneapolis Magazine* to Olivia. Mary said, "It's from a few years ago. Page thirty-four."

Letting out an impatient breath, Olivia grabbed the magazine and quickly flipped through the pages until she found the right one. And she knew it was the right one—not by the page number on the bottom right-hand corner, but by the enormous photograph of Mac and another man sitting on a stainless steel desk, a killer view of downtown Minneapolis displayed out the windows behind them. The spread was called "Workaholic, yet Woman Friendly," and featured both men holding BlackBerries in one hand and gold bars in the other. The sight of Mac, looking both handsome and arrogant as hell, didn't bother Olivia at all. It was the picture of the other man who sat beside him that had her stomach turning over.

Tim Keavy.

Her heart pounded furiously against her chest and she broke out in a sweat. The one guy from high school who knew what she truly was, knew her most shameful secret. God, did this mean that Mac knew, too? Was he going to use it against her? Against her father?

Olivia brushed a hand over her face. So much for her calm professionalism around Mac Valentine. Damn him. She hadn't expected him to go this route. She'd expected a full-out seduction—not using her past against her.

She stared at Mac's dark, dangerous face. Was it possible that he didn't know, that this was just an odd coincidence? A nervous shiver went through her entire body. She was going to have to be extra vigilant now. Watch every move he made and be prepared for it.

For a moment she thought about quitting the job, but she didn't run away from difficult situations anymore. She was no coward. She rolled up the magazine, then grabbed her notes. "I've got to go."

"Just watch yourself, okay," said Mary.

"I will." And on her way out the door she tossed the magazine in the trash.

* * *

November snow in Minnesota was said to be only the warm-up act for what was coming in January, but as Mac pulled into his driveway, his tires spinning and begging for chains as thick flakes of snow pelted his windshield, he wondered if Christmas had already come and gone without his knowing.

He pulled into the dry haven of his garage and shut off the engine. For a moment, he just sat there. He'd left the homes of many women before, but never had he come home to one. Yes, Olivia was an employee so it should have made the situation feel less domestic, but it didn't. He found her too pretty, too passionate, too smart to be just an employee.

When he entered the house a few minutes later, he heard the clanging sound of pots and pans being put away, and walked the short distance to the kitchen. His body instantly betrayed him as he spotted Olivia bending down, stacking pan lids on a shelf inside the island. Her dark hair was pulled back in a girlish ponytail and her pale skin looked flushed from all the activity. She wore a red sweater that hugged her breasts and waist, and jeans that pulled deliciously against her firm, round bottom. Devilish thoughts went through his head…like how good it would feel to be there when she stood up, to wrap his arms around her waist, to feel her backside press against him, to slip his hands under that soft wool sweater and feel her skin, her bones and her nipples as they hardened.

She turned then, caught him staring at her and gave

him an expectant look. There was nothing new in it, she sported this look quite often, but today there was something more in her eyes, as though she seemed to be silently accusing him.

He dropped his briefcase and keys and walked into the room. She'd done wonders. The space was perfect, homey, yet surprisingly modern with its green, gray and stainless steel accents. She had actually created a family kitchen for him, based on his tastes. She was damn good at what she did, and he couldn't wait to experience the aspect of the job were she had the most skill: the cooking.

"Well, Ms. Winston," he said, trying to lighten the mood. "You're going to make some man a great wife."

But the joke was lost on her. Her brows drew together in an affronted frown. "That was an incredibly sexist remark."

"Was it?"

"Yes."

"Why? I was giving you a compliment. The room looks amazing."

"So, only a husband can appreciate it?" she said, holding an incredibly large frying pan in one hand. "This is my job because I love it, not because I chose something stereotypically female. Okay?"

"Sure." He eased the fry pan out of her hand and put it on the counter. "This is not a weapon."

She stood a foot away, looking altogether too attractive, even in her ire. "I don't need stainless steel to do harm, Valentine."

He nodded. "I believe you." He reached up and brushed a stray hair off of her cheek. Her skin was so soft it made him ache to keep touching her. "Tell you what, when I go out back later and chop firewood you can say that I'd make a fine husband."

Not even a hint of a smile. He had no idea what he might have done to make her so mad at him, but he knew he was in trouble.

"I doubt very much that you chop wood," she said, picking up a pot from the sink. "But even if you did it would take a lot more than watching you to make me think that you'd be a good husband."

"Why are you so angry with me?" he said finally. "I could sense it the moment I walked in. You look damn pretty, but clearly pissed off."

"I'm not angry!" she shouted, snatching a dishtowel off the counter.

"What is it? Have a conversation with your father today?"

"Listen, buddy," she said sourly. "I don't need to talk to my father to get fired up about you."

"Fired up?" he repeated, amused.

"That's right." She put the pot on the stove top. "I am fully capable of forming my own opinions about you."

He stepped forward, making her step back, her hips pressing against the granite island. "And what have you come up with?"

"That you're a man who likes women—"

He chuckled. "Damn right."

"You didn't let me finish." Her voice was low, as intense

as her gaze. "So much so that you can barely remember their names five minutes out of the relationship."

"I don't have relationships, Olivia." He wondered if kissing her right now was a bad idea or a brilliant one. But she never gave him the chance.

"Are you proud of the way you're seen by other people?" she said. "Someone who jumps out of one bed only to charm his way into another?"

"That's the question of a woman who is in desperate need of a man in her bed."

She stared at him, her cheeks red and her dark eyes filled with irritation, then she dropped her dishtowel and walked out of the kitchen. "It's getting late."

"I'll walk you out," he said, following her to the front door.

"Don't bother." She grabbed her coat and hat and gloves and purse and opened the door. "I'll be back first thing in the morning."

Then Mac saw the snow and remembered his drive home. "Wait. It's really coming down out there."

"Good night, Mr. Valentine."

"The roads are pretty bad."

She stepped out the door and went down the path, calling back, "I'm a Minnesota native, Mr. Valentine. I've driven in worse than this."

"Damn it to hell!"

Olivia glanced over her shoulder and winced when she saw that she'd backed over Mac's mailbox. There it was, stretched out in the snow, a sad, black pole with a missing head. What a fool she was thinking that just because she had four-wheel drive and an SUV she could avoid the realities of Mother Nature. She'd just wanted to get away from that man, out of his house and the questions about how others saw him, how he had jumped from one bed to the next and all of that crap that she'd tossed at him—questions she was really asking herself.

She put her car in gear and stepped on the gas. A sad whirring sound was followed by rotating tires.

"Damn snow."

She slammed the car back into Park. This job had gone from a leap of curiosity to just plain complicated. Never had she acted so unprofessionally, and even though Mac's motives for hiring her were questionable at best, her job was to execute without getting personal, without allowing her fears to drive her actions. Well, from this point on she was going to make sure that happened.

She cranked up the heat, then reached for her cell phone and dialed information. But before the automated operator picked up, there was a knock on her window. Startled, she turned to see Mac, in just his jeans and shirt, and she pressed the button for the window.

"What are you doing?" he asked.

"I've killed your mailbox, I'm stuck in the snow and now I'm calling a cab."

He cursed, the word coming out in a puff of breath. "You'd do better to call a tow truck. No cab's coming out in this. I could brave it and try to get you home, but I don't think that'd be very smart."

"No, it wouldn't," she agreed. "You should go back

inside." She rolled up the window, then reached for her cell phone and dialed the operator once more.

Mac knocked on the glass, hard this time. Again, she rolled down her window. "What?"

"You're going to freeze."

"Only if you keep making me roll down the window. Now, go in. You're the one who's going to freeze in that getup, and I refuse to be responsible for your getting pneumonia or hypothermia or something."

"You're acting like a child. Come inside."

"I'm not acting any way. I'm being sensible. It's not a good idea for me to go back in there tonight. Things got too heated earlier."

"True, but I think we could use a little more heat in that house."

"It's too cold for jokes." She sighed. She just wanted to get home, into the tub and have a hot soak, maybe watch a few reruns of *Sex and the City*.

But that wasn't going to happen.

"It's your choice," he said, his teeth chattering now. "Nice warm fire or freeze in the car."

She heaved a sigh. "Fine. I'll come inside…but I'm going to call for a tow truck."

He helped her out of the car, and she followed him through the drifts of snow to the walkway, then up to the front door.

"If the tow truck can't get to you tonight," Mac said as he opened the door, "you are welcome to stay in my room."

She stopped inside the entryway. She wanted to scowl at him, but instead she laughed. "Are you insane?"

"Actually I thought I was being pretty gentlemanly." He turned back and grinned. "And that's a rare thing for me."

"Can I use your phone? My cell doesn't work very well in here."

"Sure." He took her coat and hung it up, then covered her hands with his and slipped off her gloves. A shot of awareness moved through Olivia, from the hair on her scalp to the backs of her knees, and she looked up to find him watching her, his dark eyes intense. He took off her gloves so slowly it made her belly knot with tension, and when her fingers were finally released from the warm leather, he took her hands and squeezed them into his cold palms.

"You're freezing," she said.

"And you're warm." His fingers laced with hers, and her muscles tensed. "I don't think I'm going to let go."

Sadly, she didn't want him to, but she wasn't about to give in to herself or to him. He was using her, and she'd allowed herself to be used too often in the past.

Olivia pulled her hands away. "I'm going to make that call now."

"You're not getting your car out tonight, Liv," Mac said evenly. "Now I'm going to be bunking in one of the leather chairs by the fire since all the rest of the bedrooms haven't been furnished yet, so if you do stay, take my bed—or don't take it. Either way, I won't bother you."

She didn't know if she believed him, but what could she do? She needed the shelter for tonight. "Thank you."

He nodded. "Good night." Then he walked in the direction of the den.

Six

The guy at the first tow truck company hung up on her, the guy at the second tow truck company actually laughed when she'd asked if he could come out and excavate her car, and her third call had gone straight to a machine.

Olivia had known it would be somewhat of a long shot to get home tonight, but after the way her body had reacted to Mac's touch earlier—a very simple, not that overtly sexual a touch—she was really hoping.

She sat on the edge of Mac's king-sized bed, her shoulders drooping forward. She was tired and cold, and disappointed in herself for caving in and taking his room. A better woman might have stuck to her guns about not bunking in Mac's sparse, octagon-shaped room, maybe grabbing a few extralong towels from his bathroom and cuddling up on the carpeted floor of one of the empty guest rooms. But she was a wimp that way. She liked her creature comforts. She'd always wondered about people who liked camping. Strange noises and bugs for bunkmates…what was the attraction? Anyway, she was sleeping in Mac's bed tonight. She just hoped he'd keep his word and wouldn't venture out of the den to find her.

She pulled the comforter off the bed and wrapped it around herself. Then again, why would he leave such a lovely, warm spot by the fire? Olivia blew out a puff of air to see if she could see her breath. It was cold as hell in Mac's house, a ridiculous kind of cold that sank deep into your bones and could only be relieved by a hot bath. She didn't know what that handyman did around here, but first thing tomorrow, she was calling in a professional heating technician. Forget all the warm, family friendly furnishings. If the house felt like an igloo, the DeBolds were going to head straight for the nearest five-star hotel.

Olivia thought about lying down and trying to sleep, but when nature called, she threw off the comforter and dashed into the master bathroom. And there she saw it— surrounded by beautiful pale brown tumbled stone was a massive box of glass with a rain showerhead above and four body sprayers along one wall. Oh, she wanted to cry it looked so inviting.

Did she dare? Maybe just a quick one? Just to get warm.

Feeling a sudden burst of happiness at the thought, she flipped on the water and turned the temperature knob to the equivalent of "hotter-than-hell." After closing the door to keep all the beautiful heat contained, she got undressed. She was just about to step inside the shower when she heard a knock on the bedroom door.

Her heart dropped into her stomach. No, no, no. Not now. Why was he here? Did he have radar or a sixth sense that told him when there was a naked woman in his room or something?

She snatched a huge white bath sheet and wrapped herself in it, then she opened the door and walked out into the frigid air.

He was knocking again. "Olivia?"

She opened the door just wide enough to accommodate her head, but hid the rest of her from his view. "Yes?"

"So you took the room?"

"Yes. I took the room. Can we not make a big deal out of it?"

"Of course." He grinned. "Are you okay?"

"Fine. Just tired." *And cold.* "What's up?"

He didn't look convinced. In fact, he was trying to assess the situation as he spoke. "I put a frozen pizza in the oven if you're interested."

She shook her head. "Thanks, but I'm not very hungry. Just tired. Very, very tired."

"All right. Good night, then." Olivia thought that he was about to leave, that she was about to finally get warm, but then he paused and cocked his head to one side. "What's that?"

"What's what?" she asked innocently, as if she didn't know.

"Is that water running?"

"No."

His mouth twitched. "Are you taking a shower?"

"Not at this precise moment," she said with irritation, which caused him to grin, full-on and slightly roguishly.

"Taking advantage of my steam shower, are you?"

She rolled her eyes. "Oh, for God's sake."

"Hey, I don't blame you, the thing is awesome."

"Well, good…then I'm going to go—"

"Have all the towels you need?" he asked.

"Yes."

She looked expectantly at him. Time to leave, Mr. Valentine. What more was there to say? After all, he'd humiliated and humbled her, what could be left? But he didn't leave, he just stood there looking sexy in his black sweater and pants.

Olivia let out a frustrated breath. "I'm freezing, okay? I need a way to warm up."

His grin widened, his gaze dropped. "No, too easy."

"Good night, Mac," she said through gritted teeth. "Enjoy your pizza."

He chuckled and pushed away from the door frame. "All right. Enjoy your shower. But," he said as he turned to walk away, "if you find that you can't sleep or you get hungry, you know where to find me."

"That, I can promise you," she called after him, "will never happen."

Mac put another log on the fire, then rescued his bottle of beer from the rutted mantel before dropping back into his chair. The book he was reading was pretty dull, but he was halfway through it and he wasn't a quitter. Just as he was about to find out why early man and an anthropoid ape had almost the same number of cranial bones and teeth, he heard footsteps behind him.

"You suck, Valentine."

Mac chuckled and turned around. "Now why would you say something like—" The words died on his lips as he caught sight of her, practically glowing in the firelight. From the moment he'd seen Olivia Winston, serving up brownies and attitude in her office kitchen, he'd found her incredibly attractive. Tonight, however, she was breath-stealing.

Her white blouse was untucked and rumpled, and re-sembled a man's shirt with the cuffs falling loose about her hands. Her long, black pants seemed a little too big without the heels and belt, but it was her face and hair that had his pulse running a race at the base of his throat. With no makeup, she looked fresh, delectably soft, her flawless skin glowing a pale peachy color. Her long, damp, dark hair swung sexy and loose, and reminded him of a mermaid. It took every ounce of control he had not to take her in his arms and kiss her until she realized just how perfectly their bodies would fit together.

She walked over and dropped into the chair beside him. "My hot shower wasn't so hot."

"No?"

She tossed him a look of mock reproof. "And it's all your fault."

"I did inadvertently ask if you wanted me to join you," he reminded her, taking a swallow of his beer.

"That's not what I mean."

"No?"

"You made me stand at the door talking to you so long the hot water was almost gone by the time I got in there."

"I'm sorry," he said sincerely. "Let me make it up to you with a never-ending fire and a cold slice of pepperoni."

She looked unconvinced at first, then she shrugged. "Okay." She took a piece of pizza from him and practically attacked it. "Oh, the fire feels so good. Your room is freezing, Valentine. This house is freezing."

"It can get a little cold, I guess."

"You sound like you don't mind turning into an ice cube every time the sun goes down."

"I hardly notice. I'm really only here to sleep."

"Well, first thing tomorrow I'm calling a heating technician. The DeBolds may sell ice, but they don't want to sleep in it."

He grinned at her. "That was funny, Liv…clever."

She shrugged. "I have my moments," she said, reaching for a second slice of pizza.

Mac grabbed another bottle of beer from beside his chair, opened it and tipped it her way. "Something to drink?"

"Sure, why not?" She took the cold bottle from him. "Thanks."

"You bet."

"Sitting in a freezing house in front of a fire eating

cold pizza and even colder beer—this night couldn't get any stranger, could it?"

He sipped his beer, then said, "How about if I tell you that when I was around nine or ten I thought—well, I'd hoped—I'd grow up to be a comedian."

She turned to stare at him. "That would be stranger."

"Hard to believe, I know. I'd put on one of my foster father's suits and tell incredibly awful jokes to these three crazy dogs they had. I was really into toilet humor at nine."

"You grew up in a foster home?" Her tone had changed from cute sarcasm to barely disguised pity in a matter of seconds.

He hated that, and rarely told anyone about his less-than-ideal beginnings to avoid hearing just such a reaction. He didn't know why he'd just blurted it out to her. Inadvertently, yes, but still… Maybe he needed to ease up on the beer. "I lived in a few foster homes. No big deal."

"What happened to your parents?"

"My mother died when I was two, and my father was never really in the picture."

She bit her lip. "That's tough."

He shrugged. "It wasn't that bad."

"Was the foster father you borrowed the suit from a good guy at least?"

"He wasn't awful. Although he did come home early one night to see me knocking around in that suit and he was pretty pissed off."

"What did he do?"

"Went for the belt."

Olivia's mouth dropped open. "What a bastard. What a cowardly piece of trash. If I had been there I would've kicked his—"

Mac's dark laughter cut her off. "It was no big deal. It happened." Even though he said the words with cool casualness, he appreciated her passion and protective nature. "You know, twenty-five years ago, there wasn't this push for fathers to be loving and gentle. 'Hands-on' had a different meaning." He took a healthy swallow of beer. "Every kid got boxed by their dad, foster or not, once or twice while they were growing up."

She sat forward in her seat, and looked at him with a strange mixture of sadness and care in her eyes. "No, they didn't."

Sure, he'd had a few beers, but he understood exactly what she was saying, and who she was saying it about. His jaw twitched. Owen Winston may have disciplined with words, but he was certainly no saint. "Well, I learned my lesson," he said tightly. "I never touched his suits again."

They were both quiet for a while after that, both drinking their beer and staring into the fire. Mac's ire subsided, and he was close to sleep when he heard her say his name.

He turned his head. "Yeah?"

"What happened to the career in comedy?"

He chuckled. "Ended shortly thereafter."

She smiled. "Bummer." Her cheeks were flushed from the heat of the fire and she looked really beautiful.

"Or a blessing—depending on how you look at it."

Yawning, Olivia curled deeper into the chair. "Well, feel free to try out any new material you've got on me."

His body stirred with her words, but he said nothing. He wasn't going to push things. Whether she wanted to admit it to herself or not, she was growing interested in him, attracted to him, and someday soon he would have her in his bed. It wouldn't make nearly the impact if he took what she wasn't ready to give. Owen Winston needed to know that his sweet, innocent little girl had come to Mac all on her own.

Mac heard her breathing grow slow and even, and after a few minutes, he closed his eyes and allowed himself to sleep, too.

Olivia woke up in a daze. In front of her the dying fire crackled softly. For a moment, she thought it was morning, but with a quick glance to the windows to her left she saw that the inky blackness of night had yet to turn to the steely gray of dawn.

"Hey."

She looked over at Mac, who was sitting forward in his chair, his dark eyes seductive and hungry under heavy lids. "What time is it?"

"Around three."

She blinked a few times, feeling foggy. "I should go back to bed."

"But it's cold in there."

"Yeah." But she didn't move. She just stared at him. Mac got out of the chair and went to her, sat on his

heels in front of her. The hot flicker in his gaze made
every bit of Olivia's tired limbs feel on edge and alive.

He reached up to touch her face. She grabbed his
wrist, that hard, thick, oh-so-masculine wrist, and he
stopped and stared at her. Her heart thudded in her chest
as he leaned in, his gaze hungry, his mouth so close.
Looking back on that night, Olivia had wanted to blame
the foggy tiredness in her brain or the cold and snow for
what she did next. But she knew exactly why she went
temporarily nuts. All the frustration she felt at her attraction to Mac, and all the years of pushing aside her
feelings of need and desire, just seemed to explode in
her face at that moment.

Her hand snaked around his neck and she pulled him
down for a kiss. And not a peck kiss, either, but a full-
blown, lip-nuzzling, teeth-raking, breath-stealing kiss.

Seven

"Holy—" Mac didn't finish the end of the curse as he took her in his arms and dropped back onto the rug, taking her with him.

Poised above him, Olivia welcomed the crush of Mac's mouth and the heat of his body against hers. It had been so long, almost ten years since she'd been touched like this, felt a man's lips on her, his warm breath mingling with hers. The delicious hard angles and clean scent of his skin thrilled her, and she pushed away any thoughts of how wrong the situation might be.

She threaded her fingers in his hair and gripped his scalp as he changed the angle of his kiss. Soft, hot, drugging kisses. All she wanted was to get closer to him, feel a new kind of heat, forget who she was for a few minutes, forget what he was after.

In one easy movement, he flipped her onto her back. The warmth of the fire made her sweetly dizzy and she arched against him. Sensing her need, Mac explored further. His hand moved down, under her shirt, and she felt his palm on her belly. Little zaps of fear warred with the almost desperate urge she had to feel his fingers brush over the skin of her breasts, hear his breathing change when he cupped them and felt the weight of them, feel the lower half of him grow thick and hard as his thumb flicked back and forth over her nipple.

Mac dragged his hand up, over her ribs and along the side of her rib cage. She arched and tilted her body toward his hand, silently begging him to go there, put her out of her misery or show her exactly what misery felt like again as he gave in to her fantasy.

He was no fool, he knew what she was asking for and he delivered with the utmost care. As he applied teasing kisses to her lower lip, his hand drifted from her ribs to her breast, and slowly—so slowly—he began to roll the hard peak between his thumb and forefinger. Olivia shuddered, and released an anguished sigh. Oh, such sweet torture. She felt as though she had just been plunged into a deliciously hot bath, and God help her, she never wanted to step out of it.

But somewhere, deep in the back of her mind, she knew if she didn't, she was going to drown.

He left her mouth and dipped his face into her neck, kissing and suckling her rapid pulse as the speed of his fingers on her nipple quickened. Back and forth, faster and faster.

Her legs were shaking now, almost uncontrollably, and she knew if he didn't stop touching her, she was going to climax. Right then and there without him even going near the hot, wet place between her thighs. And she couldn't do that—not now, not for him.

She pushed at his chest and sat up, her breathing as labored as if she'd just outrun a hungry animal.

"Why are you stopping?" His voice was ragged.

"You know why," she uttered softly.

He raked a hand through his hair. "Damn it, Liv, there's nothing wrong with being together like this, taking what you need when you need it."

She looked down at him, her body warring with her mind. "From you, there is." He looked so sexy lying there in the light of the fire with his hair tousled and a light shadow of beard around his full mouth. "From a guy who's just using me—"

"You're using me, too," he uttered darkly. "Don't pretend you're not. I could feel every moment you've denied yourself in your touch, in your kiss, the way your hips pushed against mine. You're starving, Olivia, and you want to feed so badly you're still shaking with it."

"I'm cold."

"Bull. It's hot as hell in here right now."

His words startled her. She did want him, but she wasn't altogether sure why. Was it to use him? Was it to make up for lost time and to finally feel a release in her body and a release of the past? Or was it because she was actually starting to like him?

Her body still hummed from his touch, but she ignored it and said softly, "I'm going to go back to your room now. Alone."

"Is that really what you want?"

Of course it wasn't, but she needed to step back and gain some perspective here. "Yes."

"All right. But if you get cold—"

She stopped him right there and stood. "A little cold might be a good thing right now." And without another glance in his direction, she left the room.

Mac woke up to the sounds of a snowplow and his doorbell chiming. Looked as though the streets were clear and his furniture delivery had arrived. He pushed himself out of his chair and stretched, the kinks in his back protesting. As he walked to the front door he wondered if Olivia was still asleep in his bed or if she'd slipped out at dawn.

He raked a hand through his hair. What kind of trouble would he be in if, after he let the furniture guys in, he went to wake her up, started at her ankles and worked his way up? He grinned, the lower half of him tightening at the thought. She might kick him out of bed—but maybe not.

Mac was still very deeply ensconced in that fantasy when he opened the front door. But when he saw who was on the other side, all softness and desire vanished, and his fangs came out. "Hell, no. It's way too early for this."

Owen Winston looked ready to murder him. "Where's my daughter?"

"You have a helluva lot of nerve coming here."

"Where is my daughter?"

Mac leaned against the doorjamb and raised one eyebrow. "In my bed."

The older man's eyes bulged out like a tree frog's and he lunged at Mac.

Eight

Olivia walked down the hall, an aching stiffness in her bones that came from sleeping in a chair for most of the night. If she'd had the day to herself, she might grab a massage and a whirlpool bath at the local spa, but she had a full plate today and a good soak in her bathtub when she got home tonight was about the best she could hope for.

When she got to the stairs, she heard voices below in the hall. "Oh, that's my cab," she called to Mac. "The tow truck company said they should be pulling out my car later this afternoon, so you don't have to—" She stopped talking. The voices she heard were angry and threatening, and she recognized them at once. One belonged to Mac, and the other, she was pretty sure, belonged to her father.

She raced down the hallway, but when she got to the entryway, all she could do was stare. There was her father, his back against the wall, looking like he wanted to kill Mac with his bare hands. And Mac, who was standing in front of him, only inches away, looked just as menacing.

"What the hell are you two doing?" she demanded. When neither of them answered, she walked over and stood in front of them, her hands on her hips. "Mac," she said evenly, trying to bring some sense of calm to the situation, and to the two fire-breathing men before her. "Take a breath and back up."

His jaw flickered with tension, but he didn't look at her when he muttered hotly, "Yeah. Sure. As long as your father here doesn't jump on me again."

"What?" Olivia turned to her father. "Jump on you?" When Owen didn't look at her, she put a hand on his shoulder and said in a voice laced with warning, "Dad, what are you doing here?"

Owen's lips tightened as he turned to look at her. "We need to talk."

"You could've called me."

"I tried to call you, but you weren't at home."

"Let's go outside." Embarrassed at her father's behavior, and the overly parental way he was treating her at that moment, Olivia tried to smooth things over with Mac. She felt really awkward looking at him, especially after their encounter last night, but she forced herself to. "I'm sorry about this—"

Mac put a hand up. "Don't worry about it, just get him out—"

"Don't apologize to him, Olivia," Owen said with a sneer. "He's a monster, a conniving—"

Before Owen could hurtle any more insults Mac's way, Olivia took his hand and pulled him out the door, calling over her shoulder, "I'll be back at ten for the delivery. If you'll just put a key under the mat…"

Not expecting a response, Olivia led Owen down the walkway toward her waiting cab. She was furious, and could barely contain her anger. She understood her father's need to protect her, but this was way over the top.

As soon as she believed herself to be out of earshot, she faced him, her tone grave. "Dad, seriously, what are you doing? Coming here and attacking a man in his own home?"

"He's no man, he's a—"

"He could have called the police. Hell, he still could…and I have to say I wouldn't blame him. What were you thinking?"

Owen suddenly looked very weary as he reached out to touch her hair. "I was trying to protect you, honey, stop you from making a huge mistake." His eyes clouded with sadness. "But it looks like I'm too late for that."

"Too late for what? What mistake…?" Then she understood why her father had come. She heaved a sigh. It was the same old thing—her father's desperation, and constant fear that she was going to turn out like his older sister Grace. Her poor aunt Grace, who had been way too wild, made way too many mistakes and had been totally incapable of picking a decent guy. Poor Aunt Grace who, after staying out until dawn partying with some jerk from the local college, had been killed in a car accident on her way home. She'd just turned eighteen the week before, and Olivia's father had never gotten over losing her.

Olivia understood her father's fears and his need to protect her, but she wasn't sixteen anymore. This over-protectiveness needed to stop.

Standing beside the open door of the cab, Owen was shaking his head. "That monster stood there in his doorway and smiled when I asked him where you were."

Oh, great. "What did he tell you?" As if she needed to ask.

"That you were in his bed." Her father said the words as though he had acid on his tongue.

So Mac had baited her father. What a shocker. God, they were both acting like such juvenile idiots....

"Is it true then?" her father asked, his brown eyes incredibly sad.

"Dad, I'm not going to answer that."

The cab driver opened his window. "You going to be much longer, lady?"

Olivia shrugged. "I don't know—maybe."

The man rolled his eyes and closed his window.

"Olivia, please," her father continued. "You're such a good girl. Don't act irrationally—and with a man who only wants to use you to get back at me."

"I'm not acting irrationally, Dad. And I'm not a girl anymore."

"I know...."

"No, I don't think you do." She bit her lip and contemplated broaching the subject about his fears and what the hell had happened so long ago. But his eyes still spit fire and he looked way too closed. "Listen," she said gently, "you knew I was taking this job, and that it would mean working closely with Mac Valentine."

"Helping my enemy."

"I have a company to run, too."

Owen seemed to consider this, then he said in a slightly calculating tone, "Okay, so you're helping him do what exactly? Go after new clients?"

Olivia shook her head. "That's confidential."

Owen looked livid. "The man is a conniving bastard who wants to hurt you, and you're worried about…"

She put a hand on his shoulder. "How long have I been living on my own, supporting myself?"

"Since you were eighteen." He pointed at her. "But that was not my choice."

"Exactly. I'm a grown woman who makes her own choices, and as I've told you before—respectfully—I don't have to answer to you or to anyone."

Owen wilted slightly, but it wasn't the first time he'd heard her speak this way. After her mother had died, and after Owen had emotionally checked out, Olivia had made decisions for herself. Some of them had been downright stupid, even reckless, but the majority, she'd been proud of—like her business.

Her father's gaze grew soft as he looked at her. "What happened to my little girl?"

"I left her back in high school." Olivia leaned in and kissed him on the cheek. "I have a busy day, as I'm sure you do, too." She got into the backseat of the cab and gave him a little wave before her driver backed out and pulled away.

Mac stood in the living room, watching Olivia's cab take off down the street. The glass on every window in the house was pretty thin, and he'd heard their entire conversation. Looked like he had gotten it wrong; Olivia may not be that sweet, naive girl he assumed her to be. But where her father didn't want to deal with it, Mac burned to know every detail of the past she seemed to be hiding—especially after last night.

Grinning, he left the living room and went into his study. Embers burned in the fireplace, and as he sat in one of the leather armchairs, his body twitched with the memory of Olivia in his arms, on top of him, underneath him. The way she'd responded to his touch, the silent, hungry demands. She'd felt pleasure before, but she'd been denied it for way too long. There was no need to push her, he realized. The demands of her body had started to take over her good sense and Mac was going to be there, totally available when it happened again.

After all, her father thought him to be a womanizing bastard, and Mac was ready to prove him right.

All in all a very successful day, Olivia mused, walking from one beautifully furnished room to the next. She'd quite outdone herself, and in record time, too. Each room complemented the next in leather and iron, glass and walnut.

She stopped in the living room and marveled at the classic, comfortable feel of the space. Not to mention the warm air puffing from the vents in the baseboards. She'd finally found a guy to come out in the snow and turn on the heat. A vast improvement in and of itself.

Though she'd purchased all the linens for the upstairs, the bedroom furniture wouldn't be arriving until early tomorrow morning. But they were close—well on their way to creating a very modern, very homey, very Mac-like environment.

"Ms. Winston?"

Olivia returned to the living room where Dennis Thompson, a local art gallery owner who looked rather like a short version of Ichabod Crane, was hanging several paintings she'd purchased for Mac's house.

"What do you think?" he asked, holding up two Josef Albers pieces, both in several shades of yellow. "On top of one another?"

She sat on the new distressed, brown leather couch to get a better view. "Hmm...I don't know. How about—"

"Side by side?" came Mac's voice behind her.

Dennis Thompson looked behind Olivia and beamed at Mac. "Perfect. I'll just go get my tools from the car."

Olivia turned, surprised. "You're home early, Mr. Valentine. Are you here to supervise?"

He was dressed in a tailored black suit and crisp white shirt, his tie loosened from his neck. "I came home for a late lunch or an early dinner."

"Oh, really?" she said with a grin. "I haven't stocked

the fridge yet and you ate the only frozen pizza, so what were you planning on having? The cocktail onions or that last, lonely bottle of Corona?"

He walked around the couch and sat beside her. "You're a pretty good chef, aren't you?"

"I like to think so." He smelled so good. She tried not to breathe through her nose.

"Well, then, can't you make something amazing out of onions and beer?"

"No," said Olivia succinctly, lifting an eyebrow. "Can I ask you something?"

"Shoot."

"When do you normally leave the office to come home?"

His lips twitched. "Oh, I don't know…"

"Approximately."

"Seven, eight…nine, ten."

She looked at her watch. "It's four-thirty—why are you here?" Her heart began to pound in her chest as she wondered for a moment if he was there to see her. After what happened that morning with her father, she wouldn't blame him. She just hoped he wouldn't spread the story around town. "Are you going to fire me?"

"No." He laughed. "That's over and done with." His voice turned serious. "As long as it doesn't happen again. I can't have your father showing up when the DeBolds arrive."

"It will not happen again," she assured him. "You have my word."

Satisfied with that answer, Mac leaned back and

crossed his arms over his chest. "I'm not exactly sure why I'm here. But I think the reason might be embarrassing."

"For you or me?"

"Me. Definitely me."

"Oh, well, then share, please."

He glanced around the room. "It's really warm in here."

"I know. I had the tech come this morning and it took him hours just to—"

"No, I mean what you've created here from the furniture to the artwork to all those little things on the tables and in the bathroom and on the mantels. It's all warm. I never thought I'd be comfortable with warm.…" He looked at her, surprise in his gaze. "As you start to make my house into a livable, family-friendly place I sort of want to be here to see it…and you."

Her muscles tensed at his words and she could almost feel the pressure of his lips on her mouth once again. Her reaction to him, her attraction to him, wasn't going away, she knew that. But she hoped that maybe the two of them could forget what happened last night and go on about their business.

When she found his gaze once again, Mac had that look in his eye, that roguish one that made her knees weak and her resolve disappear.

"Listen," she began, "about last night…"

"Yes?"

"I was half-asleep."

"Before or after you kissed me?" he asked huskily.

Right. Her brow creased with unease. "As clichéd as this is about to sound, it'll never happen again."

He grinned. "Are you sure?"

"Yes."

"We made sparks."

His words and the casual way he offered them made her laugh. "I won't argue with that. You're one helluva kisser, Valentine, but…" And on that note, she sobered. "You're also using me." She put a hand up as she saw him open his mouth to speak. "I know you think I'm using you, too, but I'm not. And last night, I didn't."

His grin evaporated. "Then why…"

She stared at him, wondered what he would say if she told him she was starting to like him—that even with the information she had about him and why he'd hired her to begin with, she believed he was good man. A damaged man—but, under that hard-ass exterior, a good one.

"Ms. Winston?"

Dennis Thompson had returned from his car and was standing in the doorway with his toolkit and another painting. "I'm sorry to interrupt, but before we can hang the rest of the pieces, we need you to tell us where you want them."

"I'll be right there," she told him before facing Mac again. "Now, we have guests arriving tomorrow afternoon, and I have to finish up here, then go home and plan a menu."

He nodded. "Have you decided to stay here?"

"Not yet."

"If you do, I won't bother you."

"I'm not worried about you starting anything." It was all she had to say. The flush on his neck and the stiffness in his jaw were obvious clues that he'd heard the slight emphasis on the word *you* and understood her meaning all too clearly.

She got up and was about to leave the room when Mac called her back. "Olivia?"

"Yes?"

"As far as the menu, I've invited another couple to join us tomorrow night, so there will be six instead of four."

"Okay. Anyone I know?"

He shook his head. "I don't think so. It's the DeBolds' attorney and her husband."

"Got it." She tossed him a casual, professional smile, then left the room.

Nine

If someone called Mac Valentine an arrogant jerk to his face, he usually agreed with them before kicking them out of his office. He was arrogant. But in his defense he believed he was the best at what he did and that unshakable confidence was the only way to stay at the top of his game. Today, at around three o'clock in the afternoon, he'd had that theory tested and proven correct by one of the clients who, just a few weeks ago, had been running scared after Owen Winston's foolish attempt to discredit him. After waiting for twenty minutes in the lobby, the client had sat before Mac and had practically begged him to take him back. Whether the man still believed that Mac had given preferential treatment and tips to his other clients or not, being at a competing firm had not proved lucrative and he wanted back in.

Mac pulled into his garage feeling on top of the world. When one client returned, he mused, the others would surely follow—they'd leave Owen Winston and other financial firms and come back to where they belonged.

He cut the engine and grabbed his briefcase and laptop. Today's success would by no means deter him from getting revenge on Winston. And in fact, he actually felt a stronger desire to follow through on his plans with Olivia. By the end of the weekend, he thought darkly as he stepped out of the car and headed into the house, he would have it all: Owen's little girl and a powerhouse of a new client to add to his roster.

The heavenly scent of meat and spices, onions and something sweet accosted his senses when he walked through the door. Home sweet home, he thought sarcastically, walking into the kitchen. But once there, he promptly forgot everything he'd just been thinking, plotting and reveling in. In fact, as he took in the sight before him, he realized he had little or no brain left. "You look…"

Olivia stood before the stove, stirring something with a wooden spoon. "Like a wife?"

He saw the lightness, the humor in her eyes, but couldn't find a laugh to save his soul. He cleared his throat, his gaze moving over her hungrily. "I was going to say, breath-stealing—but I suppose you could look wifely, as well."

She wore pink. He hated pink. He'd always hated

pink. It was for flowers or cotton candy. But Olivia Winston in pink was a whole different matter. The dress she wore was cut at the knee and cinched at the waist, and pushed her perfectly round breasts upward, just slightly—just enough so that she looked elegant, yet would also drive a man to drool. Her long dark hair was pulled up to the top of her head, causing her neck to look long and edible, and her dark eyes, still filled with humor, reminded him of warm clay beneath long, black lashes.

And she had wanted him to forget about the other night? Get serious. All Mac wanted was to pull her against him, ease the top of her dress down, fill his hands with her, play with one perfect pink nipple while he suckled the other. His groin tightened almost to the point of pain. He wondered, would she moan as he nuzzled her? Or would she cry out again, allow herself to climax this time?

"Well, thank you for the compliment," she said, gathering up several bottles of wine. "Would you mind setting those things down and giving me a hand?"

"Sure. What do you need?"

She nodded in the direction of the island. "Wineglasses. Can you grab them and follow me?"

He picked up the spotless glasses that were laid out on a towel on the island and followed her into the dining room.

"Well, what do you think?" she asked, setting the bottle down on an impressive black hutch.

This woman wasn't fooling around. She was damn good at what she did, and it showed in every detail.

She'd set the table with unusually modern-looking china, gleaming stemware and silver silk napkins. But the most impressive part was the centerpiece, which sat in the middle of a round walnut table. It looked as though she'd brought the outdoors inside with cut branches from his yard, white candles and small silver bells.

He set down the wineglasses and released a breath. "It's perfect."

"Good." She checked her watch. "Your guests will be here in thirty minutes. You'd better wash up and change your clothes."

"I have time."

She gave him an impatient look. "It would be rude, not to mention awkward, if you weren't here when the doorbell rings."

"Careful, or someone might think you're the woman of the house," Mac said with amusement, wondering how long it would take to kiss that pink gloss off her mouth.

Reaching for the dimmer switch on the wall, Olivia lowered the lights a touch. "For all intents and purposes this weekend, I am."

His gaze swept over her. "Did I tell you how much I like the color pink?"

"No, you didn't," she said primly, putting her arm through his and walking him toward the stairs. "But we really don't have time for that now. I have a dinner to get on the table, and I won't allow anything to burn."

He grinned. "Of course, can't have things getting too hot now, can we?"

She glared at him, raising one perfectly shaped eyebrow. "I think a shower would be good for you."

He nodded and said with sardonic amusement, "Yes, dear," then took the stairs two at a time. She was right. He needed a shower, a really cold shower. Hell, he thought, chuckling to himself, he might do better diving into one of those piles of snow burying his lawn.

Harold DeBold was one of those guys people just liked the minute they met him. Hovering somewhere around forty, he was very tall and thin, and had pale blond hair and wintery blue eyes. He reminded Olivia of a surfer, relaxed and free-spirited. His wife Louise, on the other hand, was dark-skinned, dark-eyed, completely city-sexy in her gorgeousness and totally high-strung. But she also seemed sincere, and when she was told that Olivia was going to be their chef for the weekend, instead of thinking it odd that the person Mac had hired to help him was not going to stay in the kitchen and/or serve, but was going to eat and socialize with them, she'd acted as though it were the most normal thing in the world—even adding that she was thrilled that Olivia was going to cook some down-home Minnesota fare for them.

"Honestly," the woman said to Olivia, curling her diamond-encrusted hand around her wineglass. "I feel like all I've eaten for days is foie gras, caviar and squid ink. I'm over it."

Chuckling, Harold told Mac, "We've been in New York for the past week."

They were waiting for the DeBolds' attorney and her husband to arrive as they sat in Mac's den, which had been completely transformed into a contemporary, masculine, but family-friendly retreat with his two existing leather chairs and several other pieces of dark blue chenille furniture curled around the fire. Cozy rugs dressed the hardwood floor, and lights had been installed outside to showcase the wintery-forest view from the floor-to-ceiling windows.

Mac reached over and topped off Louise's wine. "You two were in Manhattan for a week and you didn't get around to pasta?"

Louise snorted. "Unfortunately, no."

"Next time you go, let me know," Mac said seriously. "There's this tiny hole-in-the-wall in Little Italy that you've got to check out. The spiciest pasta puttanesca—not to mention the best-tasting parmesan cheese I've ever had."

"Cheese." Chuckling, Harold said with dramatic flair, "City folk think that all us backcountry Wisconsinites get to eat is cheese, so they refuse to take us anywhere that might serve it. Instead, they figure they've got to impress us with all those fancy, unpronounceable, unrecognizable *foods*." As he said the last word he mimed air quotes.

Olivia held out a tray of hors d'oeuvres. "Well, everything you're going to eat tonight is as easy to pronounce as it is to eat."

Louise sipped her wine and said, "Thank God."

Harold took one of Olivia's famous blue cheese

jalapeño poppers wrapped in bacon and practically sighed when he ate it. "Oh, my," he said to Olivia, his blue eyes so warm she couldn't help but wonder if he was flirting with her just a little bit. "If these are any indication of your culinary skill, then you might never get me to leave."

Louise agreed. "These tomato basil tarts are over the top."

Olivia smiled, pleased that her fun and flavorful finger food was such a hit. "Thank you."

"Are you self-taught, Olivia?" Louise asked.

"I actually went to culinary school, then I worked for several chefs in town before starting my business."

Harold's brows drew together. "And what kind of business is that exactly? Catering? Or are you a personal chef?"

Olivia looked over at Mac, who was sitting in a dark blue wing-back chair by the fire. He didn't appear concerned by the question, and even winked at her, so she was as honest as she needed to be. "Myself and two other women provide catering, decorating, party planning…those kinds of services to clients."

"And are your clients mostly clueless men or women?" Louise asked, her eyes dancing with humor until she realized she was including her host in that question. She offered him an apologetic smile. "Of course, I didn't mean you, Mac."

Mac laughed. "No apology necessary—I know where my skills lie and they're not in the kitchen."

"Mine, either, sadly," Louise said on a sigh.

"All it takes is a little practice," Olivia told Louise sympathetically.

Harold shook his head wistfully. "She has tried, Olivia."

"Hey, there." Louise gave him a playful swat on the arm.

The doorbell chimed over the laughter in the room, and Mac stood. "I'll get that. Must be Avery."

When Mac was gone, Harold turned to Olivia. "My lawyer and her husband are great people, and are usually very punctual."

Olivia smiled warmly. "We're in no rush tonight."

"I like that attitude," Louise said, snatching up another tomato tart. Male laughter erupted from the front hall, and Louise rolled her eyes. "Boys. We just found out that Mac went to college with Tim, fraternity buddies or something."

It was as if time slowed after Louise had said the name *Tim,* and Olivia couldn't seem to find her breath. Even the room spun slightly. "Tim?" she managed to say. "That's your attorney's husband?"

Louise may have answered her, but Olivia's ears were buzzing. It wasn't him. It couldn't be him.

"Sorry we're late," came a voice that Olivia recognized at once. She swallowed. What was in her throat? It felt like a rock. She wouldn't turn around—couldn't turn around. He was coming and she felt frozen to the couch.

"Avery couldn't decide on which shoes to wear," he said dryly.

"Don't you blame me, Tim Keavy, you know it was your fault." The woman sniffed and added, "The Vikings game was on."

"Typical." Mac chuckled. "Avery, Tim, I'd like to introduce our amazing chef for the evening."

No…. She didn't want to.

"Olivia?" Mac said.

She wasn't ready….

"Olivia?" Mac said louder, sounding puzzled now.

Her heart slamming against her ribs in a noxious rhythm of fear and dread, Olivia turned around to see the one person in the world who knew her secret—the boy who, nine years ago, had walked in on an affair between a teacher and a student. A boy who had made a young Olivia Winston feel like trash from that day forward.

Ten

For a moment, Mac wondered if Olivia was having an anxiety attack. Her face was as pale as the snow outside the window, and her eyes looked watery, as though she desperately wanted to cry, but wouldn't allow herself to go there in front of guests.

What the hell was wrong with her? Had the DeBolds said something to upset her while he was gone? The quick, almost fierce anger that rose up inside of him surprised him, as did the protective impulse jumping in his blood.

Protecting Owen Winston's daughter was hardly the plan.

His gaze shifted, and he saw Tim staring at Olivia, his lip drawn up in a sneer. It was a look Tim usually reserved for people who didn't perform to his standards, from office staff to the guy who continued to put whipped cream on his espresso at the local coffee shop. Mac didn't get it.

He watched Tim walk toward her and stick out his hand. "Wow," he said coolly. "Olivia Winston. Small world."

"Microscopic." Olivia rose stiffly and clasped his hand for about half a second. "Hello, Tim."

"How do you two know each other?" Mac asked, though the tone of his voice sounded slightly demanding.

"We went to the same high school," Tim stated flatly.

"How funny," Louise remarked with a dry laugh, clearly not seeing the discomfort between the two. "You knew Olivia in high school and Mac in college?"

"That's right," Tim said.

Mac watched as Olivia seemed to get herself under control. With a smile affixed to her face, she walked over to Tim's wife and held out her hand, "Hi, I'm Olivia. Welcome."

"Avery Keavy. It's so nice to meet you." Avery had the good sense to leave the high school talk alone, and instead gestured to the coffee table and assorted hors d'oeuvres. "These look amazing. I'm sorry we're late."

Olivia picked up a tray and offered a stuffed mushroom to Avery. "It's no problem. Dinner's almost ready. In fact, I'm going to check on it right now. If you'll all excuse me…" After she placed the tray on the buffet, she excused herself and headed for the door.

"Need any help?" Mac called after her.

She turned then and glared at him. "No. I've got everything under control, Mr. Valentine."

Mac had never seen anyone look at him with such full-on revulsion, and he had no idea why. And her palely masked anger didn't end there. It continued all through dinner. Not that the DeBolds or the Keavys really picked up on it, they were way too focused on the food—which was perfection. But Mac saw every little glare she tossed his way as he served himself another helping of her mouthwatering brisket and smashed red potatoes, and wondered why the hell she was so upset at him. It couldn't be just because he was responsible for inviting Tim to the house. What was the big deal, so he knew her in high school?

Maybe he'd have to go to Tim for the information if Olivia wasn't going to speak to him. He looked over at Tim. The guy was just going with the flow. He didn't even look at Olivia.

"Pecan pie is one of my favorite desserts," Harold was saying to Olivia, his plate nearly empty.

Olivia gave him a warm smile. "I'm so glad. Would you like a second piece? How about you, Louise?"

"Absolutely." Louise held out her plate. "And I'm not even going to ask you to force me in to it."

Avery dabbed her mouth with her napkin. "Will you force me then, Olivia?"

"Of course," Olivia said, keeping her gaze fixed on Tim's wife. "I demand that you hold out your plate, Avery."

Avery gave her a small salute. "Yes, ma'am."

Avery and Louise broke out into laughter as they

passed around the fresh whipped cream to top their pie. Mac, however, was too distracted to find humor in the situation. When he should've been selling himself to the DeBolds, talking about how he could change their financial future, he was staring at Olivia, wondering what was wrong with her and how he could fix it. It pissed him off. Why did he care if she was angry with him?

After the brown-sugar coffee and pecan pie had been completely devoured, Avery thanked both Olivia and Mac for their hospitality and she and a very unsocial Tim took off. The DeBolds, feeling a little jet-lagged and extremely full, requested an early night, as well, and retired to their room.

The night had been a successful one—on the business front at any rate. The DeBolds seemed content and happy with Mac and with his home, and wasn't that the first step to having them as clients? With the DeBolds in bed, Mac had to deal with Olivia, who had fled to the kitchen as soon as both couples had gone.

When Mac entered the room, Olivia was camped out over the sink, washing dishes at a frenetic pace, taking out her anger on a serving platter.

"Great dinner," he said, walking over to her, leaning against the counter next to the sink.

"Yes," she said stiffly. "I think you've impressed them."

"I hope so."

"Yep. One step closer to getting the big fish on the hook."

He didn't respond to her sarcasm. "Do you need any help?"

"No."

He exhaled heavily. "Are you going to tell me why you're so angry with me?"

She continued to scrub the life out of a white platter, and Mac wondered if talking right now was a stupid idea. Maybe she just needed to cool off with her soap and hot water. But then she dropped the platter in the sink and turned to face him, anger and disappointment in her dark eyes.

"I knew you were out to punish my father and use me in the process," she said. "But I had no idea how far you'd go."

"What are you talking about?"

"Are you kidding me?"

"No."

"Tim Keavy," she snapped.

"What about him?"

She shook her head. "Don't do that."

"Do what?"

"Don't act like you're clueless. It doesn't suit you. You're a shark, be proud of it."

"You're nuts, lady." He gritted his teeth and pushed away from the counter. "All I know is you two went to the same high school."

"Right." She glared at him, her nostrils flaring. "So how does this go? You think by outing my sordid past to my dad, he'll back down on whatever he has on you? Apologize?" She shook her head, then walked past him out of the room, saying, "It'll never happen. My father's even more stubborn than I am."

He followed her. "Where are you going?"

"To my room."

"You're not leaving?"

"I'm going to give this job everything I have, get you the clients you want, then get the hell out. You'll have no ammunition if you're looking to ruin my business reputation along with my personal one."

"You're talking crazy," he said, following her up the stairs and down the hall to the guest room. She had chosen the one on the opposite side of the house than the DeBolds, and Mac was thankful he didn't have to whisper.

When she got to the door, she said, "Good night, Mac," then went inside.

When she tried to close the door behind her, he wouldn't let her. He held the door wide. "Listen, you can't just throw all that garbage in my face, then walk away."

She released her grip on the door, put her hands up in the air. "What do you want to say, Valentine? That you didn't know your best friend from college knew me?"

"Damn right," Mac said hotly, walking into the room and closing the door behind him.

"I don't believe you."

"I don't care if you believe me or not, it's true."

Standing just inches from him, she held her chin high as she stared hard into his eyes. "It's going to take a lot more to humiliate me and screw with my father than tossing my past mistakes, my past humiliations, back in my face."

He grabbed her shoulders. "I'm not doing that."

"Bull."

"I don't give a damn about your past."

"I do!" she shouted, her voice cracking with emotion. She dropped her gaze, bit her lip and cursed. When she looked up at him again, she looked like a kid, so vulnerable it killed him. "I hate that part of my life."

Tears sprang to her eyes.

"Stop that." He gave her a gentle shake, for the first time feeling the guilt that came with his plan. "Stop it, Olivia."

This wasn't how it was supposed go. He was the one who was supposed to make her miserable, then send her back to her father in shame. He should be reveling in the fact that he had access to information about her past that would make her father suffer.

"Damn it." He hauled her against him and kissed her hard on the mouth. "I don't care what happened before, and neither should you." He nuzzled her lips, then nipped at them, suckled them, until she gave in, gave up and sagged against him.

"There's nothing wrong with this," he said as his hands found her lower back and raked upward. "Or this." He dipped his head and kissed her throat, suckling the skin that covered her rapid pulse, grinning as a hungry whimper escaped her throat. "Nothing to be ashamed of, Olivia."

"You don't understand," she uttered, letting her head fall back.

He held her close, his lips brushing her temple. "Help me to, then."

"I…can't. I made a promise to myself.…"

He rubbed his face against her hair. "When you were a kid?"

"Yes," she whispered.

"You're a woman now." He nuzzled her ear, nipped at the lobe. "Everything's different."

On those words, she froze. "That's the thing," she said, her voice hoarse. She drew back, her eyes filled with regret. "Nothing's different. Not at all. I refuse to make any more stupid mistakes with men who just want to…" She didn't finish, just shook her head.

"Olivia."

She disentangled herself from his grasp. "Two more days. That's it. That's all you're getting from me, so do your worst because after this weekend is up you're going to be done. Done with me and done with my father."

"We'll see about that," Mac said darkly before turning and leaving the room.

Eleven

And the winner of the worst night's sleep contest was…Olivia Winston.

Standing over the stove, she made sure her pan was hot, then carefully cracked an egg into the hole she'd made in the slice of crusty bread. Three cups of extra-strength coffee and all she wanted to do was go back to bed. But maybe that had nothing to do with being tired as much as it had to do with hiding. For someone who had gone into this job thinking it would be easy-peasy, she sure was going through a lot of difficult, trying moments. Not to mention, some sexually charged moments that she couldn't get out of her head. She'd really underestimated Mac and his desire to bury her father, and she'd overestimated herself, and her needs, in the process. She'd wanted to find out just how Mac was going to get back at her dad, and had basically given him the goods to make it happen.

She flipped the bread. To make matters worse, she wanted more—more of him, more of his touch, his kisses. She was weak and a total disappointment.

She felt him in the kitchen even before she saw him, and wanted to kick herself for the giddiness that erupted inside her at the thought of seeing him again.

"Good morning."

She spared him a quick smile. "Morning." He looked good, Saturday-morning sexy in expensive black sweats and dark tousled hair.

"Sleep well?" he asked, pouring himself a cup of coffee.

"No. You?"

He chuckled. "I slept okay."

"Yeah, guys can sleep through anything. Your brains turn off—so lucky."

"Maybe our brains turn off, but that's about it." Despite his hard, unyielding business-guy attitude, he had this obvious sensuality, this slow, tigerlike laziness that made him seem always ready for bed. "Honestly, the effects of what happened in your room last night are still with me this morning."

She ignored the pull in her belly. "Me, too—but maybe in a different way." She laid another slice of bread in the hot pan and cracked an egg. "Listen, Mac, I don't know if I believe what you said last night about Tim—if you set that up or not—but I can't worry about it anymore. I've spent too many years worrying about the past. Can we just let everything go and concentrate on what we're trying to accomplish with the DeBolds?"

"Let *everything* go?"

"Yes. Do you think you can do that?"

"Do you really think *you* can do that?" he countered, his eyes glittering with heat.

Before she could answer, Harold and Louise walked into the kitchen, all smiles and dressed like models from a Hanna Andersson catalog. "Morning," Harold said, taking a seat at the island.

"Morning," Mac said good-naturedly. "Sleep well?"

"Perfect," Harold said. "Something smells good, but that's not surprising."

Olivia glanced at Mac, who was watching her over his steaming cup of coffee, then she turned to her guests. "Eggs in a blanket, bacon and good, strong coffee."

"Are you trying to fatten us up?" Louise asked, sitting beside her husband.

"Of course," Olivia said on a chuckle, setting two cups of coffee before them. "But only so you have all the energy you need for what I have planned today."

"And what do you have planned?" Mac asked, seeming to suddenly realize he'd never discussed plans with her.

Olivia looked at them all brightly. "Ice skating."

Mac practically choked on his coffee. "Ice skating?"

Louise, on the other hand, looked as though she were about to explode with happiness. "Did you hear that, Harold?"

"I did. I did."

Clasping her hands together like a little girl, Louise cried, "I haven't been skating in ten years."

"Well, then maybe it's not such a good idea—" Mac began, but Louise cut him off.

"Not a good idea? No, no, no—it's perfect. Harold and I had our first date on a skating rink. Rounder's Pond—it was in back of my grandfather's property, a beautiful kidney bean shape and surrounded by trees. Do you remember that, honey?"

"Of course." Harold smiled at his wife, then looked over at Olivia. "You have made my wife very happy today. Thank you."

"My pleasure." Olivia beamed as she turned back to the stove. "Now, let's get you two fed."

Mac came to stand beside her.

She whispered over the DeBolds' loud chatter, "You look panicked."

"And you look happy about that," he muttered.

Laughing, she took two perfectly cooked eggs in blankets out of the pan and placed them gently on plates. She whispered, "Buck up, Valentine. Ice skating is perfect and fun, and I've planned a lovely picnic afterward with hot chocolate."

"I don't skate, Olivia."

"Well, you lucked out then." She handed him the two plates and smiled. "I'm a great teacher."

He'd been good at sports. Not the school kind. You had to spend more than a year living in one place to get on an organized team, but he'd killed at street basket-

ball and alley soccer in every community he'd been sent
to. He'd never tried hockey though, and before today had
assumed that hockey, or anything involving skates, was
a little like trying to understand German when all you
spoke was Spanish. But he'd jumped into it with both
blades. It took him about twenty minutes to really feel
his balance, but after that, he was like a demon racing
on the ice, even getting an impromptu hockey game
going with Harold and some of the guys on the lake.

After an hour, he retired himself and joined Olivia on
the bench. She was dressed all in white and looked very
pretty. She'd spent much of her time with Louise in the
center of the lake, teaching the woman how to execute
perfect little turns and spins and other girlish things
Mac didn't have a clue about—but he'd sure liked
watching her in between plays.

"Well," she began, her cheeks pink from the cold
and exercise, her eyes bright with humor. "You sure
took to that like a baby to a bath."

"You think so?"

"You had the moves, Valentine. I was very impressed."

Instead of throwing away her compliment with a
laugh, he felt an odd sensation in his gut as if he'd eaten
something past its expiration date. And he knew exactly
what that feeling was—he'd felt it once or twice in his
life and it worried him. He liked this woman.

He blew out a breath, turned to watch Harold and
Louise as they skated casually around the lake. He had
to get rid of this feeling, stop himself right here, right
now, before he did something stupid like abandon his

plans to make her father pay. He had one more night—tonight—to get her in his bed, then they were done.

"And I'm impressed," he said in a voice he normally reserved for his employees, "with your skills off the ice."

"What do you mean?" she asked, looking confused.

"You did well." Mac gestured toward the DeBolds, who were laughing and holding hands as they weaved in and out of the other couples in the "slow lane." "They look happy."

"They do," she agreed.

"Funny that you picked the very thing they did on their first date."

"Not funny at all."

He stared at her. "You knew?"

She smiled.

"How—"

"Romance breeds comfort, comfort breeds trust," she explained, taking out a thermos of hot chocolate and pouring them both a cup. "And that's what you're looking for, right? Trust in you and your skill?"

He shook his head. This woman was unbelievable. He'd had no idea how far she'd go to help him. Honestly, he hadn't expected much with her knowledge of what his true motivations were, but she'd really come through for him. Too bad he couldn't offer her a position in his company. He asked her, "How could you find out something like that? Even if you researched them, something so personal…"

She laughed as she handed him the steaming cup of

chocolate. "You really didn't know who you were hiring, did you? Silly man."

"Maybe not—but I see it now. I see you."

"Yeah? What do you see?" she asked, sipping her chocolate.

"You're a damn good wife."

"Thank you."

"And if I wasn't completely against legal unions, I might be compelled to make you marry me."

She laughed again, clearly thinking that every word he'd just uttered was a nonsensical joke. Mac wasn't so sure.

"That's very flattering, Mac, but you know I'd have to turn you down."

"Really?"

"Yep." She looked away, sipped her chocolate.

"You want me to ask why, don't you?"

"Nope."

"Fine," he grumbled. "Why?"

She turned back to face him, the humor in her gaze now gone. This time he saw the sad reality of a woman who knew and understood him—it wasn't pretty to look at.

"What?" he said. "Go ahead, say it."

"I don't think you'd make a very good husband."

Nothing shocking there. "Well, I don't know. Last night you thought—"

"That was passion, desire," she interrupted.

"You can't have passion and desire in a marriage?"

"Of course, but those kinds of needs are only *part* of

it." She nodded toward the middle of the lake. Louise was now teaching Harold how to do a spin. He looked like an idiot, Mac thought. An idiot in love.

"Look at them," Olivia said wistfully. "They're friends, true companions. They really like each other."

Mac pressed his lips together. Not that he wanted to admit it—and he wasn't about to, out loud at any rate—but he liked Olivia. He thought they made a pretty good team.

"They're coming back," Olivia said, pulling Mac from his thoughts. "And after a full morning of cold and exercise, I'm betting they're hungry."

"I know I am," Mac said softly, his gaze resting on Olivia.

She shook her head at him, but he saw that flash of hunger in her eyes—the same one she'd worn last night when he'd touched her, kissed her.

Screw friendship. Maybe what they had wasn't long-lasting, but it was real, and there was going to be a moment when she allowed herself to take it. And if he was on top of his game, that moment would come tonight.

At four o'clock in the afternoon on Saturday, Olivia was dealt some bad news. She was in the kitchen, pounding chicken breasts into thin paillards, when Mac walked in and announced, "Harold and Louise want to ask the Keavys to come over after dinner tonight for cocktails."

Olivia's heart dropped into her stomach with anvil-like heaviness. She continued to smash the chicken, but with slightly more vigor. "Okay."

"Avery's the DeBolds' attorney. It's good to have her here. I think it will get them talking and asking questions tonight, and I need that to happen. They're leaving in the morning, so—"

"You don't have to explain, Mac," she said tightly, not looking at him. "This is your home. You don't need my permission to invite someone here."

"I know that." He sighed, pushed a hand through his hair. "Damn it, I care about your feelings, okay? Too much, but there it is."

"You don't need to worry about me." She needed him to just stop talking about it, stop asking questions. But that wasn't Mac's way. "I'm a professional. I will not allow my feelings to distract from the goal of this evening."

"Screw that. What happened with Tim? Did he treat you badly? Not show up on a date? Was he…all over you on a date? What the hell happened between you two?"

"Nothing."

"I'm trying to be sensitive here, Olivia, because I can see that whatever happened in the past is upsetting to you—but it was high school. That's a long time ago."

Her head came up and she glared at him. "You've got to stop with the questions. This is none of your business, Mac."

"I know, but if it interferes—"

"It won't. I swear I'll be the perfect hostess tonight— I was just caught off guard before."

He looked as though he wanted to say more, ask more, demand more, but after a moment he turned and started to leave the room.

Thinking he was gone, Olivia faced her meal-in-progress once again, feeling tired. All she wanted to do was throw her ingredients into the garbage and go home, forget about Tim, forget about Mac. She put down her mallet, took off her plastic gloves and put her head in her hands.

"Olivia."

Her heart sank. Damn him, why hadn't he left the room like he was supposed to? He'd seen her break down, lose it a little, and that wasn't good. She felt him beside her.

"I'm just a little tired, that's all," she said.

"Come on. It won't go further than this room, if that's what you're worried about. I swear I won't use anything you tell me. Talk to me."

She looked up and melted at the concerned look on his face...she could almost believe it was genuine.

He reached for her, wrapped his arms around her. "Give me something, Olivia."

Maybe it would be easier if he knew, she thought. Then it would all be out in the open—he wouldn't have to dig for information. But...there was a part of her that didn't want him to know, didn't want him to see her as Tim had seen her, and maybe still did—as trash, as a little tramp who had been so starved for love she'd slept with her teacher.

"He knows something about me," she began, letting her head drop onto Mac's shoulder. "A mistake I made. And he didn't like me for it, simple as that." She couldn't go further than that, she just couldn't....

"Simple as that, huh?"

"Yes."

"I don't believe you."

She stepped back, lifted her head and gave him a bold smile. "I have chicken to prepare."

"Olivia…"

"Everything will be fine tonight, Valentine."

He reached out and brushed his thumb across her cheek. "You're sure?"

His touch was like the best kind of comfort food and she wanted to wrap her arms around him again and beg him to take away her anger over a past she couldn't find a way to change. But that job belonged to her alone. If she ever wanted to feel comfortable about men and sex and love again, she had to deal with her past herself. "Now, I want you to get out of my kitchen and go be with your guests. It's your last night to impress the DeBolds, and I'm going to make sure you do."

Mac regarded her without smiling. "It's their last night, and it's your last night."

She nodded, then faced the counter again and got back to work. She wasn't sure when he left exactly, but when she turned around to get the arugula from the fridge, he was gone.

Twelve

The amazing thing about Olivia Winston was that once she made up her mind not to care about something or someone, it came rather easily. When Tim and Avery joined them after dinner for drinks and a few games of Pictionary, Olivia put her nerves aside and became the professional she knew herself to be. She was in her element: a small, elegant, relaxed, family friendly get-together with great desserts and just enough spirits to make everyone smile. She and Tim had managed to successfully ignore each other and the DeBolds were happy and acting exceptionally warm and familiar with Mac.

An all-around success.

"We've had such a good time," Louise said, sipping

a second cup of Olivia's delicious hot-buttered rum as they relaxed beside the fireplace in the den.

Harold nodded in Mac's direction. "You're a class act, Valentine."

"Thank you, Harold." Mac tipped his glass in the couples' direction. "It's been a pleasure having both of you here. Maybe we can do it again over the summer."

Harold grinned warmly. "Maybe. Maybe."

Avery had excused herself to go to the ladies' room, and perhaps Tim had felt uncomfortable without her, but he, too, excused himself to have a cigar on the porch.

While they were gone, Olivia asked Louise about her New York trip and if they'd seen any Broadway shows, and as she listened to the woman's hilarious accounts of a show they saw about underpants, she saw Mac get up and follow Tim out of the room.

Her stomach rolled over, but she forced her attention back on Louise.

He was a guy. A hardheaded guy who went after what he wanted regardless of the consequences. And right now what he wanted were answers.

He knew where his friend had gone—the balcony off the kitchen—and headed straight there.

Out in the inky darkness, a light snow was falling and the air felt still and frigid. Tim was simultaneously puffing on his cigar and shaking from the cold.

Mac stepped out onto the balcony, barely feeling the below-zero temperatures. "I couldn't stand those things when we were in college and I can't stand them now."

Laughing, Tim said curtly, "Then why are you out here?"

"I need to talk to you."

"About what?"

"About her. What did you do to her?"

His nose was red at the tip, his ears, too. "What? Who?"

"Olivia," Mac said impatiently. "In high school. What happened between you two?"

"Oh, man…" Tim shook his head.

"Come on."

"I don't want to go into this," Tim said, tossing his cigar over the balcony and into the snow.

"You will go into it," Mac said through gritted teeth. "Or I'll make you dive into that snow and fish out the cigar using only your teeth."

Tim stepped back, chuckled. "What's with the violence?" He was trying to be funny, and although the clown act had worked on their frat brothers in college, it was going nowhere tonight. When Tim realized that Mac was having none of his BS, he shrugged his shoulders. "Oh, hell. Fine. It was a long time ago, junior year. I'd just finished soccer practice and I was getting a few things out of my locker. I heard a girl and a guy in an empty classroom. It was late, after five." He shrugged again. "I thought it was a couple of kids fooling around and I was going to jump out and scare the crap out of them." Mac raised his eyebrows. "It wasn't a couple of kids. It was Olivia."

"And?"

"And the math teacher."

Mac cursed.

"Yep."

"So, you didn't jump out?"

"Hell no!"

Mac could see why Olivia felt embarrassed about something like that. But hell, everyone did stupid things when they were kids. One question remained though. He stared hard at Tim. "I don't get it. Why is she so angry at you?"

Tim blew out a breath. "I didn't exactly keep the news to myself."

Anger smashed through Mac like a tidal wave. "What? You told someone about what you'd seen?"

"A few people actually." He quickly reacted to the hard look on Mac's face. "C'mon, it was high school. If you can't talk trash about the school skank, what fun is—"

Mac stopped him with a deadly glare. His voice low, he asked, "What did you call her?"

Swallowing hard, Tim dropped his gaze and tried to play it off with humor. "C'mon, man, it was a long time ago."

Mac stared at Tim as if he were seeing him for the first time—and he looked a like a major ass. He said evenly, "It was a long time ago, but you clearly haven't grown up one day since then. You need to leave, Keavy."

"What?"

"Right now."

"You've got to be kidding."

"Do I look like I'm kidding?"

"I don't get you, man." Tim hugged himself against the cold and swayed from foot to foot. "Why do you care about this? She's your employee, not your…" Tim stopped moving. "Holy sh—"

"Don't," Mac warned menacingly.

"You like her. Wow. I haven't seen you really get into a woman since…" He searched his memory. "I was going to say college, but you really just played around then, too."

Mac scowled. "I'm going inside now. I'll think up something to tell Avery, then you need to get the hell out of my house."

"Look, Mac," Tim started, changing his tune as he looked almost sincere, "I was a kid…"

"We're done here." Mac left his former friend in the cold and went inside.

"Door County, Wisconsin, is the sweetest spot in the Midwest. Beautiful wildlife. It's kind of a kitschy area with friendly people who don't try to get in your business—it's my kind of place. We bought some land six years ago and built our dream home." Louise sighed as she sat in front of the fireplace and sipped her buttered rum. "Traveling is fun and always a great adventure, but nothing feels better than going home, you know?"

Olivia nodded, but she didn't exactly feel that way about her two-bedroom apartment. Sure, it was pretty and bright and had a decent kitchen, but it wasn't exactly her dream home.

"When are you going back, Louise?" Avery asked, curled up like a pretty blond cat on the sofa, while Harold inspected a book on architecture that had been on the coffee table.

"Tomorrow morning. We want to be there in time to start decorating for the holidays. Harold and I have this thing for Christmas trees. We go to the lot ourselves and pick out one for every room in the house."

"Every room?" Olivia asked disbelievingly.

Louise laughed. "Yes."

"It's beautiful," Avery said knowingly. "And that pine scent everywhere…"

"You know," Louise said to both Avery and Olivia, "we're having all of Harold's family for Christmas." She lowered her voice. "He has an enormous and very judgmental family."

"I can hear you, honey," Harold said, flipping through the pages of his book. "I'm sitting right here."

With an impish smile she continued, "They have always taunted me about not being able to cook and take care of my man, so this year I have vowed to create the best Thanksgiving dinner anyone has ever seen." She paled. "I have no idea how I'm going to manage it though. Unlike you, Olivia, I have zero skill."

"It's not that difficult," Olivia assured her, trying to be as supportive as she could. Anyone could learn to cook, but in her opinion Thanksgiving dinner was not the best place to start. "The simpler the better. All you need are a few recipes."

"A few?" Louise repeated nervously.

Olivia laughed. "Before you go in the morning, I could give you a little lesson in—"

Suddenly, Louise's face brightened, her eyes rounded and she burst out, "That's a wonderful idea."

"Great," Olivia said. "So, meet me in the kitchen say around—"

"No. That's not what I mean."

Confused, Olivia shook her head. "I'm sorry…I don't understand."

Louise grinned widely. "You're done working for Mac tomorrow, right?"

"Yes."

"Then come with us to Door County."

"What?"

Louise looked beyond excited, like a kid, sitting forward in her seat. She put her mug on the coffee table. "Stay for a few days and teach me how to cook. In style, too—the kitchen is awesome, and I have every tool…every tool I have no idea how to use."

Still in shock, Olivia just muttered, "Wow. I don't know."

This time, Harold jumped in. "Why not? You travel for your job, right?"

"Right, but—"

Louise laughed. "I know I'm not a bachelor looking for help, but couldn't you extend your client base to include clueless, helpless females, too?"

Olivia glanced from Harold to Avery to Louise. They were all smiling. Why couldn't she do this? She was done with Mac, and she'd love to see Door County and help the DeBolds. She shrugged and smiled herself. "Okay. I'll have to check my schedule, see if I've been booked. But if not, I'm all yours."

"Great." Clasping her hands together, Louise turned

to her husband and hooted. "I'm going to wipe those evil, know-it-all smirks off your family's faces."

Harold's lips twitched. "They don't smirk, darling."

It was at that moment that Mac entered the room. He spotted Avery and gave her a terse glance. "Avery, your husband's not feeling well. You'd better take him home."

Avery looked concerned. "What?"

"Tim needs to go."

A small flicker of concern tapped at Olivia's insides. What had gone down between the two of them to make Mac look so annoyed and Tim rush out? What was said? Her heart dipped as she wondered what Tim had revealed.

"He's waiting for you by the front door," Mac told Avery brusquely.

"Oh. Okay." Slightly confused, Avery stood and offered a quick goodbye to Olivia and the DeBolds before leaving the room.

Without another word about it, Mac turned his attention to the threesome remaining. His eyes were cool and detached, but he was forcing a grin. "You all look excited about something."

"Is Tim all right?" Olivia asked.

"He'll be fine," Mac stated quickly and without an ounce of emotion.

Louise looked serious for a moment. "I hope so."

Mac nodded, then glanced around expectantly. "So, what did I miss?"

Louise didn't hesitate to switch topics, "We're talking about Harold's family and how they're going to drop their jaws when I cook and serve them Thanksgiving dinner."

"Looks as though my wife has hired Olivia to teach her how to cook," Harold informed him on a chuckle.

"Really?" He looked at Olivia, his jaw set.

"Could be. If I'm free." He didn't look pleased, but Olivia couldn't tell exactly what was going on behind his eyes. Was it whatever had happened with Tim or the prospect of Olivia working for the DeBolds that had him fuming?

"Where are you going?"

"To our home in Wisconsin," Louise said, but Mac was still staring at Olivia.

"When?"

"Tomorrow."

"No." Mac said the word so darkly and succinctly that everyone stopped and stared at him.

"What's wrong?" Olivia asked Mac.

Mac recovered quickly, his tone now ultraprofessional as he addressed her. "You and I haven't finished our business yet."

"Huh?"

Harold and Louise exchanged glances, and Harold cleared his throat. "I'm sorry, Mac. We didn't know."

It was then that Mac realized he was about to alienate the clients he wanted so badly to score. "No, no," he said, chuckling, back in total control now. "I'm the one who's sorry. My business is so all-consuming these days, I didn't get a chance to ask Olivia to continue on."

"All-consuming," Harold repeated with understanding. "Well, that's why we agreed to come here, isn't it?

And why we're considering transferring our financial holdings to you."

"Well," Mac began, "my new project with Olivia doesn't have to start immediately. But I would like a chance to talk with you both, show you the plans I have created for your future. Do you have room for one more in Door County…?"

Harold seemed to like this idea and nodded in agreement. "Kill two birds, is that it?"

Mac nodded.

Olivia sat on the floor fuming. She did not appreciate Mac's interference or his interloping ways, but before she could even get a word out, Harold was talking again—sounding pumped up and making specific plans.

"Okay," he said. "So while the women are in the kitchen—"

"Hey, watch yourself, Harold," Louise warned goodnaturedly, going to sit beside him on the couch. "Make sure you don't add a 'where they belong' to the end of that sentence."

He patted her leg. "Never, darling." Then he turned back to Mac. "While the women are in the kitchen plotting against my family, you and I can do some ice fishing and talk about how you're going to make us richer than we already are."

"Richer, more secure and totally protected."

Harold beamed. "I like the sound of that."

Olivia knew she had zero control over her immediate future. The DeBolds had found a perfect situation, and as they sat there grinning they had that rich person's, "we're going to make it happen no matter what anyone says" look on their faces.

Olivia stood and started gathering plates and cups, knowing full well that Mac was watching her, feeling like he'd won, like he had more time to get her into bed. She swallowed thickly at the thought, trying to ignore the pounding of her heart.

The only thing that could save her now was if her partners had booked another job for her.

Thirteen

All the excited chatter about Mary's upcoming engagement party came to a screeching halt when Olivia walked into No Ring Required's modern kitchen and announced her plans to fly to Door County the following day. Seated at the table, Tess and Mary listened intently as Olivia explained that she was going to Wisconsin to teach Louise DeBold how to cook Thanksgiving dinner, and that Mac Valentine was going along, as well.

Mary cupped her mug of tea and tried to be the rational one. "Okay, I personally think it's great that we're expanding to include women who don't have, or who choose not to grow, the stereotypical 'wifely' gene, it's just…" Her voice trailed off.

"I'll finish for her," Tess stated boldly, pulling her red

hair into a loose bun. "The fact that your former client, Mac Valentine, is going with you is a little bizarre."

Olivia sat beside Mary. "I know, but Harold DeBold wants to get to know him better and hear his plans for their financial future before he'll give Mac his business. So, you see, it's really two separate gigs going on here."

"Uh-huh," was all Tess said.

"Going out of town seems to be where trouble starts," Mary said, touching her belly.

Olivia frowned at her. "You don't consider little Ethan or Ethanette here trouble, do you?"

"No, of course not. I just mean, when you're out of town you're not in your comfort zone and you look to someone else for comfort—that is, if you're attracted to that someone else." She leaned forward. "Are you? Are you attracted to that someone else?"

"I refuse to answer on the grounds that this one—" she pointed behind her to a looming Tess "—might sucker punch me, or something."

Tess laid a hand on Olivia's shoulder and said sweetly, "I'm fair. I'd at least have you turn around before I hit you."

Mary laughed, and Olivia grimaced. "This is partly your fault, ladies."

"How is it our fault?" Tess demanded, sitting across from them.

"Maybe someone should've booked me for another gig starting today."

Tess snorted. "Maybe you need to stand up to this guy and tell him to take a hike."

"Maybe I will." Both women looked unconvinced, and Olivia sighed with frustration. "Look, you two, the only comfort I'll be cooking up is in the kitchen, okay?"

Tess and Mary continued to vocalize their opinions and concerns for the rest of the day. Then later, when Olivia returned home to pack, the phone call to her father didn't go much better....

"You are insane to go anywhere with that man," said Owen Winston angrily.

She had him on speakerphone, and was packing a suitcase while they talked. "Dad, I didn't call for advice, I called to let you know that I was going to be out of town for a few days."

"To the diamond DeBolds house in Door County." He made a noise that sounded awfully like an out-of-tune French horn. "Door County is a place for couples on vacation. Did you know that?"

Yes, she did, and it probably worried her more than it did him, but she wasn't about to let her father know that. "Will you go by my apartment and feed my fish...once a day? Will you?"

He heaved a sigh. "Of course. We don't want them to suffer."

She laughed at his sarcasm. "Will it hurt your masculine pride if I tell you that you're acting like a drama queen?"

"Livy, tell me you're not falling for that bastard."

She stopped packing. "No falling."

"Good. And tell me you're not going to—"

"Stop. Dad. Please don't go there." This was it.

Maybe this was it. The opportunity for her to tell her father the truth. Not the details, but the basics of what she'd done in high school, so that if Mac ever did approach her father with the information it wouldn't come as a shock.

"I'm sorry, Livy," he said, sounding sad and maybe a little lonely. "I love you and I just want…"

"The best for me, I know—I get it." She bit her lip, thought about how to say it, how to begin…then she remembered how Mac had promised not to use her past against her by going to her father, and she found an excuse to leave it alone, or at the very least, put it off until maybe she and her father were face-to-face.

She tossed a few sweaters into her suitcase and said, "I love you, Dad, and I'll see you on Thursday."

Fourteen

Mac enjoyed the solitude of a private plane. He had a rule: if he was going to be in the air for more than an hour, he always chartered a Gulfstream. He glanced around with an assessing gaze. The DeBolds' Citation was smaller than what he was used to, but comfortable enough once he was seated. He was curious to see how it felt once they got it in the air, as eight-seaters could act a little unsteady at times. The interior was ultraplush, though, outfitted with soft leather and thick carpet, and the very capable steward, Tom, had set out glasses and a bottle of sparkling water.

Just outside the plane Mac heard Tom greet another passenger. Mac glanced up from his laptop, annoyed at the jolt of excitement that ran through him when Olivia Winston came aboard.

"Morning," Mac said.

She gave him a friendly smile. "Hey." She took the single seat across the aisle from him. "Are we early?"

"I don't think so."

His gaze moved over her, from the soft chocolate-brown sweater to the jeans that stretched temptingly over her thighs and hips when she sat. His hands itched to touch her. It had been too long and he could hardly wait to have her—in his arms and in his bed. Up until this point, there had been too many distractions, and he'd been unsuccessful in his attempts to seduce her. Now that they were going away together...

The steward came out and addressed them, his large blue eyes and round face filled with practiced friendliness. "Welcome aboard, Ms. Winston, Mr. Valentine."

"Thank you," Olivia said warmly.

"Is there anything I can get you?"

"Not for me, thanks." She turned to Mac. "Anything you need, Valentine?"

He grinned at her and uttered, "Nothing that Tom can provide."

She rolled her eyes at him, then glanced back at the steward. "We're fine, thank you."

He nodded. "We'll be leaving in just a few minutes. Please fasten your seat belts."

Tom was about to head for the cockpit when Olivia called out, "Excuse me."

"Yes, Miss Winston?"

"Aren't we missing a few passengers?"

The steward looked confused and just a tad annoyed. "I'm sorry?"

"The DeBolds?"

"Oh, no, miss. They went home last night, and sent the plane and myself back for the two of you."

Olivia looked at Mac, then back at Tom. "Why?"

"I don't know, miss."

The man stood there. And Mac, growing tired of both Tom's put-out attitude and Olivia's questions, decided to step in. Sitting on the tarmac wasn't his idea of a good time. "Thank you, Tom. Now, let's get this lady in the air, shall we."

Looking relieved, the man nodded. "I'll inform the captain."

When he was gone, Olivia turned to Mac, her dark eyebrows drawn together in a frown. "Why wouldn't they call us, have us all leave together?"

Mac shrugged. "Why does it matter?"

"I'm just curious. It's a little odd."

Below their feet, the engine sprang to life with an easy vibration.

"I have a feeling they're trying to get us together," Olivia remarked, fastening her seat belt.

"We are together."

"You know what I mean, Mac."

"Ah, yes." He grinned at her over his laptop. "And what if they are? Would that be so wrong?"

She glared at him. "What is it with married people?

Why do they always feel like they need to make more couples?"

"Maybe they want others to experience their blissful state."

"Do you really believe that, Valentine?"

"Nope."

She laughed. She had a great laugh, throaty and youthful, and he had an incredible desire to always keep her laughing, keep her happy.

"Listen, Valentine, I think we need to try and remember why we're here." She was leaning back in her seat, her head tilted toward him.

"And why are we here…?"

"To work," she said, humor dancing in her eyes. "Or in your case, to work and exact revenge on my father through poor little me."

He couldn't help it—he smiled at her, and she returned it. She was something else, no wilting flower. Why did it excite him that she understood exactly what he was after and wasn't afraid to take him on?

"Speaking of revenge…" she began, her eyes suddenly not meeting his.

"Yes?"

"Did your friend give you any helpful ammunition the other night?"

Mac's jaw tightened. "No."

She was quiet for a moment, then said, "Tim didn't tell you about…what happened?"

He stared at her, hard and intense. "Listen, Olivia, I told you before, I don't care what happened in your past. I don't need to use BS hearsay from a former friend to get what I want from you."

"Former friend?"

"I'm not sentimental. I don't value friendships. And if someone crosses me, goes too far, I have no problem walking away."

She nodded. "I'll remember that."

A slow grin moved over his lips. "Now, let's get back to talking about why we're here."

"Right. To work."

Mac sighed. "I'd hoped you'd forgotten."

She laughed. "Nope. And odds are Louise and Harold are going to throw more of this—" she gestured around the interior of the cabin "—our way."

"More private planes, more romantic destinations...sounds like hell on earth."

"You don't want to take any of this seriously."

"No."

She sighed and looked away. "Well, I do. And if you have any sense you'll focus on landing this client, not getting me into bed."

Damn, he liked her—he liked her attitude, her spirit, her brains, the way she moved and how her eyes always spoke for her. But there was no way he was going to allow his feelings to interfere with the facts. He wanted payback. Of course he wasn't about to use her past or Tim's account of it against her. He would only work with what he had now—his desire for her, and to take Owen's daughter to his bed. Mac would have what he wanted: revenge and a woman he desired above all things.

The plane backed up slowly, getting in position to taxi. "Not to worry, Olivia," he said with a tone of arrogant confidence. "I'm fully capable of landing both you and the DeBolds."

Comprised of a sprawling log house, orchard and barn, the DeBolds' home was truly one of the most unique places Olivia had ever seen and she was completely enchanted by it. On fifty private acres, just a half mile north of Sturgeon Bay, the custom log home was already being dressed for the holidays. When Mac and Olivia arrived, a crew of ten or so men and women were working outside, affixing garlands, wreaths and twinkle lights to trees, doors, rooftops and anything else that didn't move.

Olivia gave a low whistle as she stepped out of the Town Car that had picked them up from the airport. "Okay, I grew up in a very nice house with very nice furnishings—most of which you couldn't touch—but this...this is spectacular."

Mac helped the driver with their luggage, told the guy that he could handle it from there, then gave him a hefty tip.

As the car pulled away, Olivia stood in the driveway and just stared at the house, transfixed. "I wouldn't think that anything so big could feel so warm and friendly, but it does." She leaned down and picked up her small carry-on, as Mac had the rest of the luggage. "I think I know where I'm retiring to."

"Really?" Mac said, sounding surprised.

"Yes, really." She followed him up the walk to the front door. "This is my fantasy home. If they have horses, I'm just going to tie myself to one of the fence posts and cry squatter's rights."

"I don't get it. I mean, it's 'cute' in a country bumpkin sort of way, but—"

"Yeah, I know it's not like that glass and stainless steel penthouse of yours in Manhattan, but—"

He stopped, shot her a sideways glance. "How did you know about my apartment in Manhattan?"

"Oh, Mac," she said on a laugh, "you never stop underestimating me. Great place, by the way, very James Bond meets Times Square."

"Thanks," he muttered as they reached the front door. "I think."

"But this place is way cooler. What could you possibly not like here?"

"It's just a little too much like a bed-and-breakfast," he said, dropping the bags onto the DeBolds' massive monogrammed welcome mat.

She snorted. "You're such a guy."

Before she could stop him, Mac snaked a hand around her waist and pulled her close. "Damn right."

Olivia gasped, and even though it was twenty degrees outside, heat accosted her skin like a blast from an oven.

"But, hey," he said gently, gazing down at her, "if you like this place, that's all that matters. I'm more than willing to accept patchwork quilts, sunflower wallpaper and raspberry-colored bathrooms if you'll share it with me."

The soft, sweet way he was looking at her made

Olivia almost believe him. And yet she chose sarcasm over sincerity. "Interesting. Sounds like you've been to a B and B a few times before. You've got the description of every bed-and-breakfast I've ever heard about down pat."

"I've been sent to a few Web sites in my time."

"By a few ladies?" His lips were so close, looked so good—and she could remember exactly how they felt.

"Women seem to think 'homespun' is romantic."

"And it's not?"

He slowly shook his head. "Not to me."

Power pulsed from him, strength and sexuality, too. It was a hard combination to resist. And again, she questioned herself, questioned why she needed to resist at all. Why couldn't she just have fun here and not hold back? She was an adult, maybe a foolish one, but hey…

"I'll probably kick myself later for asking this," she said, "but what is romantic to you?"

"Well, this doesn't suck." He grinned mischievously, then glanced up.

Olivia followed his gaze and spotted a sprig of mistletoe hanging from a beam over the porch. "Now this is just awkward," she began, laughing. "What if the mail carrier and the UPS guy got here at the same time—"

"Ah, shut up, Winston." He cut her off with a growl, then covered her mouth with his. His nose was cold, but his lips seared with heat and need, and Olivia melted into his embrace.

"You smell good," he whispered against her lips.

"It's the snow."

"No."

"Pine trees."

"No," he said, applying soft kisses first to her top lip then to the bottom one. "It's you."

Her breath caught in her throat as he kissed her again, hot, sweet kisses that made her forget where she was. Like a blind woman, searching, hungry, she slipped her hands inside his coat and ran her fingers over his trim waist to his back, then upward. The muscles in his shoulders flexed, and she gripped at them, squeezed at them as she tipped her chin up to get closer. She just wanted to get closer to him.

It was at that moment the front door opened. Like a guilty child with both of her hands stuck in the forbidden cookie jar, Olivia jumped away from Mac.

Pulling the door wide, Louise looked from Olivia to Mac, just a touch of confusion on her perfectly made-up face. "Did you ring the bell? We didn't hear anything."

Olivia quickly said, "We…just arrived." She looked at Mac to corroborate this, but he only stared at her, his eyes rife with amusement. Of course he wasn't going to be any help.

A broad grin on her face, Louise said, "That's odd. One of the decorators came inside to tell me you were here."

Which meant that said meddlesome decorator probably also mentioned what Mac and Olivia were doing out on the porch.

As Louise ushered them inside, Olivia muttered a terse, "Oh, man," back at Mac, which only made him chuckle.

"Harold," Louise called up a beautiful log staircase. "They're here." Then she turned back to Mac and Olivia. "Have a good flight?"

Trying to brush off any residual embarrassment, Olivia forced a smile. "It was great, thank you."

They followed Louise into a massive, two-level great room with hardwood floors, exposed beams and a rock fireplace that stretched all the way to the cathedral ceiling. The open floor plan was spectacular, allowing visitors to see the living room, dining area and huge chef's kitchen, with a rectangular black granite island, from the entryway.

"You have an amazing home," Olivia remarked. "I'm completely in love with it, and this area."

Louise beamed. "Well then, you'll have to get out of the kitchen while you're here and experience Door County fully—or our property, at the very least. We have horses and orchards, and cross-country skiing is a blast."

From beside her, Mac touched the small of her back. "Horses, Olivia."

"Yes, I heard. Very exciting," Olivia said, stepping away from him so her cheeks—and several other parts of her—wouldn't go up in flames from his touch.

Above them, a creaking sound echoed on the landing, and a few seconds later, Harold trotted down the stairs. He had a big grin on his face when he saw them. "Welcome, welcome," he said warmly, shaking Mac's hand, then Olivia's. "Good to have you both here."

"We're looking forward to the stay," Mac said. "Great place you have here."

Olivia shot him a look as Harold said, "Thank you."

"So, I suppose you both would you like to get settled before lunch?" Louise asked

"I'm a big unpacker," Olivia joked. "So, that would be great."

Harold looked at Louise, who looked at him with big eyes, then she turned to Mac and Olivia. "We wanted to have you stay in the house, but we're having the rooms fixed up for Harold's family, and of course they're very particular about what they want."

"Easy, honey," Harold said on a chuckle.

"Anyway, we have two small guest houses on the property, and we've had them made up for you."

"Guest houses?" Olivia said, feeling a little worried. Guest houses were a little like hotel suites. Staying in the house was far safer. "Are you sure we're not putting you out?"

Louise laughed as though this were the silliest idea she'd ever heard. "I'm going to get lunch ready. Not to torment you, but so you'll be able to see my skill level—or lack thereof—and Johnny, our groundskeeper, will take you across the pond to the guest houses."

Across the pond. Right.

Those guest houses had better be a good fifty yards away from each other, she mused as Harold called for Johnny over the intercom. It took no more than thirty seconds for the tall young man to show up, an easy smile on his thin face.

After thanking the DeBolds for their hospitality again, Mac and Olivia followed Johnny down a long flagstone path and around a small pond, which was tree-lined and frozen solid.

When Olivia saw the adjoining guest houses, her heart leaped into her throat. They were too close, only separated by a wall, for goodness' sake. But when they were ushered inside the first house, her heart sank. Decorated from top to bottom in luxurious whites and creams, soft rugs and warm lighting, Olivia knew she was in trouble. The large one-room suite screamed romance, from the small fir tree, which was dressed in white lights, to the massive stone fireplace, to the four-poster, king-sized bed with down pillows and terrycloth robe draped across the comforter, to the double whirl-pool tub not ten feet away.

Olivia put her hands on her hips and sighed. "Oh, yeah, they're trying to hook us up."

Beside her, Mac chuckled. "Want to come and see my room? Maybe it looks even more like a room at a bed-and-breakfast than yours does."

She didn't think that was possible, and she uttered, "Some other time."

"Promise?"

When she glanced up at him, saw the wicked gleam in his dark eyes and the curl of a smile on his extraordinarily handsome face, she felt her knees grow weak and knew it was only a matter of time before the rest of her followed suit. Because seriously, how much could a girl resist?

Fifteen

"I'm really sorry about lunch. I was trying to impress you, and I ended up almost killing you."

If someone were looking at Louise DeBold from the outside they'd see a confident, beautiful, sharp woman who owned every room she walked into and didn't need accolades from anyone to feel her value. But as she stood in front of Olivia, a semicooked turkey sitting on a platter of greens, she looked as though she'd shrunk in both stature and self-confidence.

Olivia took the platter from her and set it on the island. "You didn't know the turkey was undercooked."

"I would if I'd have cut into it."

Olivia laughed. "True."

Ripping off her apron, Louise sighed. "I think I might be hopeless."

"You're not."

"Harold's family is going to have a field day with this." She sat at the island. "I don't fail at things, Olivia, you know? I was an appraiser for ten years—the top gemologist in the country. Everyone came to me...." She stared at the turkey as though she'd just gone to war with it and had come back bruised and defeated. "I can't fail at this."

"You won't," Olivia assured her. "Now, get that apron back on and come over to the cutting board. We're going to try this again."

"All right."

"Poultry is a tricky thing," Olivia explained as she took another small bird out of the fridge and laid it in the sink. "I like to compare it to a relationship."

At this Louise perked up. "How so?"

"If it's not seasoned right or given enough heat, it will fail. Not to mention become boring and bland."

"Wow."

"That's right," Olivia said as she pulled out the bag of giblets and other delicious innards from inside the turkey. Then she washed it inside and out and patted it dry with paper towels.

"So," Louise began tentatively, "if I may be so bold as to ask, are you and Mac good poultry or bad poultry?"

Olivia took a second before answering to assess the warming feeling that had seeped into her belly. "We don't have a relationship."

"So, earlier on the porch…"

"Was a moment of insanity."

Louise sighed. "God, I love those."

Olivia laughed, she couldn't help herself. "Mac and me…it's complicated."

"Uncomplicate it, then—just like you're doing for me with this damn bird. Dress it, season it well, stick it in the oven on the right temp and baste, baste, baste."

Olivia pointed at her. "You've got this down, Louise."

"I like you, both of you," she said, seasoning the inside of the turkey with salt and pepper. "It would be fun to do this again."

"It would, but it might be a separate thing. While Mac is an amazing money man, he wants nothing to do with relationships."

"You never know, Liv." She paused, looked up. "Can I call you that?"

Olivia smiled. "Of course."

"Harold was a total player when we met," Louise said as she dug under the skin, loosening it from the breast.

"Really?"

"Uh-huh."

"I can't imagine it."

She stuffed the breast with sprigs of sage and thyme. "Well, it's true. Different chick every night. And look at him now." She slathered the top of the bird with butter. "Today, he brought home all this beautiful wood. He wants to build a baby crib, all by himself."

"Baby crib—are you…"

She smiled as she walked over to the sink to rinse her

hands. "My point is, you just never know what people are capable of until you give them the chance. Now, let's put this thing in the oven and get to work on the stuffing."

When Mac walked into the kitchen two hours later, Harold in his wake, the scent of Thanksgiving nearly bowled him over. He spotted Olivia at the sink with Louise, watching over the diamond queen as she carefully poured steaming boiled potatoes into a stainless mesh bowl. They looked very cozy, the two of them, almost like friends.

Harold elbowed him in the ribs and whispered, "I know it may be sexist, but look at our girls, wearing aprons and cooking their men some supper. Almost makes a guy want to grunt and scratch himself."

Chuckling softly, Mac said, "Almost." But he was hardly laughing inside. His reaction to Harold's comment worried him. *Our girls*—the phrase should've washed over him, meant nothing, hell, meant less than nothing. But the idea of Olivia belonging to him in any real, meaningful way made his heart ache strangely.

Now, as a kid he'd been put in and taken out of home after home until he was close to fourteen. Thanksgiving and family really hadn't meant anything sacred or special. So maybe it was that when he looked at Olivia with Louise in the kitchen, being all domestic and looking content—and with the smells of a happy home curling through his nostrils—it had triggered something. Something he might want at some point in his life.

At some point, but not now…

"I love this part," Louise was saying as she smashed the hot potatoes with something that looked like a branding iron. "Gets out all your aggressions."

They hadn't noticed Mac and Harold yet.

"Don't I know it." Laughing, Olivia poured the hot cranberry relish into a bowl. "The key to good cooking is to make simple food with really fresh ingredients."

"Something smells good in here," Harold said, walking past Mac and slipping his arms around his wife's waist as she continued to beat the potatoes into submission.

Glancing over her shoulder, Louise smiled. "Yes, a proper lunch. Even if it is two o'clock."

Mac looked over at Olivia. She was watching the happy couple, her eyes melancholy. Then she noticed him looking at her and offered him a gentle smile. Mac's body stirred. What would happen if he walked over and put his arms around her, kissed her neck as she stirred sugar into those plumped-up cranberries? Would she want to get lost in the fantasy that the DeBolds had created and were slowly but surely sucking them into?

"So, did you two have an interesting talk?" Louise asked Harold and Mac.

"Interesting doesn't begin to cover it," Harold said, releasing Louise from his grasp. "This guy is too damn smart. Why Avery didn't introduce us sooner, I'll never know. The amount we could've been saving in taxes…" He shook his head.

"So do we have a new financial advisor then?" Louise asked.

"It would seem that way."

Olivia glanced at Mac, gave him a tight-lipped smile. It could've been congratulatory or sad, he didn't have a clue.

"We'll have to give Avery a call," Louise said, "and have her draw up the papers."

Harold nodded. "Right."

Mac's jaw clenched at the mention of Avery. He hadn't spoken to either her or Tim since he'd tossed the latter out of his house the other night. He'd have to work out his relationship with Avery, but he was done with her husband. Mac glanced up and saw Olivia watching him, curious. He forced his mood to lighten and winked at her. Then he addressed Harold.

"Not so fast," he said, joking with Harold. "You know I'm only taking you on as a client if you can play a serious game of pool."

Harold raised his brows at his wife. "Can you spare me for a few hours after dinner?"

"You've been challenged, honey," she said. "I don't see how you can't go." She held up her bowl of potatoes. "But right now, you're going to sit at the table, eat the meal we've prepared and then promptly tell me what an amazing cook I am."

"Done." Harold growled, kissed her neck. "Then after lunch, I want you to lie down for a while, okay?"

"What about our guests?"

"We're fine." Olivia carried stuffing and cranberries to the long pine table. "I have a book and Mac always has work to—"

"No way," Louise said severely, her dark eyes narrowed. "Didn't you say you loved horses, Olivia?"

Mac took a basket of rolls from Olivia's hands and nodded before heading to the table. "Yes, she did."

"Perfect. The horses need some exercise." As if she had just solved an enormous problem, Louise smiled contently and they all sat down at the table and marveled at the delicious-looking pre-Thanksgiving feast. "A ride in the Door County snow is a must-do for every couple."

Olivia's head came up with a jerk. "Louise…"

"I meant, every*one*." But the giggle that followed completely and obviously negated her quick correction.

They weren't a couple, but as far as Olivia was concerned there was nothing more romantic than horseback riding through the snow with Mac, dipping under naked, brittle branches, galloping across an open field iced with white. For the first time since they'd arrived, Olivia understood what Mary had meant about the dangers of getting out of her element, her comfort zone, and hanging around with a guy she could see herself kissing until she was both sweaty and naked.

As she slowed her chestnut mare to a brisk walk, Olivia breathed in the cold air. She turned to look at Mac. He was like something out of the movie *Camelot,* in a modern wool coat and scarf, of course, but he had rugged, thick dark hair, and that one-with-the-horse thing going on, and she didn't even try and stop herself from imagining him sitting in front of her, her arms wrapped around his waist as they gave the mare some serious exercise.

The sky was starting to lose its afternoon warmth when Olivia stopped in the middle of a snowy field and took in the faded colors of the sunset. "Come on, Valentine, tell me this doesn't beat the Manhattan skyline by a mile."

His horse, a proud gray palomino, was a little frisky and Mac had to circle him around Olivia and her horse a few times to get him to calm down. "I don't know," he began. "What's so amazing? Fifty acres of trees, natural springs and killer views. I don't get it."

She laughed at his lighthearted sarcasm. "So, are you headed home tomorrow?"

"What?"

Their horses puffed out warm breath into the cold air. "You bagged the DeBolds. It's a done deal. Harold as much as said he was ready to sign on the *X* when we were at lunch."

"He was ready to sign back in Minneapolis."

"What?" Olivia said, confused, studying him.

A hint of a smile curved his lips. "Harold and Louise would've signed papers before they left Minneapolis if I had pushed for it."

"Then why didn't you?"

He chuckled. "C'mon, Liv. You know why I'm really here."

Catching the spark of challenge in his eyes, Olivia took a shivering breath. "You have a huge new client, and you said that one of your former clients has come back. Do you really still feel the need for payback?"

He regarded her with amused impatience. "I feel the need for you. The payback is just a bonus."

His unguarded, hungry look sent chills running through her body. Saying nothing, she turned her horse around and headed back toward the barn. With a click of his tongue, Mac spurred his horse forward to catch up with her.

When they were riding side by side again, he said, "I know you're as curious as I am."

"About what?"

"What my skin would feel like against yours."

"Mac…c'mon…"

But he wouldn't stop. "How long you could hold out before you begged me to kiss you somewhere other than your mouth. What it would feel like when I pushed inside of you, climaxed with you."

His words went straight to the core of her, and she swallowed against the tightness in her throat. She was in trouble here or she was about to allow herself a good time…she wasn't sure which. "I am curious, but I'd hoped I could hold out." She saw the gentle slope of the barn up ahead, looking like a wood-hewn salvation. She forced herself to look at him, into those dark, wicked eyes. "Honestly, I'm not so sure I can hold out—or want to anymore."

A flush that had nothing to do with the cold crossed his cheeks. "Well, that's an admission."

"Yeah."

They rode back to the barn in silence. Around them, the air swirled with new, fresh snow, and the sky grew gray as afternoon came to a close. Inside the stables, Johnny was nowhere in sight, and after climbing down and tying up his horse, Mac reached for Olivia, helping her off her horse and onto her feet.

"I'm going back to the room to take a shower before dinner," Olivia said quietly, trying to disentangle herself from his grasp.

But Mac held her firm.

She looked up at him. "What are you doing?"

"Holding you until you stop fighting."

Running on instinct, Olivia tried to push away from him, get free of the rousing feel of his body against hers. But it was no use. She growled her frustration. She wanted him. There was no more denying it, to herself or to him. Damn it, why should she have to deny herself? Sure it might be a mistake, he might be a mistake, but so what? She was old enough now to deal with her stupid choices.

She stared at his mouth, that full, hard mouth that could crush her with his words, yet make her want nothing more than to leave all past mistakes and promises in the dust. "What are you waiting for then?"

His hot gaze swept her, but he said nothing.

She laughed out of sheer insanity. "Kiss me, damn it!"

He laughed, too. But he quickly sobered, let his head fall forward against hers. "Olivia, understand that if I kiss you now, I'm not going to be able to stop."

"I don't want you to."

"And I want you more than I've ever wanted anything in my life." He pulled her against him and gave her a deep, all-consuming kiss on the mouth.

Olivia could barely breathe when he released her, grabbed her hand and uttered hoarsely, "Come with me."

Leaving the horses tied up, Mac led her down the center aisle of the stable, all the way to the end, then off to the right, down another corridor. When he spotted an empty stall, he pulled her inside and closed the door.

Clean, sweet-smelling hay blanketed the floor, but Olivia barely registered the fact as Mac pulled off her coat and took her in his arms. His kiss began soft and slow, light pressure on her lips as he swayed back and forth to music she couldn't hear. Then the pressure increased until she opened for him, gave him access to her tongue, until she murmured "so good" and other ridiculous utterances, until she wrapped her arms around his neck and kissed him back so intensely she felt as though she were drowning.

He left her mouth and dipped his head, nuzzling her neck, nibbling at the thin flesh over her pulse, making her blood race in her veins. It had been so long, and she couldn't wait to feel his skin on her skin, the weight of him as he pressed into her. Just the thought of having him inside her had her feeling weak and hot and wet.

Somehow Mac got Olivia onto her back, but the change of position barely registered. All she knew was that one moment she was standing, and the next, her body was cradled in a soft nest of hay.

"What if someone comes…?" she uttered breathlessly. "Sees us…"

Positioned above her, Mac unbuttoned her shirt. "I don't give a damn if anyone sees us."

She refused to recall the last time someone had seen

her with a man. This was different. This was right now. It was almost as if she needed to do this—this way—and she felt no shame in her actions.

His hands found her belly, and she sucked air between her teeth at the sheer pleasure of him touching her naked skin, so close to the center of her, where she ached. She wanted him to just get to it, send his hand lower and put her out of her misery. Hell, she was already so worked up it would only take ten seconds—maybe less.

But Mac wasn't going there, not yet.

She wore a bra that clasped in the front and he easily took care of it, casting aside the two pale pink wisps of fabric. The fading light of afternoon filtered through the small square window above them, and Mac looked down at her and shook his head. "You have no idea…"

"What?"

"How long I've wanted to see you like this, and touch you. And now, I feel like I should take time to just…marvel."

She laughed, but it was almost a pained sound. "You do and I'll kill you."

He gave a quick, husky laugh, then bent his head and dragged his mouth over one of her breasts, then the other, applying soft, irritatingly slow kisses over the skin around her nipple.

Feeling as though she was about to explode, Olivia reached up and threaded her fingers in his hair, tried to pull him down.

"Patience, Liv," he whispered, the heat of his breath sending sparks to every nerve ending.

Olivia waited, the muscles in her legs contracting, her toes pointing until finally she felt him, felt that electrifying sensation of hot, wet tongue against her hard, sensitive nipple. Her breath came out in a rush and she thrust her hips in the air. Sensing the urgency in her body, Mac lapped at the hard peak, finding a rhythm, groaning when he heard her moan as his free hand moved down…down her belly, over her hips and under the slip of cotton.

"No," he uttered hoarsely, his fingers burrowing between her thighs. "Olivia, you're too hot, and way too wet. I don't know how long I can wait."

"And you wanted me to be patient," she uttered.

He found the entrance to her body and thrust his middle finger inside of her. It was too much. She sucked in air, shivered and bucked against his hand. She almost didn't know what to do. Her hands fisted hay, and the way he was moving inside her, pressing against that deep, sensitive part of her, she felt tears drop onto her cheeks, down to her neck.

"What is it?" he whispered, concerned. "Does this hurt?"

"No," she uttered. "No. It's wonderful."

He kissed her cheek, her lips, her neck.

"Make love to me, Mac. Please. Now." She couldn't control her body and all she wanted was him, inside of her. She clawed at his shirt, tore a few buttons and unhooked the others, then pulled it off of his chest. He was so beautiful, the way the thick muscles of his chest rose and fell with each breath he took. With greedy hands, she found his zipper and tugged.

"Olivia, wait."

She shook her head, annoyed. "No. For what?"

"I don't have anything—not here."

"No...." Her heart sank, and her mind raced for a solution. "Can't you just let me feel you, for a moment?"

"I think I only have a moment in me," he said hoarsely. "But I'll protect you, if you want that."

She nodded, wriggling out of her jeans and underwear, not giving a damn about the risks. Mac, too, pulled off his remaining clothes and wasted no time, slipping his hands under her, lifting her hips and burying himself deep inside her.

Olivia saw stars, actually saw them on the back of her closed lids. For just a moment, she let the delicious feeling of Mac inside her wash over her, then as he began to pull out, she woke up from her daydream. She gripped his hips as he thrust back inside of her, opened her legs and wrapped them around his waist, rocked with him, moaning, scratching at him, knowing she had little time left and feeling simultaneously frustrated and desperate for release.

Then Mac leaned down, caught one hard nipple between his lips and suckled deeply. She lost it. Pumping furiously, she gave in to the fire and ice of her climax, crying out, whimpering as Mac bucked and thrust inside her, the sweet feeling rolling through her.

On a curse, Mac pulled out and hovered above her.

Hardly a second elapsed before Olivia reached for him, wrapped her hand around him and stroked the thick, pulsing length of him until he sucked in air, thrust against her hand and climaxed.

He dropped down beside her on the hay, breathing heavily, his brow damp, and wrapped his arms around her. They lay there in silence, both breathing heavily, both damp with sweat, watching the last lights of day fade into the early gray of evening.

Olivia wanted to stay with him, keep him against her, but she didn't know where they stood now and that made her feel uncomfortable, as though she wanted to steal away by herself and think things through. "I want to stay," she began. "But I need to help with dinner."

"I know. Listen, Olivia." In one quick, effortless movement, he rolled her on top of him and cupped her backside possessively. His eyes blazed with a sincerity she'd never witnessed before. "You have nothing to worry about from me."

Her throat tightened with emotion as she looked down at him. "Oh, I think I have a lot to worry about with you. Just not in the way that you mean."

Chuckling, he squeezed her backside. "You might be right about that." He leaned in and kissed her gently on the mouth. "To speak in your language, sweetheart, this was just an appetizer. And I fully intend to enjoy the next course and the next and the next...."

Sixteen

Men didn't normally notice table settings or flower arrangements. They were usually hungry when they sat for dinner and just wanted to fill their bellies with whatever it was that smelled so damn good.

Sounded cavemanish, but it was true.

Mac was no exception as he sat beside Olivia at the DeBolds' dinner table, his plate piled high with fettuccine Alfredo and garlic bread. He was perfectly content at that moment. "You should be very proud of yourself, Louise. This is amazing."

Across the table, Louise looked at her husband and grinned. "Thanks, but I think my teacher should get all the credit."

"No way," Olivia retorted, twirling pasta on her fork. "You did this all by yourself. I just supervised."

Harold put an arm around his wife. "All by yourself, honey?"

"She's exaggerating."

"I am not!" Olivia insisted, laughing.

Just hearing Olivia's voice made Mac's body stir and he turned and stared at her. Dressed in a pair of funky black pants and a white sweater, she looked like a sexy ski bunny. He had every intention of being with her again tonight. As he'd said, their encounter in the barn was like a warm-up for the real thing. They'd both been too worked up, unable to take their time and really enjoy each other. Tonight, however, he was going to make her climax over and over again.

Olivia was talking to Harold, her eyes bright and happy. "And she rolled out the pasta herself."

"You did?" Harold said to Louise.

Blushing, she confirmed it. "I did."

Harold kissed her cheek, then said, "We have a pasta machine?"

Louise laughed. "Yes. Who knew, right?"

In between bites of pasta, Olivia said, "Tomorrow morning, we'll work on a few breakfast dishes that will have your in-laws apologizing for ever doubting your culinary skills." She grinned widely. "Think crab cakes benedict with lemon and parsley hollandaise, eggnog French toast and pancetta—"

"Forget apologizing," Harold interrupted merrily.

"They'll want to stay here all the time with that kind of menu."

Louise blanched. "Hmm, maybe we'd better rethink the cooking thing."

Everyone laughed, then Harold said, "Too late, honey—they're going to want to be here more often anyway when…you know."

Mac watched all three of them grin and wondered what was up, what he was missing. "Are you three going to let me in on the joke?"

"No joke," Harold said, looking at his wife in a soft, sweet way. "Louise is pregnant."

"Wow, congratulations," Mac said, reaching across the table to shake Harold's hand.

The proud father-to-be actually blushed. "Thank you."

"Do you really think your family will want to be around more?" Louise asked, a worried expression crossing her face.

"Not my family," Harold clarified. "My mother."

"Oh, Lord."

"She'll be ecstatic, sweetheart."

"She'll be meddlesome."

Finished with her pasta, Olivia dabbed her mouth with her napkin. "Well, she'll be here, and from a girl who hopes to have a child someday and has no mother to get frustrated and annoyed with for visiting too often, I say, 'you're lucky.'"

The news that Olivia's mother was not in the picture didn't come as a shock to Mac. When he was gathering information on Olivia and her father, he'd seen the obituary. But hearing her talk about it, the trace of sadness in her voice, did something to him, made him feel protective. He knew what it felt like to lose a parent, and he didn't enjoy seeing her upset.

Louise was smiling sympathetically at Olivia. "I'm sorry. I had no idea. When did you lose your mother?"

"In high school."

Mac didn't know what made him do it, but he put his hand over hers under the table. It felt good, right.

"That's awful." Shaking her head, Louise looked over to her husband. "No matter how insane your mother makes me, I'm going to grin and bear it for this little one."

Harold downed the last bite of his garlic bread. "Glad to hear it, sweetheart." He turned and winked at Olivia, who smiled in return.

As the foursome chatted and ate, Olivia did the strangest and most enchanting thing. She rotated her hand under his so that they were palm to palm, and every once in a while she gave him a gentle squeeze.

Olivia pierced a freshly made popcorn kernel with a needle and pulled the yellow fluffy bit onto the string until it met with its cranberry neighbor. As the stereo belted out Judy Garland's version of "Have Yourself a Merry Little Christmas" and the fire crackled and spit, she sat on a thick, oval rug in front of the tree, trying to teach Mac how to make garland for the little Christmas tree in her suite. It wasn't easy. The guy was a financial genius and one helluva kisser, but when it came to a needle and thread, he was all thumbs.

Mac crushed the popcorn kernel as he stuck the needle into it. Cursing, he tossed the remaining bits into the fire. "This is BS."

Olivia laughed. "Come on. No swearing when Judy Garland is singing."

"Why not? I feel sad and it's a sad song."

"It's not a sad song," she corrected. "It's an emotional song."

"Same thing."

She settled back against the base of the chenille chaise and sighed. "This was kind of me and my mom's song."

He looked at her as though she'd just stuck her needle in his side. "Okay, you can't go there when we were joking around, it makes me look like a jerk."

She smiled. "You're not a jerk." Realizing what she'd just said, she made a face, then laughed. "I can't believe I'm saying that."

He raised a sardonic eyebrow at her. "You're very funny when you're melancholy."

"My mom loved a good laugh, so she'd appreciate the dark humor in this conversation."

"When did she pass away? I know you said something at dinner...."

"When I was in high school." It was amazing that the words were still so difficult to say, and Olivia felt the urge to leap up on the bed and burrow under the covers.

"So, you were...what? Sixteen?"

"Yep."

"That's tough on a teenage girl. Mom's gone and

Dad is…" He paused, cocked his head to the side. "Dad is what?"

The direction of this conversation was starting to worry her. Mac was a sharp guy and he was putting the pieces together as he watched her. Sixteen, mom's gone, girl looks for comfort… "Dad was devastated—understandably—and he couldn't manage to do much but breathe." He was staring at her, studying her. "What?"

"Owen left you to fend for yourself, didn't he?"

Her jaw tightened. "No. He was grieving."

"So were you, Olivia."

She looked away, into the fire, her throat feeling that all too familiar tightness. She didn't want him, of all people, pointing out that her father had emotionally abandoned her for a time. It wasn't his place.

"How did you grieve, Liv? How did you manage all by yourself?"

"I wasn't by myself, damn it!" she shouted hoarsely. Fine, he got it. She hadn't been alone—she hadn't allowed herself to be alone. She'd found a substitute for the missing affection from her father, and a way to push back the pain. She grabbed her garland and a cranberry. "I went a little crazy for that first year and a half. But I got back on track, okay?"

He nodded. "Okay."

"I don't want to talk about this anymore."

"Done." He gestured to the bowl. "Can I have some more of that popcorn?"

He granted her a soft smile, and she felt the tension in her muscles relax. She let her shoulders fall and she released the breath she'd been holding since their conversation had begun. "Here you go," she said, handing him the bowl.

"I'm going to try this again."

She watched him stab at the popcorn, one piece, then two, then three. She shook her head and took away the bowl of popcorn before he crushed every piece to bits. "I'm thinking that this activity might be a little too sweet for a guy like you."

"Damn right it is," he said, reaching for a cranberry instead. "But I figure the sooner we finish decorating this tree the sooner I can kiss you."

She laughed. "Smart man. So, did you do any of this kind of thing around Christmas when you were a kid?"

"Nope. Not until I was fourteen, anyway."

"What happened when you were fourteen?"

"I was taken in by a college professor and his wife. They weren't the home-and-hearth type, but we had nice, relaxed holidays."

"Not the home-and-hearth type…"

He'd strung five cranberries on the string and looked quite proud of himself. "What I mean is they weren't the kind of parents who baked pies, sang me to sleep or tried to give me advice about girls. But I didn't mind that—I'd had enough of people trying to make me into something I didn't want to be. These people were teachers, question askers, and they made me think. They inspired me to work my ass off. They were the reason I ended up going to Harvard."

Interesting, Olivia thought. It explained so much

about him. Why his whole life was his work—and why he'd do anything to protect it. "Did they end up adopting you?"

He shrugged. "In their way. I lived with them until I was twenty-one."

"Are they still around?"

He shook his head. "She died a year after he died."

"I'm sorry," she said softly. "It must be hard to be alone."

He stabbed another red cranberry, then glanced up at her through his thick lashes. "I'm not alone right now."

She'd never met a man like this one, never been so affected by anyone. In a matter of a few minutes he had her feeling sad, frustrated, unsure, angry, protective and now, aroused. "Does growing up the way you did make you want kids, or not?"

There was no flash of revulsion or even dislike for the idea in his gaze, only a look of frank sincerity. "I can't imagine being able to love anyone that much. I don't think I'm capable of it—you need to see love from a very early age to be able to learn how to give it."

It surprised her that he'd given the idea so much thought. "It helps, probably, but I don't think it's a necessity. I think love can be learned, just like history or reading."

"Or chemistry?" he offered, amusement dancing in his eyes.

She nodded. "Exactly." Then she leaned in and kissed him on the mouth. A soft kiss at first, coaxing him to open for her, taste her. And when he did, she sighed. He'd eaten some of the popcorn when she hadn't been looking because his lips were slightly and deliciously salty. "I'm not going to wait for you to finish your garland."

"Sweetheart," he uttered huskily, "I was about to throw the whole damn tree out the window."

The tip of his tongue ran across her lips in one silken stroke and she smiled, touched his face with one hand. He had the slight scratch of a day's worth of beard, and the rough feeling acted like a drug on her. She angled her head and kissed him hard, reveling in the wounded, turned-on sound he made as he returned her kiss, then nipped at her bottom lip.

"I've come prepared tonight, Ms. Winston," he said, his eyes blazing with hunger.

"I hope you've come doubly, maybe even triply, prepared."

A hoarse chuckle escaped his throat. "I'm glad we're on the same page because there's no way I'm letting you out of my bed before sunup."

He was just about to kiss her again when there was a soft knock at the door. Mac cursed brutally. "I might have to kill the person on the other side of that door."

He pushed to his feet, stalked to the door and flung it wide. Johnny. He looked embarrassed.

"I'm sorry to bother you, sir," he said, then caught sight of Olivia. "And you, Miss Winston—but Mr. DeBold needs to speak with Mr. Valentine immediately."

When Mac first arrived and saw Harold DeBold sitting on the couch in his living room having a beer, he wasn't sure what the man wanted to see him about. Maybe he was freaked out about becoming a dad and wanted to talk about it, or about Louise. Or maybe he wanted their financial plans to change immediately to include the child.

Then Mac noticed another beer on the coffee table, opened, sweat beading on the bottle, and for the first time since he'd met the DeBolds his confidence in having them as clients waned.

Harold gestured for Mac to sit. "I apologize for interrupting your evening."

Mac wasn't up for pleasantries—not tonight. "What's this about?"

"I didn't know Olivia's father was Owen Winston."

Mac frowned.

"He's a legend in the financial world," Harold continued.

Mac didn't like where this was going. He stared at Harold steadily. "Is there a point to this?"

Sensing Mac's irritation, Harold pointed to the bottle on the coffee table. "How about a drink? It's a great little microbrew from—"

"Harold," Mac interrupted tightly, "with all due respect, I don't want a goddamn thing except to know where you're going with this Owen Winston thing."

Harold grinned at that, then nodded. "I just got off the phone with him, Mac."

"You called him?"

"No. He called me."

"Looking for his daughter?"

"He wanted to warn me about you." Harold took a heavy swallow of beer. "But he also doesn't like that you're here with his daughter, that's for sure."

Mac grabbed the bottle of beer from the table and drained it. Then he stood. "Thank you for your time, Harold."

"You know, it was ballsy of you to hire her."

Mac shrugged. "It was calculated."

"Okay, then it was ballsy of her to take the job."

Ballsy…? Maybe the better word was unethical. Strange. Olivia had called him immoral once, but he'd never broken his client's trust—not like she just had. "I assume we're done here?"

"Of course. I don't want to keep you. But, Mac…" Harold stood, regarded him seriously. "I don't believe in rumors or the pissed-off ramblings of a jealous rival. I go on what I see. You have our business." He shrugged. "I just thought you should know."

Mac should have been thrilled—or hell, satisfied—but all he felt was the urge to shove his fist through a wall.

"Thank you, Harold." Mac shook his hand, then walked out of the room and out of the house.

Outside, the bitter wind slammed him in the face, small bits of snow pelting him from all sides. But he hardly felt it. From day one, he had been out to screw Olivia Winston, both physically and emotionally, and had ended up being screwed himself.

He spied her cottage, the lights of the Christmas tree inside glowing through the large bay window. She was a sly one, he had to give her that. But her little betrayal was going to pale in comparison with what he had planned for her next.

Seventeen

Olivia had little practice at seduction. She'd never been to a Victoria's Secret store or trolled the bookstores looking for the most recent printing of *How to Please a Man*. Instead, she was relying on the good old-fashioned art of being naked on a bed to get Mac right where she wanted him. And that would be on top of her…

On the other side of the room, the fire blazed in the hearth, warming the room and subsequently her skin. She was a little nervous. This was major exposure, total vulnerability, every flaw out there to be judged and inspected. For a moment, she contemplated greeting Mac from under the covers, but decided against it.

The door opened and Mac walked in, bringing a blast of frigid air with him. He was back so soon. Must've been nothing all that important with Harold, she thought, just guy talk. She shifted on the bed so she was lying sideways like one of those women in a Botticelli painting. Then he looked up and saw her. When he realized that she was nude, a flush of heat rolled up his neck. In one easy movement, he closed the door, then went to the edge of the bed.

Olivia's heart beat strongly in her chest. "Everything good?"

He nodded, his eyes dark and intense as he stared down at her. "Perfect." He unbuttoned his shirt and removed his pants. "Exactly what I was hoping for."

Anxious excitement played in Olivia's belly as Mac crawled toward her like an animal at feeding time. When he had her in his arms, he paused for a moment and just looked at her, her skin, her breasts. Then he leaned forward and took one soft peak into his mouth.

Olivia sucked air between her teeth and melted back onto the bed. This was what she'd wanted, what she'd hoped for tonight. She couldn't wait to have him inside of her. She closed her eyes and reveled in the feel of Mac on top of her. His skin, the way his muscles flexed and hardened as he moved down her body, planting kisses on her ribs, then her belly.

As he moved downward, Olivia smiled. She knew where he was going and she reached for his hair, fisted his scalp. His head dropped between her thighs. She felt his hands between her legs, pressing them apart, his fingers raking up her skin, opening the hot, wet folds. Her rational mind fell apart, and all that was left in her brain was the place that registered pleasure. And then he was licking her, soft, quick laps that had her legs trembling with excitement. Her fingers gripped his hair as he continued suckling her, as she bucked against his mouth. She could barely hold on. The feeling was too strong, too intense.

"Oh, Mac…I'm going to…"

He must've heard the desperation in her voice, knew she was on the brink of climax, because he lifted off of her, grabbed the foil packet that had been in his jeans and sheathed himself.

He entered her with one hard thrust. Olivia cried out, her body wracked with heat and energy as she took him fully. He slipped his hands under her hips and squeezed her closer, then pulled out and slammed back into her again. Olivia felt the initial thunder of climax coming over her and her body reacted. She bucked under him, her hands searching for his chest, her nails digging into the flesh over his muscle.

He bent his head, covered her mouth with his in a deep, all-consuming kiss. Olivia started to whimper, the core of her shaking and pulsing until her body could no longer contain the hot, decadent energy inside and she erupted. Her head dropped to one side, then the other as she cried out in several painful-sounding screams that seemed to rip right through Mac.

He pounded into her, over and over, until she thought he might rip her apart. But when she straightened her legs and spread them wide, he stiffened, groaned and thrust deeply inside of her, bucking, pounding, until he gave in and took his own release.

In the moments afterward, Mac stayed on top of her, his hips flexing and shuddering with the aftermath of release. But as soon as her arms went around his neck and threaded into his hair, Mac pulled himself away and off the bed.

Olivia stared after him, her body still achy and warm from his touch. "What's wrong?"

He sat there, his back to her. Then from deep in his chest, he started laughing. It was not a pleasant, happy sound, but dark and ominous.

"What?" Olivia asked softly.

Mac glanced over his shoulder, his gaze eerily satisfied. "I had no idea you were as ruthless as me."

A waft of cold air moved through her. "What are you talking about?"

"I have to say I'm impressed."

"Impressed with what?" He didn't look like himself. He was dark and sad, and Olivia suddenly felt very naked. Covering herself with a throw, Olivia asked, "What is wrong with you?"

"During my drink with Harold he informed me that he had just gotten off the phone with your father."

Olivia's heart sank. "No...."

"To warn him about me."

Olivia swallowed hard.

Mac stood and threw his shirt on. "I wonder how he knew I was with the DeBolds."

This was not happening, Olivia thought with deep

frustration and disappointment. How could she have made such a mistake? How could her father be such an ass? "I'm sorry. I told him where I was going, but—"

"And that I was going, too, right?"

"Yes, but—"

"I remember you calling me immoral...."

"Mac, I know you're angry and I get why. And I don't blame you. But if you look at the situation for what it is, I did nothing wrong here."

He put his pants on. "Really. How do you figure that?"

She came up on her knees, the throw pressed to her chest. "We're not working together on this trip. Our job ended when I left your house. I'm working for Louise, and I had every right to tell my father where I was."

"Where you are, yes. Not where I am." He put on his coat. "Good thing Harold and Louise don't believe lies spread by tired, envious, unscrupulous old men."

"Stop that." She hated what he was saying because now she was starting to believe it was true.

Dressed and ready to walk out, Mac paused and looked at her. His gaze was filled with disrespect. "I believe we're even, don't you?"

"*We're* even?" she repeated. "Who are you referring to, Mac? Me and you? Or you and my father."

His lips thinned dangerously, then he shrugged as if he couldn't care less. "Take your pick."

"Well, you did nothing to me," she said tightly. "I'm not hurt or humiliated. You wanted me and I wanted you. I'm done obsessing about my past, about mistakes I've made. I enjoyed every moment of us."

For one second—just a split second—his eyes softened. Then the walls closed once again and he uttered a terse, "Well, perhaps that's where the revenge lies then. There's no more *us* to enjoy."

He closed the door behind him, and Olivia just stared after him. An hour ago, that door had been the heaven's gate her lover had walked through. Now, it represented the enormous barrier between them.

She dropped back onto the bed. She had told him the truth. She felt no shame in the choices that she'd made. She had wanted Mac as much as he had wanted her, and though they were never going to be together this way again, she had no regrets for making love to him one last time.

Because, no matter how much he despised her now, she felt sure of one thing—that's what it had been for her.

Love.

Eighteen

Morning-afters were usually filled with headaches or heartaches. Olivia's was filled with both. She had struggled to get through the two-hour breakfast lesson with Louise, overcooking the hollandaise, then dropping the pan to the floor when the woman had mentioned that Mac had indeed left late last night—on his own plane, of course.

If she were a more carefree woman, Olivia mused, stepping out of the DeBolds' limousine and gathering up her bags, she'd just chock the whole thing up to a great fling, and the reason she had finally let go of her shame about the past. Mac had made her feel good—nothing wrong with that. She was an adult now, and she deserved pleasure, even if the man giving it would never love her back.

"Have a safe flight, Olivia," Louise said, waving from the window of the limousine.

Olivia shouldered her bag, then waved back. "Thanks for everything."

"No—thank you. I'll let you know what happens on Thanksgiving."

Her evil smile made Olivia laugh. "Give 'em, hell, Louise."

The woman smiled and waved again, then rolled up the window and the car pulled away. Olivia walked toward the plane and boarded. As she sat in her leather bucket seat waiting for takeoff, she thought about herself and Mac and their backgrounds, and how their pasts had totally dictated their present. He'd been abandoned, and had learned to survive in the only way he could. And he had survived—he'd gone to the top of his profession. She'd been abandoned, too, but unlike him, she hadn't fought—instead, she'd refused to deal with her pain and had looked for help in the wrong place.

So she understood his anger, and the fear behind it.

She fell asleep thinking about him, and woke up in Minneapolis with a neck cramp and a small twinge of hope that maybe she'd see him again. She got her car from long-term parking and drove home. For the first time in a long time, her apartment felt warm and safe, and for the rest of the night, she ignored the blinking light on her answering machine and settled under her comforter to watch *Bridget Jones's Diary*.

Tomorrow was a huge day. She had menus to execute

and staff to boss around. Ethan and Mary's holiday engagement ball had been in the works for weeks, but it
was the last thing Olivia wanted to think about. Cele-
brating her friend's happiness was a must-do, of course,
and she'd never shirk her duty, but because of who
Ethan was, the event was going to be a blowout. The
whole of Minneapolis was going to be there, and she
couldn't help wondering if maybe that meant a certain
financial genius was going to show up....

Olivia pulled the covers up to her chin, aimed the
remote at the TV and pushed Play.

Ah...Colin Firth.

Mac's lungs were about to explode, and his legs felt
shaky, but he didn't stop running.

It was coming up on 5:00 a.m. and he'd been in the
gym of his office building on the treadmill for over an
hour, trying to get his brain to shut down. Unfortunately,
it looked as though his body was going to go first.

He stabbed the off button on the machine and reached
for his towel. Damn it, he thought, walking unsteadily
to his private locker room. When he'd left Door County
two days ago, he'd counted on the fact that he wouldn't
have to see Olivia Winston for months.

It wouldn't be nearly that long.

Mac hated tuxedos about as much as he hated over-
the-top parties, but he was a slave to business, and after
learning that one of his former clients was going to be
at Ethan Curtis's engagement party tonight, he'd recon-
sidered the invite. Ethan Curtis was marrying Mary

Kelley, Olivia's business partner, so she was definitely going to be there.

He'd broken things off with many women in his time, and had never given a second thought to seeing them again. It was just this woman—she made him feel like a weak animal, a constantly hungry animal. He had to get her out of his system.

He stripped and headed for the shower. Maybe the best way to get Olivia out of his head was to force himself to see her again, be reminded of her betrayal. Or maybe he was just kidding himself and tonight was going to be just as hellish as the past two nights had been.

The top floor of the world-famous building rotated at the pace of one revolution per hour—that way the guests who were partaking in food and drink wouldn't get dizzy and lose their lunches in the first five minutes.

A wise plan by the architect, Olivia mused as she left the kitchen after inspecting each and every serving platter before it went out. She spotted Mary talking to Tess by the window and headed their way. Her blond hair piled on top of her head, Mary was wearing an off-the-shoulder gray silk dress, her protruding belly stretching the material in a lovely, earthy way. And looking especially glamorous in a brick-red minidress and matching heels, her red hair loose and blown straight, was Tess. Olivia watched as No Ring Required's resident hard-ass reached out and touched Mary's stomach, her smoky eyes shining with warmth.

"Well, well, well," Mary said when Olivia approached, her gaze running over Olivia's strapless chocolate-brown pencil dress. "Can I say it again, Miss Winston? You look hot."

Tess snorted. "That word should not be coming out of a pregnant woman's mouth."

Laughing, Mary remarked, "How do you think I got this way in the first place?"

Pretending to cover her ears, Tess said, "Okay, too much information."

Feeling self-conscious for a moment, Olivia smoothed the fabric of her skirt and glanced around at the party, which was packed and in full swing. She'd dressed carefully for Mary's engagement party. After all, she was wearing two hats—guest and worker—so she had needed to find the right combo. And then there was the not insignificant fact that Mac might be coming. She wasn't going to lie to herself and pretend that seeing him hadn't affected her choice in wardrobe.

"Did you see your father yet?" Tess asked, pulling her from her thoughts.

Olivia shook her head. "Where is he?"

"Over at the bar."

Olivia had been trying to get hold of her father for the past two days, but he'd been in Boston on business and hadn't returned her calls.

"So," Mary said cozily, "before Ethan steals me away, are you going to tell us how Door County went?"

"No."

Tess lifted a brow at Olivia's succinct reply. "Uh-oh."

"Was I right?" Mary asked gently. "About going out

of town together? Did you two…hmm, how to put this delicately…"

"Forget delicately," Tess interrupted. "Did you get busy with the guy?"

Olivia felt red all over. "C'mon, Tess. Jeez."

Tess gave Mary a look. "That's a yes."

"Tess," Mary said, warning in her gaze, "I hope you've learned from this—never go out of town with a guy you find attractive."

"Please…he'd have to slip something in my double espresso and carry me off for that to happen, and God help him if he did that." Tess was looking around the room as she spoke, and in a matter of seconds her whole demeanor changed. Her skin went white as milk and she stared, fixated on something.

Both Mary and Olivia saw the change and turned to see what was affecting Tess in such a way, but in the sea of people, they couldn't tell who or what was the cause.

"What's wrong, Tess?" Olivia asked.

"I swear I just saw…someone I knew a long time ago."

"Old boyfriend?"

"I suppose you could call him that. He looks so different—it can't be him."

Mary attempted to lighten the mood. "Did he look better or worse?"

"He looked bored and aloof, and utterly gorgeous." She kept searching the crowd. "It can't be him." She turned back to them, color returning to her cheeks. "Seeing people from the past is an awkward thing."

It was all she said, but Olivia knew it had to be more

than feeling awkward. Tess had actually looked panic-stricken. But Olivia didn't get to inquire further because at that moment Ethan walked over to them and slipped his arm around Mary's growing waist. "Can I take my girl? There's a coat check up front calling our name."

Mary rolled her eyes. "You are such an exhibition-ist, Ethan."

"It's one of the reasons you love me, right?"

She smiled at Olivia and Tess, then kissed her soon-to-be husband. "Of course, honey."

When they'd walked away, indeed toward the coat check, Tess quickly excused herself, too, saying that she was going to see about something.

Then, Olivia spotted her father speaking to two men by the bar and she headed his way.

Standing near the jazz band, Mac watched Olivia dance with her father. She looked beautiful tonight, and even though he'd tried to put her out of his mind, his body remembered everything. Clearly, it was going to take a helluva lot of time and effort to forget her.

She caught his eye then, and blanched. She hadn't expected him, and she looked both hopeful and worried. His hands itched to touch her, kiss her. If he had any pride, any sense, he'd walk away from the situation and never look back. But he was an idiot.

Pushing away from the stage, he walked toward her just as the song was ending.

Owen spotted him, too, and gritted his teeth as Mac walked up. "What are you doing here?"

"Retrieving an old client," Mac said easily.

"Oh, yes, I saw you talking with Martin Pollack. I suppose he's willing to overlook your—"

"Stop, Owen. This story of yours is growing so old there's mold on it. Everyone knows you lied, they're just waiting for you to admit it."

"I'm not admitting anything."

"Suit yourself. I don't give a damn anymore." He looked at Olivia. "You look beautiful tonight."

"Thank you." Her eyes glittered with warmth, and something else…something he couldn't quite name.

"Are you having a good time?"

"Not really."

Owen stared at her. "Let's go, Olivia."

But Olivia wouldn't take her eyes off of Mac. "It's okay."

Mac was confused. "What is?"

"If you need to do it, I understand. You have me and my father here."

"What are you talking about?"

She smiled, a little sadly. "The great revenge. What it's all been for."

"Oh, Liv…" Mac shook his head. She didn't get it. She thought when he'd walked out the other night he was still bent on payback. She didn't understand that what she'd done had pissed him off as a man—not a businessman.

"What did you do to my daughter?" Owen said menacingly.

"Dad, that's enough," Olivia said.

But Owen wasn't listening. "If you hurt her—"

"I'm serious, Dad. You've caused enough trouble." Olivia glared at her father. "One more word about Mac, and our relationship will be irrevocably damaged. Do you understand me?"

Owen looked shocked. "Olivia."

A surge of need moved through Mac. It was so powerful it took him completely by surprise, and he reached for Olivia's hand and lifted it to his mouth. After he kissed the palm, he spoke to Owen, but he looked into Olivia's chocolate eyes. "You have an amazing daughter, Winston. Beautiful and brilliant. I tried like hell to make her pay for your mistakes, but she'd have nothing to do with me."

Owen said nothing.

Mac released Olivia's hand. Revenge was a useless thing. He was done. He nodded at Olivia, said goodnight and walked away.

Nineteen

The party wasn't supposed to end until midnight, but Olivia just couldn't stay any longer. She asked Tess to cover for her, then grabbed her coat and headed for the elevator. Just as the doors were about to close, her father slipped inside.

"Dad, I said good night to you…." She knew she sounded peevish, but she didn't care. She wanted one thing right now and any interruptions were unwelcome ones.

"Sweetheart, I just had to tell you that I'm so proud of you."

"For what?" she asked impatiently.

"Keeping that snake away from you."

That was it. Olivia reached out and pulled the emergency stop button. The elevator came to a jolting stop, and her father looked at her like she was crazy.

"What's going on?"

"I love you, Dad, but I'm not doing this any longer. Get this straight, I'm not Grace—"

"What?"

"I'm not your sister. I'm not Grace. Her life is not mine." She looked at him, her gaze serious. "What I am is a grown woman who is not going to cater to her father's fears about a life he can't control."

Owen's neck reddened. "Olivia…"

"My personal life is my own. Period." Owen looked very stuffy in his tuxedo, very impervious, but she went on. "Now, about Mac. You're going to leave him alone. Bottom line is, I love the guy, and if we can both get past how we met and why we were brought together, I think there might be a future in it for us."

Her father looked horrified. "No…."

She took a breath and softened at the look of despair on his face. "What do you have against him, other than the fact that he wanted to punish you for lying to his clients?"

For a second, Owen looked as though he was going to deny it, then he dropped his gaze and stared at his shoes. "Getting old isn't graceful or easy. People treat you like you might break, like you can't take the heat—they think your mind isn't what it used to be."

Olivia touched his arm. She loved her father—even with all his faults, and there were many. She rolled up on her toes and kissed him on the cheek. "Do the right thing, Dad. You're a great money man, a legend—everyone thinks so. Just be that for as long as you can." She reached out and flipped down the emergency stop button. The elevator descended. "The truth will come out eventually. Don't make this foolish mistake be your legacy. Take care of it."

Owen was silent for a moment, then he nodded.

The doors opened to the lobby and Olivia stepped out. "I have somewhere I need to be. Good night, Dad."

He gave her a tight smile and uttered a soft, "Good night, Olivia," before the elevator doors closed again.

When Mac walked into his house an hour later, he felt like he didn't belong there. Every piece of furniture, every color on the walls, had been picked out by her. Why was it then that she herself wasn't here? Olivia belonged here, she belonged to him.

"Damn it," he muttered, going down the hall to his room. He was going to take a shower, then head over to Olivia's apartment. He was so tired of fighting for the stupid, inconsequential things in his life. He was going to fight for something real now. He was going to make her talk to him.

"I'm trying this again."

Instinctively, Mac prepared himself for a fight. Then the voice registered in his brain and he let it fall to the side as he looked up. There on his bed, lying back against his pillow, was Olivia. She was fully dressed, her dark hair tousled and loose, and she had a worried smile on her lips.

Mac stared at her. "How did you get in here?"

She held his gaze steady with hers. "I still have the key. You forgot to ask for it back."

He shook his head slowly. "I didn't forget."

The expression in her eyes turned hopeful and she said, "Mac, about tonight…and the DeBolds…"

He cut her off. "No."

But she was insistent. "Yes. I need to say this to you again." She pushed off the bed and walked over to him, stood before him. "I didn't think. I shouldn't have said a word about where I was. It was bad business, and I've learned from it. You could've lost the DeBolds—"

"Stop." He grabbed her arms and pulled her against him. "I don't give a damn about the DeBolds. Hell, I could've lost you." His gaze moved over her face. "From the very beginning, I put you in an impossible situation. I was a first-rate ass."

She bit her lip and her eyes misted over. "I have to tell you something. I talked with my father, and—"

"Sweetheart, I don't care," he said, truly meaning it. He'd never believed he was capable of the feelings he was having, the intensity of his feelings for her. "I don't care about any of that anymore. The only thing that matters to me is you, making you happy, making you smile, having you in my bed every morning. I'm tired of fighting, of doing battle." He reached out, brushed his fingertips across her cheek. "The only thing I'm going to fight for now is you…us."

Olivia could hardly believe what she was hearing. This was not the impenetrable tycoon she'd known when she had signed on to be his wife-for-hire. This was the loving, forgiving, generous man she'd hoped and prayed would walk into the room tonight and smile at her, accept her apology and go forward with her.

"Ever since I laid eyes on you, my life means something, Liv," he continued, taking her face in his hands. "Screw the money and the need for more, and more power to go with it. This is something good. You and me. I don't know what to do with it, but I know one thing, I'm not letting you go."

"Oh, Mac…"

He leaned in, kissed her on the mouth, a possessive, branding kiss that had her catching her breath. "I love you, Liv. I love you so much I ache."

"I love you, too." She laughed, pressed her forehead against his. "God, we're such idiots. Our intentions going into this thing were so stupid."

"True, but if they hadn't been we never would have found each other."

She nodded. "Or the way out of the past."

"Damn right." He kissed her again, a deep kiss that had her melting into him. Groaning with need, he murmured against her mouth, "Sweetheart, stay with me, love me. I want you to be mine forever."

Olivia smiled, her heart so full and happy. "Yes." She couldn't believe she was hearing him say that he loved her—it was a miracle.

Mac looked up then, his eyes burning with desire. "I'm going to marry you."

Olivia tried to fight back the tears, but it was useless. She nodded, and choked out, "Okay."

He brushed away the tear from her cheek. "Make babies with you."

"Yes. Yes." She threw her arms around his neck and held on tight. From a shameful past that had held her hostage for so long, to a light, loving future with the man of her dreams. How was it possible? She was so lucky.

Mac took her mouth in a slow, pulse-pounding kiss. "I love you, Mrs. Valentine."

"Sounds strange, doesn't it?" she whispered against his mouth, feeling so vulnerable, yet so loved.

He shook his head and nibbled at her lower lip. "No way, sweetheart. Sounds just right."

* * * * *

RICH MAN'S
VENGEFUL SEDUCTION

BY
LAURA WRIGHT

To Isa, the strongest, smartest
and most amazing four-year-old I know!

One

There was nothing more unsettling than a devil in church.

Swathed in a black chiffon Vera Wang bridesmaid dress, her red hair piled on top of her head, Tess York stared at the man in the fourth pew, her palms going damp around the base of her bouquet of red peonies. His name was Damien Sauer and he was tall, dark and fierce looking—just as she remembered him. Once upon a time they had been together, boyfriend and girlfriend, lovers and friends, but then another man had come along. A man who was mild and shy and had seemed the safe choice at the time. Back then, she'd been a sucker for safe, and had walked away from Damien and the look of seething animosity that had followed her out the door.

The scent of pine from the decorative holiday garland strewn around the church ceased being romantic and festive and instead gave way to a horrible bout of nausea. *What is he doing back here?* she wondered nervously. He didn't belong here anymore. As far as she knew, he'd gotten out of Minnesota years ago and had moved to California. Rumor had it that he'd taken on the real estate market, flipping houses at the rate of two per month. Supposedly, he was unstoppable, went into every deal without a conscience and was now worth millions.

Tess was hardly surprised by his success. Six years ago he'd worked as lead carpenter for a construction company in town. His ideas were so clever, so innovative, his handiwork so skillful and beautiful, he was wanted by every contractor in the city.

But local jobs and local pay hadn't been enough for Damien. He'd wanted more and had been willing to risk everything to get where he wanted to go.

Tess watched him sit immobile in his seat with that arrogant lift to his chin as he witnessed Mary and Ethan exchange wedding vows. Tension moved through her neck and shoulders like a snake in search of a fat mouse. She had done everything to bury her wretched, mistake-filled past, erase the so-called life she'd lived, married to the most worthless of husbands. Along with her partners, Olivia Winston and Mary Kelley, she'd helped build a winning wife-for-hire business and had created a smooth, comfortable life for herself. All she wanted to do these days was act as though the past had never existed and continue to live happily and cautiously in the present.

But the devil had shown up in church.

Behind her, someone took to the keys of the piano, playing the introduction to *Phantom's* "All I Ask of You." Everyone in the wedding party turned—as rehearsed—to watch the two performers walk to the piano, then sing.

Everyone except Tess.

She couldn't take her eyes off Damien. Maybe if she stared hard enough at him he'd get up and leave. She almost laughed out loud at the stupid thought. He wasn't a man to be chased out, scared off. He had the strongest will of anyone she had ever known.

Her gaze moved over him. He had grown leaner in the body and broader in the shoulders since she'd last seen him, but his mouth was as hard as his expression now, as though he didn't make a habit of smiling.

What is he here for? Does he know Ethan? Or God forbid, Mary?

Tess shifted, her black heels feeling suffocatingly tight. There was no way she was ready to spill her guts about the past to her partners…

Beside her, No Ring Required's culinary expert, Olivia Winston leaned in. "Hey, I know the singing's not Broadway caliber, but no spacing out, okay?"

"Yeah. Right. Sure," Tess muttered, utterly distracted.

The pretty brunette frowned at her. "What's wrong with you?"

"Nothing," Tess said quickly.

"Doesn't look like nothing," Olivia muttered.

Refusing to make a scene at her partner's wedding, Tess forced herself to face the singers. She had to get a grip here. Maybe Damien didn't even know she was there—maybe he'd forgotten all about her. Maybe he was married…with two kids and a dog named Buster. After all it had been six years. Look at all that had happened to her….

But as she half listened to the singers belt it out for the bride and groom, the music swelling and filling the church, she had an odd feeling, as though she were being watched, as though little bugs were crawling into the red curls at her hairline and nipping at her skin. It was a feeling she'd had only one time before.

The day she'd turned her back on the devilish Damien Sauer and walked out.

"Sir, would you like me to take you home?"

As his driver navigated through the congested downtown Minneapolis traffic, Damien sat in the back of his limousine, the collar of his black coat kissing the hard line of his jaw. "No. I'm going to the Georgian."

"I'm sorry sir. I don't think I heard you—"

"Take me to the Georgian Hotel," Damien said evenly. "I'm going to the reception."

"But, sir, you never go…" The driver's voice trailed off.

"Is there a problem, Robert?" Damien asked impatiently, as outside the long, black car, snowflakes pelted the windows.

"Sir?" Robert glanced up into the rearview mirror, his pale brown eyes not exactly meeting that of his employer's. "If I can speak frankly—"

Damien raised a brow. "You may…if you keep your eyes on the road while doing it. This isn't the dry and mild Los Angeles weather. The roads in Minneapolis can be pretty slick."

"Yes, sir." Robert turned his attention back to the road, two hands locked to the wheel.

Damien released a breath. "So, what do you want to know?"

"In the four years I have been working for you, this is the first wedding reception of a business associate you have ever attended."

"Is it?" Damien said tonelessly.

"Yes, sir."

"Hmm."

"Very important business then, sir?"

The car slowed, made a turn then stopped. Damien looked up, frowned. "Are we here?"

"Yes, sir, but there's a line of cars ahead of us."

They were more than a few yards from the entrance to the hotel, but Damien wasn't a man to wait. He reached for the door handle and pulled. "I'll get out here, Robert."

"But, sir?" The driver glanced over his shoulder, uncertain. "Shall I—"

"No, no. Stay in the car."

Robert nodded. "All right, sir."

Damien was half out the door when he turned back. "And, Robert?"

"Yes, sir."

"To answer your question, this reception is about something far more important than business." He stepped out of the car. "Be out front in one hour."

The ballroom in the Georgian Hotel was *the* most spectacular sight in Minneapolis for a wedding reception, beautifully appointed with gilded ceilings, crystal chandeliers and a black-and-white-marble dance floor. In any season the room could knock you off your feet, but in December, there was an extra shot of fabulous as the ballroom was decked out in white Christmas lights, spruce trees, mistletoe, and atop every black glass place setting, handmade chocolate candy canes nestled sweetly inside mini Christmas stockings.

Tess York was a self-described chocoholic, and five minutes after her arrival to the hotel her mini stocking was empty. Beside her seat was Olivia's, and the only reason a candy cane still lay safely on her plate was that Tom Radley, No Ring Required's very first client five years ago, and a family friend of Mary's, had taken Tess by the hand and forced her onto the dance floor before she could snatch it up.

On a rectangular stage beside the dance floor, a woman who sounded shockingly similar to Natalie Cole belted out love songs.

Next to Tess, Olivia and her fiancé, Mac Valentine, moved to the music. The pair were so handsome, so sharp looking they could have easily been mistaken for a Hollywood couple. Stunning in a black bridesmaid dress similar to Tess's, her dark hair long and loose about her bare shoulders, Olivia turned her brown doe eyes on Tess and cracked a smile. "You are one amazingly bad dancer, you know that?"

"Gee, thanks," Tess said dryly.

"Not true," insisted Tom Radley, sidestepping to avoid contact with the heel of Tess's shoe as she executed an awkward spin. "Don't listen to her, Tess." He glared at Olivia. "She's as graceful as a swan, light as a feather."

Olivia snorted. "As long as she doesn't step on your feet, right?"

"Easy now, my love," Mac said, pulling his girl closer.

Tess made a gesture with her hand as though she was flicking away an annoying bug. "Move along, Winston. I'm sure there are other people on this dance floor whose self-esteem you can destroy tonight."

Olivia laughed. "Right. As if you could ever be bested, Tess. You have more confidence in your little pinky than a grizzly bear at feeding time."

"Hmm," Tess said, her brow creased. "Not sure how I should take that."

Ever the gentleman, Mac jumped in. "As a compliment. And I think you dance beautifully." He attempted to look innocent, but the guy's smile had way too much rascal in it to be believable.

"Flattery won't get you anywhere with me, Mr. Valentine," Tess said, ducking her head to walk underneath Tom's arm as he led her into a spin.

Mac shrugged, then turned to his fiancé and leaned in to kiss her neck. "How about you? Will flattery get me anywhere with you?"

Olivia snuggled closer in his arms. "Yup."

Tess rolled her eyes. Leaning into her partner, she whispered, "Let's move away from the lovebirds before the cherubs flying over their heads accidentally shoot us with their arrows."

Laughing, Tom said, "You got it," and steered her away.

But when they reached the other side of the dance floor, there was a man standing there. He was clearly waiting for them, his cool blue eyes regarding them with an interested, though unfriendly stare. He was tall, wide in the shoulders and dressed in a very expensive tux. His black hair was cropped short and his full mouth looked hard and capable of cruel words.

Tess's heart leaped into her throat and remained there, pounding away unsympathetically. It was one thing to have him sitting ten feet away, his gaze trained on Mary and Ethan as they gave themselves to each other—it was another to have him in front of her, reaching for her hand.

Damien Sauer glanced at Tom, lifted an eyebrow. "If you don't mind."

Slightly nervous, Tom's answer came out sounding winded. "Of course I mind. But…well, I'm good at sharing."

"That's admirable," Damien said darkly, easing Tess from Tom's arms into his own. "I'm not."

Tess was not the kind of woman who would allow a man to call the shots—not anymore, at any rate. If anyone else at any other time had jumped in and pulled her away from her partner the way Damien had, she'd have been tempted to deck him. But this man was different, and so was her reaction to him. It was as though time had never separated them, and once in his arms, she felt so good, so warm, she didn't even attempt to pull away from him.

As the music played all around them, Damien settled into a slow rhythm, his gaze burning into hers. "Hello, Tess."

She hadn't said his name out loud in six years. Guess now was as good a time as any. "Damien Sauer. Wow. It's been a long time."

"Not that long," he said. His voice was deep, deeper than she remembered, but the tone was the same and it washed over her, bringing back a hundred different emotions. "I saw you at the engagement party, and I thought you saw me. Maybe not."

"No, I did. I mean, yes. But I didn't think…" She shrugged at her own inability to speak coherently. "I guess I wasn't sure…"

"You're stuttering, Tess," he said, arching a brow. "That's not like you."

No, it wasn't. But strange, complicated things had always happened when this man touched her. And right now his hand, wrapped lightly around hers, and his body just inches away were making her breathe a little funny. "What I was trying to say, completely inarticulately, was that I didn't know you and Ethan were friends."

"We're not," he said plainly. "He's looking to buy one of my properties and I was looking for an invitation to his wedding."

Her heart dropped. "Really?"

"Yes."

"Why?"

He gave her a sardonic grin. "I've heard that your business is quite a success," he said, ignoring her question. "You've done well for yourself."

His words sounded more like an observation than a compliment. "I think so. But not as well as you, it seems."

He nodded. "After you left town, I became very focused."

Of course he was going to go there. Make her damn uncomfortable, maybe break out in a sweat. "Well, focused can be good."

"Yes, it can. In fact, I might go so far as to say that I owe a great deal of my fortune to you."

The scent of the spruce tree to their left was overpowering. "I'm sure that's not—"

"Don't be so modest, Tess. You were an inspiration…"

It was too much. The whole thing—his sardonic compliments, her nervousness. She was not going to put herself in the position of being freaked out around a man anymore. She stopped dancing. Music played and people swayed, but she stared expectantly at Damien Sauer. "What's going on here? Why did you come?"

"I wanted to see you." There was zero warmth behind his eyes, and the look he gave her chilled the blood in her veins.

"Well, you saw me," she said, turning away. "Thank you for the dance."

He took her hand and placed it through his arm. "I'll take you back to your table."

She thought about wrenching her arm free, but she wasn't going to cause a scene, so she let him lead her. As they walked, Tess couldn't help but notice the way women stared at Damien: hungry, needy. Just the way she'd stared at him once upon a time.

When they got to the table reserved for the wedding party, Tess sat and hoped that Damien would just take off, that the dance and the verbal sparring would be the end of it. But he didn't leave. Instead he sat beside her.

"So, how's Henry?" His voice was low and cold.

She stared at him, looked into those deep blue eyes and found clarity. He wasn't here on business or to just "see" her. He'd come to the wedding to confront her or hurt her. But why now, after six years, she wasn't sure. She looked directly into his eyes and said evenly, "My husband passed away. About five years ago."

Damien nodded, but didn't look surprised. "I'm sorry."

"Are you?"

His brows lifted. "I could say no but what would that make me?"

She shrugged. "Cruel."

"How about honest?"

"How about both?"

Out of the corner of her eye, Tess spotted Mary and Olivia on the other side of the dance floor, and her heart jumped. They were staring at her and Damien, curious looks on their faces. Tess knew her partners well enough to know that in about thirty seconds they were going to be headed her way. She wasn't about to have her past and past mistakes laid bare at her partner's wedding.

She turned back to Damien, hoping that her face had not gone pale. "Dinner is going to be served soon. Maybe we can catch up another time."

"Are you trying to get rid of me, Tess?" he asked, studying her face.

"No."

"I can tell when you're lying. Always could."

"Fine." Her jaw tightened. "My partners are on their way over here and they know—"

"Nothing about me?" Damien finished for her, a flash of venomous pleasure lighting his eyes.

"They know nothing about you or Henry or my life before we started the company."

"Why is that?"

"It's none of your business." There was no time for this. Mary and Olivia were just a few feet away. "You can say whatever you need to say. But not here, not now. Another time."

He considered this for a moment, then nodded. "All right."

Relief accosted her, and she said quickly, "Okay. Goodbye, then."

He stood. "I'll see you tomorrow, Tess."

She looked up. "What?"

"I'll be at your office tomorrow at one."

"No!"

Mary and Olivia were almost upon them. Damien leaned in close to Tess's ear, the heat from his breath making her hair stand on end and her heart twist painfully. This she remembered, and long ago this she had loved.

"I'm not here to reminisce about old times," he uttered darkly. "I'm here to collect on a debt that was never paid."

Tess's head started spinning. What debt was he talking about?

"Six years ago," he continued, "you made a promise to me. One that was never fulfilled. I'm here to make sure you fulfill it. Because if you don't, everything you hold dear will crumble."

He stood just in time to greet Mary and Olivia, shaking their hands and complimenting the bride on the ceremony and reception. Dumbstruck, Tess just stared at her plate and the empty stocking. Through the din of her overactive brain, she heard Damien wish them both well, then walk away.

"Nice," Olivia said, taking her seat beside Tess. "Very cute."

"Gorgeous and charming," Mary remarked, righting her tiara before sitting in the chair designated for the bride. "And looking smitten with our girl here."

"Did you get his number, Tess?" Olivia asked.

Tess nodded and said hoarsely, "Yes. I've got his number all right."

Two

In the four and a half years that Tess York had been with No Ring Required, she'd called in sick three times. The first time was in the winter of 2004, when she'd had the flu so badly, she'd passed out on the way to her car. The second time was last summer when she'd had her wisdom teeth out, and the third time was today when she'd woken up with a nasty little hangover.

She wasn't a big drinker. Actually she wasn't even a little drinker, but last night, after seeing Damien and having the past hurled back in her face, she'd enjoyed a few glasses of champagne too many.

Garbed in ratty old sweats and stretched out on the couch with her cat, Hepburn, Tess stared at the TV. Trying to ignore her pounding head, she watched

Montel Williams take a seat beside his favorite psychic guest, who was telling one audience member after another that what they probably had in their house was a ghost who had unfinished business.

"Maybe you can give us some advice on how to get rid of those ghosts," Tess muttered at the screen.

So far, she'd only taken steps to avoid hers. Mary was already on her honeymoon, so Olivia was going to be the only one in to work today. The one appointment Tess did have wasn't on the books, and she was more than willing to skip it.

As the psychic rambled on about heaven and the light, Tess let her eyes close and her mind shut off for a while. She must've drifted off because when she woke up, there was a soap opera on the television and someone knocking on her apartment door. Her head still pounding, she padded over to the door and looked out the peephole.

When she saw who it was, she swore silently, turned around and sagged against the door.

Damien.

"Tess?"

Accompanying her headache, her stomach twisted sickly at the sound of his voice.

"Tess, I know you're there."

"What do you want, Damien?" she yelled into the door.

"You know exactly what I want. I was pretty damn clear last night. Now open the door."

"I'm sick."

"Yes, Olivia was kind enough to tell me that. After I'd driven all the way over there."

Tess sighed. This was not how she did things— hiding behind doors so she wouldn't have to deal with uncomfortable meetings and threats from an old boyfriend. That was the way the married Tess had handled herself, the Tess who'd had a reason to feel nervous and afraid. But that part of her life was over.

She flipped the lock and opened the door wide.

Damien stood there, filling up her doorway. Freshly shaven and showered and dressed in a navy blue suit so fine it probably came straight from the Gucci runway show in Milan.

Knowing she looked like her cat's chew toy after a gnarly play session, she lifted her chin and said in her most superior tone, "I never agreed to see you, Damien."

A slow, cool smile curved his lips as he looked her over. "Well, there she is."

"There who is?"

"The firecracker I used to know. The woman worthy of that mass of red hair." He leaned against the doorjamb. "After last night and hearing all that stuttering and fear of what your partners might find out, I thought she was gone. I wondered what or who had taken that fire out of her."

Well, he could keep on wondering, she thought dryly. There was no way he was ever going to know anything about her life with Henry, about the scars that remained.

He narrowed his eyes, studied her. "You look…"

"Sick?" she offered.

"Did you drink last night?"

"That's really none of your business."

"Champagne gives you intense headaches, remember?"

"No," she lied.

He crossed his arms over his chest. "Are you going to let me in?"

"I think you can say whatever cryptic thing you need to say from here."

"Fine, but I did bring you matzo ball soup…well, actually Robert picked it up." He held up a white deli bag. "And you look like you could use it. But you can't eat it standing in the entryway."

"Who's Robert?"

"My driver?"

She rolled her eyes. "There's a point at which someone has too much money."

"Not really."

He tried to walk past her, but she stopped him. "Soup first."

He handed her the bag, and she let him pass. After a quick look around her living room, he sat on the couch. She picked up the remote and switched off the television, then dropped into the leather armchair a few feet away.

His brow lifted. "Are you afraid of me?"

"Fear is a useless emotion," she began. But then she shrugged. Instead of inspirational quotes, maybe honesty…or some form of hybrid might be a better tack to take with this man. "After what you said last night, or didn't say, I think feeling apprehensive isn't a bizarre response."

His gaze grew serious, his mouth hard. "No."

She placed the deli bag on the coffee table, then looked up at him. "Enough bantering back and forth. You and I both know this isn't a social call, so let's get to it."

He sat back and regarded her. "Do you remember the red house in Tribute?"

A rush of memories flooded into her mind along with a deep burn of sadness. It had been their spot, a starter home, in a tiny town, that Damien had bought for a song as his first investment property. In the high days of their romance, they had walked the main drag of that town, sharing their plans for the future, then later they'd shared a bed.

She met his gaze and nodded. "I remember."

"I want to renovate it."

This surprised her. "You never did?"

"No."

"Okay. So, what does this have to do with me?"

"You made a promise to me in that house, one week before you left."

Tess's heart plummeted into her stomach, and she searched her memory.

"You promised to help me renovate. You wanted to make it a home, if I recall correctly." His voice dropped, soured. "I expect you to keep that promise."

"You can't be serious?"

"I am."

And then it all came back in a rush. It had happened a week before she left, just like he'd said. One week before Henry had asked her to be his wife. One week before she'd forced herself to realize that with a man like Damien she'd never have the kind of life she'd planned for herself. The kind of stable, family-friendly life she'd promised herself when she was seventeen, after her parents' deaths. She stared at him and shook her head. "But why? Why do you care now—"

"It's a chapter I need to finish," he said, his tone cool. He stood, then reached inside his coat and pulled out an envelope. "Here are the keys, the address—in case you've forgotten—and a formidable amount of cash."

"What—"

"I need you to start right away."

He was crazy. She stood. "Damien, I have no intention of—"

"I need the job done in two weeks."

She didn't even try to suppress a bitter laugh. "Impossible."

"I leave in two weeks, back to California. I want to make sure everything is done. And I want a full remodel, not just a coat of paint and new towels for the bathroom."

She put up a hand. "Stop right now. This is not going to happen. Two weeks is Christmas."

He shrugged. "You can do your shopping up in Tribute."

"Not funny, Damien. I have a business to run—"

"Yes, and if it will make you feel better, tell your partners that I hired you." His gaze moved over her hungrily. "My wife for hire for two weeks, fixing up my home."

Awareness moved through her, but she shook it off. She walked to the apartment door and opened it. "I'm not going to play this game with you anymore."

He didn't move. "Good, because I don't play games. You will go to Tribute and you will fix up the house."

"Or what?"

"Or that business of yours will have to find a new location, which will take a lot of time and money that a new business can't really afford."

"Are you actually threatening me?" The words ground out from between her teeth. "Because I don't take kindly to threats."

"I'm telling you to think about your future," he said, his tone dark with warning. "And the future of your partners."

"What the hell does that mean?"

He walked to her, faced her. "I know the owner of your building and I think I could convince him to not renew your lease in January."

Her heart took a nosedive. "How do you know our lease is up in January?" She was shaking now, her breathing uneven. "Do you have this jerk owner in your pocket?"

"I don't have to. I'm the jerk."

Tess held her breath, and silence filled the space. She was trying to process what he had said and, more important, what it meant.

"I own your building, Tess."

She shook her head. "I don't believe you."

"My company owns your building," he said evenly. "Three years now."

"Why are you doing this?"

"I have a business, too."

"What is this business of yours? Revenge? Hurt feelings because I chose another man over you?"

He seemed to grow a foot taller before her eyes, and his gaze became dark and menacing.

She looked directly at him. "You need to grow up, Damien."

His lips formed a sneer. "I'll expect you at the house tomorrow afternoon. Don't disappoint me."

"Who are you?" she called after him as he walked down the hall. "The man I used to know would never do something like—"

"The *boy* you used to know was a fool," he said over his shoulder as he walked into the elevator. "Enjoy the soup."

Tess shut the door with a little too much force. That bastard. *Never. No way.* He could take his threats and shove them where the sun don't shine. She spotted the deli bag on the coffee table and snatched it up, stalked into the kitchen. But as she dumped the soup into the sink, her rational mind started to rear its unwanted head. If he did own her building—a fact she would check immediately—he could follow through on his threat and kick them all out on their backsides.

Did he really hate her that much…?

Tess leaned on the counter and released a breath. Her headache from earlier was gone, but it looked like she was about to get another…one that would last about two weeks.

According to some major athletes and those perfect people who work out a lot, exercise is the best way of reaching a state of true introspection.

Well, Tess was counting on it.

"So, renovating a house? Like new paint and drywall? Or we talking air ducts and toilet flanges?"

It was 7:00 a.m. and Tess had met Olivia at the gym for a workout. Earlier that morning, say around 6:15, she'd sat in her office at NRR and gone over lease agreement after lease agreement, only to discover that Damien's company did indeed own her building. It hadn't taken her long to get it—there was nothing to do but face the fire. Damien was in need of some vengeance, and from the look on his face yesterday he wasn't going to hesitate to kick them all out of the building if Tess didn't comply with his demands.

So, at eleven o'clock, she was leaving for Tribute. She'd get in, do the job and get out.

"I'm not sure what I'll find when I get there," Tess said to Olivia, her breathing uneven as she picked up the pace when the treadmill inclined a notch. "Guess I'll have to wait and see."

Beside Tess, Olivia rode a stationary bike at a snail's pace. "The client didn't give you specifics?"

"He asked for a full remodel."

"Who is the client, by the way? Do I know him?"

Tess hesitated. She wanted to tread lightly here. "He's the man from Mary and Ethan's wedding."

Olivia's brows shot up. "Mr. Tall, Dark and Dreamy? The one who came into NRR looking for you yesterday?"

"That's the one."

"Wow. He moves pretty fast."

Tess bit her lip. She hated to lie to her partner, but there was no way she was going to explain the past and the present circumstances. Or what was at stake if she didn't take this job. "We spoke this morning. He needs the job done ASAP. He needs to get back to California in a couple weeks."

"He's looking to sell the place?"

"I think so."

"That's a big job to take on right before Christmas. You sure you want to tackle it?"

"Yeah. Not a problem. I'll probably do a good portion of the work myself, then hire a few subcontractors."

"You're gonna have to pay double because of the holiday." Sweat-free and smiling, Olivia stepped off the bike and came to stand by the treadmill. "Speaking of which, what are you doing for Christmas?"

Ah…same thing she did every year. Join a few people in her building on Christmas Eve for some food and music, then just relax on Christmas Day. She shrugged. "Not sure."

"I want you to spend the day with Mac and me."

Tess grinned at her partner. It was a nice offer. "That's sweet, Liv. But—"

"No buts."

Tess stepped off the treadmill and grabbed her towel. "We'll see."

"And you know," Olivia continued. "Mac has a friend…"

"That's nice," Tess said quickly. "Everyone needs friends."

Cocking her head to the side, Olivia gave her a soft smile. "I want you find the right man."

"I don't want the right man, Liv."

Olivia laughed. "How about the wrong one, then?"

Been there, done that. She tossed Olivia a tight smile. "I have to go home. Shower and change, take the cat to the vet, then get on the road."

She nodded. "I'll call you."

"Okay."

Tess owned a pretty great SUV. It was sleek and black, had four-wheel drive, leather seats, a killer sound system and an easily accessible cup holder for her coffee. It also had a panel that displayed the outside temperature.

Normally Tess glanced at this panel once during her regular drive time, but on this trip she'd checked the thing every few minutes. Mostly because she couldn't believe how quickly the temperature dropped—five degrees every thirty minutes.

Northern Minnesota in winter was as close to the Arctic as most people ever got. Freezing temperatures arrived in October and stayed around until April, making everyone up there a bit nutty. Tess shook her head. And she was about to spend the next two weeks there. Good thing she'd packed her parka.

Just before two o'clock, she pulled off the freeway and drove the short distance to downtown Tribute, which was comprised of four wide, unclogged streets with a handful of mom-and-pop stores, a gas station and a diner. It hadn't changed much in six years, and for a moment Tess recalled how she and Damien had shared a burger in the diner and a good deal of necking behind the gas station.

Tess slowed to a crawl as she drove down Yarr Lane, then pulled into the third driveway on the left. She killed the engine and stepped out of the car. The yard was three feet deep in snow, but other than that the little red cottage looked very much the same as it had. Which, incidentally wasn't saying much.

To start with it needed a fresh coat of paint, a

clean doorknob, coach lamp, knocker and new address numbers. And that was just on the outside.

As she walked to the door, she recalled thinking that Damien had bought this house for them, for a future together. But he had been quick to point out that he'd purchased the house as an investment property: the first of many—to be fixed up and sold for a profit. Hearing that had crushed her, made her realize that they'd wanted very different things from life.

She unlocked the house and stepped inside. It was completely bare, not one piece of furniture, and there was dust on every visible surface.

She did a quick walk through and found that the two small bedrooms were well maintained, just in need of a cleaning, new fixtures and a few coats of paint. The kitchen and bathroom, however, were, in a word, horrible. Outdated and showing years of wear. Both spaces needed new floors, countertops, some drywall patching, new appliances, fixtures and paint.

She stood in the living room and stared. The place needed a lot, a complete overhaul. First thing she had to do was go into town, get some cleaning supplies and the phone numbers of some skilled labor.

"So you're the city girl Damien hired?"

Startled, Tess whirled around. Walking into the house was a woman in her late sixties, bundled up in a dark-blue down jacket and matching ski cap. She had smooth chocolate-brown skin, high cheekbones and cat-shaped violet eyes. She was short and a little plump, but even at her age she was startlingly beautiful.

Tess stuck out a hand. "Hi, I'm Tess York."

"Wanda Bennett," the woman said, shaking Tess's hand with the firm grip of a lumberjack. "I'm the property manager here in Tribute, and the owner of the food market in town."

"It's nice to meet you."

The woman nodded, then glanced around. "Sweet place, but it needs some work."

"Sure does," Tess agreed.

"Never understood why Damien left it to rot like this. Not his style."

No, it wasn't his style. And he had just left the place to rot until he'd found the time to blackmail his former girlfriend into fixing it up. Tess didn't think that sharing this information with Wanda was appropriate. Of course, the woman had called Damien by his first name, so maybe they were friends, maybe she knew exactly who Tess was and what she was doing here.

"So, you're probably wondering why I barged in like this?" Wanda asked.

"You said you're the property manager…"

"Sure, I turned on the heat and water, but Damien wanted me to give you this." She took a fat envelope out of her jacket pocket and handed it to Tess. "Here."

"What is it?"

"He wired it this morning. He thought you might need more than what he gave you," Wanda explained.

"For fixing up the place. He wants it furnished, as well."

Tess looked inside the envelope. A three-inch stack of hundred-dollar bills. Good Lord. He'd already given her four times that much. But then again you never knew what problems might come up in an older house. She looked up at Wanda again. "Is there a furniture store in town?"

"Nope."

"Lighting, hardware?"

"There is a hardware store in Tribute—it's on Main, next to the diner—and you can get furniture and light fixtures in Jackson, that's about fifty miles away." She paused for a moment, then said, "But I think Damien might want this place fixed up with the local flavor. A few people make their own furnishings around here, I'd talk to them."

"Do they work quickly? I'm under a bit of a time crunch."

Wanda shrugged. "Depends."

Tess sighed. Looked as though she was just going to have to figure everything out on her own. She gave Wanda a quick smile and said, "I'm going to head over to the motel and check in, then."

"Ruby's place?"

"Yes. I saw it in the phone book."

Wanda pressed her lips together and looked at the ceiling.

"Is something wrong?"

"Nope."

Tess's shoulders fell. "What? Is Ruby an ax murder or something?"

"No. Ruby's lovely." She pointed to the envelope in Tess's hand. "It's just that before you go to Ruby's, you might want to go here first."

Tess glanced down at the address written on the envelope. "What is this?"

"Damien asked that you be there at four o'clock."

"Four o'clock when?"

"Today," Wanda said evenly.

Tess looked down at her watch. "It's three-thirty now."

She waved her hand as if it was nothing to worry about. "It's just a short drive. I'll give you directions."

On a sigh, Tess grabbed her purse and searched for a pen. She had really wanted to clean up the place before it got dark. Damn Damien and his demands. "So, what's at this address?" she asked Wanda. "A contractor or a plumber or something."

Wanda shrugged her shoulders again. "Or something."

Tess glared at her. "Did Damien tell you to be this annoyingly evasive?"

At that, a smile tugged at the woman's lips and she pointed to the pen in Tess's hand. "I'll give you those directions now."

Three

The drive took under five minutes, but it was all uphill, and the roads were slick, as daylight had decided to knock off a little early. When Tess pulled into the driveway and saw the house, she thought she'd made a mistake with the directions. She glanced down to check if she had the correct address.

She did.

Who in the world lived here? she wondered. An artist? A famous, reclusive artist who had cut off his ear, then moved to Tribute for the peace and quiet and frigid climate?

Tess got out of the car to a blast of arctic air and looked up at the massive glass fortress. Whoever lived here, she mused, had better have something to do with the renovating process.

She walked to the front door. It wouldn't surprise her if this was some kind of roadblock that Damien had put up to mess with her—picking out artwork for the walls before they were even painted, or something equally wasteful in the time management department. Sure, he wanted the house done in two weeks, but he wanted to make every move she made that much more difficult in the process.

Her teeth chattering, she rang the bell. Thankfully, she didn't have to wait more than ten seconds before it opened. For a moment she thought she'd come face-to-face with Danny Devito. Then she realized the impossibility of such a thought and granted the man a friendly smile. "Hello. I'm Tess York. I have an appointment."

"Of course." He stepped aside. "Please come in."

The first thing Tess noticed when she walked into the entryway was how warm the space was. Not the architecture. That was sleek and sexy and ultramodern. But warm in temperature. Even with the sun going down outside, the light that had been filtering in from the many windows all day heated the house toasty warm.

The man she'd mentally referred to as Danny Devito took her coat, then gestured toward the open living area. The space was perfectly outfitted with expensive, modern furnishings—some that could double as pieces of artwork—that matched the home's architecture. "Come with me, please."

Tess gave the man a grim smile. "I'm sorry, no can do." She had a rule about this kind of situation. If she didn't know where she was and who was in charge, she remained close to the exit. "I'll wait here."

The man looked a tad worried. "He wouldn't like that."

"Who is he?" Tess asked.

"My employer."

Tess rolled her eyes. This was getting nuts. Forget Damien's orders. If he wanted to have this guy's art or whatever the man was selling, then he could get it himself.

Perhaps sensing that she was ready to bolt, "Danny" said in a hopeful voice, "If you could wait one moment, Ms. York?"

Tess released a breath. "Okay. But seriously, this had better get clear real soon."

Like a fretful mouse, the man scurried away, through the double-height living room and its beautiful floor-to-ceiling soapstone fireplace. Tess started counting to sixty. She got to fifty-one before she heard the butler returning.

But it wasn't the butler.

She heard him before she saw him, and her gut went tight. "Giving the help a hard time, are you Tess?"

Tess watched him walk toward her, the master of the manor, dressed in jeans and a black sweater, looking too gorgeous, too dangerous for words.

She shook her head as he approached. "Your house, huh? I should've guessed." She pointed a finger at him. "And, for the record, I wasn't trying to give anyone a hard time. I was being firm. But maybe he's not used to strong women coming here."

"Olin," he said, walking into the living room. "His name is Olin."

Tess followed. "Right. Well, maybe Olin's not used to you having strong women around."

Damien's eyes were cool and brilliant blue as he sat in a black leather armchair. "Only one woman comes here, and she's plenty strong."

"Only one, huh? How progressive of you," she said sarcastically, taking the chair across from him.

"You met her today, in fact."

"Wanda?" Tess said.

He nodded. "She's a good friend."

"How nice."

"I don't bring the women I date here."

The women. Plural. So, there were many. Of course there were many. She pushed away the nip of jealously in her gut and got down to business. "Why am I here, Damien? And with all the mystery?"

"Mystery?" he repeated.

She put her hand up. "No, forget it. I don't need an answer for that. I get it. You wanted me to see your amazing spread, how well you've done—and I have. It's fantastic, you're successful. Okay?" When he said nothing, just looked mildly amused, she pressed on. "Now, I have a job to do—one that was forced on me—and I'd like to get it done as soon as possible."

"I didn't have Wanda tell you that it was my house

you were coming to because I assumed you'd still be pretty pissed off at me and you'd probably stand me up. And I needed you to see this house so you could see my style, what I wanted for the red house."

Oh. Well, that made a small amount of sense. "You want the red house to go modern? It's a cozy little cottage."

"Cozy cottages can and should have modern touches."

"Fine. Okay. Cozy, but modern it is." She stood. "If I could get my coat, I need to go over to the motel and check in before it gets dark—"

"No."

She stared at him, puzzled. "No, what?," she said, laughing. "I don't get my coat back?"

"You're not staying at the motel, Tess."

"Excuse me?"

"No motels or hotels."

This guy was something else. "Where am I supposed to stay, then?"

Damien sat back in his chair.

Tess crossed her arms over her chest. "If you think I'm going to stay here, then the LA smog has really rotted your—"

"No. You're not staying here."

Her hands balled into fists, and she said through gritted teeth, "What do you suggest, then? Building an igloo?"

"You'll stay in the red house." He said it as though it was the simplest, most logical solution in the world.

Her stomach churned with irritation. "The red house is filthy and unfurnished."

"You'll change that."

Nostrils flaring with anger, Tess stood there, her body rigid. She wanted to scream at him, maybe clock him with that mean left hook she'd learned in self-defense class at the Y. But that was just what he wanted—a mad, frustrated, vulnerable Tess York.

Not going to happen.

"So, more punishment, is that it?" she said tightly.

A slow smile pulled at his lips.

Tess nodded. "Have at it, Sauer. Just know that when this is all done and you're back in California making another million, the only thing that'll have changed on this end will be that small amount of regret I felt when I walked out on you."

His gaze flashed with icy contempt. "It's getting dark. I'll have Olin get your coat."

"Don't bother." She left him standing there and walked to the entryway. After pulling her coat from the stainless steel closet, she left.

Every weekend for one year, Damien had come to Tribute to supervise the building of his hilltop house. It was everything he'd ever wanted, a twelve-thousand-square-foot glass house; a modern, mini-malist fortress that overlooked the little red house he couldn't let go of. He had designed the house so that he could see the red cottage from nearly every window. It was how he'd wanted it, needed it.

Whenever he looked down at it, he was reminded of her, and the feeling of betrayal had spurred him on, had made him wise and passionless and highly successful in business.

Damien took the elevator to the roof and stepped out on the deck. Snow was falling in sweet, tiny flakes, melting at once as they hit the heated stone floor. He could see for miles from up there, but he didn't even try to look beyond the borders of Tribute. His gaze rested where it always did—on the red house. A tiny speck of a place that mocked him big-time.

Right now it was dark. Obviously, she wasn't back yet.

"Sir?"

"Yes?" Damien didn't turn around to address Olin.

"Dinner is ready, sir."

"Nothing for me tonight."

Olin paused for a moment, then uttered a quick, "Yes, sir," before he disappeared.

Damien wasn't hungry. Not for food, at any rate. What he wanted was her. Her body and her soul. He wanted to make her hate him, then make her love him, then crush her as she'd crushed him.

And, after their meeting earlier, it looked as though he was well on his way....

"Seriously?"

Ruby Deets looked suitably remorseful as she shook her head, her platinum-blond beehive shifting as she moved. "I'm sorry, hon. Wish there was some-thing I could do for you."

Starving and running out of the half cup of patience she had remaining, Tess leaned against Ruby's front desk. "You can. You can give me a room."

"Can't."

"He doesn't own you."

"No, that's true." Ruby leaned in, her double chin just hovering above the tarnished welcome bell. "But he does own the motel."

Tess grit her teeth. Of course he did.

"Is the grocery store still open?" she asked.

Ruby checked the clock on the wall. "You got another thirty minutes."

"Okay, thanks."

"You must've done something to really piss him off," Ruby remarked dryly.

"He's a man," Tess said, then turned to leave, calling over her shoulder, "They're not that hard to piss off."

Three hours later Tess sat on a blanket from her car in the red house's tiny living room. After she'd gotten rid of the cobwebs, scrubbed down the walls and mopped the floor in the one room, she'd built a fire in the brick fireplace and opened her deli sandwich and chips.

Between the rough accommodations and all the thoughts running through her brain, from Damien to the remodel to her past, she was not going to be sleeping much tonight.

For about a half a second, she'd contemplated going home and just explaining to Olivia what she was up against. Her partner was pretty understanding and very cool. No doubt, she'd pat Tess on the back, whip up a five-course meal—three of them heavy on the chocolate—then suggest they find a new office building immediately.

Oh, such a tempting thought.

But Tess was no coward, no quitter. She would take control of this situation and turn the red house into a comfortably modern masterpiece. Then, when the two weeks were up, she'd pack up and go home, put Damien behind her for good.

She took another bite of her egg salad sandwich. To make this work, she would have to stay one step ahead of him, try to anticipate what he would throw at her next. Because if there was one thing she could be sure of, it was that Damien Sauer had plans for her. Possibly destructive plans, and she had to be ready.

Four

"Bed's in the trunk, Tess."

"Thanks, Mr Opp." Tess pulled several hundred-dollar bills from the envelope stash. It was close to four in the afternoon and she was pretty wiped. She'd been cleaning since sunup. Later, on a trip into town for a late lunch, she had found the name and address of a man who sold handmade furnishings and gifts. She'd purchased a beautiful walnut bed, complete with mattress and box spring, as well as a few other pieces for the living room that she was going to pick up later in the week.

Mr. Opp took the money and gave Tess a tired grin. He was a tall, lanky man in his early seventies, who had a pack of little dogs that continually weaved their way in and out of his legs whenever he stopped to talk. "How about a few more sheets of *lefsa?* Butter and sugar on top?"

"No, thanks," Tess said graciously, eyeing the stack of round, flat potato bread. A half hour earlier she had made quite a dent in that stack. "I don't think I could eat another bite."

He grinned and said kindly, "I'll wrap up a few for the road, then."

"I'd appreciate that." With the limited selection of food in Tribute, she wasn't about to decline the offer. Especially when the food in question was ridiculously delicious.

She gave Mr. Opp another round of thank-yous, then got in her car and took off. As she drove back to the little red house, she felt better, as though she might be getting a handle on the situation. After last night and sleeping on the hardwood floor, just the thought of having a bed to sleep on tonight was a massive improvement. Sure, it was going to take every ounce of muscle she had to lug the thing inside and set it up, as Mr. Opp had no delivery service, but hey, it would be worth it.

The sun was settling itself into the horizon when she pulled into the driveway. Before bringing in the bed, she decided to grab some firewood from the side of the house first. She'd kept the heat on all day, but as she'd discovered last night, it wasn't the greatest source of warmth in the world.

After piling four logs into her arms, she pushed the front door open with her hip and went inside.

Immediately she felt something strange. She bent and gently rolled the logs to the floor, trying not to be too noisy. Her heart started pounding against the walls of her chest, but she wasn't sure why.

Was someone in the house? Something?

Animal or human?

She glanced around for something to use as a weapon. No baseball bat, and the chopping ax was outside beside the woodpile. Without thinking, she grabbed one of the logs, swung it back over her right shoulder. Her throat tight with nerves, she moved cautiously through the living room. This was crazy, she thought, stepping into the kitchen and flipping on the lights. There was nothing here, probably just her imagination.

But she let her guard down too quickly. As her arm fell to her side, someone seized her, grabbed her around the waist and spun her, then pinned her back against the countertop. The log dropped to the floor and made a crashing sound. Tess screamed, thrashed around until she saw who was holding her. Then she stopped cold and stared at him. "You!"

His face just inches from hers, Damien Sauer whispered, "Making yourself at home."

"You scared the hell out of me!" she said caustically, trying to break free of his grasp.

But Damien didn't release her. "And you almost knocked my head off my shoulders with that log."

"What a tragedy that would be," she said sarcastically.

Amusement glittered in his eyes. "You seem testy today."

"Do I?"

"Living in the lap of luxury not agreeing with you?"

"Living here is fine. It's the unwelcome guests I have a problem with."

"Then you should keep the door locked."

She ignored the truth in that statement. "What are you doing here? Aren't you supposed to be watching me jump and squirm from under that ten-thousand-square-foot magnifying glass you got up there?"

"Twelve thousand."

"What?"

"Twelve thousand square feet."

She rolled her eyes. He was one of the most arrogant, self-centered...

"I'm checking in," he said, his sapphire gaze moving over her face. "On my wife."

A ripple of laughter escaped her. "That arrangement is going on only in your head."

He leaned in, his mouth just inches from her. "And in your partners' heads, as well, right?"

How was it possible to want to kill someone and kiss them at the same time? They stood there, so close, the scent of snow and leather emanating from Damien as he baited her with his words and his full lips.

Ignoring the prickly warm sensation inside her breasts, she forced her gaze to meet his. "I want you to let me go now."

At her words, something changed in his expression. It was no longer playful, more serious, and he released her, backed up, even walked away into the living room. For a moment Tess just remained there, her back against the butcher-block countertop. She'd said those exact words to another man many years ago and many times before, but with very different results. Damien confused her. He wanted to punish her, yet his punishment was all mental…

With a quick breath, she followed him into the living room. "As you can see, I've cleaned the place. That's about as far as I've gotten in the one day I've been here. Oh, that and I bought a bed."

"A bed?"

"If I'm staying here it's at least going to be tolerably comfortable."

"Where is it?"

"In the car."

He was opening the front door and disappearing outside before Tess got a clue about what he was doing. "I don't need your help, Damien," she called, running after him into the frosty cold air of twilight time. "In fact, I don't need anything from you, except maybe…"

A foot from her car, he paused and turned around. "Except what?"

From three to five in the morning last night, she'd given this idea much thought. Damien wasn't going to be the only beneficiary in this deal. Tess didn't do things that way anymore. "I'd like you to promise me something."

He raised a brow.

"After I do this job, you'll sell the Minneapolis building."

He crossed his arms over his chest. "Which building is that?"

She cocked her head to the side. "Don't be obtuse."

For a moment he just stared at her, looking both emotionally and physically cold, puffs of warm air escaping his mouth. Then he turned around and walked to the back of her car. He had the trunk popped and the headboard out in seconds. "You didn't lock your car door, either?"

"I didn't think this was chop shop alley, Damien."

He carried the headboard up the walk, and Tess followed him. "The building I'm referring to is the one that houses No Ring Required. I want you to sell it."

"Why should I?" He put the headboard inside, then went back for more.

Again, she followed after him like a hungry puppy as he removed parts of the bed frame from her SUV and brought them inside. "Because it's the right thing to do, and underneath that badass exterior you're a good guy."

"No, seriously, why should I?" he said dryly, returning to the car and hauling out the mattress and box spring.

"Because I'm willing to walk away from this if you don't."

He snorted. "You wouldn't. I know you—"

"You know nothing about me, Damien!" She said the words so loudly, so passionately, he stopped in the doorway and stared at her.

She shook her head. "You have no idea who I am now. What I've…" She needed to go easy here. "What I've seen and experienced in the past six years. I'm willing to let you humiliate me, give orders and use me for the next two weeks, to protect my business and my partners. But I won't do it for longer than that."

He didn't move. His chin was set and his eyes narrowed.

She walked to him, her tone low and cool. "You clearly don't need the money. And after we're done here, I'd think you'd want to put me back in the past where I belong."

"That easy?"

"Yes." She held out her hand. "Okay?"

Damien didn't speak for a moment, then he reached out and took her hand in his.

The warmth of his hand instantly seeped into her body, her bones, and for just a second a flash of the past came roaring into her mind. She saw herself in Damien's arms in this very house, saw him kissing her neck, then her mouth.

She pulled her hand away, knowing her cheeks burned. "If you're done here, I have work to do."

He nodded darkly. "I'm done." He walked past her, down the path.

Then she noticed something. "Hey, how did you get here? I didn't see a car."

He glanced over his shoulder. "Walked."

She couldn't stop herself from asking, "You want a ride back? It's kind of far."

He shook his head. "No. It's just far enough."

He disappeared down the street and into the darkness so quickly she didn't get a chance to ask him what he'd meant by that.

Damien arrived home hungry and cold as hell. But all in all, the walk had been a good one. Time to clear his head, make new plans and fill his lungs with clean air. Couldn't do that in Los Angeles.

Olin was hovering at the front door when Damien walked in. "Sir?"

"You look panicked, Olin."

He took Damien's coat and tossed it gently over his arm. "Mrs. Roth is here and she brought along a Mr. Kaplan."

Damien checked his watch. "It's eight o'clock."

"I told them it was too late, but they insisted on waiting." The man leaned in and whispered covertly, "Mrs. Roth called Mr. Kaplan a land developer."

Damien chuckled. "Yes, I know who he is. How long have they been here?"

"Twenty minutes." Olin stood taller. "I'll go back and tell them you don't wish to be—"

"No. I'd told Irene to come by anytime." He should've specified anytime during the day. But this was a special circumstance, part of his plan, and he couldn't afford to be his usual overly demanding self. "Tell them I'll be right there."

"Yes, sir."

"Where are they?"

"The study."

"Fine." He started up the stairs.

"Sir?"

Damien turned. "Yes, Olin?"

"I know it's not my business to ask, but if you're thinking of selling this house, I would be most grateful to know—"

"I'm not selling."

"Oh."

"Not this house, anyway."

There were times when Tess York believed she didn't feel anything—that the ugliness and shame of her past had made her numb. Then, out of the blue, she'd get a few gentle waves of emotion. They were normally accompanied by memories, not good ones, but even so, the waves did remind her that she was still alive and able to feel. And she had to take that as a positive.

Tonight Tess sat on the new bed and rubbed oil onto the snakelike skin of her inner thigh. She was riding a wave right now, where the reality of the massive burn scar that Henry had inflicted that last night before she'd left him was meeting up with the emotions of the memory. It was an odd thing, too, because she always felt the scar, felt her jeans rub against it or the shower water pummeling it.

Tonight, however, it burned.

She couldn't help thinking it was Damien's presence in her life again, the notion that if she had picked him, her life might've been so different—that this scar wouldn't have existed. But who was to know. In his own way, Damien had turned out to be a monster, too.

Outside, snow started to fall. Tomorrow was a big day, the real renovation could begin.

Tess put her salve away, got under the covers and closed her eyes.

Five

The trouble with picking a paint color was twofold: too many choices, then there was the what-if-this-looks-hideous-on-the-wall factor. Normally Tess could get past these minor roadblocks in about fifteen minutes. In her five years with NRR, she'd chosen color for over a hundred walls, but this morning she'd been at Hardy's Hardware for an hour, unable to make a decision.

Tess stood in front of the paint chips and stared at the blur of color, a shiny bald-headed Frank Hardy beside her. She shook her head. "I just don't know."

"You could go white," Frank suggested.

"True…"

"What's the plan for the house?"

"I'm not sure." Maybe that was part of the problem here—no clear goal. Damien still hadn't told her what he was going to do with the house after she fixed it up.

Frank took a chip labeled Basic Eggshell off the board and held it out for her. "Neutral is good."

Sure. Good, but kind of boring. "The thing is, Frank, the man who owns the house is just not a neutral guy, and it's not a neutral house."

"Do I know this guy?"

"Probably."

"Who is it?" Impatience with the nutty woman was starting to register on his face. "Maybe if I knew who you were working for I could be a better help to you."

Maybe, but she wasn't experiencing the greatest luck with the people in town who knew she was working for Damien. Best to keep that information to herself. "I think I'm just going to go for it." She started handing over paint chips. "I'll take the Ryegrass for the kitchen, Toasty and Svelte and Sage for living room and dining room, Buttercream for the bathroom and Ramie for the bedroom."

He looked relieved. "And the exterior will have to wait for warmer weather."

"Yes. But even then, the house will always remain red."

The man's voice came from behind them, and both Tess and Frank turned to see Damien standing there. He looked very tall under the store's low ceiling and very handsome in jeans, black sweater and wool coat.

"For a project that's supposed to be done by me and only me, you're around an awful lot," Tess said, only mildy irritated. "What are you doing here?"

"I'm in dire need of a rake," he said with complete seriousness, walking toward her.

"Yeah, right. You were spying on my paint choices."

Damien smiled lazily. "I'd like to see what I'm getting for my money."

Tess gave him a look of mock disgust. "Where's the trust, dude?"

His brows went up. "Dude?"

Sticking out his hand in Damien direction, Frank grinned. "So, you're the not-so-neutral guy, huh?"

Damien shook it and grinned. "She was talking about me?"

"Didn't know it was you, but now that I do, I get it."

"Get what?" Tess asked Frank.

Frank shrugged, stuffed his hands into the pockets of his stained overalls. "Why it took you so long to decide. Mr. Sauer does that to all the ladies."

Tess snorted. "What? Make them crazy?"

"In a word, yup."

Tess cocked her head to the side and said in a high, breathy, girlie voice, "Well, I just can't decide anything, you make me too crazy."

Frank burst out laughing, pointing at Tess. "I like her."

"Yeah." Damien's sapphire gaze moved over her face in a hungry, possessive way, sending an electrifying jolt of awareness right into Tess's core. It had been so long since she'd felt something stir her up that way. She hardly remembered how good it was to feel turned on. How unfortunate it was that the man who had done the stirring was also the man who wanted to punish her, then put her behind him and forget she ever existed.

Frank cleared his throat. "All right. Give me a half hour for the six gallons."

Tess thanked him, then walked outside with Damien beside her. It was a crisp, winter morning with just enough sun to make being outside moderately tolerable. From lampposts to street signs to shop windows, the town was dressed for Christmas, and, feeling in pretty good spirits that day, Tess suggested they take a walk down the sidewalk to enjoy the sights.

As Damien walked beside her, he said, "I stopped by the house."

She was about to ask him once again about his ongoing involvement in the renovation but decided against it. He was here, in town, and had made himself involved. He was a man who did what he wanted and got what he wanted. Trying to stop him would surely prove fruitless.

"And how's the drywall looking?" she asked.

"Satisfactory. I see you found Jamie and Max."

She nodded. "Best drywallers in the county."

"So they say," he said as they rounded the corner. "Where are you off to now?"

"I have a date."

He came to a dead stop on the sidewalk. "What?"

His eyes were fierce and practically black as he stared down at her.

A shiver of satisfaction moved through her at his reaction. But she mentally flicked it away. "I have a date with a flooring salesperson."

She watched him process this information, then make a satisfied grunt before continuing down the street. "Driving into Jackson?"

"Yep. They have a flooring outlet there. I'm thinking maybe some prefab oak."

He sniffed imperiously. "Prefab? No. Absolutely not."

She looked him over. "You know, you've turned into quite the snob, Sauer."

"Why? Because I like good quality, natural materials?"

"Prefab can be really nice."

"I only want the best materials used on this house."

"Why?" A sudden gust of snowy wind assaulted her, and she pulled the collar of her coat tighter around her neck. "What is the plan for this house, Damien? I mean, correct me if I'm wrong, but if you're going to do your thing and flip it, isn't the rule to put in the best product for the cheapest price?"

Damien was quiet for a moment, then he said neutrally, "I won't be flipping the house."

Okay. So, he wasn't selling. Why did that make her feel so relieved? Why did that make her feel anything at all?

The town was small, and soon they ran out of

sidewalk and shops, and they were headed into the park. Neither one of them suggested turning back, and as they neared an abandoned, snow-covered swing set, Tess turned off the path and made a beeline for the swings. She brushed off the tuft of snow covering the plastic red seat and sat. Damien stood nearby and watched her swing back and forth gently.

"If you could choose anything for the floors," he said evenly. "Never mind the cost, what would you choose?"

"You mean, my fantasy floor?"

He nodded.

She thought for a moment, then sighed. "Oh, let's see. Probably, thick planks, antique wood, maybe barn wood."

He nodded. "Okay."

"Okay, what?"

"Do it."

She laughed, continuing to swing back and forth even though it was starting to make her nauseous. "That kind of floor can run twenty dollars a square foot."

"Just order it, but make sure it's here at the end of the week."

"That's impossible."

"Nothing's impossible. Pay whatever they ask for the shipping and they'll get it here in a week." His cell phone rang and he glanced at the number, seemed to deem it unimportant and slipped it back in his coat pocket. "In fact, I want you to pick everything for the house with no thought to the cost. Make all your choices fantasy choices."

She put her feet down and skidded to a stop. "Come on, Damien."

"What?"

"Make all the choices fantasy ones? To what end?"

"I'm not following."

She shook her head. "I don't get this. What are you doing?"

"Is there something wrong with enjoying your work?"

This went past enjoying her work. "Is this some show of how much money you have?"

His eyes narrowed. "I don't put on shows."

"You have to know that I'm not interested in your money and what it can buy. It doesn't impress me. It means nothing to me. Less than nothing."

He laughed bitterly. "I find that hard to believe."

"What does that mean?" she demanded.

"It's why you went with a man you didn't love."

"What?"

"Henry offered you security," he said, walking over to her. "With him you believed your future would be set, financially and otherwise. Isn't that true?"

"Yes, it's true."

"And what did I offer you?" He stood before her, his face taut, his gaze searching hers. "Not much— just a hope for a future."

"Do we really need to do this?" She pushed herself off of the swing. The paint was probably done.

Without another word, she walked past Damien. But she didn't get very far.

"And now look at us," he called after her. "Your future, your security is in my hands."

She stopped, just feet away. The past wouldn't rest as long as there were others still living in it. And Damien clearly was. He sounded so cruel, so unhappy, so delighted. It was disgusting and foolish, and she couldn't stop herself from turning around and walking right back up to him. When she was there, in his face, her breathing unsteady and her jaw trembling, she blurted it out. "Do you want to know why I went with him? Why I left you?"

"Yes."

"I loved him, Damien."

"I don't believe you."

She said the words slowly. "I was in love with him."

His jaw was clenched so tight she thought it might snap. "You were in love with what you thought he could give you."

"It's all the same."

"No, it's not."

"How would you know?"

She turned around to go, but he grabbed her arm and pulled her back to face him. "If you loved him, what was it you felt for me?"

She lifted her chin. "Lust."

His eyes darkened with rage. "Then you won't mind this."

She didn't have time to react as he leaned in and covered her mouth with his, his free hand cupping her nape.

His kiss was hard, punishing, and she wanted to be repelled by it, by him, but she wasn't. Every muscle, every inch of her skin trembled and ached. Yes, it had been a long time since she was touched this way, but it wasn't that, it was Damien. He was an artist, always had been. The way he held her, his lips taking greedily one moment, then pulling back to nibble and slowly suckle.

Tess sagged against him, her fists wrapped around the collar of his coat, her hips pressing into his thigh.

Her pulse slapped against her rib cage. She wanted more, so much more. If only they were back at the red house, not outside in the park....

Delicious, mind-numbing heat quickly turned to anxiety as she realized where she was and what she was doing and who had started it all. She released him, pushing him away as she stepped back. Her brain felt foggy and she shook her head.

"That will not happen again." She didn't look at him, couldn't, her body was still humming.

This time when she turned and walked away, he didn't reach out to stop her. But his words echoed through the snow-covered park, a dark, delicious warning...

"Don't be so sure."

"Slow down, Damien, for heaven's sake."

"I'm fine."

"You're going to choke." Her hands planted on her formidable hips, Wanda Bennett watched Damien devour the plate of food she'd just set in front of him. Inside her food store, there was a diner counter where she served the basics, from grilled cheese to pancakes. It all depended on her mood. Today her mood had run in the direction of everything egg related. Eggs weren't really high on Damien's list of favorite foods, but he never tried to persuade Wanda to do anything else but exactly what she wanted to do. She was just like him, arrogant and stubborn as hell. If there weren't such a difference in the colors of their skin, he might wonder if they were related.

"Aren't you going to Minneapolis this afternoon?" she asked him.

"Yes." He had a four-o'clock meeting with an investor. "I have to be at the airport in twenty minutes."

"Why aren't you eating on the plane, then?"

He shrugged.

"Steak and champagne is a helluva lot better than my greasy egg sandwich."

"No, it's not," he said sullenly.

She glared at him expectantly. "What's the problem? Is it the girl? The redhead?"

Damn right it was the girl. Always that girl. Why couldn't he be done with her? Why couldn't he have stopped himself from going there, kissing her, tasting her. Now all he wanted was more. "I need a napkin. Or a hose."

Wanda ignored him. "Yeah, I figured she wasn't just an employee. But she's not really your type, either."

"I don't have a type."

"No? I suppose it's just a coincidence that every woman who's ever followed you up here has weighed less than a toothbrush with a figure to match. And," she pointed out dramatically, "I swear a couple of them have shown up on the covers of those rag mags over by the register." Wanda shook her head. "Never understood why a man like you would take company with women who don't know their nose from their elbows…but it's none of my affair."

"No, it's not." He stood and tossed money on the counter. "Truth is, Wanda, those women are wonderfully uncomplicated. No strings, no—"

"No real feelings?" she interrupted.

Damien shot her a defensive look. "I have to go."

She pressed her lips together and shrugged. "Okay, go."

Wanda was the one woman in his life who never pressed him for anything more than what he wanted to give. "She is my past," he said with far too much irritation. "She made me what I am."

A slow smile touched Wanda's full lips. "And what is that?"

"A soulless, uncompromising pain in the ass."

She grinned broadly. "A devil in the bedroom and in the boardroom?"

Damien's brow lifted, and he matched her grin with one of his own. "You'd never marry me, would you?"

"If you were ten years younger…maybe."

He leaned over the counter and gave her a peck on the cheek. "It's supposed to snow tonight. Be careful going home."

* * *

It was nearly midnight, but the last thing Tess felt like doing was sleeping. She was running on Double Stuff Oreos and diet cola, and had just finished the demo of the kitchen and bathroom floors, removing all the old tiles. The installers were coming tomorrow with the antique hand-hewn limestone she'd found through Frank at the hardware store.

She cranked up the stereo she'd bought that afternoon. She had a thing for eighties music, especially Prince, and as she poured the old tiles from the dustpan into the garbage can and hauled them outside, she danced. She was in the middle of the living-room, on her last load of tile, when it happened. The floorboard beneath her creaked, then cracked, then suddenly gave way.

She had no time to react as her slipper-clad foot dropped through the subflooring. For a moment she just stood there, one foot on the floor, the other in a hole.

"Damn dry rot," she muttered, dropping onto her backside and easing her foot out. But as she did, the pain came on fast. Then she noticed her slipper had fallen off, and her naked foot was sporting a good deal of blood. Confused, she cupped her foot and rotated it so she could see the ball and heel, find the source of the blood. Her stomach clenched when she saw it. There was a nasty-looking gash on the ball of her foot.

"Crap." She took off her other slipper and pressed the soft side against the open cut, then she hobbled to the bedroom where she kept the emergency kit.

After cleaning the wound with hydrogen peroxide, she grabbed a butterfly Band-Aid. She tried to get the cut to close well, but every time she moved, it hurt like hell and blood seeped out everywhere.

She was going to need stitches. How in the world was she going to make that happen?

"Tess?"

Her heart leaped into her throat as fear gripped her. Then she recognized the voice, and relief spread through her. Before this moment, she'd never thought she'd be so happy to hear his voice. "I'm in here, Damien—the master bedroom."

He walked in, looking cold, tired and thoroughly pissed off. "Are you completely insane?"

"Is that a serious question?"

"It's after midnight and the front door is wide open."

"I was working."

"If I hadn't been driving by—" Then he saw the blood on her foot, on the slipper, on the floor. "What the hell happened to you?"

"Rotting floorboard."

"I saw it when I came in, but I thought it was demo." He squatted down and inspected her foot.

"I think I sliced it on the edge of the board next to the one that gave way, or maybe there was something sharp on the subflooring—I don't know."

"Did you clean it with anything?"

"Yes and I tried a butterfly bandage, but nothing's stopping the blood. I think I need to go to the emergency room."

He got up and went to the bathroom, came back with a roll of toilet paper. He used nearly the whole thing, but in seconds he had her entire instep wrapped up like the foot of a mummy.

She gave him a nod and a smile. "Thanks."

"Sure." Then without warning, he lifted her up and gathered her into his arms.

"What are you doing?"

"Taking you to the emergency room," he said, walking out of the bedroom.

"I can call—"

"Get serious." He stepped around the rotting floor-board and walked out the door. "An ambulance takes forever. I'm here and I'm taking you."

"Are you sure this won't mess up your plans to punish me?" she said dryly. "You know, by actually helping me?"

His jaw tightened as they headed for the black sedan in the driveway. "You got hurt on my watch. There's nothing else to say. Now, just shut up and put your arms around my neck, you're starting to slip."

Six

As Tess sat in a plastic chair in the cold half-empty emergency room, Damien paced. Waiting was not his strong suit. Sure, there were a few other people in the E.R., but none of them had anything too serious going on, none of them belonged to him, and none of them made his gut tighten with just a look.

Anger bubbled up in his blood, and he searched the room for someone who looked as though they wanted a good verbal sparring match. But no one would make eye contact with him.

"You look like a caged animal, Damien. Sit down."

He stopped and stared at Tess. He hadn't noticed

before but she was wearing a pair of red flannel Christmas pajamas and her hair was piled on top of her head, a few wavy strands falling about her neck and shoulders. Not surprisingly, she still wore the one remaining black slipper. She was a mess, but a very sexy mess.

He scowled at her. "Are you keeping pressure on your foot?"

"Yes. Now sit down. You look nuts."

"I look nuts?" he said, ire in his tone. "You want to know what's nuts?"

"I'm guessing that's a rhetorical question," she said, her makeup-free face looking very, very beautiful, yet very pale.

His voice dropped to a whisper. "Nuts is wearing slippers during demolition."

"It was late."

He threw his hands in the air. "You were knocking out tiles."

"I wore boots for that part."

"Well, why the hell didn't you keep them on for the cleanup? What did you do when you went outside?"

"I have duck shoes outside the front door. I slipped into those."

He groaned. "Women."

"We're great aren't we?" She gave him an innocent smile. "Complicated, mysterious…"

"That's not where I was going."

Her smile suddenly evaporated, and she closed her eyes and sucked air through her teeth.

Switching from anger to concern, Damien dropped down beside her. "Does it hurt?"

"Not any worse than a tooth extraction," she muttered through gritted teeth. "Without the pain meds, of course."

He cursed. "I'll be right back." He stalked over to the front desk and spoke to the nurse, "That woman with the cut foot needs to see someone right away."

Staring at a patient chart, the nurse didn't even look up at him. "We're busy tonight, sir. She'll have to wait."

"It doesn't look all that busy to me," he said with a thread of irritation running through his tone. "There's a guy in here with a cold, and another guy who's too drunk to even fill out his paperwork. The woman I brought in is bleeding."

The nurse looked up then and shrugged. "I'm sorry. Rules are rules."

Screw rules. Damien took out his cell phone and, right there at the reception desk, punched in a number.

"Sir, please go outside to use your cell phone," said the nurse.

Damien ignored her. The phone rang three times before it was picked up.

"Hello."

"Greg, it's Damien Sauer."

"Damien?" came the tired male voice. "Everything all right?"

"Sorry to call this late, but I'm having an issue at your hospital."

"You're at the hospital? What happened?"

"Not me. A friend. She needs to see a doctor, but we're dealing with first come, first serve, and to be honest there are no emergencies ahead of us—"

The man cut him off. "I'll take care of it right now."

"Thanks."

"I'm sorry about this, Damien. I'm sure they would never have allowed this to happen if they knew who you were."

Damien hung up the phone with the president and CEO of Tribute Memorial Hospital, but he didn't move from the reception desk. Seconds later a call came through on the emergency room phone that sent everyone in a panic. The nurse who earlier had brushed him off now simultaneously blanched and smiled as she told Damien she'd be right with him, then rushed away with several other members of the hospital staff.

Thirty seconds later, two nurses and a doctor burst through the double doors with the cleanest of squeaky-clean wheelchairs, and Tess was whisked away to a private room.

"All right," Tess said to the male nurse who had lifted her from the wheelchair and was gently placing her on a bed. "What did he do?"

She was pointing at Damien, who only shrugged and said, "I'm going to find you some ice chips and the best wound specialist in this hospital."

He was just outside the door when he heard Tess say, "Seriously, did he threaten you guys?

The male nurse laughed. "No, miss."

"Then what's all the fuss?"

"The man who brought you in is Damien Sauer."

"I know."

"Then you also know that he donated the new emergency wing to the hospital?"

Tess sighed. "No, that part I didn't know."

Damien drove his car up the steep hill without hitting a rock, hard chunk of snow or pothole. Pretty damn impressive. Not that the woman next to him had noticed. She'd been asleep for the past ten minutes, the painkillers they'd given her at the hospital working their magic. But as he pulled into the garage and killed the engine, she stirred, her hands closing around her purse, a soft moan escaping her lips.

He looked over at her, lifted a brow. "Hey."

She turned to him, her eyes heavy and tired. "Hi." Her foot was wrapped in a bandage and in his trunk was the pair of crutches the hospital had given them. "Where are we?" she asked.

"You're staying with me."

Tess came awake immediately, even sat up a little in her seat. "No."

"Don't be an ass, Tess. You heard the doctor. You need to stay off your foot for a few days."

"Not here."

"You need the help."

"I don't," she said defiantly. "I can handle this myself."

"How?"

She paused, then let her head fall back against the seat. "Fine, I need help." She rubbed a hand over her face. "But I'll get it from someone else."

"Who?"

"I'll go home, back to Minneapolis. You can get someone to finish the job."

There was no way he was letting her out of his life just yet. He needed so much from her: to make her love him again; to feel her mouth again; to leave her cold like she'd left him. "I don't want anyone else to finish the job." His voice grew dangerously low. "That wasn't our deal."

"Well, how do you think the house is going to get done? I won't be able to do anything major for at least two days. I have a tiling guy coming tomorrow to help me lay the tile, and there's no way—"

"I'll do it."

She stared at him. "What?"

"I'll help the guy lay tile. I've done it a hundred times."

"Not lately, I'm willing to bet."

"You think I can't get dirty?" Damien asked with a touch of heat.

Her mouth twitched with amusement and she returned bluntly, "No, I think you can definitely get dirty."

"Was that an insult or a sexual innuendo?"

She shrugged. "Who knows? Depends if it was me talking or the drugs."

He chuckled. "Perhaps a little of both. Now, tomorrow I'll meet the guy at…what time?"

"Eight," she supplied, looking unconvinced. "You sure you're up for all that manual labor now that you're Mr. Sauer, millionaire real estate mogul who donates hospital wings on a whim."

"That had nothing to do with a whim. That was a kick-ass tax deduction."

She looked at the ceiling. "Oh, that kind heart of yours, Damien."

Laughing again, he got out of the car and came around to her side. But when he got there, Tess was starting to fade a little. The twinkle in her eyes from a moment ago had disappeared, and she was sitting back against the seat, looking miserable. With supreme gentleness, he bent and slipped his hands underneath her. "I'm going to carry you."

"And I'm going to let you," she whispered.

"Pain's back?"

"With a vengeance and a hammer and some kind of hand-crank drill."

He shook his head, grinned. "You're the only one I know who can joke through their pain."

"Who's joking?"

He carried her into the house, through the living room and up the stairs to the second floor. He'd called ahead and had instructed Olin to fix up the room overlooking the garden. He'd never admit it to anyone but himself, but he'd had Tess in mind when he'd designed the room. It had a huge bed with a down comforter, a lavish bathroom and wall-to-wall windows. Even in the sea of pain she was riding, she smiled when she saw it.

"Nice room."

"It has a great view in the morning." He laid her on the bed, her back against the pillows.

She looked up at him. "Is this your room?"

"No."

"Then how do you know about the view in the morning?" She stopped herself, put a hand up. "Forget I asked."

He sat beside her. "What are you rambling on about?"

"Your stay in this room with your many guests. You have had women stay in here before, right?"

"Does it matter?"

Her face contorted with pain and she practically barked out the word, "No."

"All right. Relax now. Can I help you take off something?"

She smirked. "Cute."

A grin tugged at his mouth. She was something else, this one, he thought as he opened the bottle of pain medicine she'd been given at the hospital pharmacy. He took out a pill, then he handed her a bottle of water from the bedside table. "Take this."

"With pleasure." She popped the pill, drank the water, then sank back against the pillows, closing her eyes. After a moment her eyes drifted back open and they locked with his. "Hey."

"Hey."

"Thank you."

"For what?" He felt himself softening with her, and it killed him.

"Helping me out. It should just be the one night, then—"

"Stop, Tess."

But she wouldn't. "I'm a pretty quick healer. Tomorrow I should be a lot better, and I won't need to be watched over or—"

"I get it," he interrupted with an edge to his voice. "You don't want to rely on anyone." He reached over and pulled the covers up to her chin, then he stood. "Go to sleep now."

She nodded and closed her eyes, and Damien turned to leave.

Yes, he wanted to touch her again, make her need him, but he had to be vigilant. If he got too close, cared too much, there was a chance he might end up needing her again—and that he could not allow.

Tess was dreaming. It was one of those situations where she knew she was dreaming and she wanted to stay in it, and see it through to the end. She was dancing the tango in a competition, and her partner couldn't seem to hold her correctly. Every time he tried, she'd slip out of his arms. Around them, other couples dipped and stomped and made grand gestures with their arms, but Tess just stood there in the middle of it all, waiting,

waiting for this guy to get his act together and take her in his arms.

Not far away, at the judges' table, was Damien. He sat on a throne, a crown on his head, watching them, his eyes flared and his jaw set as though he found the whole thing repellent. As the music dissolved and the couples danced off the floor, Damien stood and walked toward her, his hand outstretched…

And then Tess opened her eyes. The music was gone, along with the activity and drama. She was in Damien's guest room and her foot was bandaged and it stung like the devil. She blinked, then glanced around. The curtains had been drawn on only one side of the massive windows, leaving the other side exposed. Outside, the sky was a bleak gray as if it was just too tired to contemplate morning….

Maybe in an hour or two, it seemed to say.

On the other side of the room, Damien was asleep in a chair by the fireplace. Tess's first reaction to seeing him there was to feel comforted by his presence. But that was no good, right? Comforted by the man who wanted her to suffer so he could get her out of his mind and his life? That mentality didn't sound like something she would ever be comfortable being around.

She just stared at him, a heart-stopping Adonis in a blue sweatshirt and jeans. Had he actually slept in that chair all night? she wondered. And why? Seriously, why was he even letting her stay at his house?

Why did he seem to despise her one moment, then treat her so gently the next?

Her gaze caught on something beside him on the floor. Her suitcase. He had gone back to the red house for her things. Her belly clenched. He was expecting her to remain there for more than a day.

She shifted in the bed, tried to get comfortable, but the bandage on her foot was awkward and the sting had morphed into a painful ache and stiffness.

Well, his expectations were going to be met, she thought. She wasn't going anywhere. A wave of panic moved into her already tight belly. She hated feeling stuck, feeling as though she were unable to get up and go, no matter how desperately she wanted to. It reminded her of those endless, or seemingly endless, days and nights in Henry's house, where he watched every move she made and pulled her back if she tried to put even a pinky toe across the line.

"You're awake."

Her head came up with a jerk. Damien was staring at her, so handsome, so devilish with his dark eyes and stubbled jaw. "I'm awake."

"You okay?"

"Can't sleep."

"Does your foot hurt?" He got up, came to sit beside her on the bed.

"Only if I move it."

"Then don't move it."

Her heart stuttered. Why did he look concerned? Was this just a way of helping her to get better faster, getting her back to work? Was he willing to be extra nice just to get her to finish the house?

As she downed two more pain pills, she thought about how her mind worked now. The belief that there was always a motive behind any action. She hated it. But wasn't there was always a motive with men?

She gestured to her bag on the floor. "Thanks for getting my stuff."

"Sure."

She took a deep breath. "You know, Damien. I'm not comfortable here."

"I know."

"With you taking care of me."

"I know."

"In fact, it makes me a little crazy."

A smile tugged at his mouth. "Too bad."

She returned his smile. "You should go back to your room, get some sleep."

He didn't move. His gaze raked over her face, then paused at her mouth. "Yeah, I probably should."

But instead he leaned in and kissed her.

Seven

Damien knew the moment he tasted her that he had just bought his ticket to hell.

Nothing—not even a bandaged, aching foot—was going to stop him from taking more. It was as if time had never passed. She smelled the same—that sweet, cool vanilla scent that had always driven him insane. He touched her face, her soft cheek, felt the skin tighten as she opened her mouth and deepened the kiss. The action tied him in knots, had his head pounding, his heart, too.

He dropped his head back, stared at her, into those large, hungry gray eyes. He'd never wanted anything more than he wanted her at that moment, and when she gave him a small, tentative smile, he crushed his mouth to hers, devouring the wet heat of her, changing angles with every breath, her long red curls tickling his face.

On a soft sigh, Tess placed her hands on either side of his head, her fingers snaking into his hair, forcing him closer.

Damien went hard as granite. This was going to be punishment for them both, pleasure for them both.

He ripped his mouth from hers and kissed her neck, nuzzling at the spot where her pulse pounded. She moaned and fisted his hair, tugging him closer. He nipped at her skin the way she used to love as his fingers madly searched for the buttons on her pajama top.

"Kiss me," she whispered. "Kiss me so I can't say no."

Her words excited him, yet were a warning, too— but he was too far gone to care. He wanted her mouth again, wanted to taste her tongue, suckle and bite and make her shiver, make her wet.

His mouth covered hers as his fingers flicked open the buttons on her top. He could hardly wait to feel her, that soft, milky skin beneath his palm. He cursed against her mouth as his hand slid beneath the flannel and over the full curve of her breast. She moaned and arched against him, and the sound filled him with longing. He liberated the buttons of her pajama top, then lowered his head and gently lapped at the soft peak, then again and again, circling the pink flesh until the nipple turned dark and hard.

Tess let her head fall back against the pillow as he continued in easy, lazy circles. Then, when his body and mind were about to explode, Damien took the hard bud into his mouth and suckled deeply. Again and again he suckled until Tess's mewling sounds turned to deep moans. He continued as he let one hand drift down her belly to the top of her pajama bottoms. Her reaction was quick. She stiffened and her hand came down over his.

His head came up and he looked at her.

She swallowed, shook her head. "It's…it's my foot. Hurts."

He turned away. "Dammit. I'm sorry." He felt like a giant ass. What kind of man hit on a woman in pain? Maybe the kind who was only looking for a little payback. He stood. "I'm gonna go."

"Back to bed?"

Not a chance. "I'm going to the red house. Get things set up for the tile job."

"It's so early."

"By the time I get there the sun will be up."

"Okay."

He raised a brow at her. "You're not to move."

"Damien…"

"If you need anything," he said, his body feeling as tight as a jackhammer. "Olin is here, and you just have to call down."

"I'll be going to the ladies' room alone," she said with a half smile.

"Of course." He walked over to the fireplace and

grabbed her crutches. "Use these only if absolutely necessary."

"Yes, sir." She gave him a mock salute.

"Now, if you get bored, there's some books on the nightstand here, and—" he gestured to the large trunk at the end of the bed "—there's a television in there. You just have to use the remote."

"Seriously?" she asked, surprised.

He nodded.

"It's inside the trunk?"

"Yes."

"Fancy."

She sat there, in bed, her cheeks flushed, her hair tousled and sexy and Damien felt as if he was going to explode.

Too damn much already. He couldn't stare at her for one more second. He turned around and walked out of the room, calling over his shoulder, "I'll be back around noon."

Once upon a time, a rabbit was caught in a trap. It sat there for hours until it felt as though it was going quite mad, then it proceeded to gnaw its foot off. Yes, it was bleeding and in pain as it limped through the forest, but it was free.

With her crutches tucked under her arms, Tess explored the second floor. It was all she could do. No up and no down. She had ruled out the stairs, as she had easily envisioned herself falling down them and being bedridden in Damien's ultramodern house long after he'd returned to California.

Slow and steady, she walked down the hallway, past a few more bedrooms, then a workout room and a billiard room. None of these rooms did anything to pique her curiosity. But then, at the very end of the house, in a large, square-shaped room, she saw a library. Heavy on charm, the space was lined in books and artwork. The furniture was a mixture of leather and chenille, and in the middle of one wall, a river-rock fireplace.

Perfect. A lively blaze danced in the fireplace, and after Tess grabbed a few random novels from the shelf, she sat in front of the fireplace on the brown leather couch.

As she was relaxing, her foot propped up on the coffee table, she saw something move out of the corner of one eye. She turned to see the man she had dubbed "Danny Devito" enter the room.

He inclined his head. "Good morning, Miss York."

"Hi, there. Olin, right?"

"Yes, miss."

"Good, because I wanted to apologize for the other day. I was pretty rude."

Olin shook his head. "No, miss."

"Oh, c'mon, Olin, it's okay. You can say it."

The man smiled, but it was a very thin-lipped one, as though he were fighting the urge to laugh. "You seemed...frustrated."

"I was. But I'm sure that's not the first time you've

seen a frustrated woman—you know, with who your boss is and everything."

Olin's smile faded. "Can I get you something, miss? Breakfast? Coffee?"

"No, thank you."

"I could help you back to the room, if you wish."

Boy, she knew where this was headed. "Thanks, Olin. But I'm good here."

Olin's brown eyes were filled with nervous energy. "It's just that Mr. Sauer said you shouldn't be out of bed, miss."

"I'm sure he did."

"I'm sensing a *but* miss?"

She smiled. "But I don't take orders from Mr. Sauer."

The man grimaced.

Tess shrugged. "I'm good here, really. No worries, Olin, okay?"

Olin didn't look convinced, but he nodded anyway. "Yes, miss." Then inclined his head and left the room.

Tess returned to her book, but after thirty minutes or so she started to get a little antsy. Propped up on crutches once again, she circled the room, not really looking for anything in particular. But when she came to an ancient-looking desk in an alcove off the main part of the library, she was intrigued. She went to the desk and sat. There were only two things on the desktop: writing paper with a modern DS embossed on the top of it, and a very nice pen. This had to be Damien's desk, Damien's chair.

She'd never been much of a snoop, but something about being at Damien's desk without him knowing made her ultracurious. She reached down and opened the long, thin drawer just under the desktop. Her pulse quickened as she searched through a few papers, a map of China and a small bag of sour candy. She didn't know what she was looking for until she found it. Two photographs. The first was of her and Damien in her college apartment, the one right off of campus. What was he doing with this, she wondered, staring at the picture.

She and Damien looked so young, and so totally happy. Why couldn't she remember that feeling?

She looked at the second photograph. How the hell had he gotten this? The photo was of her wedding day. She and Henry were standing close, holding her bouquet between them. Tess narrowed her eyes. Unlike the other picture, she didn't look exactly happy, but she did look hopeful. Things hadn't started to change yet; Henry hadn't shown his controlling side yet. Henry smiled back at her in the picture, and a shiver moved over her, settling on the scar covering her inner thigh—that hateful scar that would never go away, and would have to be explained if she ever let a man touch her below the waist.

Flashes of her early-morning makeout session with Damien went through her mind. She'd almost gotten that close with him, and he was the last person she wanted to know about her scar.

She took a deep breath and stuffed the pictures back in the drawer. Just as she closed it, she heard, "You never used to be a snoop, Tess York."

Startled, she pushed away from the desk and stood. She fumbled for her crutches.

"Need some help?" he asked.

"Nope."

He walked to her, his blue eyes glistening with mischief. "Find anything interesting?"

"Huh?"

"In my desk. When I came in you seemed fixated on something."

"Spider."

His brow lifted. "You saw a spider?"

"A big, black, hairy one," she explained, knowing full well that he not only didn't believe her, but thought her a total idiot as well. She let her head fall forward and blurted out the truth. "Okay, I was snooping and I saw the two pictures in there. I'm sorry, it was rude…"

He said nothing, and his expression was unreadable. Was he mad? Annoyed? Embarrassed? Who knew. He was giving nothing away. In fact, he changed the subject all together. "Hungry?"

"A little," she said uneasily.

"Good. I've decided that we're going to have lunch in your room."

"Okay." She actually wouldn't mind putting her foot up again. The ache had returned.

He nodded. "I'll meet you there in ten minutes. I'm going to shower first."

Tess paused, and for the first time since Damien had found her at his desk, she really looked at him. From shoes to spiky hair. He had gunk all over him, all over his hands and clothes, probably a mixture of tile adhesive and grout. Her mouth twitched as she remembered him looking like this many a time. He was a man of labor once again.

He stared at her. "What?"

"What?" she returned innocently.

"What's with the face? The grin?"

Was she grinning? That wasn't good. "You just reminded me of this guy I knew a long time ago."

"Really," Damien said in a surly tone.

She nodded. "Yep. He'd always come to pick me up with his hands and face caked with paint or something equally gross."

"Yeah, I remember that guy," Damien said, sticking his hands in his pockets. "He used to be so damn excited to see you he'd forget to clean up before driving over to your house."

"I let him use my shower, didn't I?" Tess said, grinning.

Damien's lips twitched with a faint smile. "You did more than that."

Heat rushed into Tess's cheeks, and she laughed. "Come on."

He walked toward her, his gaze eating her up. "You were damn good at getting paint off and out of the most intimate of places."

"I was a dedicated worker even then."

"I'll say." Without a warning, he scooped her up. "Too bad you've got that bandage on. I could use a little help in the shower today."

For one second she felt the urge to fight him, fight being in his arms. But the feeling quickly dissipated. She didn't have to fight him or fear him. No matter what his motives were in making her come to Tribute and fix up the house, she knew in her heart, in her gut, that Damien Sauer would never make her feel like a frightened, trapped animal.

They were nearing the door to the library when Tess called out, "Wait. My crutches."

"Nope. No crutches, no more getting out of bed."

"Fine. I'll just get Olin to swipe them for me. We're like this now." She crossed her fingers.

"Yeah, right." Damien shifted her in his arms and kept right on walking. "Come on Tess, I need you healthy and walking and back on the job."

Tess laughed as they headed down the hallway. "Manual labor getting to you already?"

"Tiling was never something I enjoyed. I liked the actual building, though." He walked into the guest room and placed her on the bed. "You might find it hard to believe, but on my jobs in California I get in there from time to time and put walls up."

"You're right. I'd find that hard to believe."

He narrowed his eyes with mock severity. "I'll be back in ten minutes."

"I can hardly wait," she said sarcastically, fighting a smile.

"I know—but you'll just have to."

For the first time in a long, long time, Tess watched a man walk away, fully enjoying the view of his lean, hard backside as he went.

The last time they'd eaten in bed, they hadn't made it past the salad.

Damien stared. And if Tess's robe crept open any further, exposing the gentle slope of her breast any more, they weren't going to make it very far today, either.

Lying on the bed, her hair loose and her face free of makeup, Tess held up her sandwich and announced, "This rivals Olivia's Croque Monsieur."

Damien grinned. "High praise?"

"The highest. This cream sauce is insane. And the ham… And these French fries," she continued, lounging back against the dense pillows. "How are they made? They're as light as a leaf."

"If you really want to know, I'll ask Marilynn."

Tess paused, stared at him, her mass of red hair falling about her face. "I can't believe you have a chef."

"Is it that you can't believe I have a chef or that I made enough money to afford one?"

She stopped eating, even put down her fry. Her eyes blazed with sincerity as she said, "I never doubted you'd be successful, Damien."

"Hmm." Why did he find that so hard to believe?

"It's true. I never thought for one second you wouldn't accomplish your goals and make a million."

"Too bad a million wasn't enough." He knew he sounded like a spoiled ass, yet he didn't attempt to apologize or take it back.

"You have the wrong idea about all of this," she said, her food forgotten as her eyes filled with melancholy. "I didn't care about money—I don't care about it now. You know my history, Damien. Losing my parents so young, and having no other family to hang on to. It was brutal. I wasn't ever looking for money. All I wanted was family, a comfortable life, a—"

"A safe life," he finished for her.

"Yes. Safe was the ultimate prize to me, it's what I felt I needed to be happy."

"I wasn't safe."

"No, you weren't. You were all about risk back then. Taking risks. And for you it paid off big-time, and I'm glad."

He didn't need her to be glad for him. He didn't want her to be glad for him. "So you made your choice based on safety."

"Yes."

"And did that make you happy? Were you happy with him?"

The expression that passed over her face was quick but very telling. Pure, unadulterated revulsion.

Damien's eyes narrowed. What the hell? What had happened when she'd left Minneapolis, when she'd left him? What had happened with the safe choice, Henry?

He was about to probe further when they were interrupted by a knock at the door.

Annoyed, he fairly shouted, "Come in."

It was Olin, looking appropriately sheepish. "Sir?"

"What is it?"

"I'm sorry, sir, but there's a problem with the house down the hill."

"What it is?"

"There's been a break-in."

"What? At one in the afternoon?"

"The workmen had gone to lunch, and when they got back the door had been knocked in."

Damien cursed. "By who?"

"A young lady," Olin supplied.

He felt Tess's gaze on him and he turned. A smile tugged at her full mouth and she lifted a brow at him. "Someone you know?"

"Doubtful," Damien said testily. "The women I know would never follow me up here and break into one of my properties."

"You sure about that?"

"Actually, Miss York," Olin said quickly, not meeting her gaze. "The woman says she's a friend of yours."

Tess looked shocked. "What?"

Olin nodded. "She was brought here. She's downstairs in the foyer. Shall I bring her up?"

Damien answered first. "Absolutely."

Eight

"You know this is insane, right?"

As she sat on the bed, in the very spot that Damien had occupied not more than sixty seconds ago, Ms. Olivia Winston's large brown eyes were filled with concern.

Tess's business partner, chef extraordinaire and, after today, nearly a class-C felon, made no bones about what was to be done. "I'm taking you home right now."

"I can't go now," Tess told her.

Olivia frowned. "Can't? Is this guy keeping you here against your—"

"No, no, no. I hurt my foot during the renovation and he's…helping me out." She wondered where Damien was now. He'd been very polite to Olivia, the woman who had broken down his door, before leaving the room.

Olivia took a deep breath and blew it out. "Jeez, Tess. When the hospital called looking for you, I completely freaked out—"

"Wait…the hospital called you?"

"Called the office. It was the number you gave on the form in the *emergency room*." She said the last two words with real feeling.

Tess leaned back against the pillows, cocked her head to one side. "I'm sorry you got scared. It's just a cut. I had a few stitches, and I should be up and moving by tomorrow."

Olivia took a moment to process the information, then seeming somewhat pacified, she asked, "So, are you okay here—I mean, barring the foot. This guy is cool?"

"He's fine."

"Yeah, he is fine," Olivia said dryly, "gorgeous even—but is he treating you well?"

Tess laughed. "Very well. Don't worry."

"Come on, Tess. You're in a client's house, a guy who's basically a stranger. It's not right. I really think you should pack it in and come home."

Tess chewed her lip. She didn't want to go there, didn't want to tell her partner the truth. But Olivia looked as though she wasn't about to let up on the subject. "Listen, Liv, Damien Sauer isn't just a client, and he's definitely not a stranger."

Olivia's brows knit together. "Oh?"

"We used to be an item, back in my college days."

Her brows relaxed. "Oh."

"Yeah, he wanted me to renovate the house. It was the first house he bought back in the day when we were dating, and we spent a lot of time there... So I really know the ins and outs of the place."

She shrugged. "Well then, it makes sense that he'd want to hire you."

Tess gave Olivia a tight smile.

But Olivia wasn't done with the questions. "Why didn't you tell me?"

The reason was right there, on the tip of her tongue, and that's where it remained. She shook her head. "I don't know."

The three partners of No Ring Required had secrets in their past and in their present, and each had done her very best to keep those secrets hidden. But as Tess knew, and Olivia and Mary as well, eventually those secrets had a way of coming out. Maybe knowledge of that was what kept Olivia from prying and pressing Tess for more. Whatever it was, Tess was thankful.

"So," Olivia said, "do you at least want me to stay and help you finish the house?"

Tess kind of did, but she knew that Damien would never allow Olivia to stay and help her. He wanted Tess, and only Tess, to make the house into a home. She smiled at Olivia. "No. Thanks though. It's some-thing...I have to do myself. You understand."

"Not really, but I'll take your word for it."

Tess pointed at her. "Hey, aren't you the only one at the office right now?"

"Yep."

"Well then, we need you there." Tess paused, thought of something that had the nerves in her stomach dancing. "You didn't call Mary when the hospital called you, did you?"

Olivia shook her head. "No. I thought I'd wait and see what was going on here before I interrupted her honeymoon."

"Good." Things had really changed with her partners. Five years ago they hardly spoke unless it was work related. And look at them now.

A bashful grin curved Tess's mouth as she looked at Olivia. "I can't believe you came here."

"Why?"

"We're business partners—"

Olivia leaned in and took a fry from Tess's plate. "If you say we're not friends I'm going to slap you—which would incidentally not be the greatest thing for your recovery."

Tess laughed. "No. It wouldn't."

Nibbling on the cold fry, Olivia said, "Listen, Tess, the three of us—you and Mary and I—we might've started out as 'just business partners,' but I think we're way more than that now. I think we've all been through a lot together. We've all come from something…maybe something not so great, something we want to continue to run from, but I think maybe it binds us."

Tess nodded. "Maybe."

"I believe we got together for a reason. And I hope we're friends now." She gave Tess a coy smile. "You know, I'm thinking that maybe it's not such a bad thing to have each other to lean on."

Olivia's words were passionate and truthful, and hard for Tess to ingest. Right now, anyway. Too much was happening with Damien and the ghosts of the past that he had brought with him. For now, Tess could only nod at her partner, but she hoped that Olivia would understand her small gesture, take it as a sign, a first step toward a future, a friendship.

And in Olivia's way, she did. Smiling, she pointed to Tess's plate and the Croque Monsieur. "Can I have a bite of that?"

"Of course." Tess handed her the uneaten half.

After taking a bite, Olivia sighed. "So good."

"I know, right?" Tess said, laughing.

"I can't believe you're supplying my food here. I left the office too quickly to make anything—you know how much I hate going anywhere without a food offering."

Tess nodded, said with mock seriousness, "I do. You're freakish that way."

Olivia narrowed her eyes. "Watch it, or you won't get any of the truffles I brought. I had them stashed in the freezer, so I could grab them quickly."

"You're such a sugar tease, Liv."

"So I've heard." She reached into her purse and

pulled out a square Tupperware, then she handed it to Tess. "Go nuts, Miz York."

Smiling, Tess settled back against the pillow, a Tupperware full of chocolate truffles against her chest. "So, how many clients are you juggling right now?"

"Three."

"Oh, man. You should get back."

"Not until I know you're all right."

"I'm fine."

Again Olivia narrowed her eyes. "You like being with this guy, don't you?"

Tess heard the question, but was too busy dealing with the shot of awareness that was rolling through her body to answer right away.

Olivia just sighed. "All three of us are raving lunatics when it comes to men. No common sense, no thinking things through—just allowing the beautiful man to sweep us away into a fantasy—"

"So, how is Mac, by the way?" Tess asked dryly.

"Wonderful. But he's such a guy. Did I tell you about his obsession with this portable driving range I bought him?"

"It's winter."

Olivia sighed. "He has it set up in the house. Three broken windows so far…"

For the first time since he'd been back in Minnesota, Damien felt a wave of apprehension move through him. Tess had a good friend in Olivia Winston, and he wouldn't be surprised if the dark-haired

beauty had already convinced her to return to Minneapolis.

He sat at his desk in the library, staring at the photograph of Tess and Henry on their wedding day.
Damien had gotten so close to finding out the truth
about their marriage. The look that had crossed
Tess's face. Pretty damn close to horror.

Damien gritted his teeth. Well, she deserved it,
didn't she? To be unhappy in her marriage? She'd
walked away from Damien for a safe, carefree life,
and he was willing to bet that it had been anything
but. Time would tell…

Damien thought about ripping up the picture and
tossing it in the trash. He didn't need it anymore. He
had her, had access to her memories, the real story.
That would fuel his fire and the need for payback.
But when he tried to rip the photograph in two, he
couldn't do it.

"Dammit," he muttered to himself. Why did he
need the thing? Was it that he had to look at them,
her in that dress and him with that persuasive grin,
to keep going, keep punishing her?

He sighed, thrust his hands through his hair.

Whatever the reason, he dropped the picture back
in his desk and slammed it shut. Then he grabbed his
coat and walked out into the hall. He heard them,
Tess and her partner, laughing in the guest room.
The sound filled him with lust and he forced himself
to turn away and go downstairs. He wanted to be in
there, in that room. He wanted to be the one who

made her laugh, see her gray eyes sparkle and fill with happiness.

Olin met him at the base of the stairs.

"I'm heading over to the red house," Damien told him. "I'll be back around six."

"Yes, sir."

"If Ms. York asks…"

Olin nodded. "Yes, sir. I'll tell her."

Only for a guy who had donated millions for a new emergency room, Tess thought as she watched Tribute Memorial's chief of staff change the bandage on her foot, all from the comfort of her bed in Damien's guest room. Doctor Keith Leeds had descended on Damien's home twenty minutes ago, medical bag in hand, ready to give Tess a thorough checkup and see how she was healing.

This was an odd occurrence, to say the least, Tess thought. After all, it took a good month for her to get an appointment with her regular doctor—forget her ever-vacationing gynecologist.

"So, what do you think?" she asked him when he'd finished dressing her foot.

Dr. Leeds was short, kind and hovering around fifty. He had a full head of gray hair and liked to fiddle with his glasses when he talked. "Looks good. Really good. But more important, how does it feel?"

"Sore. But the intense pain is gone."

"I'd take things slow. No more than a few hours on it at a time."

"So, I could walk on it?"

He nodded. "Tomorrow, you should be able to get around quite well without the crutches. Just listen to your body. If the pain graduates from sore to more—"

"Nice rhyme."

He laughed. "Thank you. Sore to more, take a break, okay?"

She nodded. "Got it."

It was at that moment that Damien walked into the room. He was dressed in jeans and a black shirt and looked as though he'd just showered, his dark hair wet and spiky. Heat moved through Tess's body at the sight of him, and she turned her attention back to the doctor.

"I'll make sure she takes it easy," Damien said, holding out his hand. "Thanks for coming by, Keith. I know house calls aren't your thing."

The man shook his hand and granted him a smile. "No problem, Damien. It's on my way home."

"So, did I hear you say Tess could walk on her foot tomorrow?"

"I did."

Tess smiled broadly at Damien. "That's right, sir. Back to work."

Doctor Leeds's brow went up, and he said to Damien, "Interesting situation you have here."

Damien chuckled. "You have no idea." He walked the doctor to the door, then said, "Olin is waiting downstairs. He'll see you out."

Dr. Leeds waved at Tess. "Take care, now."

"Will do." She smiled. "Thanks again."

When he was gone, Tess settled under the covers, then proceeded to ask Damien about the new tile. "Is it all in and grouted?"

"Yes." Damien sat on the edge of the bed. "Looks good. The stone you picked out is perfect. Modern, yet warm enough for a cottage."

"Good." With large, excited eyes, she pressed a button on the remote control that was half hidden in the comforter and watched the television slowly rise out of the chest at the end of the bed. "This is the just the coolest thing." When she looked up, she caught Damien staring at her, his eyes heavy with amusement. She heaved a dramatic sigh. "Don't worry, Mr. Sauer, I'm not getting too comfortable."

"What does that mean?"

"Just because I'm fascinated with the elevator television thing doesn't mean I don't understand what happens tomorrow."

"What happens tomorrow?"

"I go back to work, and back to living in the red house."

"Back to work, maybe," he said. "For short bursts. But you're not living in that house."

"Yes, I am."

"No." He crossed his arms over his chest and waited for her to acquiesce.

She didn't. "I think it's best."

"Not for me. You've had one accident there. I'm not taking any risks with a second."

"Not taking any risks, huh?" she said slyly.

"Not with you." A wicked glint appeared in his blue eyes.

A jolt of heat flashed into her belly. Great, she thought. Twice in five minutes.

It was back—the lust—back with a vengeance. She wanted him to kiss her again, touch her, taste her.

Fear gripped her heart, went to war with the sparks of desire heating her blood. What would he think if he saw her scar, that disgusting reminder of a past they both wanted to put behind them?

But as it was, she didn't need to worry. At that moment Damien was thinking about something completely different. "If you go back to the red house and something worse happens," he was saying, "you could sue me."

He was thinking about business.

"Right." Feeling like a jerk, she turned back to the television and started flipping through the channels. "Can't have that."

They were silent for a moment. Then Damien pointed at something on the TV. "Hey, what's that?"

"What's what?"

"Go back two stations."

Curious, she did, but once there, she shook her head vehemently. "Oh, no."

"Oh, yes."

"Hey, we're not dating anymore. I don't have to pretend I like this movie."

He turned away from *Dirty Harry* and tossed her a sardonic look. "How many times did I have endure

Meg Ryan and that Barrymore girl? *French Kiss* was not about what I thought it was going to be about…"

She laughed. "Are you saying I owe you?"

"Yeah."

"You know, you could watch it in another room—you have a media room, for God's sake."

"And not see your horrified face when Clint Eastwood says that, 'Do you feel lucky? Do yah, punk?' line? What fun is that?"

"You're a sadist."

He didn't answer, just leaned over and pressed the intercom on the table by the bed.

"Yes, Miss York?"

"We need popcorn, Olin."

The man was silent for a moment, then he said quickly, "Ah, yes, sir."

Damien looked over at Tess, raised a brow. "Butter?"

She snorted. "Are you kidding? Not that much has changed in six years."

He laughed. "Extra butter, Olin."

"Very good, sir."

Damien kicked off his shoes and got in bed beside her. Not all that close, but close enough for Tess to breathe in the clean scent of his hair and skin. Close enough for her skin to tighten and feel prickly, feel desperate for his touch.

"Can you turn it up?"

She turned back to the screen and pressed the volume button. "Just so you know," she began, "*Last of the Mohicans* is on after this."

He groaned. "No way. That's not just a chick flick, that's a period chick flick."

She laughed. "After this classic here, you're gonna owe *me.*"

"Fine." He reached over to press the intercom again. "But we're going to need a few beers to go with that popcorn."

He was screwed.

It was midnight, the movies were over, the beer and popcorn consumed, the room was lit by a full moon, and Damien was still in bed with Tess. She wasn't naked and sitting on top of him, but he felt as though he might explode just the same.

Halfway through the *Mohicans* movie, she'd fallen asleep, rolled in his direction and now here they were: Damien on his back and Tess curled up beside him, her arm around his waist, her head on his chest.

He was no sap, but tonight had been fun, sexy in an odd, sweet way—like old times. And he didn't want it to end. Maybe it didn't have to.

Could he just close his eyes, fall asleep and wake up with her next to him? Could he? He dropped his chin and kissed the top of her head, the soft, red curls that were scented with apples from her shampoo. He grinned. It was the same shampoo she'd used in college.

She stirred then, her knee escaping the confines of her robe and sliding up his thigh. An inch higher, he mused, and she'd feel every hard inch of him.

She moved again, her head lifting, her eyes, groggy and heavy, opening and trying to focus.

"Damien?"

He ran his thumb over her bottom lip. "Yes, sweetheart?"

"I wanted you." She spoke softly and slowly as though she was still in a dream state. Then her eyes closed again and she shook her head. "I wanted you so much."

His body went still. His fingers went under her chin and he lifted her face to his once more. "What did you say?"

Her eyes opened again and she looked like she was trying to focus.

"What did you just say, Tess?"

She licked her lips. "I want you."

Disappointment roared through him, but he dismissed the feeling. It wasn't what she'd originally said, that was for sure, but it was enough—enough to put flame to sun-dried brushwood.

He dipped his head and kissed her, gentle and slow, trying to coax a response from her. She was cautious at first, her kisses guarded and quick. But as he rubbed the back of her neck, nuzzled her lips with his own, her body relaxed and she opened for him, lapping at his tongue, matching his speed and the pressure of his mouth.

It took every ounce of self-control for Damien not to pull her on top of him and have his way with her. Every nerve ending, every muscle was alive, inside and out, and when she slid her hand up his chest, to his neck and around his head, he allowed himself to take her.

Like a possessed animal, he rolled, sending her to her back and settling himself above her. For a moment he just looked at her, watched her eyes glisten, her lips part and her chest rise and fall with every breath.

She belonged to him.

He would have to let her go soon, but for now, right now, she was his.

He bent and kissed her, her mouth, her chin, then down, his lips searing a path from her neck to her collarbone. He wanted to feel every part of her, taste every inch, make love to her until they were both too exhausted to speak about the past or even think about it.

Maybe then she'd be out of his system and he could go back to California and breathe again.

His hands moved over her collarbone and he pushed aside the white terry cloth robe, revealing her pale chest and her heavy, full breasts. She arched her back, thrusting her breasts and tight, pink nipples forward. Damien cupped them firmly, then rolled one taut nipple between his thumb and forefinger. He dipped his head and took the other into his mouth, rolled the tight peak against his tongue, lapped and suckled, then ever so gently bit down on the tip.

"Damien," she moaned, her head thrashing from side to side against the pillow, her hips thrusting, trying to meet his.

But Damien couldn't keep things slow and relaxed. He needed to be inside her body, needed to consume her. He cursed his frustration and reached down for the knot that held her robe together. But just as he'd gotten it undone, Tess put a hand over his and squeezed.

"Damien. Please. No more. I can't." She sounded like an injured bird, and Damien watched as she covered herself back up with the robe.

Like a hammer, the blood in Damien's veins pounded inside his head and chest and groin. But he wouldn't make demands or beg her to put him out of his misery. That wasn't his style.

Instead he moved off her, off the bed, stood there with his erection pressed against the zipper of his jeans.

Tess stared at the comforter. She wanted to die.

She sat there in the bright light of the round moon, not looking at Damien, not wanting to face what was coming next. She had allowed things to go too far. Again. What was wrong with her? Did she have no self-control when it came to this man?

She grabbed for the comforter and pulled it over her legs. What a fool she was. Damien had been unbelievably close to touching her scar.

"Tess?"

"Yes."

"Look at me."

Cowardice was not a part of her makeup, and she lifted her chin and looked at him. Her stomach clenched. Never had a man looked so sexy, his hair tousled, his eyes heavy, his cheeks flushed.

"What's wrong?" he asked darkly.

"This can't happen."

"It is happening."

He was right. They'd started something, and how was either of them supposed to go back? "I was half-asleep, Damien, too comfortable…"

"Don't try and pretend you didn't want this, Tess, because—"

"I'm not." She shook her head. "I did want it, but now…"

His eyes were devil-black and menacing. "And now? What?"

She stared at him, trying to think of what to say next. If she lied, was cruel, would it stop him from wanting her? Would it stop the flirtation and fun and frivolous moments?

Is that what she wanted?

No, but she couldn't have him find out her secret. And she would protect herself at all costs.

"Now I know that it's not fair to you to continue this," she said evenly.

He lifted a brow. "Oh? How so?"

She squared her jaw. "Because when I was kissing you, I was thinking about…" She stopped. She couldn't.

He looked ready to kill as he ground out, "Finish your sentence, Tess."

"No."

He stared at her for a moment, then he turned to leave.

Her heart pounded against her rib cage. This was

ridiculous, insane and juvenile. She was a grown woman, for God's sake.

His hand was on the door when she called, "Stop. Wait, Damien."

He glanced over his shoulder, said with a bored tone to his voice, "What?"

"It's not true."

He said nothing.

She continued, "It's not true." She released a breath. "I needed you to stop touching me, so I lied. You were right. So right. I loved it, every second that you were kissing me and touching me. I haven't felt that good in a long time. But I needed you to stop."

His jaw hard, he leaned back against the door. "Why?"

She shook her head. "I can't tell you."

His fist shot back, pounded the door. "Dammit! Come on, Tess. This is bull."

"Maybe. But to me it's my life."

He cursed.

"Damien, I'm going back to the red house tomorrow."

"You're not going anywhere," he said in a dangerous voice, his gaze fierce. "And I'm warning you, don't push me on that again."

He said nothing more as he turned, gripped the door handle and threw it wide. He was gone in seconds.

Tess dropped back against he pillow, feeling miserable and lonely. And what made it worse was that the faint scent of him lingered on her pillow.

Nine

As the first week of renovations drew to a close, the little red house had taken on a whole new look. New windows, new tile, new tub and toilet, new cabinets and new light fixtures had been installed. Tess had worked hard with some help from Damien and of course the labor of several subcontractors.

Today the beautiful vintage floors that Tess had ordered were being put in. Normally a house was painted before the floors went down, but with her injury things had gotten a bit turned around.

After an hour or so at the red house, making sure everything was going as planned, Tess had asked Damien to drive her into Jackson to pick out the new kitchen countertops. Though her foot was much better, driving was still an issue.

They hadn't spoken a word about last night, not at the red house, not on the drive to Jackson and not as they walked through Hubbard's Tile and Stone. Tess figured it was just as well. Best to get the job done and get on with it. No entanglements, no regrets and no secrets revealed.

But then again, she missed the intimacy they'd shared last night, the fun they'd shared—and the heat of his mouth when he kissed her senseless.

As the salesman hovered at her side, Tess rubbed her hand over the honed black granite she had picked out. She sighed. "This is gorgeous." Then she pointed to the clean, white Corian. "But this is practical."

Damien finished a call on his cell phone, then stated dryly, "You know my opinion on practical."

"I do."

"Well then, you know which one to get."

Tess asked the salesman to excuse them for a moment, then she turned to Damien. "Are you like this with every project?"

"Like what?"

"Impractical. I can't see you making much money if that's the case."

His gaze turned intense and personal. "This isn't every project."

She didn't want to go there, and didn't acknowledge the look. "If you're just going to sell the place, what's the point of such personal taste?"

He lifted a brow. "Who says I'm going to sell it?" His cell rang again. He checked the number, then let the call go to voicemail.

"So, what are you going to do with it, Damien?" she asked with perhaps too much interest. "Keep it as an investment property?"

"I don't know."

"Pass it down to the next generation of Sauers?" she pressed.

He shrugged. "Perhaps. But that could be a while. I'd have to get married first."

"You don't have to get married…"

"If I'm going to make little Sauers, I do."

Tess stopped talking, stopped asking questions she didn't want the answers to. The thought of Damien having children with anyone else made her feel physically ill. Not just the act that it would take to create them, but the thought of him sharing a life, a day-to-day life with a woman and their children… she couldn't conceive of it.

Oddly enough, she'd never been able to. It was one of the things that had gotten her through the past six years, settled her with Henry—believing that Damien Sauer would never get married and have babies.

And now, here he was talking about it as though it could actually happen.

Tess turned back to the granite. "I just don't see it. You and a family. No, don't see it."

"I'm an old-fashioned guy, Tess."

"Sure." She laughed, but it was a heavy, sad sound. "The millionaire jet-setter with a glass compound and a penchant for making women pay for their mistakes."

"Just one woman," he said, his gaze intense.

"Right."

He added, "And when did you decide that leaving me was a mistake?"

She opened her mouth to deny it, then stopped, ran through what she'd just said—what had accidentally popped out. How she felt that leaving him was a mistake…

She sighed inwardly. It was a truth she hated to look at, much less admit out loud, and she pressed on, changed the subject. "Are you going to tell me what you plan to do with the house or not?"

He frowned. "I'll decide what to do with it when the work's completed."

Frustrated, she shrugged. "Fine."

"So, do you want the granite?"

"Yes, I want the granite."

Damien gestured to the salesman. "She'll take the granite." Then he walked off, his cell phone to his ear.

He couldn't sleep.

Again.

Damien glanced at the clock. Midnight. What was up with midnight? His body just couldn't seem to shut down, and his mind couldn't seem to shut off. All he could think about was her. The fact that she was down the hall, sleeping, and he wanted to be next to her again, feel the warmth of her body, her arm draped over his chest.

He rolled off the bed and threw on a T-shirt and sweats. He was a jackass, thinking he could go to her and she would welcome him into her bed as though nothing had happened, as if it was six years ago and she was waiting up for him.

But he was out his door and down the hall and knocking on her door before he could talk himself out of it.

When she didn't answer, he knocked again, even said her name. When there was still no answer, he contemplated going back to his room. But then he got a strange feeling, a worried feeling, that maybe something was wrong, and he decided to go in— deal with her ire if he had to.

He opened the door silently. It wasn't terribly dark in the room. The shades were pulled back and the moon was brilliant and nearly full, illuminating the furniture. He walked over to the bed, blinked to make sure he was seeing things clearly. Then he leaned down and flipped on the bedside lamp.

His gut clenched. The bed was made, and all of Tess's things were gone.

He muttered a curse, stalked out of the room and went to find Olin.

With a large hoop of painter's tape circling her wrist like a bracelet, Tess moved on to the next window. Tomorrow was priming and painting day, and she'd wanted to get a head start.

Well, that was mostly true.

Staying in Damien's guest room was starting to feel a little too comfortable, and kind of uncomfortable at the same time. Lying in that bed, she'd wanted him beside her, watching a movie, feeling his warmth….

She ran the tape over the window molding and snapped it off. The paint colors she chose were going to be amazing, especially with the new floors.

Oh, the floors.

They were so beautiful that when she'd gotten there tonight, she had actually sat in the middle of the living room and stared at them for a full thirty minutes. If she ever won the lottery, the beige carpet in her apartment was going into the trash and these floors were going in.

Suddenly the front door burst open and Damien stood there, looking diabolically sexy and ready to do battle.

"Holy…Jeez!" Tess gripped her chest, felt her heart slamming against her ribs.

"Get your things, we're going," Damien said, his voice low and menacing.

She glared at him. "You scared the hell out of me."

He closed the door and walked into the room, his long, wool coat trailing behind him like a villain's cape. "As if you didn't know I'd come after you."

"Well, sure I did. But I thought it would be in the morning." She was starting to believe that there was no escaping this man. "How did you even know I was gone?"

"Doesn't matter."

"Olin squealed on me, didn't he?"

Damien lifted his chin. "His loyalty should be to me."

She sighed. The poor guy. She shouldn't have put him in such an awkward position. "Don't be mad at him. I begged him to drive me, told him it was sort of a life-and-death thing."

"Whatever the reason, he made a mistake and he's fired."

Damien bent and pulled back the tarp covering the floors. Tess bent next to him, her sore foot aching a little with the movement. He looked at her. "Floors are beautiful."

Awareness moved through her, sent chills to the outside of her body and heat to the inside. Her voice was easy and intimate as she said, "You're not really going to fire him, right?"

His blue eyes softened, and he gave a small shrug. "No. But I should."

"Thanks." She sat on her backside.

Damien followed suit, looking far too handsome and put together to be sitting amongst drop cloths and paint buckets. "You don't just disappear, Tess. I told you to stay in—"

"Please, Damien," she said, putting up her hand to stop him from saying anything further. "I am not your prisoner and you are not my warden."

"This isn't about keeping you captive, Tess."

"What's it about, then?"

"Keeping you safe, dammit!"

She sighed. "That was one freak accident. It's not going to happen again."

His eyes glimmered with heat. "You're right it's not, because you're coming back with me."

"No," she said firmly.

"No?"

He looked so shocked, so vexed, she couldn't help but laugh. "I know that's hard for you to hear," she said, sobering slightly. "I'm sure you don't hear it very often."

"Tess—"

"I like this house. I feel comfortable here."

"You don't feel comfortable in my house?" he demanded darkly.

She sighed. Didn't he get it? "Damien, I can't stay there…with you."

His mouth curved into a wicked grin. "Afraid I'm going to finish what I started last night?"

"Frankly, yes."

He reached over and took her hand, then bent and kissed the inside of her wrist. "Sweetheart, it doesn't matter where we are. In that house or in this one."

"So why fight it, is that what you're saying?" The heat from his mouth had branded the skin on her wrist and she felt weak. Clearly he still remembered where her most sensitive spots were.

"Why not go with your instincts, Tess?"

She forced herself to return to reality, to remember the past and what it had taught her about instincts. "I did that once before, and it didn't turn out…it didn't turn out as I'd planned."

His brows knit together. "What are we talking about? You and Henry?"

She nodded.

"Do you want to tell me what happened?"

"You only want to know so you can use it against me."

He said nothing. Didn't agree, didn't deny it.

She pulled her hand away and shook her head. "I'm right, aren't I? There's something in you that wants to really hurt me?"

Silence met her query. Damien stared at her for a good long time before he finally said, "If I'm honest with you, will you be honest with me?"

A shot of panic went through her. How honest did he want her to be? How honest would she allow herself to be?

But even as the questions circled her mind, she looked at him and nodded.

"Yes, I want to hurt you," he said softly. "I want you to feel just a fraction of what I felt when you left. And even after we're together, after we make love—because you and I both know that's going to happen—I'll still want you to hurt because I'm an ass, a miscreant." He reached out and touched her face, his fingertips brushing gently over her cheek. "When you left, I became someone else, a machine, a man with no soul."

His words cut deeply into her, fisted around her heart. Six years ago she left the man she loved for a promise of what she'd always believed would make her happy. The mistake had cost her in so many ways.

It was her turn, and he was waiting. She knew she wouldn't go all the way with the truth, but Damien deserved to hear as much as she could give him. "My marriage was a lie." She saw the surprise register on his face, but just kept going. "I wanted the perfect little life, the perfect family. Henry promised me that, and I believed him. When we knew each other in college, he was uncomplicated and sweet, but one week after we got married he showed me who he really was."

"And who was that?" Damien asked softly.

She swallowed the knot in her throat. "A mean, manipulative, controlling monster."

Damien said nothing, just stared at her, expressionless.

She said shakily, "You think I got what I deserved, right?"

He stood, held out his hand for her. "Come on, Tess."

"Henry took away my faith and my hope." She felt so tired all of a sudden. She put her hand in Damien's and let him pull her to her feet.

"You think I deserved it..." she started weakly.

But Damien was clearly done with the conversation. "Get your things," he said. "We're going back to the house."

* * *

Damien sat on a stool at the minidiner inside Wanda's store. It was hours past closing time, but when he'd shown up on Wanda's doorstep a few minutes ago, she hadn't turned him away.

With wild graying hair and a robe so thick it could double as a winter coat, Wanda poured them each a cup of coffee, then took the seat beside him at the Christmas-festooned counter. "Well, well, well…"

"I know. It's late."

"Never mind that," she said. "Are you going to tell me what the problem is or do I have to guess?"

The problem. He wasn't exactly sure himself. He just knew that after dropping Tess off at the house and getting her settled—then tossing out some threats to Olin regarding the penalties given if he ever offered Tess a ride to the red house in the middle of the night again—he'd needed to get out of his house.

Wanda grunted at him. "Fine. I'll guess. Business?"

"No."

"Must be personal, then. Not my favorite thing to discuss, but I'll do it. Spill."

The cat clock above the griddle meowed twice. Two o'clock in the morning. Damien shoved his hands through his hair. "You know how I got so successful, Wanda?"

She grinned at him. "Fine brain, fine man."

He chuckled halfheartedly. "No. Try follow through and a killer instinct."

"My second guess."

"I made a plan and I followed it through to the letter. No second thoughts, no kindness, no compassion."

"And?"

"And I'm having second thoughts about my plan."

She stood, reached over the counter and grabbed a small bottle. "Why?"

"I don't know." But he did, actually. After hearing Tess's confession about her bogus marriage and Henry being a monster, he was having second thoughts about his plans to hurt her. If she'd been hurt already, how could he…

"Come on, Damien," Wanda said, pouring the liquid from the small bottle into each mug of coffee, which, knowing Wanda, was probably whiskey. "You just don't want to admit the reason because it'll make you feel like less of a man."

Damien grinned at her over his hootch-laced coffee cup. She never let him get away with anything. He'd been parentless for more than fifteen years now, and had done just fine on his own. Then he'd met Wanda, and she'd offered her friendship and sage advice and over the years had become a motherly figure to him.

"It's the woman you met—the redhead," he admitted darkly.

Wanda nodded. "Thought so. But, Damien, hon, you can't let love influence your decisions."

"You're the only woman I know who'd say that."

Wanda just smiled and sipped her coffee.

"And incidentally," he added, "this isn't about love."

"No?"

"No." Then he amended the statement. "Well, not love now. There was love in the past and it was thrown back in my face, and you know how well a man takes something like that."

"I do. So use it. Use the anger and pain and stomped-on pride. Use that to regain your momentum and stop those second thoughts."

"Why aren't you trying to talk me out of my plan and into the flowery world of forgiveness?"

Wanda poured the rest of whatever alcohol had been in the bottle into her empty coffee cup. "Hell, Damien, if I advise you to forgive and move on, then I've got to do it myself."

"Who are you talking about?" Wanda had been seeing her produce supplier for a few months now. Damien didn't know the guy all that well. But he did know the man's name. "Is it Paulo? Did you two have a fight, because I will break him in two if he hurts you—"

"No, no." She shook her head. "This is way before Paulo."

"Well, who was it then?"

"You don't know him, my first husband—"

"You were married before?"

"That's enough now. My past is my own and I don't like 'sharing time.'" She drained her cup, then stood. "I need my beauty sleep and you need to get back to your life." She leaned in and kissed him on the cheek. "Lock up when you go, all right?"

"Sure."

Damien drank the rest of his coffee, but didn't move from the counter. Wanda was right. Every time he felt connected to Tess, felt sorry for her, he needed to go back in time and remember how she'd walked away without giving a damn about how he felt.

He needed to revise his plan. He needed to remember that he hadn't come back to Minnesota to rekindle a romance, but to get close to Tess again, make her love him, then make her pay.

And as soon as her foot had totally healed, that's just what he was going to do.

Ten

Stitches out and foot feeling good.

Tess walked out of the doctor's office, sans crutches and Band-Aid free. The doctor, who, even after Tess had assured him that it had been no trouble getting there, had insisted that he could've come to Damien's house for the final checkup.

But Tess wasn't an invalid anymore and she didn't want to act like one. She could walk and work and drive again. And Damien, thank goodness, hadn't given her any trouble, even when she'd told him that she was going to take a cab to the doctor's office and not his town car.

In fact, Tess mused as she walked out of the building and down the sidewalk toward the waiting cab, Damien hadn't made any trouble or made any passes at her in the past few days.

After coming home from painting the red house, he'd basically checked in on her, then disappeared. Could the reason stem from all those things she'd told him about Henry and her marriage?

As she sat in the back of the taxi, she wondered if Damien had given up on her, didn't want to deal with her baggage and had his sights set on someone else. The thought of him even looking at another woman made her lungs feel as though they were having the air squeezed out of them.

When her cab pulled into the driveway of the little red house, the first thing Tess saw was Damien, looking very sexy under the December sun. He had shoveled the snow off of a large patch of grass and had put down a tarp. On top of the tarp were the kitchen cabinets. Damien had work clothes on, and he didn't look up when she got out of the car.

Not until she was practically upon him.

"Hey," she called as she walked toward him.

He glanced up, over his shoulder. "Hey, there." Even with the slight warmth of the sun, the cold, clear morning had brought color to his cheeks, and his blue eyes glittered like sapphires.

"What are you doing?" she asked him.

"Sanding the cabinets."

"They look good."

"They're a work in progress."

"Well, I just came from the doctor and he said I'm good to go."

"What does that mean?" he asked.

"That means you don't have to do this anymore. Go home, get back to your regular life, and I'll take over here."

He paused, thought about this, then said, "I don't think so."

"Excuse me?"

He stood, looked down at her with a resolute expression. "I've decided that we're going to finish this house together."

Her heart started to pump faster. "You have?"

"Yes."

"Why?"

"Could be fun."

"Yeah, but doesn't that defeat the purpose?"

He cocked his head. "What purpose is that?"

"Making me suffer, making me work my backside off as punishment for my sins."

A wicked smile tugged at his lips. "I think your backside is pretty perfect the way it is."

Heat swirled in her belly and her legs felt shaky and weak. She tried not to smile too broadly.

"The truth is," he began evenly. "I need to get back to California sooner than I expected."

"Oh." She tried to mask the disappointment she felt, but she wasn't sure if she'd pulled it off.

"I need everything done by Wednesday."

Her jaw dropped. "That's two days away."

"That's right."

He seemed so blasé about the whole thing, but Tess just wasn't up for pretending she was, too. "I'd better get on the phone and see if we can have the countertops and furniture delivered ASAP."

As she walked toward the house, Damien called after her. "Throw money at the problem. That always works for me."

Tess didn't get it. Who was this guy? This chameleon? Warm and vulnerable one moment, then cold and demanding the next.

She went inside and took out her cell phone, dialed the number for Hubbard's Tile and Stone. As she spoke with the manager about changing their delivery date, she tried not to think about how in just two days Damien would be out of her life for good.

It had been a long, dusty day, but much had been accomplished. The cabinets were sanded, stained and affixed to the newly painted kitchen walls. The bathroom was completely done, the bedroom, too. The only things that needed to be done were the countertops, moldings, outlet covers, a few fixtures and the furniture. Tess had already brought back the three pieces she'd bought from Mr. Opp, and the other two delivery companies had jumped at the extra cash, and were going to be at the red house tomorrow before noon.

Tess stood in the living room and sighed. She hadn't expected to fall in love with the house all over again. It had always been cute, but now it was modern and charming. It was how she would redo her home if she had the funds. It was perfect, and no doubt some perfect little family would stumble upon it and make it theirs.

Just moments ago Damien had gone out for pizza, and Tess decided to get cleaned up and get off her feet at the same time. She headed into the bathroom. The soapstone spa tub she'd picked out looked inviting. Would it be so wrong if she tried it out?

She sat on the edge of the tub and turned the knobs. Water gushed from the tap. Hot, steamy water. Just the sight of it made her muscles relax.

Ten minutes later, she was up to her neck in bubbles, daydreaming about a man with dark hair and blue eyes, who was hovering over her, ready to explore every inch of her body. Just as she was about to let him, there was a knock on the bathroom door.

"Tess?"

Damien's booming voice brought her instantly back to reality and she sat up, sloshing water over the sides of the tub. "Yes. What?"

"You okay in there?"

"Yeah. Of course. Just cleaning up."

"In the new bathtub?" She heard the amusement in his voice.

"I had to make sure it was…"

"Seaworthy?" he supplied.

"Comfortable."

"I have the pizza, and I got those garlic knots you like."

She smiled at the thoughtfulness of his gesture. She called out, "You can go ahead and eat if you want."

"No, I'll wait. Take your time."

Yeah, as if she could just lie back and relax with him out there waiting for her. Not possible.

"I'm done," she called, standing and stepping out of the water. But in her rush, she knocked the bar of soap she'd just used off the holder and onto the floor. It made a loud thud of a sound. She called out a rather terse, "Dammit," as she leaned over to retrieve it.

She knew her mistake the minute she stood up again. She heard his footsteps, then the door opened before she could even grab a towel. Her heart slammed against her ribs and a silent scream escaped her throat as she realized that he was going to see— her leg. The scar on her leg.

No, no. She couldn't let him.

But it was too late. He was coming through the door. "What was that? Are you okay?"

"Damien get out!" she shouted, full on panic in her tone. "Out. Please."

But like anyone with a disaster in their sites, Damien couldn't look away. "Tess?"

She felt weightless, out of her body.

He cocked his head to one side and his eyes narrowed, he stared at her inner thigh, at the massive burn scar that had eaten up her smooth, beautiful skin five years ago. "What the hell happened to you?"

Misery gripped her and she shook her head. "Please go."

His gaze found hers. "Was that an accident?"

"No. Now please go."

"Someone did this to you? He looked horrified. "Who—" He took a few steps closer. "Holy sh—"

"Damien, please don't." She grabbed the towel off the hook and wrapped it around herself.

"Why didn't you tell me?" he demanded, going to her, pulling her into his arms. "Oh, my God, why didn't you come to me?"

She shook her head. "I couldn't."

"You could have."

Her towel slipped, and she tried to retrieve it, but Damien stopped her.

Her eyes implored him. "I need it."

"Screw the towel." He looked into her eyes, his own so stormy, so intense and she saw the man, the boy from long ago. And he was thoroughly pissed off. "I'm going to kill him."

"Too late."

He wrapped his arms around her and held her close, kissed her hair, her neck, her mouth. Against her lips, he uttered miserably, "You should've come to me."

Wearing nothing, the air hitting her scar, she felt so vulnerable. "And what would you have done, Damien? Tell me I deserved it?"

He tipped her face so she could see him, see the passion in his eyes. "Never, do you hear me? Never." Before she could respond, he slipped an arm under her legs and lifted her up, then he headed out of the bathroom.

She wrapped her arms around his neck. "Where are you taking me?"

"Somewhere where I can kiss you properly," he said, leaving the bathroom.

"You *were* kissing me."

He paused at the bedroom door, his gaze moving over her mouth. "I need you on your back for this kind of kissing."

Excitement warred with the panic in her belly. She'd dreamed about him touching her, kissing her, spreading her legs apart and using his tongue to drive her mad. But in every fantasy, her leg was unblemished, smooth and perfect.

She didn't want him to see her, touch that part of her....

He placed her on the bed and bent his head, applying soft, teasing kisses over her toes, then little nibbles at her ankles. Up he went, suckling her calves and the soft spot over her knee. Tess wanted to enjoy it, but she couldn't allow herself to let go. He was so close to seeing it, feeling— So close to her scar.

"No, Damien, please." She put her hand over the rough skin on her inner thigh.

"Sweetheart, let me touch you, please." His warm hand moved up her leg, gently forcing her hand off her scar.

Tess could barely breathe. "I'm not...can't...it's ugly..."

"No, sweetheart. You're beautiful."

And then he was there, applying soft kisses to the rough, sensitive surface of her scar, and Tess loved it and hated it at the same time. While her mind roared with thoughts and fears from her past, Damien kept talking to her, whispering sweet, erotic words as he soothed her with his hands.

So many nights she had dreamed of this, wondered if she'd ever feel sexual, if she'd feel desired by a man. On a hungry groan, Damien moved upward to the wet curls between her legs. She could feel his breath on her, and she released a tense, excited sigh.

"My Tess," he uttered as he reached beneath her and cupped her buttocks, squeezed the round flesh until she lifted her hips. Then he lowered his head.

Tess stared at him, at his head between her legs, electric heat flickering inside of her at the erotic sight.

And then he touched her with his tongue, soft, slow circles over the hard bud that she'd thought for so long was dead.

"Damien, please…" She didn't know what she was asking for.

But Damien responded to the ache of desperation in her voice by nuzzling her, lapping at the tender bud with his deliciously rough tongue, suckling it deep until she wriggled beneath him, called his name again.

Tess pumped her hips, feeling as though she could cry, it felt so good. She wanted the incredible heat and pressure to last forever.

As she fisted the white comforter, pointed her toes and mewled like animal in pain, Damien's mouth teased and twisted. Beads of sweat broke out on her forehead as his hands gripped her buttocks. No matter how desperately she wanted to, Tess couldn't hold on to the sweet feeling for much longer.

It had been so long, and the pressure was building and had to be released. And then she called out, thrust her hands in his hair and spread her legs as wide as she could.

Damien gave a guttural sound of approval, then sank his tongue deeply inside her. Blinding heat surged through her as she shook with climax. Her body was out of control and on fire and she pressed against his mouth, taking his tongue into her body, then out again. Over and over until the pressure eased, then subsided.

When it did, Damien sat up. His gaze was thunderstorm dark, and he looked ready to pounce. Quick as a jungle cat, he pulled off his clothes, grabbed a condom from his pocket then sheathed himself.

Unable to breathe, to think clearly, Tess watched every move he made, watched his hand glide over his thick, hard erection, watched the muscles in his chest and abdomen tighten when he did.

The muscles between her legs quivered with anticipation. She remembered how well their bodies fit together, and the wait was torture. She'd waited too long. They both had. She wanted him on top of her, his shaft inside of her.

When Damien was poised above her, the long, hard length of him bobbing sensually against her belly, she licked her lips. She had been starved for so long.

Not anymore.

Her legs were weak and shaky, but her body craved more and she opened for him, no longer self-conscious about her scar. The slick evidence of her need dripped from the center of her onto the bed sheets, and as Damien watched, his eyes glittering with need, he reached out and touched her, played with the damp curls above until he found the wet folds beneath. Tess's breath caught in her throat as his fingertip circled the entrance to her body with slow, torturous strokes.

Panting and dizzy, Tess let her head fall to one side as she pressed herself into his hand. "Damien, please. I want you."

Damien was over her in seconds, the hard tip of his erection poised at the entrance to her body. And then he entered her, slowly, one delicious inch at a time, stretching her, giving her body what it craved, what it remembered.

When he was all the way inside of her, he hovered there, his gaze locked to hers. "Hey."

Her arms went around him and she smiled. "Hey."

As she stared up into his eyes, their breath mingling, their bodies joined, she knew she had fallen in love with him. Or was it *back* in love with him?

Maybe she had never stopped.

The heat inside of her continued to build, demanding that she take it and release it. She wrapped her legs around his waist, and he starting moving, slowly pumping inside of her until she caught his rhythm, the perfect rhythm. Her hands drifted down his back and over his buttocks. She loved the way his muscles flexed as he thrust deeper and deeper inside of her.

Damien bent his head and kissed her, nuzzled at the entrance to her mouth until she opened for him. His tongue lapped at hers, mimicking the movement of their bodies.

Tess was growing restless again as the building pressure of orgasm was upon her. Heat and pleasure swirled through her, and when Damien slipped his hand between them and spread her wide, pressed himself against her and rode her hard, she felt her mind slipping away and the slow, booming fire of climax returning, taking over every muscle, every limb, every inch of her hot skin.

Damien must have felt it, too, because his thrusts turned from tame to wild, his forehead glistened with sweat and he reached underneath her buttocks and lifted her higher.

His erection slammed against the sweet spot inside of her, the core of nerves that had only ever been turned on by this man.

"Oh, yes, Damien," she called, thrusting her hips upward in a wild, jerky motion as he thrust into her. Her skin was slick, hot and she ached for release. Damien gave it to her with one hard thrust against that soft, aching spot deep within her and she cried out, gripping his back, thrusting her hips.

Damien shuddered, his body racked with the spasms of climax. Saying her name over and over, he lifted up and plunged back down, burying himself as deep as he could go. Then his body gave one last tremor and he collapsed on top of her.

Tess held him close, breathing heavily, her eyes closed tightly as she felt small aftershocks of her release play through her. Feeling so close to Damien, Tess stroked his back and buttocks, even lifted her hips to feel him deep inside of her again as their bodies cooled.

After a few minutes Damien tried to roll to one side, but she held him there.

"I'm going to smother you," he said softly, gently.

She shook her head and held tight. "No, I love it."

This man's weight on her was pure heaven and she just wanted to feel him for as long as she could have him. But after a few minutes his prediction was correct and her chest started to grow weary from the pressure.

She let him roll to his back, and smiled when he took her with him. He held her possessively, curled her against him, and as they started to breath normally again, he played with her long red hair, his fingers dancing in her curls.

"Damien?"

"Hmm?"

"There's something I have to say."

He paused, then said softly, "Okay."

She closed her eyes, snuggled deep into his arm. "Back then, six years ago, when we were together, I had so much passion for you, so much love. I thought that such a deep love, such an intense attraction couldn't last. Honestly, I thought a real, committed relationship, the kind that went on for fifty years, had to be something tamer and more sensible."

"Oh, Tess. That's silly."

"I know. I was an idiot."

"You were young."

"Yes, I was a young idiot."

He chuckled softly. "Doesn't matter."

"Sure it does."

"No, sweetheart. All that matters is what you believe now."

She'd never felt so safe, so happy. She knew the feeling was probably a temporary one, but she didn't care. She was going to enjoy it for as long as possible.

She ran a hand over his chest, played in the sprinkling of damp hair. "I believe that love is the most important gift. I believe in second chances and that being afraid of your feelings can only lead you down the path of unhappiness and regret. And I'm done with regret."

Damien pulled her even closer and kissed her hair.

Tess nuzzled his chest. "You know, I was leaving him when he got in the accident. It was the day after he gave me the scar. He was following me. He swore he'd always follow me. That's when he got into the car accident."

"Oh, Tess." Damien kissed her hair softly. "Don't think about it. It's done."

She rose up on her elbow and looked at him, deep into the dark-blue fire of his eyes. "What about us, Damien? Are we done?"

Damien's eyes turned hungry and his jaw clenched, but before he could say anything, Tess put her fingers over his mouth, his full sexy mouth, which just minutes ago had made her body ache with pleasure. "Don't answer that. Not tonight, not now."

On a growl he pulled her to him and kissed her hungrily.

"Stay here with me," she whispered against his mouth. "Don't go back to the house tonight."

He nipped at her bottom lip, uttered hoarsely, "I'm not going anywhere."

She smiled, then dropped her head back down and snuggled into the crook of his arm. "We'll work together, be together…for now."

He held her tightly and she closed her eyes, let her heart relax and her heartbeat slow, until finally she gave in to sleep.

It was close to dawn when Tess climbed on top of Damien and eased herself down on his thick, hard, shaft. Outside the bedroom window, snow fell to the ground, blanketing the earth, the glistening white color illuminating the walls of the room and the naked skin of the two people making love in it.

His back to the warm sheets, Damien stared up at her. His body rigid with need, he watched her eyes dance with hunger, her breasts rise and fall and her hips sway back and forth. He had been here a hundred times in his mind, had planned this moment, but nothing could compare with the reality.

She brought her legs forward, bracketing his shoulders, and settled her hands back on his thighs, giving Damien perfect access to her swollen cleft. As he watched her move his erection in and out of her body, the perfect connection that he would die before breaking, he placed his thumbs on either side of her wet folds. Gently, he opened her and began to circle the tender bud.

Tess sucked air between her teeth and dropped her head back, moaning with pleasure. The light played off her skin, turned her hard nipples into a ghostly pink and the scar on her thigh to a blatant reminder of a horrible past she wanted so desperately to leave behind and never revisit.

And he was planning on hurting her again….

He was a monster.

Her thrusts quickened and Damien's mind turned off. She was close, so close, and as he flicked the sensitive, white-hot bud back and forth, over and over, she let go, arched her back and called out.

The sound and the heat were too much for Damien. As she pumped and moaned, her muscles fisting around his erection, he finally allowed himself to go, fly, follow her over the edge into the sweet ecstasy of climax.

Eleven

It was nearly nine in the morning. Damien and Tess stood in the newly remodeled kitchen, wearing next to nothing. As they waited for the coffeepot to do its thing, they jovially debated some of Tess's choices in her purchases for the home.

Grinning, Tess wrapped her arms around Damien's neck and tried to help him remember their initial deal regarding the furniture-buying decisions. "I seem to recall you saying—many times, in fact—that I should consider this my house when I do the design."

His hands went around her waist. "That was before I saw the pot rack."

"What's wrong with the pot rack?" she asked,

mystified. "It's stainless steel. Who doesn't like stainless steel?"

"I hit my head on it this morning when I was getting a glass of water."

She laughed. "You are very tall."

"Hey, you're supposed to be sympathetic."

"I am?"

"You're my wife, after all."

"Wife for hire," she corrected.

He shrugged. "Technicality."

Her heart tugged at his words, and she rolled onto her toes and gave him a quick kiss. "I can have the pot rack taken up—"

"You mean taken down?"

"No," she said, giving hive a playful swat.

"And then there's the sink."

She turned her head and stared at the white porcelain farm sink. "What's wrong with the sink?"

"It's a bathtub."

"It's beautiful."

"You could get two kids in here!"

"Well, maybe I'll have two kids, then," she teased.

But the teasing part was lost on Damien. His smile died instantly, and a cloud moved over the brightness of his eyes.

"I just meant someday," she said lightly, noting the stiffness in his arms as he held her. "Someday I'll have a sink of my own like this, and maybe someday I'll have a couple kids to stick in it."

Not much better, Tess.

Damien's blue eyes narrowed. "Who are you planning on having kids with?"

She didn't know what to say. "I don't know. I was just playing—"

"Yeah." He released her, walked over to the sink. "I don't like it."

Neither did she. She didn't want to think about him being with someone else either or having kids…. But this was their last full day together and he hadn't given her any indication that he wanted the relationship to continue after he went back to California tomorrow.

"Coffee's ready," she said, trying to force a light tone into her voice. "Counters should be here in a few hours." She glanced around. "This place is so great, so fresh. You know, you could rent it out if you wanted to. Hang on to the property, if you wanted to. Someone might like it for a getaway. Tribute's got that cute, charming, small-town feel."

"We'll see," he grumbled, his dark, irritated gaze raking over her.

"Why are you looking at me like that?"

"I can't get the thought of you and another guy and kids out of my head."

Sighing, she put her arms around him and pressed herself against him. "You know what? I'm a little tired from last night. How about you?"

"No."

She smiled to herself. "I think you are. I think you could do with a nap."

When she glanced up, his eyes were changing from frustrated to ferocious as he got her meaning. With a hungry growl, he lifted her up and held her in his arms possessively. "I'm taking you to bed."

"Good."

His brow lifted wickedly. "But just so we're clear, there'll be no napping going on."

By the time the sun went down that day, the house was complete. From soup to nuts. And Tess had never felt so proud yet so cheerless in her life. Not that she was going to let Damien see how sad she was. In fact, she had planned a lovely night for them. Dinner by the fire, then a repeat performance of that morning.

Tess heard the shower running as she put the water on the stove to boil. In her mind's eye, she could see Damien, naked and wet, the water sluicing over his skin.

One thing was certain, a night or two of sleeping with him, making love with him, wasn't going to be enough, and she imagined that after he left for California her life would return to that empty shell it had once been.

She turned into the cutting board and set to work chopping tomatoes for sauce. She wished she knew how Damien felt. But he didn't give her much. Sure, he didn't want to think of her with another man or having another life, but he'd been tight-lipped about the future and what he wanted.

Was it possible that he might want to continue seeing her? Long distance? Or maybe moving to Minnesota part-time?

She stopped chopping. One thing she did know for certain was that being here together, in Tribute, had changed them both. And the red house represented that change. From something that was broken-down, messed up and battle-scarred, the little red house had been transformed into a clean, warm, safe, happy place. And Tess and Damien had been transformed along with it.

Tess turned off the burner and left the kitchen. She needed to see Damien, feel him, feel his arms around her again.

The shower was still running, and as she entered the bathroom, she was engulfed in hot, wet steam. Her heart pounding with need, Tess stripped off her clothes, then pulled back the shower curtain.

Damien looked even better than she could possibly imagine, every inch of his hard, muscled body dripping with water.

He grinned at her and offered his hand. "Dirty mind or just plain dirty?"

She took his hand and stepped inside. "A little of both."

"Good answer," he said, turning her so her back was to his front. He pulled her against him, against his already-hard shaft, then took the soap in his hand and began to wash her. Down her neck and over her collarbone.

"You let me know when you're clean," he whispered in her ear.

She smiled.

He moved the slippery bar over her breasts, over each tight, hard nipple. "How about now?"

She shook her head and uttered a shaky, "No."

He slipped the soap over her stomach, down over her hip bones, then between the wet curls at her core. "Here? Is this where you need my help?"

She nodded, unable to speak as he stroked her with the slippery soap, as he washed away the feelings of sadness and uncertainty, as he sent her to the moon again and again…

The phrase *eating in bed* had taken on a whole new meaning for Damien tonight. Like the perfect wife, Tess had served him spaghetti and champagne, pausing every so often to kiss him, nuzzle him and tell him she couldn't stop thinking about what he had done to her in the shower.

It was pure hell.

And total heaven.

He was leaving for California tomorrow night and everything inside of him was screaming to stay, to forgive her, let it go and try to be happy for once in his miserable life. But there was a force stronger than his feelings for Tess at work here, something that had been six years in the making, an undeniable force.

Damien downed his glass of champagne, then

turned to look at Tess. He had never seen her look more beautiful. Happiness and the glow of great sex radiated on her face.

The sucker, the fool inside of him could only think how great it would be to see her look like that every day, every morning when he opened his eyes.

He inhaled deeply, trying to quell the sudden feeling of being pissed off. "Hey, Tess, can I ask you something."

"Sure."

"Do you have any regrets?"

She laughed. "Tons."

"No, I mean, about coming here."

"I didn't have much choice, if you recall." She smiled over her glass of champagne. "But no, I'm glad I came here." She shrugged. "Maybe this started out as payback for you, maybe it still is, but whether you like it or not it's ending up being the best thing that could ever happen to me."

His brow creased. "How's that?"

She looked up for a moment. "I feel free, for the first time in six years…even longer, maybe."

He stared at her. Dammit! He had a plan in motion already, an anvil poised and ready to crush the dreams they'd built over the past two weeks. But what? She had made her peace with him already, with being here? She'd found freedom by being here and he was responsible for that?

What the hell? Did she deserve to feel free after what she'd put him through? And did he still have a right to want to make her pay? After everything he knew and had seen.

He didn't know. But as she put her glass down and slid the sheet off of his body, as she kissed his ear, then his neck and his chest, he decided he didn't need an answer tonight.

What he did need was her, her heart, her eyes locked with his as she scattered kisses over his chest, down his belly, down to where he ached for her with granitelike hardness….

Twelve

Tess woke to bright sunshine streaming through the bedroom window, and a Damien-less bed. At first, she panicked, thinking he had already left for California, but as she read the note on his pillow, her tension eased.

He had a meeting, and he'd be back by one.

Five hours…what could she do? The house was done, furniture in, appliances up and running. Sure she could pack, but what fun was that?

Then an idea popped into her head. A Christmas gift for Damien. The perfect gift.

With her pulse pounding, she jumped out of bed and headed into the bathroom. She just hoped she could find someone with enough skill to make it, to create the perfect representation of what had happened here in this house, between the two of them.

She knew that trying to find that perfect gift in such a short amount of time was a long shot, but it was something she had to do.

It was just business.

He would tell himself that until the day he died.

Damien pulled his sleek, black car into the driveway and shut off the engine. Before he got out, he stared at the little red house, testing himself. Did the place evoke any feelings that were useless to him now? Warmth, caring, vulnerability, comfort?

Of course they did, and Damien instantly hardened himself.

From day one, his plan had been to make Tess love him, make Tess love the house, then sell it without a thought. He had been a cold bastard then. And over the past two weeks, he had surprised himself by allowing Tess to get under his skin and melt his icy heart.

But the truth remained; she had hurt him once, screwed him over big-time. What guarantee did he have that she wouldn't do it again?

Better to cut things off here, cut her loose, and if it had to be in a blatantly obvious and hurtful way, so be it.

He stepped out of the car into the freezing air and walked to the front door. The offer that had just been made to him was highly lucrative, and needed to be acted on immediately.

When he came through the door, everything that was Tess cried out to him. The happy fire in the fireplace; the peaceful furniture in the living room; the quiet, sensual paint colors on the wall; and that damn sink in the kitchen.

Then he heard her. She was in the bedroom, talking on the phone in a merry voice. He stepped into the doorway and lifted his chin in a silent hello.

Sitting cross-legged on the bed, her hair loose about her shoulders, Tess caught sight of him and waved. Her gray eyes were bright, and she was clearly happy to see him.

"No, the foot is fine," she was saying to whoever was on the other end of the line. "I'm so much better, Liv. All healed." She looked up at Damien then, a smile tugging at her perfect mouth. "He's been wonderful." Her smile widened and she winked. "I do. Even more. Honestly, I've never felt this way before."

Damien's gut twisted as he realized what she was saying. She loved him.

Damn her. She loved him. Now. And she had said it out loud, to his face.

She'd never felt this way before.

Anger bubbled inside of Damien and he walked out of the room. He went into the living room and stood by the fire. He *had* felt this way before and look where that had gotten him.

It played like a broken record in his head. He had loved her and she had walked out on him, and even though he'd tried to bury it these past few weeks, those wounds were still fresh.

Maybe selling the house, tearing this little world to bits right in front of her would help heal him—maybe not.

But it was done, the deal was done.

He heard her walk up behind him, felt her hand on the small of his back. "That was Olivia."

"I guessed."

Her arms went around him. "How was your meeting?"

"Fruitful." Unlike the crackling fire beside him, Damien's voice lacked warmth, and was completely emotionless.

"Well, that's good," she said, sounding a little confused by his tone. "Was it about a house?"

"Yes, this one."

"Oh." And that's all it took. She released him.

He turned to face her. It killed him to see the disappointment and worry in her gray eyes, but there was nothing for it. "There was an offer made on it."

Her brows went up. "Wow. Without even seeing the place?"

"They didn't need to see it."

"Seriously, with all the work we've done. That sounds odd."

"They don't care about the renovations," he said, being careful to keep his voice casual.

"Then they're idiots because—"

"Tess." He stopped her right there. "They don't want the house."

Her eyes narrowed and she shook her head. "I'm sorry, you've lost me."

"They want the land."

"Well, the house is on the land, so—"

"They want to build a motel here, and they've offered me a considerable amount of money."

The doubtful, sad look she'd worn just moments ago was now replaced with the glare of a woman who understood what it was like to be hurt and was ready for it to happen again. "They have to tear down the house to do that, don't they?"

He nodded. "Yes."

She released a weighty breath and crossed her arms over her chest. "So what did you tell them?"

"I told them nothing," Damien said evenly. "I asked them where I should sign."

Tess stared at him. She felt numb, except for the scar on her inner thigh. For some reason, the skin there burned like the devil.

Maybe because she was dealing with the devil.

She left Damien standing beside the fire and walked to the couch to sit. She felt like the world's biggest fool. Her happy mood, her trusting spirit—the gift she'd spent hours designing for him. But mostly, for even thinking that there might be a future for them.

Clearly, it wasn't in the cards, never had been.

His back to the fire, Damien attempted to explain. "It's business. A great deal."

"I'm sure it is."

"And I know you worked hard on the property, so there will be a substantial compensation—"

"I don't want your money, Damien," she said, her gaze and tone reflecting the insulting offer he'd just made.

But Damien didn't get it. "Why the hell not? You could use it for your business or—"

"Or nothing," she uttered, disgusted.

But, for whatever reason, he wouldn't let up. "Take the money, Tess."

She stood and stalked over to him, faced him with her jaw tight and her lower lip quivering. "What is wrong with you?"

His blue eyes were almost lifeless in their apathy. "What do you mean?"

"A few hours ago you were nuzzling my neck."

"Things change," he said coldly.

"What exactly changed for you?" She lifted her brows. "Come on, I can take it. I'm no schoolgirl anymore, as we both know."

His gaze dropped and he turned to the door. "I have to get back to the house. But you should be aware that the bulldozers are coming tomorrow. Eight a.m."

"What?" she called after him.

"Eight a.m." he repeated, then walked outside.

She followed him out, into the cold afternoon air. "I heard the time part, Damien."

"They wanted to move fast, Tess."

She watched him walk away as her socks grew damp from the snow on the walkway. Then it finally dawned on her. Stupid, silly Tess, who had allowed herself to be whisked off into a fairy tale, minus the happily-ever-after part.

Tearing down the house had been his goal from day one. Have her build her dream, her perfect family home, then tear it down—while tearing the girl who'd hurt him to shreds in the process.

Damien was nearly at his car when she shouted, "Stop right there!"

He did, then turned and stared coldly at her as she walked toward him. "You're going to freeze. Go back inside."

She was in his face, feeling nothing but a burning desire to punch him. "You knew from the beginning that there was a good possibility that this house was going to be torn down, didn't you?"

"There were many possibilities."

"And you had me picking out the most beautiful materials…" She shook her head. "My fantasy materials."

He leaned against the open door. "I wanted you to feel what it was like to have something you loved ripped from you."

She just stared at him, not believing what she was hearing. "Oh, Damien. You really think I'd be emotionally destroyed because this house is gone?"

He didn't answer, but his jaw went hard as steel.

"You don't get it, do you?" she said, her warm breath making small clouds in the cold afternoon air.

"Get what?" he muttered.

"What the true payback is. You did hurt me, Damien. Make no mistake about that—you succeeded there. The true payback is that I actually thought we had something…real. I thought we'd both grown up enough to get over the past and start something that was so amazing." Her throat felt tight, but she refused to cry. Not in front of him, she wouldn't give him that. "Remember how I told you that with Henry the last bits of my faith and hope were gone?" When he didn't answer, she continued, "These weeks, I found it again. I had some faith—in us."

She smiled self-deprecatingly. "And, fool that am, I was ready to give my heart to the wrong man again."

She didn't give him time to respond. She said, "I hope you can finally leave the past in the past and move on at some point. I really do. Maybe when this house is nothing more than concrete ash…I don't know. But I'm done. I'm going home."

And with that, she turned around and went inside, to pack her things and to leave the red house and its sweet memories and unfulfilled wishes behind.

For good.

Thirteen

Christmas was supposed to be the happiest time of the year, and for most people it was. Presents and trees and Santa, happy couples and baby's first holiday bibs. How could anyone not smile at a neighbor and hum the chorus of "Jingle Bells." But for Tess, she just wanted to run out of NRR's office every day after work, get in her car and head home—hide under her bed until the whole holiday blew over.

It wasn't that she was a Scrooge or anything. She wanted to smile and sing, but it just wasn't in her.

Four days ago she'd left Tribute and the little red house and the man she had come to love once again. Today was Christmas Eve and that house had probably been bulldozed to the ground and that man was probably having a snowless holiday season in sunny California.

With a folder of new client information tucked under her arm, Tess walked by Mary's office.

When Mary spotted her, she called out, "Hey, Tess. Come here a sec."

Mary and Ethan had returned from their honeymoon a few days before, and Mary had been walking around the office like she was on cloud nine ever since.

Tess went in and sat across from her partner. There was a two-foot grinning Santa on the woman's desk, and Tess had to stop herself from knocking it to the ground. "What's up? I have someone waiting…"

"Oh, it won't take long." Mary flipped her blond hair over her shoulder and smiled. "I have something I want you to think about."

"Okay."

"You like kids, right?"

Tess laughed. "Of course I do. Mary what's this about?"

"I want you to be my baby's godmother."

A strange sadness moved over Tess. She was flattered, and incredibly honored by the offer—so pleased that Mary deemed her that close a friend. But right now the suggestion just served as a reminder of the family that she herself was never going to have.

She gave Mary her best smile. "Thank you for

thinking of me. It's an honor and a great responsibility. I need to think about it, okay?"

"Of course." Mary returned her smile. "After the holidays we'll talk."

Tess nodded. "After the holidays would be perfect."

She was just about to leave when Olivia walked in to Mary's office.

"Oh, good, Tess, just the person I wanted to see."

If Olivia was pregnant and wanting a godparent, too, Tess thought inanely, she was going to pretty much lose it right there.

But pregnancy was not what the pretty brunette wanted to see her about. "Your...client," she said with a half smile, "sent payment for service, but not a return address to send the receipt."

Tess asked, "Which client is that?"

"Mr. Sauer."

Her heart dropped. "He sent payment?"

"A rather large one."

Mary eyed her. "Have you upped your fee without telling us?"

"No." She turned to Olivia. "Listen, I don't want that money. Send it back."

"I can't."

"Then rip it up."

Mary came around her desk and touched her arm. "Tess, what's wrong. What's this about?"

"I knew he wasn't cool," Olivia said, staring at Tess's face. Then she looked at Mary and explained,

"Her client was also a past boyfriend, who obviously jerked her around."

Mary took Tess's hand but nodded at Olivia. "Rip up the check, Olivia."

"You bet," Olivia said quickly.

Tess looked up and gave her friend a thankful smile.

Olivia nodded. "Whatever you need, girl, okay?"

Tess took a deep breath. "Thanks, but I'm going to be fine." And she meant it. It might take a while to get there, maybe next month or next year, but she was going to be happy again.

"I'd better get going," she told the women. "I have a client waiting."

Mary squeezed her hand before releasing it. "Then go, we'll talk later."

Tess went into her office and sat at her desk. The man across from her was handsome, she noted. But in a boyish way. The man across from her had blue eyes, but there was no anger there, no arrogance there, no passion.

She was almost thankful for it.

She stuck out her hand. "Mr. Sumner, I'm Tess York. How can I help you today?"

The man looked grim and said, "I promised my mother I'd be married by New Year's Eve."

"And I take it you're not."

He shook his head. "Not yet."

"Do you have a girlfriend? Someone you're thinking about asking?"

He shook his head.

"And how would you like my help?

"Can you be my pretend fiancée?"

She smiled. "No, but I'll help you find the courage to tell your mother the truth."

He blanched. "How much is that going to cost me?"

Tess laughed, and it felt good. "Not a cent. This one's on the house."

He'd put it off another day. Soon they were going to give up on him and back out of the deal altogether.

Maybe that's what he wanted.

It was near midday, and Damien sat in front of the red house like a protester without a sign, staring at the bulldozers that were unmanned and stuck in the snow. They had been sitting there for days, and he had not allowed them to get any closer. He didn't know what was wrong with him. He should've been in California, back to work and on the road to recovery. Not sitting with his ass in the snow and his head on a cloud.

Damn Tess York. She'd ruined him again.

A car pulled into the icy driveway—a pickup truck, actually—and came to a skidding stop right in front of the walkway.

Damien had known it was only a matter of time before she would show up.

Dressed like Mrs. Claus, which she did every year for the kids who came into the store, Wanda got out of her truck and bellowed at him, "I don't have time for this, Damien. It's Christmas Eve."

"I know," Damien called dryly. "Shouldn't you be helping someone get dressed and on his sleigh right about now?"

Her eyes narrowed as she walked over to him and sat on the stoop. "Don't get smart with me, Damien Sauer."

"I'm sorry."

"Good. Now, what the hell are you doing?"

He shook his head. "Acting like an ass."

"I'll say. Four days of stopping that truck from doing its job…"

"Yeah…" He plowed his hands through his hair.

Her voice dropped, even softened a touch. "Do the deal, Damien."

"Can't."

"Why not?" she asked. "End it. Get it, and her, out of your system."

"The problem with that is I have a sneaking suspicion that taking down this house will not get her out of my system."

"What will, then?"

"I have no idea."

"It's freezing out here." She clicked her tongue. "This deal is sweet. It's a helluva lot of money—"

"I have enough money."

She snorted. "Please don't say, 'But I don't have her.'"

He threw her a sideways glance. "You are one sarcastic broad, Wanda."

"Damn right." She looked at him, studied him.

"Tell me you weren't foolish enough to fall in love with her again."

"I don't think I ever stopped loving her." It was the first time he'd admitted it, out loud and to himself, and it cut deeply.

Beside him, Wanda cursed like a race car driver.

"What are you going on about?" he asked her.

"I have to give you something," she said, thrusting a medium-size brown box at him. "Here."

"What's this?"

"Present."

"Wanda, you didn't have to—"

"I didn't. It's from the girl. Christmas present she ordered a few days ago at Remi's place." She frowned. "He asked me to get it to you."

Damien's heart twisted, and he felt like ramming his fist through a wall. After all they'd been through, after all he'd said, she'd gotten him a Christmas present.

He opened the package and his heart sank. It was a handmade snow globe with a model of the red house inside of it. Lights glowed from the inside and there was a Christmas tree and presents and two people by the fire.

He looked at the card. It read: "So you'll always know where you began, where you ended up and where you are always loved. Tess."

A muscle twitched in Damien's jaw, and he turned away.

"You could use it to knock out the window," Wanda said beside him. "Get the ball rolling.

Damien turned and stared at her. "What are you so angry about? Always expecting the worst, hoping for the worst. What is it? Did someone leave you heartbroken and pissed off, too?"

"Yes."

Her mouth was thin and hard, but her eyes held the sadness and pain of a lost love. Damien knew what she was feeling, and for the first time he saw what life, what his future, would be like if he remained as bitter as Wanda.

It wasn't a pretty picture.

He wanted what was in the snow globe.

He wanted her.

He dropped an arm around Wanda's shoulders. "What are we going to do, huh?"

"Not we." She faced him, lifted her chin and pretended her eyes didn't sparkle with tears. "I'm too old for forgiveness, but you're not."

He turned back and faced the bulldozers for the last time. "No. I'm not."

The word on the street was that Christmas day was to be spent with family. The women of No Ring Required might have started out as just partners, but in the past few months they had grown into so much more—friends. And if you asked any one of them, as they sat around the Christmas tree in the NRR office, family as well.

It was midmorning and all three women had left their homes, cats and sleeping fiancés, and had come to the office to eat Olivia's challah French toast and open their secret Santa gifts. A few days ago they had drawn names telling them which partner they would be picking out a present for.

Olivia had drawn Mary's name, and she went first. "Here you go, Mama."

Like an excited little kid, Mary took the small box and ripped it open. She squealed when she saw the pearl-and-diamond earrings inside.

"I love them, Liv," Mary said, giving her friend a huge grin. "Thank you."

"Pearl is the baby's birthstone," Olivia explained. "The diamonds are for you."

"As they should be." Mary laughed. "Thank you so much!"

"Okay. I drew your name, Olivia." Tess got up and pushed an enormous box toward the excited-looking brunette. "For you."

"Wow, thanks. Is someone going to pop out of here?"

"Yeah, Mac would just love that," Tess joked.

Grinning, Olivia tore at the Santa wrapping paper, then stopped and stared at what was inside—twelve bottles of what Olivia had always deemed the best Sicilian Olive Oil ever made. "Oh, my goodness, how did you find it?

As Olivia leaned over and hugged her, Tess said, "One of my clients this year is an Italian importer."

"I can't believe it," Olivia began, her eyes dancing with excitement. "A dozen bottles. Where to begin? Well, first thing I'm going to make will be Panzanella salad, then a basic tomato sauce, then of course—"

"Ease up there, Chef," Mary said on a laugh. "The culinary masterpieces can wait for five minutes. It's Tess's turn."

Olivia's cheeks turned pink. "Of course, sorry, Tess."

"No problem, Liv," Tess said with a smile as she took the box Mary held out in her direction. "We all know how deep your obsession runs."

"I hope I got the size right," Mary muttered.

The wrapping paper came off easily, and Tess knew right away that Mary had gotten her shoes. But when she opened the box and saw the rich red Jimmy Choo pumps she nearly fell over. They were beautiful. Something she'd never buy for herself, but always craved.

She looked up. "Thank you, Mary. They're stunning. And my size."

"They're supposed to be ruby slippers," Mary said with a little shrug. "My version."

"Like in the *Wizard of Oz?*" Olivia asked, confused.

Mary nodded, her eyes on Tess. "'No place like home,' you know? I just want you to always feel that way about this place and us. Whatever happened before, whoever came before, me, you and Olivia— we'll always be a family."

Heat shot into Tess's throat. She didn't want to get emotional in front of them, but it was too late. She swiped the tears from her eyes and shook her head. "Damn you both for making me cry," she said, laughing. "And thank you. Five years ago when I got into this business, I never would've thought I'd gain two best friends in the process."

Olivia grabbed her hand. "Me, neither."

"I say we make this a tradition," Mary said, her blue eyes brimming with emotion. "Every Christmas morning."

Tess nodded. "I second that suggestion."

"I'm in, too," Olivia said, picking up the torn wrapping paper to stick it in the trash. But as she passed by the tree, she paused. "Hey, there's something else here." She reached down and came up with a long envelope. "This has your name on it, Tess."

"Who's it from?" Tess looked at Mary.

She shook her head. "Not me."

Olivia shook her head, too. "Not me." She then looked down at the envelope again. "It says, 'Tess, keep the faith. Love, Santa.'" Olivia glanced up again. "What does that mean?"

A mixed bag of fear and warmth and wonder churned in Tess's belly. She knew exactly who the envelope was from. What she didn't know was what was inside and she was scared to find out. But both women were pushing her.

"Open it," Mary urged.

Olivia thrust the envelope into her hand. "Yeah, Tess. Come on."

Tess swallowed the hard lump in her throat and tore

open the envelope. There was a group of papers inside and she slipped them out, uncurled them and read the first page. Her pulse picked up speed and her head felt heavy, dizzy. It was the deed to the little red house. Damien had put it in her name. He had given it to her. He hadn't destroyed it.

"What is it?" Olivia asked softly.

I don't know, Tess thought wildly, tears building. What was it? An apology? Forgiveness? A final farewell. Tess looked up at them both and smiled. "I think it's a peace offering."

Olivia's brows lifted. "From a certain ex-client/ex-boyfriend?"

Tess nodded.

Mary looked from one to the other. "Okay, no more snippets of information. Someone better fill me in with the whole story."

Olivia laughed. "I will. But I think Tess has somewhere she needs to be right now."

With a quick smile at both of them, Tess grabbed her coat and purse and, as she was heading out the door, heard Olivia explain, "Remember that superhot guy with the blue eyes from your engagement party? Not that you should have, because you were only supposed to be looking at Ethan, but this man was hard to miss. Turns out he and Tess used to date…"

Traffic was light, just a few cars out on the road, heading for grandma's house or the airport or the 7-Eleven to pick up another carton of eggnog.

Tess made it to Tribute in two and a half hours. Her heart beat frantically as she got off the freeway and sped into town. But as she turned onto Main Street, then onto oh-so-familiar Yarr Lane, a sudden fear gripped her. What would she find when she got there? Would the house be just as she had left it, or had the bulldozers gotten to any of it? What about the inside?

And, God help her, what about Damien?

The answers to some of her questions came quickly as she pulled into the driveway and saw her sweet little cottage perfectly intact. There were even twinkle lights hanging from the rooflines and railings. The nerves in her belly eased, and she turned off the engine and got out of the car.

The wistful scent of turkey met her at the door. Not knowing what was inside, she decided to knock.

Damien opened the door, and his blue eyes glittered when he saw her. "Hey."

She nodded. "Hey."

"Welcome home."

His words, and the warm way he said them snaked through her. But she was too afraid to hope, to wonder what he was thinking and feeling.

She walked in, past him. He looked too good in jeans and a black sweater, his jaw clean shaven and his black hair thicker than usual.

"Merry Christmas," she said, noticing everything inside the house was just as she'd left it, and designed it—except for the blue spruce tree in the corner, heavily and oddly decorated with bubble lights, blue bulbs, paper ring ornaments and garland that was made out of pine cones and strawberries.

It was a mess, a homemade mess, but it made Tess smile. Clearly, Damien had done this.

She faced him. "I thought you'd be in California by now."

"And miss snow on Christmas? Not a chance. By the way, thank you for the snow globe. It was…perfect, exactly what I needed." He stared at her, his gaze heavy with longing. "You look good in this house."

She smiled tentatively. "So do you."

"You got the deed?"

"Yes." Her pulse jumped. She didn't want to ask, but she had to. "Was it another way of putting me and the past behind you?"

His eyes searched hers. "The past, yes. You, never." He reached for her hand, and when she gave it to him, he brought it to his mouth and kissed her palm. "I'm so sorry, Tess. I was such an idiot."

His touch made her weak, and all she could do was look at him, wait for him to say everything he needed to say.

"Fear makes people do crazy things," he said, lacing her fingers with his. "I thought I needed to hurt you to make myself hurt less. And that's just a load of bs— yet it's what I had to tell myself to stop myself from wanting you." His sincere gaze remained locked on her. "What I did was so wrong, Tess, and I almost lost you a second time because of it." A muscle twitched in his jaw and his voice dropped with emotion. "Tell me I have another chance to make it right."

His apology, his understanding of what had happened and why, stunned and amazed her. But she was still afraid to believe.... "Damien, I can never take back what I did—"

"Oh, sweetheart, I'm not asking you to. That's over, done. Doesn't matter. What matters is right now. What matters is that I love you."

She stared at him, her lips parted. "You love me?"

He nodded and pulled her into his arms. "Then, now and always." He kissed her neck, whispered in her ear, "Tell me you love me, too, before I go completely insane."

She smiled against his shoulder. "I love you, Damien. More than you'll ever know."

"I want to know." He pulled back so he could look at her. "Be my wife, Tess? Marry me and have my children. Let me give you the family you've always wanted."

Her heart soared with happiness. She couldn't believe what she was hearing. Never in a million years did she think this man would come to love her this much. She nodded, kept nodding.

"Is that a yes?" he said, laughing.

She stood on her tiptoes and kissed him squarely on the mouth. "That's a 'in a heartbeat.' That's a 'how about right now!'" She grinned. "Yes, Damien Sauer, I'll marry you."

He pulled her to him, his mouth covering hers

tenderly. When he eased back, he took her hand. "Come open your presents."

"I already have everything I could ever want. You and our little red house."

"Darling, there's so much more for you to enjoy." He led her over to the tree. "As you may have noticed, I'm not great with decorations. But there is one thing, right there in front of you that I am pretty proud of."

Tess looked at the branch sticking out in front of her, and her breath caught in her throat. Hanging on a thin length of pine was the most beautiful diamond ring she had ever seen.

Damien slipped it off the branch, then slipped it on her finger.

Tess stared at her hand. "It's so beautiful."

"You're so beautiful."

She looked up, felt as if she were floating on a cloud. She couldn't believe this day, this perfect Christmas day.

A holiday that had started off without a hope had turned into a season of true blessings.

Damien held her close as they stood by the tree. "Anything you want, it's yours."

"All I want is your love," she uttered with rich emotion.

"You have that, Tess."

And then he kissed her again. Not a soft sweet kiss this time, but a deep, heart-tugging, gut-clenching, knee-weakening full-mouth kiss.

"Damien," she uttered against his lips.

"Hmm?"

"You said I could have anything I want…."

He nuzzled her mouth, nipped at her lower lip. "Yes, my love. Of course. What is it?"

"That family you were talking about," she whispered.

"Yes?"

She grinned, brushed her lips teasingly against his. "Can we start making it right now?"

Damien slipped his hands beneath her and lifted her up. "Yes, my love," he said carrying her toward the bedroom. "Right now."

Epilogue

Dressed in a slightly over-the-top pink maternity bridesmaid gown, Mary glanced around the room. "Hearts, flowers and chocolate."

"Oh, my," Olivia finished, laughing.

The NRR threesome sat at one of the round reception tables, watching the wedding guests boogie on the white marble dance floor. The ballroom at Le Grande Hotel in downtown Minneapolis looked as though it had gone through a pink-and-red-and-white froufrou machine with all the ribbons, roses, hearts and toile. The wedding planner Tess hired had gone a little overboard with the *love* theme, but Tess didn't care. It was Valentine's Day. She had a beautiful white dress, great friends around her, a wonderful man who loved her and, for the first time in her life, a genuine enthusiasm about her future.

"This is one crazy wedding, Tess," Olivia remarked, pointing to the cupid ice sculpture.

"I think I like crazy," Tess said, grinning.

"You know you could've waited until the slow season, and Mary and I would have been happy to plan everything."

As the warm and familiar tune "We Are Family" blasted out of the speakers, Tess smiled widely at her girls. "Nope, I really couldn't wait."

"What do you mean?" Mary asked, confused.

Tess touched her stomach and shouted over the music. "Bun in the oven. I mean, a little Sauer in the oven."

Olivia squealed and hugged Tess. Mary smiled and shook her head. "Sorry, I'm just too big and uncomfortable to lean over."

"You're only six months pregnant, Mary," Olivia said, laughing.

Mary glared at her. "Just wait."

Olivia grinned, her brown eyes sparkling. "We are waiting. For a little while, anyway. I want my man all to myself."

"I hear that." Tess laughed. "Speaking of your man…and ours, too…"

"What?" Olivia said, her dark brows drawing together.

"Here they come."

All three women turned. Walking across the dance

floor toward them, looking tall, handsome and oh so wicked in the strange light cast by the red and pink decorations, were Ethan, Mac and Damien.

Mary gave a low wolf whistle.

Olivia muttered a dry, "Wow."

"Did we land some seriously good-looking man flesh or what?" Mary remarked dryly. "How lucky are we?"

"Very." Tess laughed. "But then again, they got pretty lucky, too."

The three women turned back to each other and smiled, They understood now that, through this newly found friendship and the stories of the past that they had shared with each other, they were forever linked. They had an unspoken promise. They were family, partners and there for each another always.

For Tess, it was not just a happy wedding day, it was a hopeful one—for all of them.

The future looked very bright indeed.

* * * * *